W9-BJV-382

THE
AMERICAN DREAM
AND THE
POPULAR NOVEL

THE AMERICAN DREAM

AND THE

POPULAR NOVEL

ELIZABETH LONG

Routledge & Kegan Paul

Boston, London, Melbourne and Henley

First published in 1985
by Routledge & Kegan Paul plc

9 Park Street, Boston, Mass. 02108, USA

14 Leicester Square, London WC2H 7PH, England

464 St Kilda Road, Melbourne,
Victoria 3004, Australia and

Broadway House, Newtown Road,
Henley-on-Thames, Oxon RG9 1EN, England

Set in 10/12 pt Palatino
by Columns of Reading
and printed in Great Britain
by St Edmundsbury Press Ltd,
Bury St Edmunds, Suffolk

Library of Congress Cataloging in Publication Data

Long, Elizabeth, 1944-
The American dream and the popular novel.
Bibliography: p.
Includes index.
1. American fiction—20th century—History and
criticism. 2. Best sellers. 3. Literature and
society—United States. I. Title.
PS374.B45L65   1985   813'.54'09   84-24828

British Library CIP data also available

ISBN 0-7100-9934-7

To my family
for their loving kindness

Contents

Acknowledgments

Many people have helped me during the years I have worked on this book. As teachers and colleagues, they gave scholarly counsel with generosity and wisdom; as friends, they gave even more generously of themselves. I consider this book, in part, a distillation of these relationships and of a community, however fragile-seeming, that affirms the interconnection of matters personal, political, and intellectual.

The book grew from graduate work at Brandeis. Egon Bittner, George Ross, and Charlotte Weissberg helped me discover the problem, name it, and write about it. They and Kurt Wolff encouraged me not only to think about theory but to trust my own thoughts. Their teaching will always be with me. Friends in the Merleau Ponty group and the Telos group heard early versions of some chapters and gave unstintingly of their criticism and support. Bill Norris helped me define the task more clearly, and Katherine Stone, then and throughout, gave superb advice and unqualified encouragement.

At Rice University I redefined and broadened the project. I am especially grateful to the other members of the Sociology Department, Chandler Davidson, Chad Gordon, Stephen Klineberg, and William Martin, for helping me with all aspects of that transition. Their comments, questions, and warm collegiality were crucial. Collectively, they reread the developing manuscript almost as much as I did. Other members of the Rice community also deserve special thanks: Linda Adair,

Susan Clark, Michael Fischer, Thomas Haskell, George Marcus, and Allen Matusow all gave wise and trenchant advice. George Lipsitz and Bruce Palmer from the University of Houston gave invaluable help over many months. Bruce's magisterial editorial skills are manifest on almost every page of the final manuscript. I am thankful, too, for sustained and sustaining assistance from Carolyn Bruse, Peter Rabinowitz and Janice Radway, who commented on many sections of the manuscript, and from Douglas Harper, Henrika Kuklick, and David Nye, whose readings of certain sections were very helpful.

A grant from the National Endowment for the Humanities made it possible for me to attend their 1980 Summer Seminar, 'New Directions in American Studies,' at the University of Pennsylvania. I am very grateful to Murray Murphey, who led the seminar, and the other members of the group for challenging my thinking in ways that have enriched this book and will influence any future work I do. The National Endowment for the Humanities also awarded me a 1981 Summer Stipend, which gave me much-needed time and freedom to complete a draft of the manuscript.

In the course of the research, I spoke to many people in publishing. My thanks to them all for their generous cooperation. Special thanks to Judith Appelbaum, John Dessauer, and Daisy Maryles and to my colleagues at Alfred A. Knopf and Simon & Schuster.

Our department secretary at Rice University, Alicia Mikula, not only typed the final manuscript, but also assisted with parts of the substantive research: her mind as well as her hands are part of the manuscript. Student assistants Ame Battle, Mark Fowler, Laurie Kyle, Michael McKinney, and Sylvia Wang also helped above and beyond the call of duty and the minimum wage.

1

Introduction

The story of America has been the story of success. From the time of *Poor Richard's Almanack*, individual enterprise has been our national anthem, and our achievements as a nation have seemed its mirror and collective manifestation. Only three decades ago, few would have disputed the description of America as 'the achieving society,' and of America's mission as the dissemination of the entrepreneurial gospel to less fortunate nations around the world.

Indeed, the end of World War II marked the beginning of what has been called the American quarter-century – a time of clear global hegemony for our country and unprecedented affluence for millions of its citizens. Yet the period when the American Dream seemed closest to fulfillment was, paradoxically, the first time when the limits and contradictions of that dream became widely apparent. Widespread affluence, and the very conditions that permitted its attainment, increasingly set the entrepreneurial ideal at odds with the realities of aspiration, achievement, and the experience of the successful life. Structural trends towards economic concentration, bureaucratization, service sector growth; rising consumer credit, new attitudes towards work and leisure; and the vast migration to the suburbs – all challenged older values of entrepreneurial independence, thrift and self-discipline, and cast doubt on the old equation between material and social advance.

1

These structural changes were accompanied in American life by a reexamination of traditional concepts of success, a broad-based and many-voiced attempt to characterize what differentiated post–World War II America from the more distant past. Both affluence and success – keystones of the American Dream – have been central categories in this discussion, and their meaning for both the nation and its people has been at issue.

From the time of the Korean War – when American troops and especially prisoners appeared demoralized – through the late 1950s, pundits and politicians debated whether Americans had 'gone soft,' mourned the decline of the small businessman and farmer, and discussed the ill-effects of affluence on the national purpose. Kennedy's famous inaugural speech reaffirmed that purpose, Johnson's 'Great Society' programs attempted (echoing the New Deal) both to open opportunities for affluence to all Americans and, at the same time, to move the definition of social success and purpose away from the entrepreneurial mode. Many of the minority groups vocal during the 1960s excoriated success as a mystificatory, even dangerous, ideology, while variously attempting reform, revolution, or 'counter-cultural' alternatives to a social system they perceived as being founded on a hypocritical or soullessly materialistic definition of success. The material hardship of the 1970s brought back an ideal of competitive individualism and corporate, if not entrepreneurial, success. Yet in the wake of the sixties, which had unsettled traditional social forms and mores – from the Presidency and the executive branch of the federal government to the inmost manifestations of individual sexuality – the tone and texture of both individual and collective 'success' felt different from what people remembered of the past.

In the 1980s, questions about personal and national purpose were asked with new insistence. Different groups proclaimed widely different models of the good life. President Reagan's image of the 'city on the hill' invoked a quasi-mythical past; gurus resettled their followers on communal ranches in Oregon; popular writers told their audiences how to dress for success or negotiate the crises of adult development; management consultants urged Americans to follow the Japanese

2

example, and political interest groups offered first principles ranging from biblical literalism to solar power.

The very diversity of such responses testifies to the urgency of a common plight: an ideal that once gave people direction, and bound their individual endeavors to a broader sense of American mission and progress, has lost its resonance and its power to inspire. The promise of the early postwar years has dissolved into a period of cultural confusion and volatility – a time that offers, along with doubt and dismay, at least the hope of reframing our basic goals and values so that they will be more fruitful for us as people and as a civilization.

To gain some purchase on the present, it is crucial to elucidate what has happened to the American Dream in the years after World War II. This book contributes to that task by examining how popular novelists have written about the dream of success in the period from 1945 to 1975, three decades that witnessed the onset of extraordinary affluence, the working out of its social and personal consequences, and the beginning of its erosion. Not surprisingly, these issues are central to the work of many novelists writing at the time, and their work provides a major source of information about widely held cultural assumptions, attitudes and beliefs, a remarkable opportunity to explore the processes of cultural change.

Novels are an especially fruitful mode of access to the subjective dimension of collective life in part because they explore the meeting-places of self and society, of inner desires and external constraints. They are preeminently stories of individual lives. Novelists discuss their heroes' and heroines' inner lives, family backgrounds, motivations, hopes and dreams, beliefs and actions, and the personal, moral, and social consequences of those actions. They show their characters developing over time through complicated series of perceptions and decisions and, often, through an equally complex dialogue with various aspects of their internal selves. Novels thus provide an unparalleled mode of access to an experiential world of finely shaded 'innerness.'

As a literary form, novels are also remarkable because they depict society with complexity and particularity. Although an individual, or several individuals, provide the narrative focus for most novels, the individual is seen as most explicable, or 'readable,' in the terms of novelistic conventions, when acting within networks of personal and social relationships and in a variety of institutional settings. In a sense, novels detail the many levels of interplay between the subjective and the objective world. They describe how individuals take the world in; how it subtly and unknowingly shapes them; how they, with various levels of accuracy or illusion, perceive the world; and how the world presents them with choices and constraints. They also illuminate, in turn, how individual desires, fears, and dreams impinge on the lives of others and stretch or tear the moral fabric of the social universe. Moreover, novels show an awareness that even these private yearnings and despairs may imply the social in their innermost parts. Thus novels provide fictional representations of the very inter-relationships – between inner aspiration and action in the world, between the personal and the social – that have both fascinated and eluded anyone who is trying to understand how modern America has changed.[1]

Moreover, novels and especially popular novels, operate within the conventions of literary realism, so they are built in part on a set of perceptions about the world that are shared with their audiences. This does not mean that novels provide a mirror of the external world, or should be judged as useful cultural evidence according to how accurate a reflection of the world they generate. But novels imply a community of shared meaning.

Not only the author's own perceptions of the world, but the perceptions of the hypothetical audience to whom the author writes, are implicated in every novel. As one thinker who has studied the linkages between fiction and the social world says, there are connections between the 'authorial audience' (the audience authors have in mind when they write) and the beliefs of actual readers, shared meanings indicated not only by how the author describes characters and their motivation, but by what the author leaves unsaid, as well. For instance, audiences in our culture understand that certain physical descriptions connote beauty, and that a certain ending is to be taken as 'happy' or 'unhappy.'[2]

4

If we grant with interpretive social thinkers like Clifford Geertz or Peter Berger and Thomas Luckmann that the social world is not a simple reality, but a web of significance built in part on our perceptions of the world, then the novelistic conventions of realism point to areas of commonality between the imagined world of the novel, and perceptions of the world held by real people in the audience – perceptions that form an important part of the social world beyond the world of novels. Moreover, these perceptions and evaluations of the world – beliefs, values, taken-for-granted assumptions – lie at the heart of the American Dream. Realism, then, provides a set of conventions that make a country's literature a fruitful source of evidence about its cultural ethos.

Bestselling novels are particularly important cultural artifacts because they are primarily a social rather than a literary phenomenon. Although they are books, their status as 'bestsellers' is socially constituted. Two implications of this fact, both related to their advantages as cultural evidence, are particularly important.

First, bestselling novels are defined by their success in finding audiences, or, to put it another way, are defined by audience demand, however distorted by the influence of large advertising budgets or a narrow choice of novels on the market. While it is impossible to tell exactly who reads each novel and what each reader gleans from a certain book, problems I will explore in more detail in Chapter 2, bestsellers become bestsellers because they have found resonance with large segments of the reading public. They are themselves successful books; and they achieve success in the marketplace because they are in tune with popular demand.

Thus, bestsellers are important cultural evidence because of their link to the social world of readers and their reading, not because of their literary merits, or lack thereof. The roots of cultural-literary studies in the field of literature have often made it difficult to separate issues of esthetic evaluation from those of cultural or social importance. Often, cultural analysts have conflated the two, assuming that the essence of a given culture of historical period could be best understood by analyzing its few great books or great ideas. This position, problematic for several reasons, seems particularly unsuited for examining a complex and fragmented society in which the hegemony of traditional cultural elites is uncertain, and the cultural hierarchy itself is under challenge. Similarly, popular novels have often been characterized as ideological or stereotypic and dismissed accordingly. If they are, however, then surely they are an appropriate source for investigating widely held beliefs about the world and their relationship to social change.[3]

Second, the wide popularity of bestsellers suggests that they are finding resonance with broad segments of the reading public, rather than appealing only to certain subsections of the audience. They run the gamut from 'mass' to 'high' culture, which assures various levels of sophistication in thematic presentation and also permits discovery of similarities and differences between novels that probably appeal to different groups – discoveries that may point to trends within the audience that are relatively generalized. The bestseller lists also include representatives of different literary genres, from war novels to historical romances. In looking at bestsellers, one can see not only whether the generic 'mix' among the most popular novels changes over time, itself an interesting cultural fact, but also whether thematic changes emerge across generic boundaries over the years. If this is the case, such shifts, once again, point to general cultural developments. In other words, I am arguing that bestsellers are a particularly useful source of evidence precisely because they represent a sort of common denominator of our literary culture. If, on the whole, they are relatively conventional stories (and may not be on the horizon of this era's novelistic vision), this makes them the more likely to be in tune with the values and attitudes of middle-class Americans. And if, as is the case, most bestsellers are not only conventional but relatively ephemeral in influence, this quality, too, is a positive one for my purposes, since it makes them an especially interesting source of data for investigating the complexities of short-term sociocultural change.

The annual lists of ten hardcover bestselling novels compiled by *The Bowker Annual of Library and Book Trade Information* provided the sample of books for analysis.[4] These lists are compiled under the auspices of the R. R. Bowker Company from industry sales figures exclusive of book club sales, and have attained preeminent status within the publishing industry. Because of Bowker's unofficial position as information-gatherer and arbiter of the book world (it serves libraries as well as publishers), its lists are the most accurate ones available to retail booksellers, librarians and researchers alike.[5]

In spite of the obvious centrality of the theme of success and the good life in American society, my research became focused on it primarily because of the attention it was given in the books under study. Even a superficial reading of these texts reveals that success is a recurrent concern and a matter of almost obsessional importance in bestselling novels. The novelists' preoccupation with success directed my attention to definitions of success, its social location, patterns of reward and sanction, the importance of success to plot and character, and how these factors changed. An understanding of success from a sociological perspective raised questions of motivation, social structure, and the relation of achievement to gender, ethnicity and class – all issues that are implicit in the novelists' construction of a fictive universe rather than an explicit focus of their narratives.

It is in a sense not surprising that bestselling novels, themselves successful books, often produced by authors also in search of success, should manifest a concern with success, but I want to emphasize that in this research I did not turn to novels with that theme on my mind (thus forcing them into my own Procrustean framework). Rather I found myself, in the course of examining novels in search of quite different themes and issues, confronted with the striking centrality of success in many of the narratives, and with the patterned nature of the taken-for-granted assumptions about success and its meanings for individuals and the social world even in novels in which it was not the central narrative focus. This study is, in turn, most centrally focused on novels whose themes concern success, its consequences, or its lack. Yet almost every novel under study is predicated on certain views about success, motivation, and social mobility, so I have drawn on the entire sample in order to analyze various components of the social worlds 'described' by their authors.

Textual analysis was holistic and inclusive. Questions of narrative structure, character development, setting and novelistic tone were all considered relevant. In some cases, I have used a group of novels to elucidate thematic parameters and variations; in others, I have concentrated on one particularly effective and representative fictional statement and merely indicated examples of similar views or novelistic presentation.

Since novelistic perceptions of success did undergo dramatic change during the thirty-year period, it seemed useful to have a flexible typology to characterize emergent patterns of success. For example, at the beginning of the period, I refer to an 'entrepreneurial' conception of success that unites individual and social amelioration. Later, as the sense of limitless expansion fades, what I have called a 'corporate-suburban' pattern emerges: work and family-centered leisure are seen as conflicting priorities. Later still, there is a significant shift from concern with occupational success to the personal rewards it brings. At this point, as heroes venture into the wilderness of 'success as self-fulfillment,' some continue the search for success, but less as an end in itself than as a means to attain very private goals of domestic happiness or immediate sensual gratification. Others equate achievement with an inner voyage of self-discovery marked less by worldly success than by a felt sense of creativity or experiential intensity. By the end of the period, both achievement and its rewards seem deeply problematic, and heroes confront individual and systemic failure to an unprecedented degree. With the American Dream in disarray, even an informal typology of success does not exhaust the material under analysis.

If success and its vicissitudes provided grist for the mills of popular novelists during the decades after 1945, social scientists were also captivated by the phenomenon of American affluence, and questioned what its consequences might be for values like individual achievement. Indeed, the amount of attention sociologists have given to achievement and success suggests that the novelist's preoccupation with success is just one manifestation of a generalized social concern. Even before World War II, sociologists enshrined achievement as the keystone in the overarching cultural value system, and either condemned the ideology of success, or attempted to unearth its intrapsychic dynamics to foster motivation, revealing beneath the multiplicity of their views a deep professional fascination with success.

In the years since 1945, social scientists have examined changing cultural assumptions about success as an important social-psychological concomitant of the dramatic institutional and occupational developments that have transformed American society. Like popular novelists, they have identified success as a key component of American identity. Like many Americans, they have identified its changing cultural meaning as a valuable indicator of the 'main drift' of modern American society.

As early as the 1950s, this concern was reflected in the work of David Riesman, C. Wright Mills, and William H. Whyte. More recently, Daniel Bell, Christopher Lasch, and Richard Sennett have extended the discussion. Each of these thinkers lays claim to different territory. Riesman, for example, speaks of social character; Sennett, of the erosion of public life; Lasch, of the culture of narcissism. Their theoretical projects and conceptual predispositions also differ. Nonetheless, all are attempting to get hold of the subjective and cultural manifestations of more easily quantifiable social developments in modern society. And, despite their differing terms and theoretical perspectives, all are coming to terms with the effects of affluence on the meaning of success.[6] Because of their concerns about our society, I refer to them as social critics, though 'humanist social thinkers' would be as appropriate a term. Their work, which I discuss in Chapter 6, provides an important counterpoint to novelistic perspectives on success.

Social thinkers, like novelists, write about the complex interplay between individuals and their social milieux, but, unlike novelists, they base their work on systematic studies of social life. Ideally, explicit canons of conceptual and evidentiary validity govern both their writing and its professional evaluation. Such work may have imaginative power, but social thinkers at least aspire to truths that are different from the imaginative 'truth' of novelists. While both seek to reveal dynamics that underlie the surface of the phenomenal world, social thinkers attempt to delineate an orderliness at work in society similar to that in nature. Correlatively, their work is held accountable for accuracy and explanatory power rather than being judged by esthetic standards.

If the sociological endeavor differs from that of novelists, so too does the sociological perspective.[7] Individuals and their lives are in the foreground of most novels. Social thinkers, on the other hand, tend to look for the regularities within and across lives. They show how the world of groups and institutions subtly conditions each person's choices and opportunities. In this perspective, the patterns of social life spring into sharp focus. This gives a critical view on individualism itself, by laying bare the social-structural determinants that shape our modes of working, loving, and playing, our inmost motives and desires. Yet, paradoxically, there is a liberating thrust at the heart of the effort to anatomize social constraints. Social thinkers hope that understanding these patterns will bring the possibility of restructuring society so it can better meet human needs.

Examining the social landscape after World War II, social critics were struck by the difference between mid-twentieth-century America and the industrializing nation of the nineteenth century. It seemed to them a 'new age,' one no longer governed by the entrepreneurial ideal because both work and leisure had been drastically transformed from the era of the expanding frontier and the small enterprise. As I detail in Chapter 6, David Riesman, William H. Whyte, and C. Wright Mills, social critics of the 1950s, feared that the organizational leviathan was eroding individual freedom. They characterized white-collar bureaucratic work as routinized and meaningless, encouraging skills of manipulation instead of open competition. Affluence offered leisure, but no relief from the pressures of conformity, in their analysis, since they thought that people's old values and traditions had disappeared, leaving only a 'lonely crowd' of isolated individuals who had no defenses against the siren call of media-propagated materialism. By the 1970s, social critics like Daniel Bell, Christopher Lasch, and Richard Sennett felt that the bureaucratic order of work and leisure had not only destroyed all organic forms of community, but was corrupting even the ideal of freedom by harnessing people's most primitive appetites to a voracious consumer culture. The 'culture of narcissism' promised free-dom, glamor and personal growth, but nurtured only a shallow, hedonistic self-involvement.

There are clear differences between the analyses of social critics of the 1950s and those of the 1970s. Earlier writers thought affluence masked a subtle form of social tyranny: conformity. Later critics feared not social pressure but the false freedom of unchecked self-indulgence.

But underlying these differences there is a striking unity: the social critics agree that the disappearance of the entre-preneurial world and its ethos has left individuals and society in disarray. They cite symptoms of this disorder, ill-masked by affluence, in every area of public and private life, and above all draw attention to its moral dimension. By the end of the period, social critics are urging Americans to rethink their most basic values.

In common with the social critics, bestselling novels during this thirty-year period chronicle the disappearance of the entre-preneurial reality and ethos. Of course, the fact that the American dream is tarnished cannot be news to anyone who has lived through the aftermath of affluence. Yet the fact that both novelists and social scientists bear witness to this dramatic cultural transition indicates its centrality to middle-class lives. In fact, the novelists write about many of the same themes analyzed by the social critics. From Sloan Wilson's man in the gray flannel suit, who speaks to us from the mid-1950s, to Joseph Heller's Slocum, complaining in the 1970s that some-thing happened to his American dream, heroes of bestsellers inhabit a world of ever more abstract and meaningless work within large companies. By the end of the period, novelists also describe a public world frighteningly out of control, where true and false, good and evil have become almost indistin-guishable. They write with anguish about the problems of private life, showing the suburban compromise between work and family either corrupted by an almost consumeristic sexuality, or buckling under the intense desire of men and women to invest more than conventional suburban meaning in the life of the emotions.

If there are significant parallels between the portrait of

11

postwar America drawn by novelists and social scientists, so too are there parallels between novelistic and social-scientific readings of the institutional causes for the failure of American 'success' to bring individual wellbeing in its wake. Novelists refer to the abstract nature of modern work, to people's powerlessness in a world of large organizations, to outmoded family roles, and to the erosion of traditional forms of authority as social contributions to the individually experienced malaise that increasingly pervades bestselling novels during this period. These references are usually embedded in novelistic narrative strategies and character descriptions, while the social critics systematically articulate such institutional problems and their interrelationships: therein lies the strength of the socio-logical perspective, and its contribution to our understanding of American society.

By the same token, the social critics' tendency to stress the power of social determinants over individuals leads them seriously to underestimate the complexity of the cultural response to the institutional shifts they anatomize. All contend that a new ideology or cultural ethos and a new American character structure have emerged almost as a reflex of the new institutional order. From William Whyte, who analyzes the conformist Social Ethic and the 'organization men' who are both its ideologues and its victims, to Christopher Lasch, who outlines the corrosive effects of the 'culture of narcissism' on the American personality, all are operating with a vision of individuals and their culture as a simplistic mirror of social-structural trends. In part this reflects, in the world of ideas, the tremendous importance of large-scale institutions in modern lives. Certainly it is easier to grasp the ways that individuals are conditioned by their backgrounds than it is to appreciate the small and subtle ways that those same individuals, in response and reaction, alter their environment. But one consequence of this perspective is that the individual is construed, for the sake of convenience if nothing else, as the passive object of broader social forces, thus a one-dimensional reflection or a cipher in what social thinkers have defined as the main drift on the institutional level. A fundamental difficulty with this strategy is that it generates a description of society that gives short shrift to processes of evolution or change, except in their most dramatic or institutionalized form. To understand social change – except when it is expressed in organized social movements – it is necessary to see what people make of the social structures that are the pre-given, taken-for-granted bedrock of their lives.

A serious attention to cultural evidence, such as bestselling novels, could correct this lacuna in sociological accounts of modern America. For the novelistic response to social-structural change is strikingly varied. To take just one example, the findings of this study show that the disappearance of the entrepreneurial ideal has been gradual, not disjunctive. Indeed, certain of its core elements have been tenaciously maintained in the face of dramatically changed social circumstances, reaffirmed by redefinition through literary, imaginative conventions. For example, by the mid-1950s the heroic entrepreneurial tale of conquest, uniting individual self-interest and social amelioration, had begun to disappear from realistic bestselling novels, but organizational melodramas, more formulaic and conventionalized, continue to show heroes reaffirming entrepreneurial values and faith in American individualism through two more decades. More realistic novels from the 1950s on reformulate success in corporate-suburban terms: the hero faces a limited universe in which he must integrate disparate roles and rewards, and chooses a balanced life and familial happiness over single-minded vocational dedication. This represents a new definition of both society and success, but the new choice is validated in traditional terms as a demonstration of independence – independence *from* work rather than *through* it.

As this one example shows, the systematic examination of bestselling novels extends, and in some cases revises, the characterizations of American values, aspirations, and personality structure advanced by the social critics mentioned above. An explicit focus on success as an evolving sociocultural construction reveals complexities in the process of short-term cultural change often obscured by descriptions of American culture as a simple reflection of large-scale institutional developments. Yet two characteristics of the sociological perspective have hindered even the social critics most attuned to the 'innerness' of our culture from effectively using cultural evidence.

The first has to do with the relationship of social critics to their culture. On the one hand, because they are part of the social world of the American middle class, these social critics apparently believe they can intuitively understand its cultural ethos. Certainly, as I shall later discuss in more detail, they treat cultural evidence rather casually, making an idiosyncratic choice of examples from literature and other kinds of popular culture to illustrate what they have already concluded to be the significant shifts in American attitudes. Casual selection of evidence not only raises questions about the social critics' characterizations of contemporary American culture, but reveals assumptions that our culture is both univocal and relatively transparent. So, this random and haphazard fashion of dealing with the potshards of our cultural 'midden' trivializes the very attempt to understand modern America, yet it also points to ways in which the sociological perspective on culture could be enriched.

On the one hand, then, social critics seem to think that they intuitively understand American culture because they are part of it themselves. On the other hand, their accounts of modern America are suffused with a sense that their esoteric knowledge of society sets them definitively apart from other people. In this view, the social critic, by virtue of professional training, stands reflectively outside society, while others, if not aided by the social critics, remain trapped within its organization and ideologies. Such a perspective, as I shall show, makes it difficult for social critics to attend carefully to independent sources of conceptualization or interpretation, like popular literature, because it is difficult for them to see that other people, too, are reflective rather than mere objects of an abstract historical process. Here, I am not claiming that social critics do not have valuable insights to offer, or that popular culture is wholly enlightened. But unless social scientists recognize that they, like others, are not fully transcendent subjects and that others, like them, may be capable of some critical distance from the environing culture, descriptions of sociocultural change will suffer.

A second characteristic of social thought – the use of schematic cultural typologies – has also inhibited social critics from effectively using cultural evidence in the effort to understand social change. Traditionally social scientists have distinguished industrial society from earlier modes of social organization by dichotomous typological comparison. Redfield spoke of folk vs. urban society, Durkheim of mechanical vs. organic solidarity, Tönnies of *Gemeinschaft* vs. *Gesellschaft*. In much the same way, the social critics mentioned above have characterized contemporary cultural formations by implicit or explicit contrast with nineteenth-century ideologies or modes of behavior. This conceptual strategy leads to several difficulties, of which the most serious may be the temptation to characterize the present as a simple antithesis of what has been defined as 'the old.' This is particularly troublesome since social critics have idealized the nineteenth-century past, making it a repository for all the values they feel are missing from their world. So the method of typological comparison also makes it hard for social thinkers to escape from the circle of their own convictions about the present.

By examining the contours of the American Dream in bestselling novels over a thirty-year period, this study restricts the period for comparison. This highlights the processes by which elements of the old are reformulated and recombined, by which cultural innovations are made part of conventional assumptions about the self and the world. Implicitly, this approach constitutes a demand for considering the imagination to be a central part of social construction rather than a reflector of structural events. Moreover, the diversity within the set of cultural artifacts that are my data urges recognition of the variety in subjective responses to change on the institutional level, of the heterogeneity within even the realm of the conventional. In turn, this points to the necessity of multi-dimensional characterizations of the emergent social order. This analytic perspective is especially appropriate for consideration of a highly differentiated society whose affluence and complex division of labor – and leisure – may indeed permit individuals to invoke a wider range of personal and social metaphors for their lives than has heretofore been the case.

It must be clear by now that the systematic examination of popular novels challenges social-scientific views of contemporary American culture. Substantively, it shows middle-class

15

culture to be much more complex than social critics have assumed it to be. It also reveals novelists as more 'sociological' than is generally assumed, since it chronicles their active involvement in reinterpreting their social world, in generating metaphors for the social process of self-description independently of intervention from social scientists.

Correlatively, by pointing out that the social critics' 'sense' of American culture is often based on intuition, and that their use of certain conceptual categories is problematic, this study claims that their work is more 'novelistic' than it is generally construed to be. Their conceptual predisposition and theoretical projects, and in particular the increasing interiority, relativism, and pessimism of their analyses, express the very cultural changes they seek to elucidate. Thus, after discussing the evidence from the novels, I analyze the social critics' 'maps' of the same terrain as cultural artifacts, showing the ways in which the cultural developments recorded in popular novels permeate the work of these thinkers.

The modern problem of meaning and values that each of these critics grapples with is also, for the intellectual, a crisis of knowing, for it challenges the conceptual categories that are themselves part of the traditional order in dissolution. By examining both popular novels and the social critics who have been especially important in defining modern America to itself, this book contributes not only to a new reading of American culture and a new method for analyzing short-term socio-cultural change, but also to a reformulation of the task of the social thinker. I hope that this, in turn, can help us better understand and more effectively participate in our common effort to reconstitute an American Dream – or dreams – that can be life-giving for us as a people and as people.

2

Success in bestselling novels: the social context of thematic content

In the Introduction I took social critics to task for the inferences they made about middle-class values and beliefs from analyses of popular novels and other cultural artifacts like magazine stories and television programs. One of my criticisms was that the way they selected and interpreted cultural evidence such as bestselling novels ignored the social context of their production, dissemination, and reception by other readers, and that this lacuna led to impoverished characterizations of American culture.

I, too, want to make inferences about American values based on an analysis of textual evidence. But in this chapter I will examine the texts as part of a communicative process, involving not only the books themselves, but also their authors, their audiences, and the institutional matrix within which they are published and distributed. In other words, I will explore the ways in which popular literature is grounded in social life. This narrows the gap between the fictional world and the social world. It also permits both a more careful discussion of the cultural meaning of texts and an appreciation of the theoretical and empirical difficulties attendant on making inferences from texts to the world beyond them – difficulties that point, in turn, towards areas for future research.

The view that literature is an institutionally mediated process of communication between authors and audiences, and that knowledge of the entire process is necessary for understanding the relationship between textual content and the environing culture, has gained currency recently. In part this may be because the rise of mass market literature has undermined the romantic understanding of the author as a genius working in splendid isolation. Certainly, early statements of the 'context-ualist' view – the view that the cultural meaning of a text can only be understood by examining the social process of its production and reception – claim that only mass culture is embedded, as it were, in a social or institutional context that requires attention. For example, Leo Lowenthal, a member of the Frankfurt School of social research who carried their interest in the mass media and propaganda to America in the wake of Fascism's spread in Germany, wrote in an early discussion of the sociology of literature that great novels were individual creations that expressed the essential truths of their time. These epochal assumptions about human nature could be revealed by historically informed textual analysis. He character-ized mass culture, on the other hand, as part of the system of commodity production, and thought, therefore, that its content and cultural meaning could only be understood by reference to the institutional context in which it was created and marketed.[1]

In later formulations, the sharp dichotomy Lowenthal proposed between high and mass culture, and appropriate methods for their analysis, has blurred. Raymond Williams in *The Country and the City*, for example, makes an eloquent argument for the usefulness of understanding even the familiar canon of 'classic' eighteenth- and nineteenth-century English novelists by reference to the communities to which they belonged, the trajectories of their own lives and their changing reference points as authors, and the evolution of the reading public who constituted their audiences. Those interrelation-ships, he contends, shaped the 'structures of feeling' – such as a facile nostalgia for a lost pastoral existence – that mark our own response to the rural and urban worlds.[2]

Similarly, Robert Escarpit, a French sociologist of literature, claims that 'In point of fact, there is no such thing as a literary work: there are literary phenomena – that is, dialogues between a writer and various publics.' He makes this claim in order to discuss the 'many ties' between good literature and 'sub-literature,' contending that social factors may be more important than aesthetic factors in influencing a book's classification as literature rather than as something that is less than literary in nature. His analysis implies that students of the sociology of literature must examine the interrelationship between authors, channels of distribution, and the wide range of reading publics, in order to understand the cultural significance of books.[3]

For my purposes, this perspective is important because it implies that one must examine these interrelationships over time before contending that thematic changes in popular novels accord with changes in attitudes or beliefs within the audience for the novels. If one aspect of this interrelated communicative process changes drastically, thematic changes may reflect *that* change, not a more generalized cultural shift. Conversely, the argument that novelistic content is symptomatic of a general cultural change will be stronger if the background and intentions of the authors, the channels of production and dissemination, and the composition of the audience change very little over the thirty years under study, or if the changes are congruent.

This, in a sense, extends an argument Raymond Williams makes at the beginning of his book *Culture and Society*, in which he studies conceptual or ideological changes that came with industrialization by an examination of the emergent, and often radically new, meanings of certain words like 'culture,' 'society,' and 'democracy' that are central markers of the categories through which we perceive the world. As he says: 'The importance of these words, in our modern structure of meanings, is obvious. The changes in their use . . . bear witness to a general change in our characteristic ways of thinking about our common life.'[4]

This study follows a similar process, tracing the evolution of one centrally important cultural theme – a larger conceptual unit than a single word, yet in some ways a linguistic category. My argument begins with the contention that after World War II a large number of novels embodying a certain understanding of success became very popular. Since that time, perceptions of success in popular novels have changed, in a patterned way. This pattern can be used, as Williams used the pattern of change in the meaning of important words, as a cultural grid through which we can look again, and with more understanding, at the wider changes in life and thought that these changes in the universe of popular fiction both spring from and refer back to.

To concretize this point, obviously both the universe of the authors and that of the audience for these novels have also changed over the thirty-year period under discussion, if only because of the biological processes of mortality and regeneration that mark the passage of generations. But even if the changes are not merely biological, the argument can still hold. Although the separate components within the communicative process may change, their variance may correspond, thus leaving them in a similar relationship to each other. For instance, let us suppose that, on the whole, the educational level of the audience for bestsellers rose over this period, and that a larger percentage of the audience came from urban or suburban backgrounds in 1975 than was the case in 1945. Moreover, suppose more well-educated and urban-born authors published bestsellers in the 1970s than in the late 1940s. These are areas in which the lives of authors and audiences would reflect more generalized changes in the conditions of middle-class American life, changes which may have given rise to changes in values and beliefs, and to changes in novelistic depictions of success. Thus, this would not necessarily mean either that the congruence between a novel's popularity and its audience's beliefs would be less in 1975 than in 1945, or that in describing a bestseller of 1945 and 1975 we would be referring to a vastly different kind of cultural product. Rather, in examining bestsellers we would implicitly refer back to the large-scale shifts in life and thought that this study illuminates.

Only if there were quite gross shifts in the universes of both bestselling audience and authors would we be examining a sociocultural phenomenon so different over this period that comparison between 1945 and 1975 would be meaningless. This would be the case, for instance, if no upper-middle-class readers bought bestsellers at the end of the period, or if the profession of authorship made it impossible for a specific group of authors with a specific kind of message to be published. Similarly, the assumptions on which this study rests could be questioned if the apparatus of production and dissemination of bestsellers shifted so profoundly as not only to skew authorship and audiences very differently, but also to severely constrain the kind of novels that could become bestsellers by, for instance, limiting the universe of choice or increasing the possibility of taste manipulation.

With these issues in mind I will briefly examine the publishing industry that marketed bestselling novels during this period, and then discuss what can be discovered about their audiences and authors. In each section, I will be concerned with whether, or how, one can infer general shifts in the cultural ethos from thematic shifts in bestsellers.

Publishing hardcover bestsellers: the industry 1945–75

Several groups within the literary community, most notably the Authors' Guild, various independent booksellers and trade publishers, and some analysts of the publishing industry, have recently expressed great concern about economic concentration within publishing and book marketing. They cite developments such as corporate acquisitions of publishing houses, the growth of highly rationalized bookstore chains like B. Dalton and Waldenbooks, and the close partnership between television, Hollywood, and certain sectors of publishing as evidence of an increased 'massification' of the book business. Most express special concern about first novels and slow-selling books. They argue that if the industry is structured so that only 'big books' are heavily promoted and widely distributed, then cultural diversity and innovation, serious literature and critical ideas, may be suppressed just as effectively by the mechanisms of mass marketing as by more visible forms of censorship.

It is possible that the same developments that have endangered first novels or 'mid-level' books may have affected even hardcover bestsellers, though they are usually seen as symptoms of the increased commodification of books, rather than as cultural products that themselves may have changed because of it. For instance, if economic concentration within publishing has meant that the book-buying public is being

21

offered an increasingly narrow and low-quality range of novels from which to choose, then thematic shifts in bestsellers might signify constraints on choice, rather than shifts in a cultural ethos. More subtly, if recent bestsellers are the product of media packagers who develop media 'properties' marketed as books, television programs and movies in a cleverly orchestrated atmosphere of hype, these books might reflect not the values and beliefs of authors and audiences but only the manipulations of the multi-media entrepreneurs. If so, the hardcover bestselling novel of 1975 would be a rather different cultural product from its counterpart of 1945, and could reveal less than earlier novels about the beliefs of middle-class Americans. Since what has happened to bestselling novels can be understood within the broader context of what has happened in publishing since World War II, I will address this broader question, but selectively, concentrating on bestselling hardcover novels, and on what implications industry-wide changes may have for this study of thematic changes within bestsellers.

First, and perhaps most important, the hardcover bestseller lists themselves reveal few changes over the thirty years under study, either in the 'mix' of serious and lighter novels, or in the fact that a small number of companies published most bestselling novels. At both the beginning and the end of the period, most bestselling novels were entertainment literature, though the popular genres and artists changed, with F. P. Keyes's regional stories and Frank Yerby's historical sagas giving way to Harold Robbins's jet-set melodramas and Frederick Forsyth's thrillers. Moreover, well-respected authors achieved bestsellerdom both early and late in the period under study. Marquand, Steinbeck, Sinclair Lewis, Mailer, Sholem Asch, and Hemingway are among the 'serious' bestselling authors of 1945–50; John Fowles, James Dickey, Graham Greene, Updike, Solzhenitsyn, Vonnegut, Heller, and Bellow, however, are among the authors whose books appeared on the lists between 1970 and 1975.[5] In other words, the hardcover bestseller lists have accommodated much the same range of entertainment fiction and more serious works from 1945 to 1975, so the range of taste displayed by the audience for hardcover novels has not changed a great deal over the postwar years. More significantly, this suggests that hardcover bestselling novels were not a fundamentally different entity in 1975 than in 1945, and thus that their content was relatively congruent with the attitudes and beliefs of their readers throughout the period.

Admittedly, it is possible that hardcover entertainment fiction has become more 'trashy' over the years. Aside from noting that cultural mores have also changed, this is a hard question to adjudicate. Certainly reviewers were making remarks fully as snide about Lloyd Douglas's *The Big Fisherman* in 1948, Frank Yerby's *The Foxes of Harrow* in 1946, or Thomas Costain's *The Moneyman* in 1947, as those elicited by Jacqueline Susann's *Valley of the Dolls* in 1966 or James Clavell's *Shogun* in 1975.[6]

The bestseller lists also show that a few large publishing companies had already begun to dominate the market for hardcover bestselling novels in the years immediately after World War II. In fact, the number of companies accounting for a substantial percentage of bestselling fiction titles has changed hardly at all from the years between 1945 and 1950 to those between 1970 and 1975. In the former period twenty companies accounted for all of the fifty-six hardcover bestselling novels, nine for forty-one of them (or 73 percent), and five companies for twenty-nine of the novels (or 51.8 percent). Figures for the latter period are somewhat more complex, because some of the imprints listed, once names of independent companies, were already in the process of being merged with other publishing companies or acquired by corporate conglomerates. Using companies rather than imprints as the basic unit of analysis, nineteen companies accounted for all of the fifty-six hardcover bestselling novels, eight for forty-one (or 73 percent), and four for thirty of the novels (or 53.6 percent).[7] These numbers imply that the bestseller-oriented sector of the publishing industry was not significantly more monopolistic in 1975 than in 1945, or in other words – and I will discuss this in more detail below – that certain aspects of contemporary bestsellerdom, such as the domination of the market by a few large companies, were already established by 1945. The figures also imply that the readers of bestsellers were probably not faced with less choice of what books to select in 1975 than in 1945, since even in the immediate postwar years a few large companies had captured much of the market for popular fiction.

Even though the hardcover bestseller lists show great continuity during this period, mainstream publishing did undergo striking changes between 1945 and 1975. And, although many of these changes appear to have increased the domination of the blockbuster, they may also have contributed both to a decline of more serious literature – which would mean future bestseller lists with no leavening of 'quality' novels – and to the rise of a mass-oriented, homogenized form of literary production more closely linked to television and the movie industry than ever before. Many industry analysts fear that this, in turn, has already increased the possibility of audience manipulation and lack of consumer choice, and is making books a very different cultural product than in the past. Either development would call into question whether shifts in the content of novels indicate shifts in the values of their audience, or are simply a reflex of these changes in the industry itself.[8]

Publishing analysts from both within and outside the industry point to several interlocking developments that have certainly changed the internal structure of the hardcover trade book – or general-interest – sector of the publishing industry and publishing as a way of life for its practitioners. These same developments have also affected the relationship of publishing to other media and to the audience for books. First, in the past twenty years a number of independently owned mainstream trade publishers have either gone public, merged with other publishers, or been acquired by large corporate conglomerates. In the 1960s the conglomerates tended to be electronic companies like RCA hoping to benefit from the expansion of education and a marriage between old and new technologies of instruction. In the 1970s media corporations like Gulf and Western or Warner Communications, and European publishers seeking broader markets, were responsible for most publishing acquisitions.[9] Though effects of big mergers or conglomerate ownership vary, there is some consensus that they entail rationalized managerial practices in financing and marketing, and often more formal editorial accountability and more attention to the bottom line.[10] In the booming 1960s, this may have contributed to pressures to expand title production (thus making it hard to give every title attention), and in the leaner 1970s it may have pressured publishers towards category fiction and bestselling novels, because both offer the hope of large and stable profits.[11] Restrictions on editorial choice, and attention to 'big,' mass-marketable books, of course, may adversely affect budding literary talent, driving serious authors off the bestseller lists and perhaps away from literary careers.

Second, at the same time that mainstream trade publishing was becoming less like a 'cottage industry,'[12] hardcover publishers were becoming more and more dependent for profits on the sale of subsidiary rights. Paperback publishers, television, and the movie industry have been buying rights to hardcover novels for some time, but in the 1970s aggressive entertainment agents – sometimes lawyers – were able to make bigger and bigger deals for their authors, in part because traditionally undercapitalized publishers could draw on money from their corporate parents. Moreover, perhaps because some sectors of publishing were more closely integrated with other media in large communication conglomerates, entertainment brokers who dealt with books as one aspect of multi-media packages began to initiate media 'concepts' or 'properties' and orchestrate their production and marketing to film or television studios and to trade publishers as well.[13] Publicity departments were already discovering that television talk shows could significantly boost certain authors and their books, allowing media hype and the cult of personality to make inroads into what many publishers had thought of as a quiet and genteel industry.

It is clear that these developments have altered the status hierarchy within some publishing houses, benefitting subsidiary rights and promotion departments.[14] They may also benefit certain kinds of authors – not only celebrities, but those who are willing to promote themselves aggressively. More subtly, editors may be less oriented towards authors and their traditional audience than towards the mass market paperback houses, television, movies and their audiences – a shift that may further endanger the prospects for serious literature. Also, the very fact that huge sums are being invested in certain book deals probably intensifies the pressure on publishers to concentrate on blockbusters to the relative neglect of more modest books. Finally, the people who generate 'novelizations' as part of a media package released to the public amidst multimedia hype are creating and marketing books differently – and perhaps more manipulatively – than traditional authors and publishers. This may result in bestselling novels whose content represents only what the media entrepreneurs have succeeded in foisting off on the public. If such is the case, it would be hard to claim that hardcover bestselling novels continue to reflect the values and beliefs of audiences, or that they are the same kind of cultural artifact that they were forty years ago.

Third, the distribution of even hardcover books appears to have become more rationalized and economically concentrated. Large chains of suburban bookstores are accounting for an increased percentage of trade book sales, and independent bookstores are accounting for an ever smaller percentage. The two largest chains, B. Dalton and Waldenbooks, now sell about one-third of the trade books marketed.[15] In one sense, the chains have merely brought bookselling into line with demographic shifts, following retailers to large suburban shopping malls. Yet they have also removed any taint of high culture from their stores, pioneered displays that treat books like any other consumer commodity, and introduced sophisticated computer systems that generate quick and accurate sales records, enabling stores to winnow out slow sellers very efficiently. Since the chains are very accurate in ordering and have a low return rate, a crucial variable in publishing, some publishers rely on their orders in setting print runs and even in the editorial decision-making process. Some analysts fear that this may lead to a short shelf-life for all but the most popular novels.[16] While cultural diversity would be the main casualty of this process, if it leads to a narrower universe of choice for the consumer, even bestselling novels may become less congruent with what people want to read.

If these three developments have indeed affected publishing as some industry spokesmen and analysts have claimed, then they would not only call into question the assumptions on which this study rests – that novels become hardcover bestsellers because they resonate with the values of their readers, and that this link between audience and hardcover

26

novels did not change appreciably over the years between 1945 and 1975 – but would also augur ill for the future of serious literature, cultural diversity, and critical thought in our country. But I am reluctant to accept this interpretation of recent publishing history. While publishing has clearly changed in the past twenty years, the cultural effects of developments within the industry are much more complex and difficult to assess than is indicated by the interpretation I have outlined above. In part, this is because many analyses of publishing suffer from historical shortsightedness, which distorts the meaning of current trends.

For example, historically informed discussions of the industry reveal that publishing has always been a commercial as well as a literary endeavor, and that some, if not all, publishers have been oriented towards mass markets whenever possible.[17] For instance, the boom in mass market paperbacks – an important aspect of the transformation of modern publishing – is the third American 'paperback revolution.' The first dated from the 1830s, and ended between 1843 and 1845, when the Postal Service reformed its rate structure, so that story newspapers and 'supplements' containing complete novels could no longer profitably be mailed to readers. The second – which followed the Civil War – prefigures our own in several respects.[18] It was, like that of our times, linked to a generalized expansion in publishing caused by wartime demand for books, and a postwar period of affluence and population growth. It ended in glutted markets and a series of mergers. Although these mergers failed to exert oligopolistic control over publishing, they enabled some houses to become bigger and more structurally complex. From the 1890s on, large houses were divided into different divisions and departments, and some, for a time, were under outside financial control, sparking turn-of-the-century debates within publishing about the future of competition that have a curiously modern ring.[19]

Publishers have not only been commercially oriented, for as long as they have been dependent on the market for survival; they have also always tried to rationalize the publishing process to assure stable profits. Well before the twentieth century, publishers had attempted, with some success, to establish a reliable market by publishing category fiction. The

Beadle Brothers, among others, flooded the markets in the 1860s with the infamous dime novels, mostly domestic romances or blood-and-thunder stories.[20] Nineteenth-century publishers also tried to reach customers directly through the mails, and tried to develop a steady demand for certain authors, like Mrs. E. D. E. N. Southworth, who could be relied on to produce similar and very popular products.

Many features of contemporary bestsellerdom were firmly in place well before the beginning of the period covered by this study. Literary agents, trying to make as much money as possible for their authors and themselves, entered American publishing in the 1890s. Bestseller lists date from 1895, and are evidence that both old and new publishing companies of the post–Civil War period were taking a more openly commercial stance.[21] O. H. Cheney's *Economic Survey of the Book Industry 1930–1931* shows that by 1930 a few large publishing companies had begun to dominate the market to a limited degree; between 1925 and 1930, four companies accounted for an estimated 20 percent of the titles published, and approximately twenty companies accounted for 49 percent of them. And there is some evidence that this concentration has not greatly changed, for publishing as a whole.[22] Even before World War II, publishers had begun to rely on some titles to generate subsidiary rights income from magazines, book clubs, and an expanding movie industry.[23]

Certainly by the late 1940s, at the beginning of the period this study covers, trade book publishers had already begun to defray a sizeable percentage of their costs by selling subsidiary rights and editorial decisions were already somewhat influenced by that dependency.[24] Although television had yet to become a dominant medium, and multi-media entertainment brokers were still a thing of the future, by 1949, as William Miller's excellent description of trade publishing reveals, the movie industry had already become actively involved in the process of generating literary properties that could be released as books and movies in carefully orchestrated campaigns. MGM, for example, agreed to share costs of 'scouting out' manuscripts with Farrar, Straus & Co. in 1947, and paid half the salary of two Random House editors who searched the country for manuscripts suitable for MGM. Movie companies also sponsored prizes, fellowships, or awards in contests for novels. Occasionally, they had a hand in the final revision of award-winning books, and they sometimes subsidized book production costs, understanding that the novels functioned as good advertisements for the movies. Although the practice is more common now, Miller also decribes several examples from the 1940s of movie scripts being rewritten as novels. Then, as now, movie and book club deals tended to favor big publishing companies and their 'big' authors, which means that then, as now, certain novels had an advantage in the competition for bestsellerdom.[25] This also means that the choices of present-day readers are probably no more constrained or manipulated than was the case in the late 1940s, so if hardcover bestsellers were congruent with their readers' values then, they were probably no less so by 1975.

Certainly bestselling novels were extremely important to hardcover trade publishing by 1949. In fact, Miller's discussion of the trade book industry begins by anatomizing the 'star system,' showing that publishers were already attempting to secure one or two bestselling authors to lead their lists and devoting a relatively large percentage of promotion budgets to publicizing potentially bestselling books. Promotion departments had developed strategies to sell books by selling their authors as personalities, and though the electronic media came to play an increasingly important role in this process, authors were already making city-to-city tours, signing copies of their novels in large book or department stores, and giving interviews for radio, newspapers, and magazines. Moreover, a bestselling novel could account for a sizeable proportion of a hardcover publisher's yearly income. Sales of Kathleen Winsor's 1947 novel, *Forever Amber*, for example, accounted for about 10 percent of Macmillan's gross business in one year.[26]

Even book distribution was relatively economically concentrated by the late 1940s. Though bookstore chains were not as important as they are now, department store book departments served very much the same function for cities as the chains now do for the suburbs. Like the chains today, they 'sold books fast or not at all.' Those retail outlets accounted for 38 percent of bookstore sales in 1930–1, and Miller estimates that they were even more important in 1949. These fast-turnover outlets contributed to worries among industry spokesmen, then as now, about the short shelf-life of modestly selling books and about the possibility that innovative books would 'die' before finding an audience. Intractably high production costs, too, worked against keeping backlist titles in print for long periods of time and raised the break-even point for individual titles from 2,500 copies before World War II to somewhere between 6,000 and 10,000 copies in the late 1940s. This pressured editors to cut backlists, limit the number of new titles, and focus on the 'big book.'[27]

In combination with the postwar boom in mass market paperbacks, these factors led some publishers to worry about the possible massification of literature as early as the mid-fifties. As Harold Guinzberg, founder of Viking, said in 1954 at the American Scholar Forum on 'The Future of Books in America': 'My worry is that you may repeat in the book field what has happened in other fields – in entertainment and communication – you may make it increasingly difficult to do anything that is not geared to large low common denominators.'[28]

Of course, again, the bestseller might benefit from such a process, yet if serious authors were unable to be published, the quality of the bestseller lists might change as a result of market pressures instead of broader cultural shifts, and the possibility of consumer manipulation might also lead to a more tenuous link between the content of bestsellers and the values of the audience.

Statements such as Guinzberg's from the 1950s and several quoted by Whiteside in his 1980 analysis, *The Blockbuster Complex*, point to the possibility that mass-oriented publishing may be winning dominance within the industry (whether in terms of money or influence), and bringing certain sectors of publishing into closer connection with other industries of mass entertainment. In the extreme, this raises the specter of homogenized and degraded literary production. Less extremely, it gives rise to questions about the relative position of serious literature and mass literature in the contemporary cultural hierarchy.

One can speculate, for example, that high culture, which used to be seen as *the* culture, is now being dealt with in publishing as one specialized aspect of a less hierarchical and more fragmentary cultural totality. But it is hard to determine whether this is in fact happening, and, if so, what the ultimate effects will be. If this large-scale cultural shift is taking place, it has certainly been a much more gradual process than many contemporary observers think. As discussed above, historical evidence indicates that many of the developments decried in the 1980s were already well under way by the late 1940s. Moreover, while hardcover trade publishing may feel to its practitioners like a different way of life than in the past, what they produce has not changed a great deal.[29] A 'massification' model is, quite simply, inadequate to account for developments in the publishing industry, because countervailing tendencies within publishing and the social world it serves work against massification and because publishing is not a monolithic industry.[30]

The issue of economic concentration in publishing shows this very clearly. Though good historical statistics on publishing are hard to come by, the U.S. Census reveals little change in concentration either for book publishing as a whole, or for trade book publishing, between 1947 and 1977.[31] While the new mergers may be different in kind than earlier ones, publishing has historically had a relatively high merger rate, in part because it has always been an undercapitalized industry. This same factor – that it requires very little money to enter publishing – means that the tendency towards concentration is offset by a tendency towards new company formation. The number of publishing establishments has grown, in fact, at about 2.6 percent for the years between 1933 and 1978, and in recent years these new, smaller houses have captured a significant percentage of industry sales.[32] Small, special-interest, or regional companies have sprung up across the country, and while many of them do not publish fiction, others have nurtured young novelists. Increasingly, too, they are either using distribution channels of bigger publishers, which helps large companies by 'feeding' the book dissemination system (a necessity when operating at the mass level), or developing alternate distribution methods.[33] These companies do not usually compete for broad markets in fiction, but they do assure cultural diversity and provide an outlet or even a training ground for aspiring authors.

Even with large companies, bigness does not automatically lead to a loss of diversity. All industry analysts agree that the subdivisions of large communications corporations do not practice inside dealing between, for example, their hardcover and paperback imprints. This assures competition not only among publishers but within them. Large companies have also begun to spin off specialized subsidiaries or personal imprints, recognizing that they can profit from editorial independence.[34]

Certain characteristics of publishing, therefore, limit the tendency towards concentration and dilute its effects. In fact, the number of new titles for every 1,000 Americans almost doubled between 1955 and 1977. While there may be some dispute about what kinds of books these are, these figures indicate no clear-cut trend towards lack of choice for the consumer.[35] Rather they point to the tremendous expansion of the industry after World War II. This expansion was partially based on the boom in mass market paperbacks and was, in part, made possible by capital generated by mergers. More significantly, it also reflects the growth in the American population, and its literacy, during those years. The expanded market may have engendered fears of massification among the cultural elite. But the rise in affluence and education that accompanied the 'baby boom' has given rise to a much more diverse and sophisticated set of reading publics than is predicted by mass culture theorists.

If the effects of publishing mergers are difficult to gauge, the same is true for the growth of bookstore chains. I have already noted that department stores used to be very comparable to the chains. Moreover, it is unclear what these large, rationalized stores mean for consumer choice. In some ways, they offer quicker customer feedback, thus *more* consumer influence, but that may lead to standardized bookstore fare. At present this is hard to know. Most chain outlets stock more titles than the average independent bookstore, which might give consumers greater choice, but numbers are not enough, in and of themselves, to show this. Research is needed to determine what kind of titles each is apt to have and keep on the shelves.[36]

The proliferation of specialized bookstores, especially in

large cities, may somewhat undercut the domination of centralized bookstore chains. While 'genre' stores like science fiction, mystery, or feminist bookstores seem to predominate, the 'traditional' personalized bookstore might be considered among this group as well. Located in gentrified urban areas or chic suburbs, they appeal to the cosmopolitan professional upper-middle class, perhaps the closest modern analogue to the social stratum who used to be at home in traditional bookstores of the nineteenth and early twentieth century.[37] So, although distribution is becoming more rationalized, there are countervailing pressures towards diversity in this aspect of publishing as well.

Just how the fabric of multi-media deals linking books to other mass entertainment markets has affected the hardcover publishing, its range of products – especially bestselling hardcover novels – and the issue of consumer choice (or manipulation) is as difficult to determine as are the effect of mergers and bookstore chains. It would be strange indeed if the rise of new entertainment media had not changed the relationship of books to other modes of communication. Evidence points clearly to some changes, but what they signify in relation to the evolution of cultural products like bestselling novels – or indeed novels in general – is much less clear. For example, there probably are more media-generated or 'packaged' books now than in the 1940s. Hardcover publishers are more dependent on subsidiary rights income than they were forty years ago, and the 'mix' of subsidiary rights has changed. Now publishers rely primarily on subsidiary rights income from mass market paperbacks, movies and television.[38] The growing numbers of spectacular inter-media deals have certainly led publishers to focus a great deal of attention on big books, and while this may not be new, a different reference group (the new media brokers) may have a growing influence over editorial decision-making, so bestselling novels may be filling a different cultural niche than they did in the past. If this is so, shock waves from this cultural shift might affect the book world as a whole. But this process is not a simple one, and we simply do not know enough about it at the present time to assert that cultural massification is the result, or to know what the results, whether for bestselling novels or for literature in general, will be.

Publishing is not a monolithic industry, nor is it likely to become so. Few hardcover bestselling novels are packaged books even now, and more traditional literary and publishing careers exist side by side with the new Hollywood–New York media nexus. That nexus may also produce book packages that reach rather different readers than those of most hardcover novels, which would explain why the hardcover bestseller lists show such continuity over the period of this study. Moreover, while one sector of the industry – mass market paperbacks in particular – is drawing closer to other mass entertainment industries, other developments offset this. New printing technologies are making it easier to handle short-run books more efficiently.[39] And behind the new technologies stand a group of talented editors and editorial consultants who have begun to formulate strategies for nurturing first novels and mid-level books, implicitly recognizing that they cannot sink or swim at the mass level, but must find a special audience. They are making efforts, for example, to build up local or regional fans for serious writers from different areas of the country.[40] While these tactics are born of desperation, they may result in a healthy reconstitution of more communal support for authors, of authorial and audience involvement with literature as a face-to-face dialogue. In turn, this increases the prospects for hardcover bestseller lists with a continuing mix of entertainment literature and more serious novels, and calls into question prophecies of a homogenized and degraded literary culture.

It is also important to remember that even though the publishing industry spends vast amounts of time, energy, and money attempting to impose its definition of what should achieve bestsellerdom, this process has not been and is not automatic. Publishers' attempts to maximize profits by controlling and predicting the market for novels do not always succeed. Indeed, some recent media deals have been expensive failures. Many heavily promoted books do not sell nearly as well as expected, and numerous books are very successful without the backing of major publishing houses.[41]

Perhaps more significantly, the whole process of publishing is structured to be in tune with popular demand. In itself, this gives credence to the assumption that there is a strong link between bestselling novels and the values of their audience. Editors become successful themselves by being attuned to what the reading public will buy, and processes of both formal and informal training are aimed at heightening this sensitivity. If editors attend to new media and possibly new audiences, *what* gets published may change, but demand is still crucial. Moreover, I know from my experience in the 1960s at Simon & Schuster and Knopf that the processes of creating a bestseller involved 'testing' a book on an ever-widening group of people. After identifying a potential bestselling novel, editors would give it to the in-house staff to read, forward publisher's galley proofs to other authors and literary opinion-leaders, and then send the book itself, with accumulated internal enthusiasm displayed in quotes or highlighted in letters, to knowledgeable reviewers, salesmen, and bookstore owners. If the momentum of such campaigns faltered, publishers would cut back print orders and promotion budgets and sell subsidiary rights before potential purchasers could detect the scent of failure. Such marketing techniques permitted flexibility and real attentiveness to what people wanted to read. While the significant actors in this process may have changed – one can hypothesize that independent booksellers are less important now – and the process itself may be influenced by heavier involvement of other media, research is needed before we can say that publishers' responsiveness to consumer demand has given way to audience manipulation.[42]

Two things, however, remain to be said. First, the people who work in trade publishing are, like most potential readers of hardcover novels, middle- and upper-middle-class.[43] The industry and the processes described above are therefore limited to a certain social class, and the people in publishing as well as in the audience have all the biases, blind spots, and limitations of that class. Second, publishing is an insular world within the middle class. People who work in major New York houses – those responsible for most bestselling novels – are bookish, and tend, for example, to be insensitive to people who use books primarily as 'how-to' guides. They tend to be liberal, secular and middle-to-highbrow as well.[44] So publishers stand at a certain distance from many members of the audience for books, even within the middle and upper-middle class.

The class composition of publishing and the literary world in general may explain the high cultural prejudice that has suffused the decades-long debate about the cultural meaning of changes within the publishing industry. I think that I have shown enough evidence to support my claim that these changes have not so transformed hardcover bestselling novels that they are noncomparable cultural artifacts at the beginning and the end of the period covered by this study. I hope that I have also shown that the cultural implications of changes in the book industry are complex, that the simple 'massification' model is inadequate to describe them, and that much more research is needed to adequately understand what is going on.

In conclusion, I would like to speculate that what we think of as high culture may be losing its hegemonic position in the cultural hierarchy. The new media have certainly expanded the cultural universe, reached mass markets untouched by books, and pulled some writers towards a new mode of communication, and new audiences. I think this has affected literature, but I am not sure that the effects are or will be inimical, either for literature or for cultural creativity. If not obvious over the short run, the fruitfulness of a connection between literature and a relatively broad and heterogeneous audience seems clear when examined over time. Harbage has made this argument quite brilliantly in relation to Shakespeare and Dickens. Raymond Williams's work points in the same direction.[45] The novel's development is so closely tied to the rise of the middle class and its role as audience and critic, legitimating the very form itself as art, that the current despair about literature seems informed by a curiously exclusive perspective. Its roots both in the critical stance inherited from the modernist movement and in literary and intellectual dismay at the immense power of the mass production of culture, or non-culture, are understandable. Yet the interstices from which invention springs are mysterious. The bestseller lists, providing examples of books accepted by the critics that have found resonance with a larger public and 'category' books that are sometimes enjoyed by those same critics, may be a node where the next creative melding of subliterature and fine literature, or literature and other media, take place.

Authors of hardcover bestselling novels, 1945–75

In order to determine whether the kinds of people who wrote bestselling novels had changed a great deal during the period under study, I examined several readily available short biographical sources.[46] This rather preliminary investigation leaves many questions both about the profession of authorship and about authors, especially of popular literature, unanswered. We clearly need much more research. However, even this survey of biographical data does strongly suggest, first, that throughout the period most authors came from the middle and upper-middle class. Second, changes in authors' social backgrounds, education, career patterns and even their sense of mission, insofar as the data allow discussion of these factors, appear to reflect larger demographic and institutional shifts that were transforming American society and culture during the twentieth century. In other words, authors and authorship have changed somewhat, but in a fashion that neither undermines the supposition that the content of bestselling novels is relatively congruent with readers' beliefs throughout this thirty-year period, nor suggests that best-sellers of 1945 and 1975 are a very dissimilar kind of cultural product.

There were 156 authors of bestselling novels published betwen 1945 and 1975. No data could be found for three, only the birthdate for two others, and no date of birth for two of the women. One 'author,' Penelope Ashe, was in fact an elaborate hoax: several people collaborated on 'her' novel, *Naked Came the Stranger*. To be able to discuss change, I divided this already rather small group into four generational cohorts: 1875–1900, 1901–20, 1921–40, 1941–60.[47] The largest cohort, that of 1901–20, includes seventy authors. So, although the notes refer to numbers and percentages, this section discusses patterns and 'trends' without elaborate quantification.

Four kinds of information seemed particularly important: data relating to social background, education, occupation, and sense of authorial mission. Social background included parents' occupations, religion, whether foreign or American, and for American authors, regional background and whether the author was raised in a large city or a rural/small town setting. Education included secondary education, public or private, and higher education. For Americans, four categories of colleges and universities seemed relevant: Ivy League schools, other elite private institutions, less prestigious private colleges, and state colleges or universities. Graduate education was also noted. Many authors earned money doing something other than writing novels. 'Occupation,' then, was divided into writing fiction only, writing for print media (e.g. newspapers and magazines), writing for or involvement with non-print media (e.g. movies or television), allied fields such as publishing and academic jobs, and other professions or jobs. 'Mission' was a category that I hoped would yield information about authors' self-avowed purpose in writing, and perhaps about their intended audience. The sources used were not extensive enough to give anything but a superficial impression of authors' purposes, but even authors' brief remarks do change somewhat over time. Again, more research is needed.

Although data on parents' occupation is unavailable for a surprising proportion of authors, especially those born between 1901 and 1920 and between 1921 and 1940, it seems reasonable to say, from the existing information on parents and data about authors' education, that most authors of bestselling novels came from middle-income or relatively affluent backgrounds throughout this period. Authors known to have had parents who were laborers, skilled craftsmen, or relatively poor tradesmen and white-collar workers never account for more than one-fifth of the authors of any period, and sometimes for no more than 10 percent.[48] This is hardly surprising, yet it is worth noting, given the similar class composition of the publishing industry and the audience for bestselling hardcover novels.

Within the middle- and upper-middle-class group, parental occupations fall along a continuum from high school principals, bookkeepers, and grocery store owners to rural doctors, professors, bankers, surgeons, Wall Street lawyers, industrialists, and ambassadors. Among those whose parents' occupations are known, a large proportion of authors came from families of professionals throughout the period, and literary, academic or artistic professions proved important within the professions in general.[49]

38

The distribution of these bestselling authors by sex changed somewhat across cohorts, but this is very difficult to interpret. Seventy-two percent of the bestselling authors born between 1875 and 1900 were men; of those born between 1901 and 1920, 69 percent were men. But 88 percent of the authors in the 1921–50 cohort were men, and the three authors of bestselling novels born after 1941 were all men. Examining bestselling lists until 1980 for authors born after 1941, seven of the total of eight proved to be men. These figures on the whole can only be suggestive, but even if one considers them meaningful, their meaning is unclear. Perhaps fewer women were able to get published; perhaps women eschewed writing as other opportunities opened, or turned to mass market paperbacks with the rise in popularity of, for example, romances. Possibly, also, women have turned to writing later in life than men, so the period I examined may not reflect the contributions of women born after 1921. At best, this ambiguity signifies, again, a need for further study of a much larger group of writers.

Examining the birthplace of authors who published bestselling novels between 1945 and 1975, one can see a gradual decline in the numbers of foreign authors of books that became bestsellers in America. Slightly over 60 percent of the bestselling novelists born between 1875 and 1900 were American, while over 80 percent of those born between 1921 and 1940 were American, and the distribution for the next period, though the numbers are very small, suggests that this pattern continues. British writers, and those from Commonwealth countries, have been a particularly important source of American bestsellers, but their numbers show the same decline.[50] These figures reflect the growing hegemony of American popular culture, a phenomenon that can be observed not only on the American bestseller lists, but beyond the borders of the United States as well.

Within the United States, the regional distribution of bestselling authors over time demonstrates the growing cultural ascendance of New York very dramatically. In the period between 1875 and 1900, writers came from New England, the Midwest, the South, and New York City in almost equal numbers; already New York City had almost regional status. By the period 1901–20, a little more than one-fourth of the bestselling authors came from New York. This period also witnessed a sharp rise in numbers of authors from the Midwest. Chicago alone could claim more writers than New England or the Mid-Atlantic states, and over one-third of the authors came from the Midwest as a whole. During the next period, the numbers of authors who came from the Midwest again resembled the numbers from the South and New England. However, one-third of the bestselling authors born during this period came from New York City, and if one counts towns or cities in the suburbs of New York, the city's privileged position is even more marked. Though the numbers of authors on the bestseller lists, even if one looks at titles published until 1980, born between 1941 and 1960 are small, they suggest that New York's preeminence continued during those years.[51]

Generally, the background of American authors shifted from rural areas or small towns to large cities and suburbs over the course of the twentieth century, in synchrony with demographic shifts for the nation as a whole. Over half of the authors with birthdates between 1875 and 1900 came from distinctly non-urban backgrounds, and a little less than one-third were born and raised in large cities. These proportions were almost precisely reversed during the next cohort. Strikingly, though this is not surprising, all of the growing number of Jewish writers who were born between 1901 and 1920 came from large cities, suggesting that this group, as writers, came into their own as did their milieu. By the next period, 1921–40, even fewer authors came from rural backgrounds. Almost two-thirds of the authors of bestsellers came from large cities, and a significant number appear to have been born in suburbs of large cities. This pattern does not seem to have changed for bestselling authors after 1941, though the numbers are too small to be of significance.[52]

Searching for the religious affiliation of these bestselling authors proved frustrating. Perhaps the most significant piece of information is the fact that these data are unavailable for approximately half of the authors. It is hard to interpret this lacuna, except as suggestive of the pervasive secularism of modern life. The authors themselves, or their biographers, may have considered it irrelevant to their work, uninteresting, or a private matter. It appears that a higher proportion of Jewish authors are identified by their religion than is the case for Catholics and Protestants, and several of these authors speak of wanting to describe the Jewish experience, suggesting that their religion, culture and ethnicity were more powerfully integrated aspects of their identity as writers than has been the case, with some notable exceptions of course, for Christian bestselling authors.

Data about authors' secondary education are even more sparse, suggesting that for this predominantly middle- and upper-middle-class group university degrees were seen, either by authors or their biographers, as the educational credentials of paramount importance, even for authors born between 1875 and 1900. From that period, however, comes the trace of one educational pattern that has the charm of a bygone era: four of the women authors were tutored at home; three then went on to private schools.

Patterns of education for bestselling American authors show rather clearly the increasing importance of higher education. Elite private colleges and universities, especially the Ivy League, figure in a large number of authors' backgrounds, and in later periods graduate education becomes more common. All of these patterns are consonant with developments in American society at large, especially within the middle and upper-middle classes, for whom college education became seen as a necessity during the course of the twentieth century. There is an interesting dichotomy among bestselling authors born between 1875 and 1900. Over one-fourth of this group apparently had little education beyond secondary school, and they include some of the most prestigious writers of this cohort. On the other hand, almost half of the American bestselling authors of this period attended Ivy League colleges. This number drops for authors born between 1901 and 1920: including those who did graduate work at Ivy League universities, about one-third passed through these institutions. However, many others attended prestigious private institutions (e.g. Stanford, Wellesley, the University of Chicago), so well over half of the authors born during this period were educated at elite schools. A much smaller number than in the previous period failed to

41

go to college, suggesting that higher education was becoming increasingly crucial for the 'profession' of authorship, as indeed was the case for other professions at that time. The hold of elite private educational institutions appears to have lessened for authors of bestsellers born between 1921 and 1940, for almost one-third of this group attended colleges that were not among the elite group. However, two authors did graduate work at Ivy League schools, and a little more than 40 percent of the entire group appear to have attended graduate school, marking a sharp increase in education beyond the bachelor's degree.[53] Of course, the numbers are small, so one cannot generalize from this group to all authors, but such patterns are certainly not out of line for the middle classes in the United States as a whole, which witnessed an enormous expansion of higher education after World War II.[54]

Higher education and occupation were the two categories for which there was the most information about these bestselling authors, indicating that the authors themselves, or their biographers, may have placed the most emphasis on the relevance of these experiences for understanding the authors' lives and work. Certainly, understanding the shape of writers' later education and careers enables a less mechanistic analysis of their development than plotting 'social influences' based only on their background, since people make very different uses of their past, and cannot be explained by simple reference to where they have come from. By the same token, looking at the web of institutions with which people are enmeshed during their productive lives can give some insight into the ways that the 'desire to write' is channeled by available opportunities for making a living by writing. Through the periods in which authors who published bestsellers between 1945 and 1975 were born, raised, and wrote, a significant number of authors were, in fact, involved with other kinds of writing, or other professions or jobs, as well as fiction writing. Approximately one-fifth of the bestselling authors practiced professions or jobs that had little to do with their vocation, such as banking, medicine, nursing, the military, the law, civil service, clerical work, or (for a much smaller number) a variety of odd jobs. A slightly larger group was active in what I have called 'allied' professions, such as translating, publishing, or, much more commonly, academic life. Most interesting to me are the numbers who made a living by writing, but wrote for, or edited, magazines and newspapers. Of the authors born during the years between 1875 and 1900, almost 40 percent were reporters, feature writers, literary critics, columnists or editors for newspapers and journals. This number declined somewhat for authors born between 1901 and 1920, in large part because bestselling authors were becoming involved with other entertainment media, such as the movies, and later television, as screenwriters, film actors, script readers, directors, or producers. Almost half of the authors of this cohort were involved in writing either for other print media or the newer entertainment media. For the period 1921–40, this total decreased slightly, but more writers were involved with other entertainment media than with newspapers and magazines. Although the numbers of bestselling authors born after 1941 are very small, this pattern appears to have continued: other media and academic life were increasingly important ways to supplement income from fiction writing. This lends credence to the assertion that a new media nexus, implicating television and movies, may be influencing the kind of fiction written recently. However, it is fascinating to see the numbers of authors who were able to move between two or three of these categories, not only writing novels and screenplays, but teaching writing, or working as magazine writers and scriptwriters, as well as writing novels, and perhaps also holding occasional academic posts.

The data gives two slightly different impressions. One is that most writers, with the significant exception of the group working in unrelated fields, have lived in relatively bookish worlds, or a milieu of wordsmiths, even if they have not been limited to fiction writing. In this, they resemble many publishers, though most publishers intersect with the institutions of the word very differently than do authors. Yet, within these bounds, many authors have moved between quite different milieux, as if their talents were protean enough to take on different shapes according to the opportunities at hand. The first impression may imply some cultural distance between writers and their audiences, who are in all probability less absorbed in the many aspects of the writer's craft. The second implies the need for much more research on the profession of authorship in recent years, particularly on the relationship between authors and the universities, on the one hand, and authors and the new entertainment media, on the other.[55]

My interest in the sense of mission or purpose expressed by authors of bestsellers grew out of an interest in the relationship between authors and audiences: who did these authors wish to reach, and what kind of message were they trying to get across? Authorial intention is important to understand, for what books mean to their authors is one aspect of their cultural meaning. An investigation of this issue beyond the superficial level lay beyond the bounds of this study, but even the authors' short statements about their purposes revealed some intriguing developments. Throughout the period, bestselling authors expressed a great variety of motives and concerns. Yet, there were some common themes. Authors born between 1875 and 1901 tended to speak rather grandly about illuminating the spirit of modern times, lifting people's hearts, or expressing the truth, rather than discussing writing as a means to money or success, or their own self-fulfillment. Authors from the next period continued to express a concern for illuminating moral and ethical dilemmas, expressing universal humanistic themes, or teaching people to overcome prejudice and work towards self-understanding. A growing number of authors, however, simply said they wanted to tell entertaining stories, sometimes as part of what they saw as an old-fashioned tradition. Perhaps they were becoming more unabashedly devoted to popular entertainment literature; perhaps, too, they felt a need to differentiate themselves from more experimental modern writers. Authors born during the years between 1921 and 1940 also discussed storytelling, but in growing numbers referred to writing as a means of satisfying their own inner needs: they mentioned a desire for catharsis, self-revelation, self-understanding, or authenticity as a motivating force. Presumably, the reasons for writing have always been a complex blend of inner needs, and desires to reach other people, but it is an interesting cultural indicator that more authors verbalized self-oriented motives in this latter period, or that the standardized biographical articles selected this kind of statement more often.

It is consonant with some developments in the content of popular novels during the 1960s and 1970s, and certainly with other cultural developments of the times. Yet, from the data I consulted, it is almost impossible to tell what such shifts signify. Surely this aspect of authors' lives, which taps their own subjectivity and sense of personal and literary identity, deserves far more extensive investigation. All that I can say is that in this regard, as in other aspects of their lives, authors of bestselling hardcover novels may well have changed since the latter part of the nineteenth century, but they do not appear to have fallen out of tune with the environing culture of the American middle classes.

The problem of the audience

This study is more closely tied to the world of the people who buy and read books – their wishes and fears, their hopes, uncertainties, desires, and dreams – than most descriptions of American culture based on textual evidence, simply because it is about bestselling novels. Large readerships make bestsellers, so the very category itself entails some reference to the audience. To put it another way, readers are by definition central to this study, since they played an active role in selecting the group of novels under consideration. Nevertheless, two further questions about the audience must be addressed to justify generalizing from the content of the novels to the values and beliefs current in the society whose members produce and read bestsellers.

First, who reads bestsellers? And, is the contemporary audience for hardcover bestselling novels drawn from the same social strata, by and large, who were reading bestsellers in 1945? If so, one can argue that a shift in the content of bestsellers over time reflects a more generalized cultural shift, not merely a drastic change in the social composition of the readership for bestsellers.

Second, what has this audience 'taken' from the books they have read? Obviously, if each reader gets something entirely different from a given novel, one cannot generalize about the values and beliefs of the audience. But I will argue that,

45

although interpretations vary somewhat from individual to individual, they are structured by the books themselves. By this I mean that novels are symbolic creations that refer to, or draw on, literary, cultural, and linguistic conventions that are themselves rooted in the realm of 'common meanings' that makes intersubjectivity possible. A corollary to the question of what readers get from books is whether it is justifiable to assume enough similarity in response to generalize from the academic analyst's reading to what other people find in the same books. While my reading is not necessarily the same as that of the audience for bestsellers, I will argue that it is closely related, so inferences about what other readers get from bestsellers are plausible.

Readership

The data that are available on readership in America make it impossible to determine exactly who the audience is, not merely for specific bestselling novels, but also for bestsellers as a whole. Publishers themselves have not undertaken such research, because of the nature of the publishing industry and its products. Unlike television, magazines, or newspapers, publishing houses, themselves relatively small businesses, issue an extremely varied range of books every year, most with small profit margins. And unlike other media, their products – books – are sold only to the public, not to advertisers. Given this, the costs of market research on individual titles clearly outweigh its benefits. Only when a publisher issues a line of relatively standardized products – such as formulaic romances like the Harlequin or Silhouette series, where the formula *is* in a sense the product, does the incentive for research on its market outweigh the cost. In such cases publishers have had readership surveys conducted to map out the parameters of what they hope will be a relatively stable demand for a relatively 'fixed' type of narrative, of which each book is merely an example.

The fact that there are no formal studies of the market for specific titles, or even for formula fiction other than the most rigidly constrained kind, does not mean that there is no knowledge in the world of books about who reads what.

Salesmen and editors are successful insofar as they can keep in touch with the shifting tides of demand for certain kinds of books, but in general this knowledge has not been systematically researched. Publishers learn sensitivity to the market informally, in the course of doing business, and it is often so taken for granted by practitioners, who speak of hunches that a given book will or will not sell, as to seem to them to lie in the realm of intuition rather than that of a 'science' of the marketplace.

Individual publishers' interests coincide with and indeed meet with the interests of educators, librarians, intellectuals, and their sponsors in foundations, business and government, in the area of readership in general. All these groups share a broad concern with the future of the life of the mind, for all are both invested in it and dependent on its continuation, in subtle as well as obvious ways. Thus, over the years since World War II several broad surveys of readership and library use have been mounted. These studies give an impression of who, in general, book readers are, and some equally general information about reading choices and patterns. Though it will not elucidate specific questions about the audience for bestselling hardcover novels, some of this information is clearly pertinent for placing that audience socially, because it is, *a priori*, drawn from among the group of those who read books. Since the surveys of readership conducted over the past thirty-five years were designed by different people for slightly different purposes, it is not always possible to compare their results. In the brief discussion that follows, I will present results from the most recent study, conducted by Yankelovich, Skelly & White, Inc., for the Book Industry Study Group in 1978, and whenever possible refer to findings that deal with similar areas of questioning from earlier studies.

The Yankelovich study investigated the reading habits of adult Americans (aged sixteen and over), and discovered that 55 percent of the population had read at least one book in the previous six months. This represents a slight increase over earlier studies. For example, in *The Library's Public*, Bernard Berelson concluded from a 1948 survey that about 60 percent of adult Americans had read at least one book in the previous year.[56] All of the studies identify a core group of

47

'serious' or 'heavy' readers, who make up between 25 and 30 percent of the population.[57]

Book readers, and especially heavy readers and book purchasers, have come disproportionately from 'the higher end of the socio-economic spectrum' throughout the period under study. They have a somewhat higher income than the rest of the population and, more importantly, have had more education. Completion of high school appeared to be an important watershed in earlier studies: those who did not finish high school were much more likely to desert books in later life than those who completed high school, or went on to college. Book reading also tends to drop off with age, especially after fifty. Researchers hypothesize that physical disabilities may account for some of this attrition, but mention that older people tend to be less well-educated and more socially isolated than younger people, and both these factors tend to depress reading.[58]

Women are slightly overrepresented among book readers (as compared to the population in general), and the same is true of single people – but children in the house appear to have a positive effect on adult book reading. Employment is not a deterrent to reading, though some people experience tension between reading for work and for pleasure. And though availability of books influences reading patterns, in general book readers are geographically distributed very much like the population as a whole.[59]

Moving a step beyond the demographic correlates of reading, all the studies show that book readers tend to be an especially active and socially involved group of people. Berelson's early study shows that book readers are more 'plugged in' to all other media of communications than those who do not read books – and are more critical of their content.[60] In the years since 1949, television has become an important activity, and although Yankelovich found that book readers do not watch quite as much television as other groups, his study shows that book readers are more actively involved in a greater number of leisure time activities than nonreaders or those who read magazines or newspapers but do not read books. Book readers also participate more in organizations, especially professional and service organizations, than other groups, although nonreaders are relatively quite involved in religious congregations.[61] Jan Hajda's 1962 study of reading in Baltimore, and McElroy's analysis of data from a 1965 NORC survey, also point to the importance of general social involvement for sustaining and nurturing the activity of reading. People with whom to discuss books, and a social context where books are 'in the air,' apparently make the act of reading, though solitary at its core, flourish.[62]

Since the audience for bestsellers is drawn from the nation's book readers, these broad surveys of readership generate a useful – though indirect – portrait of the people who read bestsellers. At the very least, they establish that the audience comes from a group that is somewhat more educated, affluent, and socially involved than the 'typical' American, and that this has been the case since the end of World War II. Changes in the thematic content of bestsellers, then, are probably not due primarily to a shift in the social composition of the audience.

Beyond this rather crude description of readers, studies can also provide information about book selection and reading patterns. What these findings imply about the audience for bestselling novels must, again, be teased out from more general discussions. One can, however, infer both that the audience for bestsellers is larger than might be assumed from the numbers of books sold and that, although the audience for books is rather fragmented, bestsellers may be our nearest approximation to a literary 'common denominator.' If these influences are valid, it would mean that the cultural change described in this study is relatively broadly based.

Results from the Yankelovich study that refer to patterns of book selection show that novels, and perhaps especially bestselling novels, are read, though not purchased, more often than nonfiction books.[63] This suggests that whether they are borrowed from a library or passed along from person to person, they reach more people than their sales figures indicate. Category choice and dissemination patterns among lighter readers seem to confirm this. Light readers tend to choose books from among the most popular categories, many of which are represented on the bestseller lists, and also tend to borrow books from friends and relatives. These social networks may keep light readers in the reading public, in fact, and ensure that novels, and perhaps more especially popular ones, catch the attention of even relatively uninvolved readers.[64] One can infer that some such mechanism is at work from Yankelovich's findings about the 'last book read.' Although the last book read is equally likely to be fiction or nonfiction, if it is a novel it is more likely to be a bestseller. If not purchased, this 'last book read' is apt to have been traded with or borrowed from a friend or relative. Also, the most important source of information about 'the last book read' is a recommendation from friends or relatives, and this is especially important for light readers. Of course, people informally recommend and pass along many books, but publicity for bestsellers is geared specifically to set this kind of word-of-mouth 'advertising' and circulation in motion. While some of it may not result in the purchase of books, it does ensure that bestsellers reach more people than actually buy them. Thus, if one can infer a cultural shift from thematic changes in bestselling novels, it will not be limited to the relatively small numbers of people who purchase hardcover bestsellers.[65]

Though the audience for popular novels is broader than their sales imply, each novel probably reaches a somewhat different group of people, because even the rather scarce data available make it clear that there are different audiences for different books. Such a statement is intuitively obvious to anyone who reads, yet relatively little research has been done on reading choices and patterns. Two kinds of sources, however, establish both that the audience for books is quite fragmented, and that bestsellers probably overcome that fragmentation more than most other books.

The growing numbers of specialized book clubs imply that the American reading public has become, in Philip Ennis's words, 'a series of subpublics insulated from each other by the boundaries of their tastes and the absence of a general forum bringing together all book readers.'[66] In 1982, the *Literary Market Place* listed 175 adult and 21 juvenile clubs. However, the three largest book clubs account for about 80 percent of book club sales, and their selections are heavily larded with bestselling novels.[67] So although Ennis is right about audience fragmentation, bestsellers probably represent the closest approximation we have to that 'general forum.' More than any other socially defined literary category, except perhaps 'the classics' which are not only read by adults but are part of school curricula, bestsellers represent that part of the world of books that Americans, in general, participate in as readers. Bestselling novels, then, are those works of current written fiction Americans have most in common with each other.

The three detailed studies of reading patterns undertaken since the 1940s underscore the immense variation in reading choices, even among people of similar ages and occupations. In-depth interviews reveal that every person selects and uses books differently, in a complex synthesis forged of background, interests and temperament.[68] Reading is expressive behavior, as everyone knows who stops to reflect on how they choose what books to read and how they make each book a part of their ongoing life. In other words, reading patterns embody each individual's life-print, as fascinating to decipher as any other manifestation of personality. And, like individual lives, these patterns are also profoundly social, for they reflect not only the influence of schooling or occupational and leisure time involvements with other people, but also the bonds of community, kinship, friendship, and marriage. Books are the foundation for discussion groups in churches, suburban neighbourhoods, and professional associations. More informally, they link parent and child, husband and wife, friend and friend. People affirm, extend, and limit their social involvement by their choices of broad subject categories and individual books. From what is known about these choices one can speculate that if people read fiction at all, bestselling novels are the books that tempt people across their usual literary boundaries, for bestsellers are a social phenomenon. Reading bestsellers is a social rite as well as an individual exercise, and reading books that are 'in the air' is often the token of membership in a given social group – a ritual, as it were, of social integration.

In sum, we know all too little about the audiences for bestselling novels. Clearly, there are a number of overlapping groups reading each individual title. However, by virtue of their very popularity, bestselling novels probably represent those works of fiction most Americans read in common. If bestsellers resonate with their readers' values and tacit assumptions, as seems very probable, this study describes a cultural shift of some significance.

Book readers in general, however, come from the middle and upper-middle classes, while the average American, according to the Yankelovich study, more closely resembles the reader of newspapers and magazines but not books.[69] Book readers also display a tendency towards active involvement in social networks centered around a variety of occupational, service, and leisure time interests, including an interest in other kinds of communication. This group does not represent all Americans, in other words, but it is the same social group addressed and described by the social critics who discuss modern America.

It may also be a group for whom success, social mobility, and visions of the good life have particular importance. One of the marks of achievement in America has been to acquire membership in the world of books, insofar as self-improvement through education, and the leisure and money to cultivate the life of the mind, have served as metaphors for success. Further, a certain degree of common ground exists between the audience for and the authors and publishers of bestselling novels, since all are members of that amorphous group, the middle and upper-middle classes. This gives discussions of the communicative process within which novels become bestsellers an oddly circular quality: authors writing for an audience rather like themselves, publishers knowing 'intuitively' what will sell because they have a certain similarity to the pool of potential customers, and an audience easily finding novels that mesh with their values because the books were written and brought to their attention by their kind of people.

Interpretation

The preceding section delineated the broad parameters of the audience for hardcover bestsellers, and established that it has not changed much since 1945. This means that thematic shifts in the novels are not simply a function of a dramatic change in the social composition of the audience. But in order to claim that changes in novelistic content reflect changing attitudes or beliefs within the audience two further questions must be answered. First, is there any commonality in people's readings? Second, is the culture critic's reading of a bestselling novel sufficiently like that of other people's to permit an inference about what others find in the books? Both questions are essentially empirical, but exceedingly difficult to answer empirically.

I will argue for a certain level of commonality in readers' responses to bestsellers, and a certain level of similarity between my interpretation of these books and those of other readers, on both theoretical and limited empirical grounds. With the following caveat. One individual can never know exactly what other people 'get' from a book. A moment's reflection on your own reading will show how subtle and mysterious the processes of textual appropriation are. Which characters in a novel do you respond to, how, and why? Which parts of the various novels you have read come to mind, and in what situations? How have the novels you have read more than once changed with each rereading? Even self-knowledge in this area is difficult, in part because all readers move through a world full of cultural products that are in some sense experienced individually, yet are also part of a social process of discussion and evaluation.

Researchers have found it difficult to discover how much, and in what ways, people digest from the bouillabaisse of books, television, popular music, movies, and magazines that they are served by the industries of cultural dissemination. Studies that address this problem by observing people in everyday life, rather than in laboratory settings, show that people generally pay attention to messages that accord with their existing attitudes, screening out communications they do not want to deal with. This heightens the probability that popular novels are in line with the values of their readers, for they are the novels that people have chosen to be open to.

Yet, a group of influential literary thinkers and culture critics have recently pointed out that even one text can generate a variety of responses among its readers. Hermeneuticists like Gadamer, European literary theorists and semioticians such as Wolfgang Iser, Roland Barthes, and Umberto Eco, and American 'subjectivist' critics like Norman Holland, David Bleich, or Stanley Fish, whose work is more sociologically grounded, have all begun to explore the implications of this fact for the study of literature and its cultural meaning. The issues they raise must be addressed, for if there is no common ground of response to books, inferences about readers' values based only on textual evidence are questionable.[70]

The growing focus on reader response is itself contingent on developments within the community of literary scholars and their relationship to other communities of readers and thinkers. Three aspects of this complex interrelationship are especially germane to how critics are thinking about literature. First, as literary critics have become increasingly involved with the abstruse texts of the twentieth-century literary canon, they have become more and more self-conscious about the difference between their reading and that of other people. They are also becoming aware that the interpretations and evaluations generated by the literary community may not be hegemonic in the world beyond universities and literary magazines. The loss of interpretive authority may make literary theorists see differences in interpretation less as a function of right and wrong readings than as a reflection of social and individual diversity. In other words, cultural relativism has entered literary thought as the relationship of the literary world, and its reading, to the broader social world, and its readings, has shifted.

Second, modern literary critics read difficult texts. Serious modern novels violate conventions, unravel plot and character, and play with esoteric allusions to other texts and cultural fragments. Roland Barthes calls these texts 'writerly' because they require the reader almost to assume the creativity of a writer in order to accomplish a reading. I think the open-ended quality of the texts that engage contemporary critics urges recognition that every book may provoke a variety of interpretations, each quite tenable according to the criteria by which the literary community judges interpretive adequacy.

Third, literary theorists are part of a larger intellectual community. And, like their colleagues in philosophy, history, and the social sciences, these theorists find it hard to maintain belief in nineteenth-century ideas of progress or of an easily discernible objective reality. Many literary thinkers, who once expected progress towards ever better interpretation, are now aware that texts call forth variable responses that may have as much to do with the environing cultural climate as with the text itself. Similarly, the view that a text is an empirical fact has begun to dissolve into a haze of doubts as literary thinkers realize how much textual interpreters bring to the construction of textual meaning.

This new, reader-oriented perspective in literary theory is especially useful for investigating the cultural meaning of texts because it forces consideration of the social and individual processes by which books are reconstituted by their readers each time they are read. Reader response theorists stress, for instance, that readers approach each text with certain expectations – that it is fiction or nonfiction, that it is written by an author who intended to communicate something – which powerfully influence how a book is understood. Indeed, the interaction of those expectations with what Holland calls 'only a series of words' allows us to experience the involvement and pleasures of reading.[71] To stress the interactional quality of reading highlights the active partnership of reader with author in the reading experience. Moreover, if what a text means depends on what readers bring to it, then those readers' motives and desires, social backgrounds and situations, and cultural assumptions must be understood in order to understand the text that they, in part, are creating as they read. So this perspective reveals a new horizon for culturally oriented studies of literature. This territory includes the entire set of social practices adumbrated by the individual act of reading – from the institutions that inculcate reading skills and taste, and the people and processes that create the literary canon, evaluate contemporary authors, or shape readers' expectations, to the social relationships that motivate individual reading needs and choices.

Yet, at their most extreme, reader response theorists are so eager to show that individuals assimilate texts differently that they forget the social and cultural commonalities that enable books either to be read or indeed to be written at all. David Bleich and Norman Holland represent this 'subjectivist' position. Although they deserve applause for venturing into empirical investigations of actual readers reading, their work shows some of the contradictions that can arise when individual differences in interpretation are the sole focus of analysis.[72] In *Five Readers Reading*, for example, Holland explains the varied reactions of five students to Faulkner's story 'A Rose for Emily' as a function of their different 'identity themes.' To do so, he 'reads' the students' personalities through interviews and thematic apperception tests. He then constructs an underlying 'lifestyle' for each student, which he grants an objective existence while assiduously denying a similar facticity to the story they read.[73] In other words, Holland accords the reader's personality an ontological status he denies the text. Personality is unified and coherent, and it determines what a reader will get from a text, while the power of the text to constrain response all but disappears.

Although Bleich and Holland are fascinated by differences in interpretation, and highlight these differences in their descriptions of readers' responses to poems and stories, the responses show a remarkable similarity. The student responses to 'A Rose for Emily,' for example, all focus on the social structure of Faulkner's South, relationships between Miss Emily, her father, and her lover Homer, and issues of sexuality and authority. Miss Emily's character emerges rather clearly from student discussions of the story, though each student gives it quite different nuances. Similarly, one can garner a relatively complete rendering of several of the stories and poems featured in Bleich's book *Readings and Feelings* from reading only what he reports of student responses to them.[74] In other words, reading their collage of student responses to a story is rather like listening to people tell you about a person you do not know. Each account may accentuate or downplay different aspects of the person's character, or express a different emotional tone, yet the responses delineate a portrait of a particular person.

In fact, both theorists implicitly recognize that there are certain limits to the subjective variation in response. Bleich shows how people add to poems in their readings, for example. Surely this assumes some consensus about what is there to begin with, even if we grant that the text is itself dependent on pre-existing linguistic and cultural codes that are the symbolic distillate of social practices. Holland, too, grants that 'the words can't be just anything. Miss Emily . . . cannot be an Eskimo – at least not without doing violence to the text.'[75] In an earlier work, Holland is even more explicit about the framework that constrains interpretive variation, contending that there is a 'range of sensible responses, but within that range, everybody has his own response.'[76]

For this study, it is important to gauge how broad or narrow the range of culturally sensible interpretations for bestselling novels is, since only if responses are similar can we assume that novelistic content indicates anything about readers' values. Here, the work of Stanley Fish is helpful, for he focuses on the social context of interpretation. He argues that texts have neither an infinity of meanings nor a lack of meaning, but rather that meaningfulness is always dependent on an 'interpretive community.'[77] He is most particularly interested in the literary establishment, a community that decides not only which textual interpretations are academically respectable, but also which texts are 'worth' interpreting to begin with. But his work suggests that we must investigate the institutional mechanisms that shape audience expectations about popular novels, as well, and the range of response that they either imply or help to create.

The ways bestsellers are produced and disseminated show that publishers assume a relatively similar response among readers nationwide. Certainly they orient their marketing nationally, tailoring advertising and publicity campaigns as if there were a quite homogeneous audience. Identical ads are released in major metropolitan newspapers across the country, or in nationally circulated magazines. Authors appear not only on local talk shows, but on network television, and a few novels, especially formulaic series like Harlequins, are advertised on national television as well. Similarly, bestseller lists are tabulated nationally.[78] This all implies that there is enough similarity among the bestseller audience for nationwide marketing to succeed commercially. Either this similarity exists, or the very mechanisms of publicity help to create a rather homogeneous set of expectations among the public, enforcing constraints on variation of response.

Whether because of publishers' efforts or because of more subtle influences, I would also argue that people regard bestsellers as relatively conventional entertainment literature, and thus read them rather differently than they read the predominantly difficult texts that form the modern literary canon. Literary critics develop a plethora of interpretations for texts because they are confronted by texts that demand great creativity on the part of the reader. Critics are also reading for production: originality of response is tied to chances for publication, and hence to one's critical reputation and scholarly success. The standard critical essay, in fact, begins with a summary of previous criticism and an assertion that something new and better will follow. Most bestsellers are packaged not as literature but as entertainment, and I think that, unlike books read in college English classes or in scholarly studies, they are usually seen as relatively transparent narratives, easily consumed communications from author to reader. Book jackets and advertisements even shape the reader's expectations about what kind of story lies within the cover (though most readers are alert to the possibility of false claims), so people know in advance what specific form of entertainment they will be experiencing as they read.[79]

In order to test my sense that such books are perceived relatively similarly, I chose several novels from the broader sample of bestsellers under study, and looked at their reviews. Obviously, this can only be suggestive. Reviewers are not the whole reading public, though they probably help to shape other readers' conceptions of what the books are about. The reviews do suggest a *relative* uniformity of response. In every case, reviewers agreed about the content of the novel. They were much more concerned than I about evaluating each novel's esthetic worth, however, and their critical judgment varied widely. They also often discussed the author's development as a writer, and commented on how a particular novel contributed to his or her career – issues that lie beyond this study. Nonetheless, their responses and mine show a high degree of agreement, at least on the level of what each novel was about.

If contemporary responses to these conventional books tend to be, by and large, unproblematic and unsurprising, evidence exists that response becomes even more conventionalized over time. Studies by psychologists of learning indicate that people's memories of stories or essays tend to reduce them to ever more formulaic clichés; individualized features or peculiarities of style and content are flattened and blurred. Recent studies of the processes of oral transmission of stories also support this conclusion.[80] Thus it is probable that the commonalities in response to and interpretation of these books will persist over time, insofar as the books are remembered at all. Most of the bestsellers probably settle easily into the sediment of their readers' past experience, becoming part of their tacit and taken-for-granted ways of viewing the world, the structure of assumptions that seems so natural it hardly ever rises to conscious awareness.

Since it is precisely this level of attitudes and beliefs I am trying to elucidate through textual analysis, my own readerly intuitions are quite different from those of the majority of people who read bestselling novels. This difference must be acknowledged and its consequences explored, but first I would like to mention an obvious demographic similarity. As a well-educated, middle-class female who formed the fiction-reading habit early, I am part of the same loosely defined social group from which book readers are drawn, though I am separated in time from those who read the bestsellers of 1945 when they were first issued. As reader, then, I bring to those books a similar set of social and cultural experiences, of perceptual categories, of expectations not only about the books but also about the social world. And it is worth noting here that the scholars who have been most vexed by the problem of textual interpretation have also been the most conscious of differences between themselves and the people who formed the 'natural' audiences for the texts under study. Nineteenth-century hermeneutics was founded by biblical scholars aware of the gulf that separated them from the historical Jesus; intellectual historians have been concerned about the 'presentist' blinders that distort our understanding of old texts; anthropologists know that the people they study approach the world with conceptual categories unfamiliar to the modern West; and literary critics are painfully aware that other people – including their students – read different books, and read them very differently, than they do. In this case, however, audience and analyst have some social similarity.

Yet I turned to bestselling novels as a basis for systematic cultural analysis. The intentions that informed my reading were not the same as the intentions and reading experiences of the audiences who made these novels bestsellers. They presumably approached the novels as entertainment, looking for diversion, or escape, or in some cases the pleasures of reading an acknowledged literary master. I read the same novels as evidence. This difference in intention is potentially a source of both strength and weakness. On the one hand, the analyst may, by virtue of a more attentive and repetitive reading of bestsellers, be able to discover thematic patterns, or what Raymond Williams calls 'structures of feeling' that remain in the background of consciousness for the ordinary reader. What is taken for granted or implicit may emerge into clarity because of a shift in focus. Any analyst of contemporary culture will of necessity be in many ways a part of its environing web of assumptions and beliefs – the web that in this case seems to entangle authors, audiences, and analysts in a remarkably circular configuration. A difference in focus, implying a difference in stance towards that which one is part of, gives a chance of seeing with greater clarity – as if one had stepped back from a group of friends and were looking in from the outside.

On the other hand, as anyone knows who has played the observer at a social gathering, distance can encourage an idiosyncratic interpretation as easily as allowing clarity of sight. The specific danger, in endeavors such as this one, is that the readings of cultural critics and ordinary people are so different that they are not experiencing the same 'book.' When this occurs, the critic's analysis of a book's meaning or significance for others may be elegantly reasoned – yet entirely off base.

This often happens when critics with literary training look at popular fiction, and it is particularly obvious in two kinds of analysis, which manifest similar critical strategies although they express very different value judgments. First, when a critic approaches popular novels with contempt and presumes that their effects are deleterious, one can sense that the critic thinks other readers are either misled, manipulated, or simply stupid for not realizing what pap they are reading. Much of the feminist discussion of popular romances and their ideological function takes this stance.[81] These judgments are suspect because the critic's reading and that of the audience may be very dissimilar – each noticing, remembering, interpreting, and valuing very different parts of the book, and each integrating the book very differently into their ongoing lives. A similar problem arises when the literary critic feels positively about a popular novel and seeks to elevate it into the ranks of books deserving serious consideration by showing that its effects on its readers are good. In such analyses the literary critic hunts down metaphor and symbol, draws parallels to great writers, and places the novel within one or another literary tradition. He or she shows approval by reconstituting the book as *literature* – a strategy that may legitimize the critic in the eyes of his or her peers, but will not elucidate what the significance of the book is for other people who do not require such justifications for their reading pleasure.

If my readerly intentions are different from those of most readers of bestselling novels, they are also different from those of literary critics. I am not trained in that tradition, and am not part of that 'interpretive community.' In particular, I am free from the mission of esthetic evaluation that is so central a part of the literary endeavor, but may be only a marginal issue in sociocultural analysis. Similarly, literary critics must prove themselves masters and mistresses of the rules and conventions of literary analysis – a different game with a rather different audience than that of sociologists.

Moreover, I am the kind of reader who is swept away by the story line and characters in a novel. When I begin a book, I am caught up in its world. I forget the time and resent the telephone. The story pulls me along at a hectic pace. It was frustrating to do the research for this book, because when I would open a novel, my sociological concerns would retreat to a small, dark corner of my mind. Rarely could I take notes while reading; usually I would turn down corners of pages or put bits of torn paper between them as markers, then winnow through passages after the book was done. So, although the books did become evidence and I never entirely forgot the preoccupations of the cultural analyst, my attitude towards the novels was very similar to those of other people for whom novels provide a magical escape into another world.

In sum, while recognizing the power of each reader to constitute texts differently, I am arguing for enough similarity in interpretation among the audience for bestsellers, and between myself as analyst and other, less research-oriented readers, to support generalizations about what others 'make of' these books based on my own reading of them. I have read bestselling novels as evidence, approaching them differently from the people who pick them up for relaxation and entertainment. But on the one hand, this difference in stance may be fruitful and, on the other hand, despite it I probably have enough in common with other members of the audience to make our readings quite similar. In like wise, although different individuals and subcultures within the national audience for bestsellers experience these books somewhat differently, it seems reasonable to assume a large area of shared response.[82] This common ground testifies not only to sociocultural similarities within the audience, of course, but to efforts on the part of publishers, reviewers, booksellers and others involved in the book business to disseminate books. This process involves telling potential customers – in the subtleties of packaging as well as more overtly – what each book *is*, so one of its unintended consequences is the manufacture of a set of shared expectations that shape response. The book business, in other words, either taps into or elicits shared responses among readers in order to make a novel a bestseller.

3

Bestselling novels 1945–1955: from entrepreneurial adventure to corporate-suburban compromise

The bestselling novels published at the beginning of the decade 1945–55 celebrate a vision of entrepreneurial success. The story of individual achievement is at the center of many plots, protagonists are men in search of success, and the overriding tone in the universe of bestsellers is optimistic and confident about the forward march of social progress and America's rightful place in its vanguard. Slightly over one-fifth of the decade's ninety-eight hardcover bestsellers are stories of success, and elements of the formula figure strongly in another twenty-one novels. Many of the other books, as well, though stories of adventure or romance, take for granted entrepreneurial assumptions about the individual and the social world. The eight war stories are one significant exception to this tendency. Often they celebrate the warlike virtues and a vision of brotherhood in combat that goes against the entrepreneurial grain.

It seems fair to label as 'entrepreneurial' the implicit assumption about success that suffuses character, plot, setting, and tone in these novels, because it, like Adam Smith's invisible hand, strongly links the individual's saga of independent self-improvement to the triumphant advance of world progress. Because the individual contributes to ideals and a community beyond himself, his achievement transcends the limits of the narrowly personal, and its effects may surpass the limits of his lifespan.

63

The individual's quest for achievement, however, remains at the center of these stories. Heroes tend to be successful men, and their careers tend to be independent and self-made, whether in business or in the professions. But these self-sufficient lives are in harmony with an expanding world that sets few limits on what heroes can attain, and more importantly, allows success to be won without any personal cost. Instead, success, and more personal rewards such as happiness and love, are conceived as being in synchrony rather than in opposition, so the successful man need feel no inner conflict, need make no choice between irreconcilable demands. These men seem to stand free of constraints from institutions and the social context of their achievements. The world is a field for their conquest, and they create their own destiny in splendid isolation, though their individualism paradoxically serves the common good.

It challenges all simplistic 'mirror' theories of literature that success is thus heroically construed in fiction appearing at the end of World War II, the time when America was passing into a new phase of corporate integration, when white-collar bureaucracies were proliferating, and when the educational credentials attesting to specialized competence were becoming increasingly important determinants of social mobility. It seems reasonable to see these novels as another expression of the well-documented desire for a return to 'normalcy' after the upheaval of the war and the Depression that preceded it, a comfortable reassurance that people could still apply traditional ideals in a new context. The entrepreneurial definition of success in bestselling novels immediately following the war represents, then, a powerful source of cultural continuity, a look backwards into an idealized golden age, like Norman Rockwell's magazine covers of small-town American life, or the ethos of the small businessman characterized by C. Wright Mills in *White Collar*.

Perhaps because of its idealization – or distortion – of the complexities of postwar life, the entrepreneurial definition of success is celebrated in its most pure and fabulous form in historical novels and novels about religion. These stories, set at one remove from the mundane world, provide an exotic shell in which one can see the operation of contemporary values in exaggerated form. Several qualities of the entrepreneurial definition of success are, therefore, highlighted by novels in these genres. For example, the importance of the *quest* for success, as adventure or agent of character formation, is obvious.

Two historical novels of 1945, *Captain from Castile* by Samuel Shellabarger and *The Black Rose* by Thomas Costain, exemplify this theme. Both books tell the story of young men of good blood who must make their way in the world because their families have fallen foul of the backward-looking institutions of the time. In *Captain from Castile*, the de Vargas family is victimized by a large landowner working in concert with the Inquisition. In *The Black Rose*, Walter of Gurnie's family has been cheated of its ancient holdings because of the iniquities of the feudal system: the grandfather followed Simon de Montfort against the king. The young heroes both embark on voyages of conquest. Pedro de Vargas accompanies Cortes to the New World, and Costain's Walter of Gurnie crosses Asia to Cathay with the Mongols. Along the way, both face trials of strength, discipline, and fortitude, and at the end of their adventures they have won not only riches, fame, and love, but a finely-tempered maturity and strength of character. Adria Locke Langley's story of Huey Long, *A Lion Is in the Streets* (1945),* and Irving Stone's tale of Jesse Fremont, *Immortal Wife* (1945), also portray the adventure of seeking high achievement. Other books with less exotic settings, like Henry Morton Robinson's *The Cardinal* (1950), or *Not as a Stranger* (1954), Morton Thompson's chronicle of a doctor in the making, concentrate in more detail on the self-discipline and dedication that lead to accomplishment.

Many novels of this period show their heroes' achievement in the context of, and contributing to, an expanding world. Pedro de Vargas opens up America for imperial Spain, for example, causing his father to reflect:

'The New Age, an age turned westward across the Ocean Sea. How different from his own! How unimaginable!'[1]

---

* Dates in brackets following titles in the text indicate the year in which a book first appeared in the bestseller list.

And in Thomas Costain's *The Moneyman* (1947), Jacques Coeur, the protagonist, is cast as the First Entrepreneur. He says of his attempts to extend commerce and manufacture in the hostile environment of feudalism:

> 'my enterprises are different from anything the world has ever seen before. There is no limit to the growth I foresee.'[2]

His story makes it clear that his vision of ever-expanding commerce enables him to unite self-aggrandizement with the altruistic goal of making a better world for all. In Costain's words:

> he had sensed the chance to revolutionize the whole face of trade by a new type of shop, one in which goods of every description would be offered for sale. . . . It was not solely the desire for power and wealth which had urged him on. The thought was firmly lodged in his mind that this was how things should be. . . . Commerce must be bound together, taking in the whole world if necessary, so that goods would be brought from all the far corners of the earth and then sold at prices which all people could pay. He had said on many occasions, 'I want the wife of the artisan to wear silks like the fine lady of the court and the poorest tinker to have spices in his wine.'[3]

Expansion alone is not at issue, for in these novels social progress is the inevitable corollary of growth. In the classic formulation that suffused postwar thought, Jacques Coeur describes the American way to world peace through a better standard of living. He is

> convinced that the world would never grow out of its interest in war and killing until life itself was made more comfortable and interesting and worth while. That was what he was striving to do. . . .[4]

The Cardinal (1950) sets Stephen Fermoyle's rise in the Catholic hierarchy firmly within the context of an ecclesiastical success story centered upon American Catholicism, its rising influence within the Catholic world, and its progressive contribution to the institutional development of religion. At the beginning of the book, Lawrence Glennon misses a papal election because the laws for attendance make it impossible for an American prelate to reach Rome within the appointed time. But by the book's conclusion, laws are being changed to accommodate the New World churches, and ecclesiastical gossips speculate that Stephen himself might become the first American Pope. American Catholicism's brilliant performance rests, in part, on a very materialistic foundation: she cares for many souls, and she garners large revenues. But the American church has also, through religious pluralism and the separation of church and state, given a distinctive touch to the historical evolution of the church: the American way of Catholicism. Even Jett Rink in Edna Ferber's *Giant* (1952), a man who remains nasty and unscrupulous throughout the book, contributes to social betterment by exercising his entrepreneurial drive. In developing the oil industry, he not only opens up the Texas economy, but also shatters the despotic ranch-based power structure. On the heels of his accomplishments will come (it is supposed) fair elections, unions, and increased social justice for Mexican-Americans.[5]

A belief system that equates personal achievement with expansive social progress gives selfishness the aura of self-transcendence, for each hero's entrepreneurial quest not only improves his life and the lives of his immediate community, but also adds to the momentum of world progress. While this equation is familiar to anyone who has studied American individualism, these novels make the cliché concrete, showing how entrepreneurship almost literally opens each individual's personal horizons, pulling him into synchrony with the forward march of history, and fusing his life with the totality of human achievement. As Costain's Walter of Gurnie examines a paper factory in China, making plans to introduce its manufacture to Europe, he imagines

what it would mean if this substance called paper were introduced into England: how all men in time would learn to read, and messages writ in honest black and white would travel all over the land to the greater glory of God and the betterment of mortal minds and bodies as well. The yard ceased to be a small enclosure of hard-baked clay. The tanbark walls seemed to vanish and shining horizons surrounded him on all sides.[6]

The act of individual achievement is paradoxically an act of communion. It affirms a connection with others, albeit in very abstract terms. This abstraction may be the symbolic expression of an increasingly complex postwar socioeconomic order, but community, however tenuous, is still implied. So, too, is an almost mystical sense of limitlessness. Jacques Coeur, Pedro de Vargas, even Jett Rink have gained a certain kind of immortality for their achievements reverberate with far-reaching consequences. These heroes act on the broad stage of world history. In so doing they live on beyond their time, and perhaps more crucially, are infused with a self-transcendent sense of purpose. Their lives have an enduring moral weight on the world's balance scales precisely because they have pursued their own entrepreneurial ends.

The pre-eminence of this entrepreneurial definition of success to the exclusion of other ideals and moral standards is also particularly evident in religious and historical novels, for in their pages the alternative codes of values one would expect to find are curiously conflated with the American business ethos. Historical novels, for example, are almost devoid of cultural relativism and appear to represent thinly veiled idealizations of present values. Protagonists of these novels look forward with naive optimism to a future very near the 1950s, celebrating their own achievements as harbingers of what was to be (at least ideally) realized in twentieth-century America. Thus not only does Jacques Coeur prophesy that peace will come with middle-class affluence (an ironic comment on the power of ideology, two years after the second worldwide conflict between industrialized countries), but Walter of Gurney speculates on the advantages of widespread education and universal literacy, Sinuhe in Waltari's book *The Egyptian* (1949) looks forward to the future when monotheism and religious freedom will become universal, and Andrea Orsini in Shellabarger's *Prince of Foxes* (1947) eagerly anticipates the widespread acceptance of science and technology. In this one sense, these historical novels are incurably present-minded. Yet they transpose the entrepreneurial story and its moral code into the past. Perhaps only then – set at a safe distance in exotic lands and faraway times – can it assume its fullblown panoply of mythic attributes. If so, it may indicate some pessimism among authors and audiences about the entrepreneurial dream of fabulous success and imperial adventure, for historical idealization at once legitimizes the contemporary dream and removes it from everyday reality.

Religious novels show that God requires something different from material achievements, but characterize those who rise to glory in God's terms very much like successful businessmen, investing religious protagonists with all-American entrepreneurial virtues. In Russell Janney's *The Miracle of the Bells* (1946), for example, the hero becomes an effective fighter for Christ precisely because of his talents as a publicity agent. When he 'sells' Jesus to apathetic coal-miners and hard-hearted mine-owners, he is likened to St. Michael, and no conflict appears between his earthly and heavenly success.

Lloyd C. Douglas's religious novels also focus on the hero as self-made man. The hero of *The Robe* (published 1942; a bestseller in 1942, 1943, 1944, and 1945), a young Roman soldier of good family, must make his fortune on the dusty outskirts of the Empire because his betrothed has refused the Emperor's advances, and his hard-headed pragmatism keeps him from embracing Christianity for some time. Douglas's *The Big Fisherman* (1948) discusses the conversion of St. Peter in similar terms. According to Douglas's account – which lies outside the biblical record and therefore tells us a great deal about the imaginative world of the author, and perhaps his audience – Simon Peter has achieved independent success as a fisher-businessman:

> Beginning as a mere roustabout and chore-boy on a dirty trawler, his wages paid in low-grade mud-suckers which he peddled from door to door among the very poor, Simon had gradually made himself useful enough to be in a bargaining position among the fleet-owners; for he was strong as an ox and fearless to the point of foolhardiness. . . . And so it was

that before he was twenty-three Simon owned a half-share in a fairly good fishing-smack. At twenty-eight he owned it fully and had taken on a crew of four. And now he was master of the most prosperous and best known fleet on the lake. . . . As his self-made success increased, the Big Fisherman's character reflected both his earlier frustrations and his current achievements, not always to his credit.[7]

Yet the very talents that brought him worldly success – strength, fearlessness, initiative – make him a mighty servant of Christianity, even though he must tussle with his materialism before embracing Christ:

Everything was going wrong for Simon, lately; everything! It had all stemmed from this mad Carpenter who had taken it into his head that the people would be better off if – if – they weren't quite so well off; that's what it came to; own nothing – and be happy.[8]

Robinson's *The Cardinal* is more attuned to the contradiction between entrepreneurial materialism and spiritual achievement, but even it depicts successful prelates as very entrepreneurial souls. Ned Halley, the one priest in the book who 'wears a shining circlet of purity above his head,'[9] cannot raise money. Though his parishoners love him for his saintliness, his clerical colleagues repeatedly refer to him as a 'conspicuous failure'[10] as a pastor. Stephen Fermoyle, the self-made Cardinal, on the other hand, has energy, ambition, intelligence, and spectacular acumen and drive. Metaphors of the business world color portraits of all the church leaders, including the Pope:

The Supreme Pontiff, like any other executive easing muscular tension before an important interview, adjusted the bibelots nearest him on his desk.[11]

Robinson's portrait of Halley pays token remembrance to a moral order built on more spiritual values, but even Halley is only rewarded in the afterworld. The novel implies that in this life the church rewards the same behavior and character traits as does any other organization, and that the ways one climbs the ladder of ecclesiastical success greatly resemble those by which people ascend the business hierarchy.

But the familiarity of this model, and of the kinds of men who are heroes in popular stories of religion, blurs the distinction between Christianity and the business ethos. Like the football players who take the stand at evangelical rallies and urge us to get God on our team, these characters and their stories serve to strip religion of its potential to undermine the established secular standards of morality. Their presence testifies to the pervasive power of entrepreneurial models of success.

The successful man is central not only to religious novels, but to many novels of this period. Whether or not they are primarily concerned with success, the sweet smell of success demonstrably pervades the books under consideration. Embodied in historical fantasies, or in more realistic accounts of professional, ecclesiastical, or artistic life, the story of success is a popular motif. Morerover, the successful man, like the beautiful woman, holds center stage even when the achievement of success is not the central issue of a book. (The successful woman is more problematic.) This analogy cannot be carried too far, for unlike the beautiful woman, the successful man is much less object than subject, but like her, he is a conventionally appealing figure, who gives a welcome familiarity and sense of moral soundness to the literary scenes he graces with his presence, and like her, he engages the reader's interest and sympathy by virtue of his attributes and actions. He is at once the stock figure and the secular saint of the times. His life is an exemplary one; his example is both inspiring and comfortably familiar.

Typically, the successful man in this decade's popular novels tends to be either a self-made man or successful in a career that affords him great autonomy. In historical novels the heroes, who must 'make their way' in periods when social mobility was unusual, appear in positions of atypical social marginality. Andrea Orsini in *Prince of Foxes* (1947) is a peasant turned artist, soldier and diplomat; the artist hero of *The Silver Chalice* (1952) is an urchin adopted by a wealthy Levantine family, and Sinuhe, in *The Egyptian*, is an orphan who becomes

71

a doctor. All, in other words are cut adrift from their times and see their social world from a very critical and individualistic perspective. Contemporary novels also tend to center on individualistic occupations and autonomous careers. Men are entrepreneurs, lawyers, doctors, publicity agents; women are film stars, writers, and in historical novels, courtesans. Because of their autonomy, these individuals are relatively untrammeled by institutional pressures. In a sense they are not embedded in a social-structural context, for their entrepreneurial drive overrides its constraints. In society, yet somehow beyond its fetters, they forge their own character through their achievements, and in so doing reshape their world.

An understanding of success as freedom and personal efficacy may have had particular resonance in the immediate postwar world. Careers were becoming less autonomous, large organizations were swallowing up small businesses, and Americans were beginning to realize they were only one part of an interdependent global economy. This entrepreneurial vision may have shored up the ideology of individualism, increasingly at odds with social reality. Whether or not it served such a purpose, the vision is reiterated over and over again in bestselling depictions of successful men.

These male heroes (women are more complex) are gifted with innate vision and drive. Energetic and untormented by conflicting motives, their inborn talents seem to unfold naturally in their achievements. Like Calvinists predestined for salvation, they are earmarked for success. Usually, authors do not even explore the sources of their hero's ambitions, especially in historical novels. For example, Costain accounts for Jacques Coeur's amazing career in this fashion: 'His was the type of mind which sees far beyond the range of vision of the ordinary man.'[12]

On occasion, novelists do mention motivational factors. Sometimes an exceptional family – poor, hardworking, honest – lies in the background, invoking the familiar theme of parental sacrifice for the next generation. The warm glow of nostalgia suffuses such family portraits. For example, Bill Dunnigan in *The Miracle of the Bells* tells the heroine he had never married because he had never met a girl

72

'who could measure up to my mother. She took in washing to put me through grade school – and a year in high school. I wasn't born in any palace either. A tenement on Houston Street. . . . My mother was the real McCoy. . . . She died after she got me through that high school term. I didn't realize how hard she'd been working – washing in the daytime, cleaning offices in a skyscraper at night. . . .'[13]

This nostalgia taps into one of the most moving of all American stories, but it obscures the pain and conflict that also marked the process of intergenerational mobility. Moreover, it explains social mobility in a stratified society – how could a swan come from a family of ducks? – by asserting that the successful hero's immediate family were *not* ducks, just deprived swans who struggled under adverse circumstances, enabling their children to realize the swan-potential in the family. This leaves stereotypes about the general worthlessness of other members of that class or ethnic group unquestioned.

More often, the hero's gifts are quite simply genetic. This formulation, of course, also provides an easy resolution to questions of social mobility. In historical novels, especially, heroes are of 'good blood,' often illegitimate sons or daughters of aristocrats, like the hero of *Lord Vanity* (1953) or the heroine of *The Moneyman* (1947), or children who have become separated from high-born parents, like Amber of *Forever Amber* (1947), or the hero of *The Egyptian*, who is a rightful son of Pharaoh floated down the river, like Moses, by a jealous co-wife. Similarly, Langley's Huey Long figure seems to be a descendant of the Virginia Breckenridges.[14]

Even the more realistic contemporary novels sometimes invoke this almost biological assumption about the sources of success. Morton Thompson accounts for his protagonist's desire to be a doctor in *Not as a Stranger* (1954) in this description of Lucas Marsh as a young boy following the town doctors on their rounds:

This was the stuff on which his days were fed. This was his hunger. This was his necessity. This activity of Hominidae was for him its prime activity and all the rest were corollary. . . . This had been so from his beginning. The

73

minor surgeries neither awakened nor quickened him. They fed him. They fed the hunger which was Lucas Marsh, a named mechanism of cells in which by accident or design this hunger was the summed and ordered craving of the cells themselves.[15]

Lucas was *meant* to be a doctor; he was born with a vocation locked into the very cellular pattern of his being. This understanding of talent and drive draws close to a secularized notion of the Protestant calling. The 'elected' have an inborn tendency towards achievement; like Bunyan's Christian, they must embark on their quest alone; like the bearers of Weber's Protestant Ethic, their success in the world is closely linked to their moral worth.

One reason why this decade's successful heroes respond to their calling without ambivalence, and tend to lead uncomplicated inner lives, is that their success demands few sacrifices. They are not perceived as making difficult choices between different possible ways of living their lives, because success brings interpersonal rewards in its train. Nonetheless, because of their absorption in their work, many of the protagonists are essentially isolated. This is particularly true in historical novels where, simply because they are self-made, the heroes fit into none of the established social strata: but in these novels their isolation is usually mitigated by a woman or a faithful servant-companion.

In novels set in the present, the heroes are not usually prey to circumstances that isolate them as much as their historical counterparts. Nonetheless, they often stand in an attenuated relationship to the world of other people because of their strong drive to succeed. For example, the young Lucas Marsh feels curiously distant from his rather ordinary roommate because Lucas spends so much time working:

To Alfred each hour of the day was an hour for play, each moment that could be borrowed or stolen or pre-empted. . . . Little by little Lucas realized that most of the boys at college were like Alfred. . . . When Alfred fell behind, as he frequently did, Lucas was relieved to loan him his notes, to work with him. Helping Alfred made him part of the cosmogony of youth, of the youth around him, of the circle he contacted but inside whose circumference he did not live. He felt no superiority. He felt a difference between himself and them. But as his difference had always existed he did not feel set apart by it; it was his relation to the group.[16]

Most realistic novels, however, adduce a more complex relationship between isolation and success. In novels describing an enterprise, such as Edna Ferber's story of cattle and oil in Texas, *Giant* (1952) or Frances Parkinson Keyes's tale of Louisiana sugar cane, *The River Road* (1946), the hero who controls the business is only as isolated as the head of a patriarchal clan. Men 'on the way up' are more alone, but this is as natural to them as other fundamental components of their individualism. Jett Rink in *Giant*, for example, is friendless until he can use his wealth to compel social acceptance, but his isolation is not shown as a sacrifice; he is simply a driven man. To generalize from these admittedly disparate portraits of successful heroes, one might say that although not all of them are seen as being isolated individuals, their emotional ties to other people are not overwhelmingly absorbing ones, especially in comparison to their work. Strong affective bonds are structurally at odds with a successful career.

Yet a career-dominated life brings substantial rewards that ease the hero's isolation. In these novels, success usually leads to happiness, love, and the benefits of interpersonal power, or a more generalized sense of having contributed to the common good. If Jett Rink can look with pleasure down a hotel banquet table at the social elite of Texas assembled on his whim, so Stephen Fermoyle can enjoy an almost godlike beneficent power over the lives of other people. At the end of *The Cardinal* he listens to a concert on shipboard. The pianist is his niece: he made the decision to sacrifice his sister's life that she might be born. The violinist is a young Polish protégé of his from his first diocese, and he plays on a violin made by Rafe Menton, the son of a French-Canadian *luthier* whom Stephen befriended in an impoverished parish.[17] In one sense Stephen has created these people, for without his intervention, they would not be who they are. So Stephen can rest at ease in the knowledge that his personal success has brought him companionship and gratitude from the people his life has transformed.

For women, success in any career other than wife and mother is problematic, and the rewards for success are much more dubious. In their portraits of 'selfishly' successful women, bestselling novelists draw a strong connection between ambition and sexual promiscuity. These women may find glamor, but rarely love. In historical novels, like Daphne du Maurier's *Mary Ann* (1954), or Kathleen Winsor's *Forever Amber* (1945), they are mistresses to the great. In more realistic novels, they are entertainers. In either case, they provide titillation, and at the end suffer the sentence of conventional morality. Amber, for example, suffers the torments of the damned when the aristocrat she loves comes home with a beautiful and virtuous bride. Winsor implies that Amber's ambition makes her both unlovable and unloving, so she has little chance of happiness with any man.

If women desiring worldly success are not whorish by nature, they tend to be peculiar in other respects. The heroine of Winsor's second novel *Star Money* (1950), for example, feels an outcast in her own family; she turns to a writing career in rebellion against them. She also has a neurotic terror of death and is self-involved to the point of narcissism:

> 'I'm not nice at all. I don't really care about anything on earth but myself. And the worst of it is – the only reason I'm even sorry about it is because I know someday I'll have to suffer for it.'[18]

Suffering is indeed the final lot of most ambitious women. A woman confronting the world directly and on her own undermines the accepted sexual division of labor. She also casts into doubt a host of other assumptions about women – their essential helplessness and need for male protection, for example – which reinforce the relations of dominance and submission between men and women that bestsellers proclaim as natural and inevitable. Some heroines are altruistically ambitious, like the heroine of Mary Jane Ward's *The Snake Pit* (1946), who writes to help support her husband, or Olga Treskovna in *The Miracle of the Bells*, who explains her reasons

76

for becoming a movie actress to her friend and publicity agent Bill Dunnigan:

> 'Whatever made you want to "go on the stage," as they say?'
> 'I didn't exactly want that at first,' she said. 'I didn't even know about theatres! But I did want to give something worthwhile to the world – something beautiful and clean and good – for everything I knew seemed the other way round.'[19]

Nonetheless, even the most selfless careers seem to place women in positions of personal vulnerability. Mary Jane Ward's heroine is institutionalized with a nervous breakdown, and Olga Treskovna's delicate constitution quickly succumbs to tuberculosis.

Bestsellers generally reward only those women who remain within the bounds of wifely supportiveness, firmly ensconced in the domestic sphere. Women authors, in particular, describe the home in such loving detail that it emanates an aura of wealth, ease, and contentment. An example from Frances Parkinson Keyes's *Joy Street* (1950) makes a tempting display of the housewife's material rewards:

> Fresh frilled curtains appeared in the bedrooms and richer draperies on the ground floor; the well-rubbed mahogany in the dining room was brightened by an array of wedding silver; the library furniture was arranged and rearranged until it was placed in the way most conducive to complete comfort. And one afternoon Emily led her husband to the spacious linen closet and, throwing open its double doors, revealed pile after pile of snowy sheets and pillowcases and towels, gartered with satin-covered elastic to insure perfect regularity, and scented with small bags of lavender nestling between each pile.[20]

Such passages – and there are many in this decade's bestsellers – convey to readers that this is true womanly success, that the definitions of womanhood within which these wives move so gracefully are entirely natural, and that a world with such a house and such a wife at its center is truly in order, at peace, secure.

The social world in which the successful heroes, and even their more conflict-ridden female counterparts, display their drive for achievement, is an uncomplicated backdrop, on the whole. It is interesting to examine however, if only to reveal novelistic assumptions about the class structure and social order within which the self-made hero's mobility takes place. Such assumptions provide the 'stage set' not only for stories of success, but also for novels about adventure and romance as well. By showing the perceived social context for descriptions of success, an analysis of these assumptions makes the terms of success more comprehensible.

For example, the novels of this period describe society from positions near the top of the social hierarchy. In historical novels about great regional enterprises, history is almost invariably seen through the eyes of those who control wealth and property. For instance, the story of cattle ranching is not that of the ranch hands, or even of the ranch hands and their bosses, but of the ranchers, their families, and the families who own the neighbouring spreads. In contemporary novels, towns, suburbs, and cities are described through the inter-locking lives of pillars of society: judges, doctors, bankers, mayors, executives. Novelists center on their concerns, des-cribe the fine nuances of their social relationships, explore the recesses of their subjectivity, and elaborate their moral dilemmas in great detail. People below them fade into insignificance and near invisibility: the working classes and the poor stand on the edges of the world of bestselling novels.

While this is not surprising, given the class composition of bestselling authors and their audiences, one consequence of this perspective is that the social world of these bestsellers is almost class*less*. These books both reflect and perpetuate the myth of the classless or the wholly middle-class society; they constitute one of the cultural products that not only expressed the commonly held notion that poverty, social conflict and a divergence of interests between rich and poor were not present in America in the 1950s, but also reinforced that restricted vision of society. A range of social phenomena – the residential segregation fostered by suburban growth, industrial zoning, high school tracking, as well as cultural products from elementary school readers to television advertisements – lent plausibility to the world of the bestsellers, a world characterized by consensus, commonality, and homogeneity. In the world beyond bestsellers, this skewed understanding could not only confirm the self-satisfaction of those who were well-off, but could also stunt the growth of any alternative visions of society among people who were less comfortable and less satisfied. Within the universe of bestselling novels, this fictive classless society provides a congenial setting for untrammeled entrepreneurial individualism, for few social structures affect individual life chances.

Another consequence of this view of society is more directly related to the definition of success *per se*. Though most characters in bestsellers are conventionalized, the lower classes (when they appear at all) are most simplistically stereotyped. They are shown as faithful servants, drunken louts, or streetcorner rowdies leering at heroines. A passage from John O'Hara, in *Ten North Frederick* (1955), exemplifies this view:

A well-built man in his thirties, obviously half drunk, dressed in his poor best and with newly trimmed red hair and beard, came out of Rinaldo's barber shop as Charlotte Chapin reached the entrance to Dutch Amringen's next door. At first he seemed to be trying to make way for Charlotte, but as he moved to his right, she moved to her left, and when she moved to her right, he moved to his left.

'Girlie's playing,' said the man. 'Give us a little kiss.'

'Get out of my way, you disgusting man,' said Charlotte.

'Get outa my way, you disgusting man. You got a pretty little pussy? Have you?' Now he was deliberately blocking her way.

'Get out!' she said.

'Me see your little pussy,' said the man.[21]

This working-class man's language, at once bestial and childlike, categorizes him as almost subhuman – an animal whose sexuality will threaten middle-class women, and thereby the entire social order of kinship and possession of the female, unless he is kept in his place.

Novel after novel characterizes working-class men as almost a different species than men of the middle class. Whether good or bad, they are creatures of strong instinctual drives and little capacity for reason. Brinkley's *Don't Go Near the Water* (1956) gives a humorous turn to this animalistic stereotype in a description of the 'typical young Navy man,' Farragut Jones:

> He looked like some fearsome sea monster come to shore.
> His flesh suggested scales and barnacles. . . . Beneath his
> pushed-up sleeves his hairy, bulging muscles were
> engraved with more thoroughly visible tattoos of naked
> women. His eyes watched the officer as a natural enemy,
> animal-like.[22]

But a strong animus lurks behind this picture of the ordinary Navy man, and other passages of its ilk, suggesting that stereotyping and trivialization are necessary novelistic strategies for dealing with the realities of a stratified society. Class poses a threat to the entrepreneurial vision of the social world – a threat that may have had particular resonance for the middle class in the years immediately after the war, when a wave of labor militancy swept the country until it was recontained by restrictive labor laws, the Cold War, and what appears in the novels as a contentment born of affluence. For good working men figure in these novels as well. They are still men of action, and still lusty and devoted to the pleasures of the flesh rather than the life of the mind, but they have been tamed, their aggression and sexuality contained by economic security and the prosperous beer belly of bourgeois life.

Sometimes the poor become objects of compassion, in which case they generally are of interest for what they can reveal about the sensibility of their patrons: they do not exist in or for themselves, but as foils for the middle-class conscience. An example from *Giant* by Edna Ferber (1952) describes Mrs. Leslie Benedict, who serves as the book's voice of liberalism, ministering to the sick wife and child of one of her husband's ranch hands:

> She felt like someone in a Victorian novel. Lady of the
> manse. How old-fashioned. She ought to have – what was

it? – calf's foot jelly, revolting stuff it must have been that they were always bringing in napkin-covered baskets for the defenseless poor. The floor of the little wood and adobe hut was broken so that you actually could see the earth over which it stood. Rats just come through those gaps, Leslie thought, looking at the squirming infant. Rats and mice and every sort of awful creeping thing.

She returned the child to the basket and his screams were shattering. The woman on the bed looked up at her submissively. Leslie felt helpless and somehow foolish.

'What is your name?'

'Deluvina.'

'What does your husband do here – what is his work?'

She wished she didn't sound like a social worker invading someone's decent privacy.[23]

Sometimes the poor fall into less tender hands, and become the victims of unscrupulous con men or demagogues, but bestselling novelists blame their plight on their own lethargy: passive and incapable of self-help, they await whatever changes exceptional men or women may bring to their world. The Huey Long figure in Adria Locke Langley's *A Lion Is in the Streets* (1945) justifies his demagogue's career by reference to the general shiftlessness of the poor:

'Folks blame me 'n men like me – 'n we got a lot t' answer for, mebbe. But the people, Verity – the people – they're so dang slothful.'[24]

Because lower-class characters are so overwhelmingly categorized as almost subrational, the rise of the self-made man from their ranks is difficult to explain except in almost biological terms – a mutation, as it were. This reinforces the genetic understanding of talent, drive and entrepreneurial individual success.

If social class presents a dilemma mostly solved by denial, ethnicity is also often dealt with in remarkably simplistic terms. For example, in books like *Earth and High Heaven* (1945) or *Gentlemen's Agreement* (1947), which are essentially pleas for liberal tolerance, Jews are shown as being just like everyone else, only perhaps morally superior. A chapter in *Auntie Mame* (1955) serves the same purpose. In *Joy Street* (1950), the heroine is a Beacon Hill Brahmin who sits in her beautifully appointed home and watches members of newly arrived ethnic groups (Italians, Jews, Irish) gradually step into her living room; they appear before her (and our) eyes as they achieve entrée into Boston's most restricted social circles. It is presumed that their backgrounds will invigorate the elite, but they certainly do not threaten the Protestant entrepreneurial consensus. So, uncomplicated by a social-structural understanding of success and failure, or by alternatives to entrepreneurial values from different ethnic groups, different historical periods, or even from religion, the social world as depicted in bestselling novels in the immediate postwar period reinforces the entrepreneurial definition of success and provides a setting in which self-made heroes can confidently exercise their talents.

Towards the end of this decade there is a fundamental shift in attitude towards this entrepreneurial mode of success. Several novels suggest that a consuming devotion to work may be overdriven and compulsive, and very likely to ruin the possibility for other, more personal rewards. Such novels begin to describe the individual's life and the world in general as limited and finite. Choices must be made between work and leisure, family and the public world. The individual becomes dependent – on others for happiness, on an organization for a job. A new view of success emerges, one I have called the 'corporate-suburban' model, in which the hero's saga is less one of conquest than one of integration of a set of disparate tasks and roles. Work is described as a fragmented and abstract process rather than as the creation of a product, and the hero's search for a sphere of mastery draws him increasingly into the private world of domestic and affective ties. Success is redefined in terms that approximate 'the good life,' a balanced whole in which work is valued only insofar as it permits material comfort and familial happiness.

I want to explore the thematic dimensions of this 'corporate-suburban' definition of success in Sloan Wilson's *The Man in the Gray Flannel Suit*. Although a detailed exposition of one book goes against the methodological grain of this study, it does not mean that my analysis rests on a single novel. Indeed

Brinkley's *Don't Go Near the Water* (1956) and Patrick Dennis's *Auntie Mame* also embody the new understanding of success. However, a reformulation of success stands at the center of Wilson's novel, and its publishers claimed that it expressed a central dynamic of the time. As the jacket copy says:

> Although this novel is about the Rath family, the man in the gray flannel suit is a fairly universal figure in mid-twentieth century America. The gray flannel suit is the uniform of the man with a briefcase who leaves his home each morning to make his living as an executive in the near-by city.

The novel was certainly greeted by critics and the public as a tellingly accurate portrayal of an almost ideal-typical representative of a new breed of man, the well-educated white-collar worker in a large corporation, who commutes to his job from the suburbs. The book's title, in fact, became a catch phrase independent of its novelistic origins, much like the title of William Whyte's book *The Organization Man*. But while William Whyte's term defined the man by his role at work – his place as a well-honed, other-directed, conforming cog in the corporate machinery – Wilson's phrase emphasized the person inside the occupational uniform, a person trying to make sense of a world where work meant sitting behind a desk performing something with no inherent logic or concrete results, worthwhile only in terms of monetary reward, since at least the money could be used, in Wilson's words, 'to create an island of order in a sea of chaos.'[25]

The island of order is, of course, the small privatized world of the family. Family responsibilities, in fact, push Tom Rath, the hero of the book, to look out for a new job, one that offers at least some chance of success. At the beginning of the book, both Tom and his wife Betsy feel trapped in their suburban house, a house whose 'thousand petty shabbinesses bore witness to the negligence of the Raths,'[26] a house he thinks of on the June day in 1953 when a friend of his mentions an opening at United Broadcasting Corporation.[27]

From the time that Tom Rath decides to apply for the job at UBC, *The Man in the Gray Flannel Suit* becomes a story of his drive to the top, his chance to become a corporate leader, and finally his refusal to make the necessary sacrifices. What is interesting about the book is the new twist to the old story, the deployment of virtues established by the old ideology of success in the service of something new. Such cultural reformulations are at the heart of social change. Every time social groups assert a new vision of the world or of what is right they make it understandable and justify it to themselves and others by plaiting into its fiber some strands of what is old and accepted. Groups as disparate as mid-twentieth-century American communitarians, German Fascists, and the leaders of Zionism have all harked back to the past in the service of social innovation. The new, after all, is built by people enmeshed in the old, people who glance knowingly or unknowingly over their shoulders into the past for precedents that are paradoxically both reassuring revivals and constituents of the unprecedented.

Novels, of course, do not set forth precedents and justifications in logical argument. Instead, novelists construct characters and motivations according to familiar and stereotypic patterns. Then, the reader can enter into the newly conceptualized situation in trusting empathy with the protagonist. Especially if the reader's life already bears some resemblance to that of the hero, the novel will simply be expressing in fictional form a set of moral and social relationships that the reader is already predisposed to feel at home with; the novelist will be speaking for a stance towards the world which the reader has already taken up or has been groping towards in 'real' life.

Certainly, Tom Rath is a sympathetic hero. He loves his wife; is still amazed at her beauty,[28] and respects her courage and optimism. He is also a warm and caring father, who not only wants to be able to give his three children the kind of education he had, but tells them bedtime stories at night. If he is dismayed by the postwar world of work, it is not because he lacks toughness. In the war he killed seventeen men as a paratrooper, with regret for the necessity, but without shirking. But in spite of the fact that Tom is smart, brave, and honest, his is not a story of entrepreneurial success.

One crucial reason for, and feature of, the difference between this and more traditional stories is that the world Tom inhabits is not a simple backdrop for heroic initiative. Instead, it is problematic, fragmented, and full of conflicting memories, responsibilities and demands. As Tom puts it:

> There were really four completely unrelated worlds in which he lived. . . There was the crazy ghost-ridden world of his grandmother and his dead parents. There was the isolated, best-not-remembered world in which he had been a paratrooper. There was the matter-of-fact, opaque-glass-brick-partitioned world of places like the United Broadcasting Company and the Schanenhauser Foundation. And there was the entirely separate world populated by Betsy and Janey and Barbara and Pete, the only one of the four worlds worth a damn. There must be some way in which the four worlds were related, he thought, but it was easier to think of them as entirely divorced from one another.[29]

Perhaps the most searing contradiction comes from the war, since the war led Tom, and many other men, to actions incomprehensible to their civilian friends and relatives, taught them skills which had no place in the orderly corporate world to which they returned, and took them into a world which was not amenable to rationality or planning, a world in which chance dealt you life or death, where each step you took was over the abyss of total uncertainty. Tom's protection from wartime chaos was founded on a typical buddy relationship with a man named Hank Mahoney. When Tom himself kills Hank by throwing a grenade a few seconds too soon even this tiny bubble of security is destroyed. For Tom, 'the final truth of the war' is that

> it was incomprehensible and had to be forgotten. Things just happen, he had decided; they happen and they happen again, and anybody who tries to make sense out of it goes out of his mind.[30]

This experience shatters Tom's confidence in a benign and sensible world and burdens him with a dragging weight of memories. He feels a profound loss of nerve as he contemplates his prewar dreams of success. Remembering how he sat

85

and listened to his wife 'talk brightly about the future' on their first night together after the war, Tom reflects:

> The trouble hadn't been only that he didn't believe in the dream any more; it was that he didn't even find it interesting or sad in its improbability. Like an old man, he had been preoccupied with the past, not the future. He had changed, and she had not.[31]

The nature of work in the glassy corporate skyscrapers also makes success problematic for Tom. Work is no longer something concrete and comprehensible. It is slippery, hard to pin down, and because it is related less to a product than a process, it is very difficult to tell when you are doing it well. Tom continually finds himself bewildered about his exact duties and position at United Broadcasting Corporation. His immediate boss hates him, but Ralph Hopkins, President of the vast company, is a small, polite, deferential man who seems genuinely impressed with whatever Tom does. Tom's actual work ranges from writing and rewriting a speech, to arranging Hopkins' accommodation at a hotel in Atlantic City, where he is to give this speech to a group of mental health professionals. Gradually Tom begins to sense that performing specific tasks is less important than sorting through the maze of the corporation and what it wants of him.

Not only is there little of substance in the work, there is also little of direct relevance to Tom's personal life. So work, like the war, is another splinter in a fragmented life. In a sense, Tom's task is less that of conquest than of integration. Tom's task is to bring discordant parts of himself and his world, at odds through no fault of his own, into some kind of harmony. This is in striking contrast to earlier books.

In spite of these conflicts, Tom does manage to launch himself on a drive towards traditional success, and reaches the point where it is within his grasp. His intelligence, independence, and honesty pay off, and Ralph Hopkins, the head of UBC, offers Tom a chance to train as his successor. But Tom eschews traditional success for success of another kind. In justifying his refusal, Tom illuminates some of the implicit assumptions encapsulated in the newly legitimated 'corporate-suburban' definition of success:

> 'I don't think I'm the kind of guy who should try to be a big
> executive. . . . I don't think I have the willingness to make
> the sacrifices. I don't want to give up the time. . . . Nobody
> likes money better than I do. But I'm just not the kind of
> guy who can work evenings and week ends and all the rest
> of it forever. . . . I can't get myself convinced that my work
> is the most important thing in the world. I've been through
> one war. Maybe another one's coming. If one is, I want to
> be able to look back and figure I spent the time between
> wars with my family, the way it should have been spent.
> Regardless of the war, I want to get the most out of the
> years I've got left. . . . If I have to bury myself in a job every
> minute of my life, I don't see any point to it. . . . I want to
> get ahead as far as I possibly can without sacrificing my
> entire personal life.'[32]

Tom's statement expresses a new recognition of the costs of
success, a new conceptualization of work and personal
happiness standing in opposition to each other rather than
forming a mutually reinforcing totality. This formulation of the
possibilities and constraints of life posits a much less expansive
universe than did the earlier formula. The world is finite, and
the hero, with only so much time or energy, must choose
family or job, work or leisure, or at least balance them against
each other within the context of his own life. Before, the hero
could have both success and happiness because energy and
time were conceived of in less static and limited terms. The
world itself was expanding, and the hero's own natural drive
for success led him into accord with the world. His life as an
individual organism could then duplicate the larger and more
universal processes of growth in such a way that desires in
apparent conflict could be subsumed in a totality that resolved
contradictions by expansion. Perhaps this is why the heroes of
earlier books addressed themselves to a future beyond their
own lives: since they were building for the future, their life
work contributed to a process bigger than their own lives, and
therefore they could in a sense live beyond their span of years.
There is an expansive sense of immortality and collective

purpose which is lost in the retreat of the gray flannel men to their privatized family worlds, where life is seen, not as a process, but as a pie to be divided between a man's different roles, as breadwinner, paterfamilias, and so on.

The Man in the Gray Flannel Suit legitimates this new 'corporate-suburban' model of success in that Tom Rath is amply rewarded for his decision. Not only does Hopkins admire his forthrightness and give him a tailor-made position within the corporation, but some inherited land brings Tom a fortune. But the novel also describes more traditional modes of achievement, presenting, as it were, a pluralistic view of society congruent with social-scientific paradigms of the day. For example, minor characters are earnest self-made second-generation Americans, recapitulating in their lives an earlier American dream. Their careers have an old-fashioned entre-preneurial ring, and seem to be justified within the novel's moral universe both because they have had to overcome poverty and because they are successful at a local level. They are among the powers-that-be in a Connecticut town, and they strive no higher. Tom Rath has had the possibility of success in its transcendent corporate form, and the novel implies that the new corporate-suburban model applies most specifically to men at work in such organizations.

The head of the UBC, Ralph Hopkins, also represents the single-minded drive towards achievement. He is shown as an overdriven man whose addiction to work has ruined his family, but may be necessary for a captain of corporate enterprise. When Tom repudiates Hopkins's version of success, Hopkins is stung to reply:

> 'Somebody had to do the big jobs! . . . This world was built by men like me! To really do a job, you have to live it, body and soul! You people who give just half your mind to your work are riding on our backs!'[33]

While Hopkins's single-minded devotion to work may be necessary for a corporate chieftain, Tom Rath garners Wilson's complete approbation. The pluralism of *The Man in the Gray Flannel Suit* is thus heavily weighted in favor of the corporate-suburban ideal. The vision of alternative possibilities is also limited, for even Hopkins, the most successful man in the book, has had to choose between family and work – a reaffirmation of assumptions about life's limitations.

The corporate-suburban view of success is also formulated as a critical revolt against the older generation in Wilson's novel, since the relationship between Ralph Hopkins and Tom Rath is described in almost father–son terms, and Tom's refusal to be Hopkins's successor is heralded as a defiant and risky decision. This formulation of the shift to a new definition of success may on the one hand express a generalized perception of a sharp social transition, but on the other hand, it also masks the quality of accommodation in Tom's choice. The development of America into a corporate society, and the transformation of independent small businessmen into suburban-dwelling corporate employees who had to devise life strategies for coping with a new range of occupational possibilities, must have seemed abrupt to many people. The crisis of the Depression, followed by the hiatus of the war years, may have influenced a widespread understanding of this transition – in fact, a gradual process – as an overnight transformation. The sense of intergenerational friction between two competing visions of success may have been true to life as many Americans perceived it.

Yet, the decision to give up the entrepreneurial ideal of unlimited aspiration in favor of a balance between work and privatized familial happiness is not merely a revolt against the old, but also an accommodation to the constraints of the new. The corporate-suburban definition of success meshes very well with the occupational and organizational structure coming into being after World War II. Certainly, it would be futile for everyone to attempt to reach the few pinnacles of success in a world of increased monopolization and conglomeration: the times called for a redefinition of success that allowed for satisfaction with a life a few notches down from the top. Seeing success in terms of a healthy balance between different activities may have been a useful formulaic shift to justify abandonment of a frustrating and increasingly unrealistic desire to be the best.

At the same time when the entrepreneurial ideal of success was challenged in bestselling novels, novels began to appear on the bestseller lists with revised ideas about social mobility as well. *Marjorie Morningstar* (1955), for example, can be read as the tragedy of a world where children go astray because their parents have climbed the social ladder so fast that they are no longer 'at home.' Their success, which has cast them out of place, means they cannot discipline their children or enforce adherence to values with the authority necessary for bringing up a child well; their code of ethics is hopelessly old-fashioned, and they are somewhat bewildered by the strange customs of the new world. As Marjorie's father says:

'Nowadays they make jokes about the marriage brokers. . . .
All the same, with the old system she'd be meeting nothing
but boys of exactly the right age and background, and no
guesswork. . . . I'm just saying that this is also a strange
system. It's going to cost us plenty, putting her near these
good families of yours. And one night at one of these
dances, what's to stop her from falling for a good-looking
fool from a rotten family?'[34]

The human costs of social mobility and rapid ethnic assimilation have been part of America for many years, but rarely did books expressing this complex vision of American society find their way to the bestseller list. It is conceivable that only after the positive attitude towards entrepreneurial success lost its unconditional quality could a more complex understanding of social mobility be expressed by popular writers and appreciated by their audience. Perhaps the costs of social mobility only became visible concomitantly with the costs of success.

4

Bestselling novels 1956–1968: the varieties of self-fulfillment – the goal achieved

The bestsellers published in the period 1956–68 show a dramatic thematic shift: a rupture in the connection between individual success, personal happiness and social progress. Success appears to have lost its dynamic power to mobilize the individual and to suffuse a personal quest for achievement with a sense of transcendent collective purpose. In the earlier period, success was in a sense self-justifying, because it was assumed to be both personally and socially rewarding; now bestselling novelists critically examine its content and costs and justify success itself by other standards, primarily that of self-fulfillment. This represents a trivialization of a hitherto unquestioned goal, and a profound shift in the meaning of achievement.

This reformulation of success was introduced in *The Man in the Gray Flannel Suit*, and indeed many books published in 1956–68 extend the thematic assumptions at work in Wilson's novel. Wilson's book was an attempt to come to grips with certain aspects of an emergent postwar social order. Similarly, the books of this period can best be understood as fictional explorations of the landscape on the far side of affluence. Before World War II that landscape was rarely described, since in conditions of scarcity success stood at the horizon of individual endeavor. But in the postwar era, the success people had hungered for was becoming more generally attainable because of the organizational and structural transformation of

91

society. Widespread relative affluence, expanded production and marketing of consumer goods, even the development of the suburbs, gave Americans access to the objects and experiences that had symbolized success to earlier generations, not so much as the rewards of extraordinary talent and drive, but in mundane and thus unspectacular fashion.

With the traditional appurtenances of success an experiential – and relatively pedestrian – reality for large segments of the audience for these novels, the metaphorical power of success as a moral imperative appears to have waned. Inspirational and cautionary tales centered on the quest for success give way, during this period, to books describing success as a state of being or a mode of existence, often itself problematic. Moreover, in the absence of success as a dynamic organizing metaphor (no longer dynamic because it has, as it were, shifted from the far horizon to the suburban backyard), complexities both in the external social world and in private life increasingly come to the fore in novels of the time. Once an exclusive focus on idealized, because unrealized, success is lost, the ambiguities and tensions obscured by that focus come to light.

The social world is portrayed as more heterogeneous, conflictual, even alienating than in the preceding period. Rather than reproducing on a social level the individual's expansive sense of achievement, the world increasingly stands against and impinges upon the individual, demanding by its complexity a more complex range of individual responses. Given this perception of the external world, and the lack of a central metaphor such as success to tie the individual to society, it is understandable that many novels turn towards a newly privatistic concern with self-fulfillment. In fact, as mentioned above, even success is legitimated by highly elaborated references to the personal fulfillment it brings. This chapter focuses first on this new understanding of success, and then describes the social and internal landscape that emerges in the wake of affluence and the trivialization of success.

One of the most striking developments of this period is the almost complete disappearance of traditional stories of individual entrepreneurial success. Only two novels maintain the heroic tone of earlier years: Thomas Costain's *Below the Salt* (1957) and Ayn Rand's *Atlas Shrugged* (1957). Both of these authors sound embattled and somewhat defensive. For example, Ayn Rand's book chronicles the defeat of America's great entrepreneurs at the hands of government bureaucracy and parasitical socialism. The defeat is not final; the giants of industry will return from their mountain fastness when the economy collapses from incompetence and they can restore order untrammeled by regulations. Her book is a shrill, prophetic call for the re-establishment of free-enterprise capitalism.

The heroic entrepreneurial saga appears to have lost plausibility as a fictional construction because of the widespread attainment of affluence, which is seen in other novels of this period as problematic both for the individual and for America as a whole. As the hero of Adela Rogers St. Johns's *Tell No Man* (1966) says to his wife about their successful friends, 'You've seen how much *emptiness* there is under all the never-had-it-so-good . . .'[1] The father of the family in Mary Ellen Chase's *The Lovely Ambition* (1960) has similar fears about the fate of society as a whole:

> 'There's something in America. . . . Perhaps *hope* describes it better than any other single word. I'm not at all sure it's going to last. I don't like all this wealth and prosperity. Perhaps – we can't know – the hope for all men will be swallowed up in the greed of the few. . . . Complacency and apathy can be even more deadly than actual corruption.'[2]

This sentiment is echoed in many books of this period, whether or not they are centrally concerned with success, and provides some insight into its disappearance as an ideal.

Success is also less ubiquitous as a central novelistic theme. It was the narrative focus for over 20 percent of the novels published from 1945 to 1955, and elements of the formula figured strongly in another 21 percent. Only 10 percent of the 120 bestsellers published in 1956–68, however, are explicitly centered on success. In almost all of them, moreover, success *per se* is less intrinsically important than are the personal rewards it brings.

Personal fulfillment, then, becomes the standard by which

success is judged, and self-fulfillment is itself conceived of in two very different ways. On the one hand, morally self-conscious heroes justify their success by reference to the comfort it brings their families and the altruistic gratification it brings them in their role as providers. In such books the content of success is critically examined and the costs of social mobility are apparent. On the other hand, unabashedly adventuristic and self-seeking heroes – usually shown in positions of great power and wealth – enjoy the luxuries that are the perquisites of successful men. In both cases, the goal of success has lost its power to suffuse the individual's life with a sense of moral purpose, its ability to meld self and world into a progressive and meaningful totality.

John Steinbeck's *The Winter of Our Discontent* (1961) and Jerome Weidman's *The Enemy Camp* (1958) represent an evolution from the corporate-suburban accommodation Tom Rath makes in *The Man in the Gray Flannel Suit*: a humanistic search for fulfillment in a world where business success has lost much of its meaning. But both are more critically cast. Men who achieve great success are not merely overdriven, but deeply immoral, and business success entails betrayal not only of other people, but also of one's ethnic heritage, or of the ideals of social amelioration it was once seen as furthering.

Steinbeck's and Weidman's books are set, like *The Man in the Gray Flannel Suit*, within the bosom of a warm and loving suburban family, but in both the comfortable balance between family and work is undermined, though *The Enemy Camp* is more concerned with past difficulties engendered by social mobility and ethnicity than is Steinbeck's book. Both are also self-consciously concerned with the problems of modern America, and synthesize views of success found in other books of this period in a particularly articulate fashion.

George Hurst, the hero of Weidman's *The Enemy Camp*, has found happiness in a moderately successful commuter routine:

> Unlike most commuters, George Hurst did not find the
> process of getting to work every morning the hysterical
> sprint against time that it was painted by comic-strip artists
> and television playwrights. . . . He enjoyed the hours just
> after dawn and the small chores with which he filled them:

putting on the coffee; taking in the newspapers and the mail; . . . pouring Mary's first cup of coffee; tiptoeing upstairs with it and nudging her awake as he set the cup on the small table between their beds; then coming downstairs again for his shave and shower.[3]

Every morning, his first sight of his wife and children reaffirms his familial happiness, a deeply felt sense of wonderment and delight that is flawed only by his ambivalent feelings about his impoverished Jewish background and the unresolved bonds tying him to Dora, his first love, and Danny Schorr, his earliest friend. Danny, now fabulously wealthy, reappears in Hurst's life in the course of an attempt to win support as a Congressional candidate, and in debating with himself about how he should respond, Hurst reflects on his past involvement with Danny and, by extension, on the nature of American success and social mobility. Danny's life exemplifies one route to success: personal dishonesty, sharp dealing and total unscrupulousness. His career is founded on a robbery. With the money, Danny purchases goods in George Hurst's name, then flees with George's girl, Dora, whom he ditches when he cannot make her a singing star. She comes back to George, but Danny reappears, tries to blackmail George for his earlier 'involvement' in Danny's shady deal, ruins George's chance at a law career, and steals Dora again. Finally George realizes that Danny is 'a smooth operator to whom friendship was a tool, to be used the way a safecracker uses nitroglycerine, for getting what he wanted.'[4] Danny has escaped his ethnicity in the same fashion he escapes his poverty: by lying and betrayal. He asserts that his dead parents were Christians, and changes his name to Shaw on his way to fame and fortune. George Hurst's own chance for great success appears, paradoxically, because of his honesty. 'W. P.' Prager, a Jewish multimillionaire, wants George as a son-in-law because of his refusal to become a yes-man. Yet, without love, a marriage to Prager's daughter would have been another form of dishonest pandering, and George instead marries Mary Sherrod, a Gentile, and in so doing enters the enemy camp. In spite of his mixed marriage, he is shown coming to terms with his background, and his triumph at the end of the book consists in a full admission – to Mary and himself – of the depth of his terrors of the Gentile world and of the powerful pull of his past. His confession is therapeutic, freeing him to go to his lovely wife 'with no strings attached.'[5]

In this formulation, the hero's impulse towards moral (and ethnic) integrity stand in direct opposition to great worldly success. In place of earlier triumphantly moral and successful heroes, Weidman gives us a triumphantly successful and immoral villain, and an appreciation of the immense costs of both success and social mobility.

Steinbeck's novel *The Winter of Our Discontent* (1961) is a series of variations on the theme of success and what motivates men towards it, set in motion as the hero assesses the way the business world operates and how he might begin to take part in it. Reflecting back on his New England family's past fortune, and his father's loss of the family wealth, the hero, Ethan Allen Hawley, characterizes success in every era and in all its forms as robbery, murder, even a kind of combat, operating under 'the laws of controlled savagery.'[6]

> There is no doubt that business is a kind of war. Why not, then, make it all-out war in pursuit of peace? Mr. Baker and his friends did not shoot my father, but they advised him and when his structure collapsed they inherited. And isn't that a kind of murder? Have any of the great fortunes we admire been put together without ruthlessness? I can't think of any.[7]

To mobilize himself to succeed, Hawley must acknowledge his own animal ruthlessness, an ability to fight and kill masked by the conventions of his mundane life. He remembers a fleeting desire to destroy his brother-in-law during his final illness, of killing during the war, of slaughtering small animals as a boy. Then he launches his own career by destroying two other men: Marullo, the Sicilian grocer he works for in a store his family used to own, and Danny Taylor, his oldest friend. He anonymously reports Marullo to the Immigration office for illegal entry, and receives the store almost as a gift. Destroying Danny Taylor is a deeper betrayal, for Hawley still thinks of him – grown into an alcoholic – as a brother. His decision to 'succeed' is a decision to give up the ideal of brotherhood, and is thus an incontrovertible acknowledgment of the costs of success. Danny trades Ethan his family property (suitable for an airport) for $1,000, with which Danny can either buy a cure or enough liquor to kill himself. Both men know he will choose the latter course; Hawley becomes rich from his death.

> I knew what I had done, and Danny knew it too. . . .
> Maybe it's only the first time that's miserable. It has to be
> faced. In business and politics a man must carve and maul
> his way through men to get to be King of the Mountain.
> Once there, he can be great and kind – but he must get there
> first.[8]

Ethan Hawley's motives for engaging in business are complex, even tortured. Nowhere is there a sense of the simple delight in work and its intrinsic rewards that permeates earlier success stories. Now, once the bloody foundations of competition are acknowledged, an intricate series of rationalizations are brought into play. One is the social status money can bring, and Hawley justifies success as a means to that end:

> I do not want, never have wanted, money for itself. But
> money is necessary to keep my place in a category I am used
> to and comfortable in.[9]

More important is his family's need for comfort and social worth. Hawley doesn't want his wife to be 'poor Mary Hawley' any more. As he says:

> Temporarily I traded a habit of conduct and attitude for
> comfort and dignity and a cushion of security. It would be
> too easy to agree that I did it for my family because I knew
> that in their comfort and security I would find my dignity.
> But my objective was limited and, once achieved, I could
> take back my habit of conduct.[10]

In both books, then, limited success is necessary for the sake of one's family and the fulfillment that comes from providing for them, but the moral foundations of success in general are treated very critically. There are two consequences of this understanding of success in the taken-for-granted universe of these books; both represent something new. First, the old certainty that morality and success walk hand in hand is shattered. In its place enter moral relativism and doubt. Both books question the rational foundation of the social world. In Steinbeck's novel, for instance, Hawley thinks about the forces of progress in Baytown:

> Now a slow, deliberate encirclement was moving on New Baytown, and it was set in motion by honorable men. If it succeeded, they would be thought not crooked but clever. . . . To most of the world success is never bad. . . . Strength and success – they are above morality, above criticism. . . . The only punishment is for failure.[11]

A second consequence of the newly critical view of business success that appears in these novels is that the family and the private realm are simplified and idealized. In particular, the wife for whom the protagonist sacrifices his moral purity is bathed in a radiant light of wholesomeness, purity and warmth. This suggests a moral arrangement that assigns different standards to family and work. In *The Man in the Gray Flannel Suit* these two spheres made conflicting demands on the hero's limited time and energy, but business was uninteresting rather than immoral. In Steinbeck's novel, business is evil, and this formulation creates a moral dilemma for Hawley that almost drives him to suicide.

The moral and human costs of success are now clearly visible in a way foreign to the novels of the previous decade. Perceiving these costs, novelists accord a new importance to the familial contribution and personal fulfillment of the breadwinner. This marks a more privatistic moral justification for success than prevailed when the individual and the social order progressed in lock step. The costs of success also compel Steinbeck's and Weidman's heroes to engage in critical introspection and moral reflection about the social order; their search for a meaningful life marks them as representatives of a 'humanistic' formulation of the fulfillments to be gained by success.

In more adventuristic success stories, this critical note is absent; indeed morals, whether worldly or private, are barely considered. Strength and cunning are the basis of individual success, and right is what the mighty can get away with. This represents a retreat in moral seriousness from earlier popular literature, in which the successful man is righteous as well. In this group of books, nine of the 120 bestselling novels of this period, seriousness of purpose and confidence in the liberal values of progress and reason are replaced by a concern with sex, glamor and high living. The quest for success has been unseated by stories about the pursuit of the good life that comes after success has been achieved. Three of the protagonists are, in fact, born rich. For instance, Jonas Cord, the hero of Harold Robbins's *The Carpetbaggers* (1961) inherits a fortune from his father's explosives factory. But even the heroes who must make their way in the world from a position of early poverty – a situation reminiscent of the books from the previous decade – are shown, for the most part, in the positions of great wealth and comfort they have achieved, rather than during the struggle for its achievement. The hero of *Youngblood Hawke* by Herman Wouk (1962) rapidly gains acceptance into the lush entertainment world of New York and Hollywood; the *Tai-Pan* of Hong Kong in James Clavell's novel of that name (1966) was born penniless and powerless in impoverished rural Scotland, but we meet him as the richest and most influential European in the Orient, and Ruark's hero Craig Price in *Poor No More* (1959) marries wealth early both in his life and in the plot, and thereafter piles fortune upon fabulous fortune.

Whether on their way up or already close to the top, as in Harold Robbins's novels, the protagonists of these books move in settings of great luxury and glamor. Not for them the hardships of commerce, the trials of voyages into the unknown. The character-building quests for success of the earlier period give way to stories set in gleaming offices or sumptuous nightclubs, and fixated on the rewards that follow achievement. The mode is of the celebrity rather than the pioneer.

Indeed, successful women in novels of this type are all involved in some facet of entertainment. For instance,

Jacqueline Susann's heroines revivify almost every clichéd Hollywood scandal. As for the successful men, the Tai-Pan moves among the silks, opium and intrigues of nineteenth-century China; Hawke writes his way through Manhattan boudoirs; Price makes his money in oil, but spends his time on African safaris; Dax, the hero of Robbins's *The Adventurers* (1966), is a polo-star diplomat; and Cord produces movies and uses the airplanes he designs as a record-breaking pilot. Heroes shuttle between world capitals, sample exotic milieux (the Paris art world, the Riviera, New Orleans fancy-houses) and brush the edges of the wars and revolutions of our times. Both what is excluded and what is included in these books indicates clearly that a central cultural message has shifted. No longer is hard work at least partly its own reward. Now achievement is worthwhile because those who succeed gain entrée into a magical world of beauty, culture, power and influence. They can touch the pulse of worldly glitter and delight.

The rewards of success are excitement, immediate gratification of every impulse, and freedom from the mundane. Work, if it is mentioned at all, is shown as just another adventure – a matter of masculine power-plays and daredevil risks – as if the successful man's rewards included liberation from the realities of a white-collar world. Indeed, many of these successful protagonists find desk work hard to take. What they enjoy are lion hunts, hard-riding polo games, or honest fistfights. As *The Carpetbaggers*'s Jonas Cord says: 'I got to my feet and stretched. This sitting at a desk for half a day was worse than anything I'd ever done.'[12] And Craig Price in *Poor No More* has to fortify himself with bourbon and branch water whenever a stint at the desk is called for.[13] This represents a demystification of work – heretofore idealized as a proving ground of intelligence and self-discipline – that is in itself indicative of the trivialization of success.

No longer do bestselling novelists depict the process of achievement as worthwhile in and of itself. Instead, they measure success by the access it grants to the almost magical experiences of the privileged, providing experiential legitimation for what used to be an overriding and self-evident goal. Moreover, the successful hero, described by novelists in the previous period as replicating in his life the larger forces of world progress, now moves without any vision, almost without 'character' in the old-fashioned sense, in a world of luxurious objects and objectified sexual gratification. His loss of the older 'rational' virtues of discipline, patience, and intelligence, reduces him to the level of a sensate object himself, a testament to the power of a commodified social order to remold the individual in its image. This is the second novelistic response to an alienating world: a surrender to the very terms of the marketplace.

At the same time that traditional entrepreneurial success declines in importance as a fictional construct, the understanding of the social world as a simple arena for entrepreneurial conquest begins to disappear. Just as the changing understanding of success in American bestselling novels of this period seems related to the widespread affluence of the times, so this newly complex understanding of the social world bears some relation to the social conditions under which America achieved affluence. The metaphor of success lost its ability to meld ideals of individual and social amelioration into a mutually reinforcing totality not simply because of a generalized attainment of affluence, but because of the qualities of the social-structural developments that enabled that affluence to flower.

The 'world' presented here is a generalized and impressionistic construct, a mosaic drawn from the individual novels examined as a whole. Among the qualities that make it different from the homogeneous society portrayed in bestsellers of the previous decade are a new heterogeneity and relativism, organizational complexity, bureaucratic concentration, and social unrest. For example, ethnic groups from Italian peasants to antebellum slaves appear in increasing numbers, and express their cultural idiosyncrasies not just as objects of liberal tolerance but in voices of their own. Novelists of this period often shatter old ethnic stereotypes. For instance, though author William Styron is white, the black hero of his *Confessions of Nat Turner* is certainly neither servile, dumb nor laughable. Often, however, the old ethnic stereotypes are merely replaced by innovative but no less limiting stereotypical views. The Jews in Leon Uris's *Exodus*, for example, are brave, smart, and loyal – and they know their Talmud. The limitations of diversity in bestselling novels point to their social function of conventionalizing elements of social change that they incorporate. Nonetheless, all these novels show some diversity and cultural relativism.

Novelists also reward other standards of excellence besides entrepreneurial success. The boys in Chaim Potok's *The Chosen* (1967) become educated, not wealthy, and the Italian peasants in Robert Crichton's *The Secret of Santa Vittoria* (1966) enjoy their simple and materially impoverished life. So even though the middle-class bias of the bestseller lists remains intact, and a variety of ethnic groups may be portrayed rather simplistically, the very distinctiveness of their life styles and life choices implicitly questions the central entrepreneurial values of the American melting pot.

Novels with historical settings also add heterogeneity to the social universe of bestsellers. Other cultures and other times are shown as more than past reflections of the present. For example, in his novel *The Source* (1965), James Michener traces the history of a Middle Eastern *tel*, eschewing a religious Darwinism that assumes Christianity's truth in triumph, and refusing to equate history with progress. Moreover, historical novels tend to focus on times of social change without assuming that change means improvement. Kantor's *Andersonville* (1956), for example, explores not only the underbelly of the Civil War, but the ways in which the war has disemboweled what went before. Ethnic and historical contexts thus provide vehicles for a new cultural relativism that subtly undermines American entrepreneurial values.

The social world also appears much more complex and fragmented in novels of this period. There is a decline in the number of family sagas of industrial and regional development (though examples by Ferber, Keyes, and Michener appear on the bestseller lists), and a sharp rise in 'organizational melodramas' that focus on the specialized compartments of a highly differentiated society – airports, political conventions, hotel chains. Organizational roles and a bureaucratic division of labor seem to have become a more plausible perspective from which to view the inner workings of society. The shift from kinship to bureaucratic organizations as a fictional lens is accompanied, as well, by a shift away from assumptions of certain social progress. Ferber's 1958 novel *Ice Palace* (Alaska), F. P. Keyes's 1957 novel *Blue Camellia* (Louisiana rice), and Michener's *Hawaii* (1959) all tell optimistic tales of settlement and agricultural or regional development; all show society improving as it moves forward into the future. Organizational melodramas, on the other hand, resemble a novelistic examination of one part of a very complicated machine, and a machine does not evolve historically. Arthur Hailey shows us how a hotel works; Irving Wallace anatomizes a summit conference or the awarding of the Nobel Prize. Such novels are optimistic in the conventional sense that they reward good people and punish bad people, but there is no sense of general social achievement in their descriptions of the organizational components of society, for their plots are devices for novelistic penetration of one cell of the intricate social organism we live in, rather than vehicles for exploring the causes and consequences of progress. Often, in fact, as in *Hotel*, the central characters heroically resist social processes of concentration and monopolization. At the end of Hailey's novel, the great family hotel has changed hands and modernized somewhat, but managed to remain independent of a large corporate chain.

All in all, many bestsellers from this period regard society as increasingly uncontrollable and threatening to individual well-being. Impersonal technological forces endanger institutions celebrated in earlier books, such as education and political democracy, and indeed threaten to destroy the world altogether. Burdick and Wheeler's *Fail-Safe* (1962) and Uris's *Topaz* (1967) describe humanity's narrow escape from a nuclear holocaust, Nevil Shute's *On the Beach* (1957) prophesies global destruction, and even religious books like Taylor Caldwell's *The Listener* (1960) worry about our species's capacity to destroy itself. Often these same authors call into question what earlier novelists saw as clearly progressive human accomplishments, such as modern science, exemplifying another strand of cultural doubt about social success or progress.

Large-scale bureaucracies also impinge upon protagonists. Whether in religious novels that lament unwieldy hierarchies, or in espionage thrillers, like those of Ian Fleming or John le Carré, that show the modern state manipulating protagonists, vast bureaucracies penetrate the most intimate aspects of people's lives, often in inimical fashion. Novelists usually describe social unrest, too, as inimical and incomprehensible, whether it springs from ill-defined collections of malcontents, as in the novels of Helen MacInnes, Allen Drury and le Carré, or from nationalist movements in the Third World, which are described by authors like Robin Moore, Nicholas Monsarrat and James Michener. Since social movements provide no beneficial counterforce, no positive collective solution, an embattled individualism still reigns over the cosmos of bestsellers. But the world is no longer a benign field for entrepreneurial initiative; now it is in the grip of vast and incomprehensible social forces that render individual lives increasingly insecure.

The sharp difference in the 'social world' as it is imaginatively perceived and transmuted into fiction during this period, in contrast to the previous decade, raises questions about perceptions of social change on two levels. First, although the decade immediately following World War II witnessed immense changes in the world at large, bestselling novels of the time register very little social conflict, and are almost untouched by the chill of the Cold War and McCarthyism. The only significant change they chronicle is an awareness of the problems of large corporate bureaucracies, and a sense of an end to limitless expansion.

In contrast, the period 1956–68 was also one of change, but now social changes enter the fictive world with great force. The cultural turmoil which was manifestly in the forefront of people's lives during the 1960s had begun to penetrate the world of bestselling novels by the late 1950s. The novels of the latter part of the decade encompassed much more conflict and ambiguity than can be understood by reference to the bland suburban family and the smooth public consensus which are central to our collective memory of the 1950s in America.

Cultural artifacts like bestselling novels, then, can be useful in unearthing social perceptions of reality that are at odds with our received assumptions about earlier periods. Yet the perceived social reality that bestselling novels express does not always mesh with more objective reconstructions of society and social change. This indicates a complex or multifaceted relationship between social reality and culturally expressed social perceptions of reality, and speaks to the need for more subtle formulations of the relationship between popular literature and the social world than have often been the case. Moreover, it speaks to the need for understanding how social perceptions of reality intersect with social-structural changes in the intricate processes of social change. For example, one can speculate that by the late 1950s social changes were more deeply felt by many Americans than had been the case immediately after World War II, when occupational, residential, political and educational shifts could perhaps have been dismissed as temporary postwar readjustments, and when the ideal of individual success exerted a more powerful sway over the collective imagination. In fact, a social scientist would be hard pressed to say with finality exactly when 'social change' occurs, especially in reference to such short periods of time, but it remains an interesting problem to determine when and how changes are socially perceived and how these perceptions relate to later social and political action. Obviously, the authors of bestsellers felt their world was in significant ways different from what it had been during the decade before, and perhaps this feeling was shared by those who read the novels, since the books of the previous decade convey a much more consistent and unified view of a world described as itself forming a unified and harmonious totality.

Confronting a newly problematic world, many protagonists of bestsellers act without the hope of triumphant social advancement and individual success that seemed plausible in the first decade after World War II. Sometimes novelists hope for limited reform. Books like Bel Kaufman's *Up the Down Staircase* (1964), about inner city schools, or Lederer and Burdick's *The Ugly American* (1959), about difficulties in American foreign policy, are fictional accounts of problems that may be solvable. However, the reforming teacher cannot sort through the educational bureaucracy in her school in spite of a year's dedicated efforts, and finally must content herself with the hope of reaching just one or two children. *The Ugly American*, which gave impetus to the foundation of the Peace Corps, is more optimistic and programmatic, yet the kind of independent innovators the authors urge exporting from America to help the Asians, are precisely the kind of small inventors and businessmen who are feeling increasingly embattled and threatened in the bestselling novels of this time.

Often, progress seems unimaginable, and heroes stoically stand their ground, trying to survive with dignity despite their disillusionment. As Jakov, an Israeli of 'stern stoicism,' says in Morris West's *The Tower of Babel* (1968):

> 'I work. I do what a believer does, without belief. I practice loyalty and impose discipline. I am paid to command and I command. I am trusted to give honest judgments. I render them as best as I can . . .'
> 'Is that all the hope you have?'
> 'It's all I count on. Hope is a different matter.'[14]

The heroes of these outward-looking books, thwarted in their efforts to shape the world and avoid manipulation by social forces of almost mysterious complexity, often turn in the end to the private sphere. James Bond collapses in the arms of a voluptuous woman, le Carré's heroes attempt this solution but are often denied it, Nevil Shute's atomic victims die in each other's arms, and in West's *The Ambassador* (1965), a frustrated American ambassador to Vietnam searches for enlightenment in a Japanese Zen temple.

Certainly, given the new and more problematic understanding of the social world and of success described in these novels as a whole, it is understandable that many individual novels focus on spheres of private life and personal fulfillment that have little to do with worldly success. This focus is an implicit corollary of changed novelistic perceptions both of success and of its social context, and must be examined to understand both what has supplanted aspirations for success in the protagonists' attempts to make meaningful lives and what this shift implies, in turn, about the evolution of success as a metaphor.

I have discussed the increasing trivialization of success, and its justification by two varieties of self-fulfillment: the immediate gratifications of a luxurious lifestyle, and the more 'humanistic' moral gratifications that come from being a good provider for others. These two aspects of personal fulfillment also appear in books about private life, whether the small interpersonal world of domesticity, romance and sexuality or the realm of spirituality and the inner life. Thus the focus on private life, which is one response to the rupture between individual self-interest and more generalized social progress, is permeated by the tension between the objectified self-as-sensation-seeker and the self as seeker for a humanistic inner meaning to life. This personal quest for meaning is proffered, in turn, as a possible way not only to reconstitute fragmented individuals, but also to end their estrangement from the world. I would like briefly to discuss the way this tension is played out in relation to sexuality, then to describe some components of interiority.

In several bestsellers, sex is construed as the ultimate moment in the immediate gratification of impulse, the central metaphor in an ethos that celebrated leisure and the commodities that signified its pleasures. During a decade marked by the rapid expansion of consumer goods, consumer debt, and consumption-oriented media, the consumption of sex in literature proliferated as well. As legal definitions of pornography changed, one could read about any kind of sexual behavior. The choice, as in the supermarket, was dazzling, and all brands, from sodomy and gang bangs to voyeurism and delicate masochism, were available to the public even on the relatively stodgy bestseller list. Within the enveloping atmosphere of a sexually manipulative consumerism, in which luxuries and necessities were, and are, sold by sex, it is not surprising that sex should take on the characteristics of its social context and become itself translated into a commodity. Its commodified form in popular literature reproduces the fragmentation and alienation of the wider social order on an intimate level. Sex is split off from human needs for intimacy, friendship, security, and love, and becomes a pure expression of hedonism, self-involvement, and the free play of impulse. As such it perpetuates the isolation of individuals from each other and from their own deepest desires.

Novels that describe sex as only one among many forms of self-fulfillment through sensory gratification tend to manifest a constellation of characteristics that make them very different from more serious books about passion. Many, for example, feature glamorous settings almost as a stageset for sensual delights. Marcia Davenport's *The Constant Image* (1960) is set

107

among jet-set Italian aristocrats, Harold Robbins's *The Adven-turers* (1966) wallows in exotic settings across Europe and Latin America, and *Myra Breckenridge* (1968) by Gore Vidal, Henry Sutton's *The Exhibitionist* (1967) and *The Carpetbaggers* (1961) by Harold Robbins brush the edges of Hollywood, the ultimate seat of wealth, youth, and the commodification of the flesh.

Moreover, the scenes and characters are often described entirely in terms of objects. For example, here is a passage selected almost at random from Mary McCarthy's *The Group*:

> Both Mr. and Mrs. Davison had an emphatic distaste for show. Mrs. Davison wore no jewelry, except for her wedding and engagement rings and occasional Victorian brooches set with garnets, her birthstone, fastened to the bosom of her coin-print or polka-dot dresses. Helena had a set of moonstones, a cat's-eye brooch, an amethyst pin, and an Add-a-Pearl necklace that had been completed on her eighteenth birthday, when she was presented to society (that is, to the family's old friends) at a small tea given by her mother in their house, which was called 'The Cottage' and had a walled garden and English wallflowers.[15]

Books by Mary McCarthy and John Updike establish a critical edge with such descriptions; if people disappear behind a haze of objects, it is because of a shallowness of character (in the nineteenth-century sense) that comes from lives spent buying a surfeit of possessions and trading pleasures of the flesh. At the end of Updike's *Couples* (1968), it is hardly possible to mourn the social eclipse of an older group of couples, since the ascendant couples only differ from them in minor terms of taste:

> So the Reinhardts, and the young sociologist who had been elected town moderator, and a charmingly yet unaffectedly bohemian children's book illustrator who had moved from Bleeker Street, and the new Unitarian minister in Tarbox, and their uniformly tranquil wives, formed a distinct social set, that made its own clothes, and held play readings, and kept sex in its place, and experimented with LSD, and

espoused liberal causes more militantly than even Irene Saltz.[16]

Harold Robbins's books and Ian Fleming's brand-saturated stories lack such self-consciousness, but also point to the substitution of consumer choice (sex as the transcendent commodity) for an older notion of character built by moral choice.

A tone of self-involvement is also common among these books. In Marcia Davenport's *The Constant Image* (1960), the narrator's watchful but finally approving eye is never far from pandering to the protagonist. We are told through her lover's eyes how well she skis; she also drives beautifully and captivates Milan society by her beauty and intelligence. In the end, her love affairs seems only to have made her more secure in her self-love. Often the lover becomes merely the instrument for achieving new kinds of experience, fresh revelations about one's self. As the heroine of Françoise Sagan's *A Certain Smile* (1956) says:

> It's always through someone else's body that, first warily and then with a rush of gratitude, you discover your own, its length, its smell. . . .[17]

More obvious forms of objectification are also at work. James Bond thrillers describe the women he encounters according to the same standards as every other kind of property the hero possesses: like his guns, they are beautiful 'pieces.' And Harold Robbins's women all have large jutting breasts, narrow waists, and slim yet flaring hips: the perfect female chassis. Robbins's descriptions of sexual intercourse – and he speaks for many others – are also standardized. They clearly show the displacement of virile aggression from the war room or the board room to the boudoir: the men have it, the women resist it or beg for it, and when they get it (sometimes with a little slapping around), they love it. This they demonstrate by clawing men's backs in their ecstasy.

Two books step over the boundaries of heterosexuality, and look back with a critical eye at this kind of objectification, which is not limited to the heterosexual world. Gore Vidal's *Myra Breckenridge* (1968) plays mocking tricks on virility and success: his heroine has a sex-change operation, rapes a promising young male star in the anus with a dildo, and spends her time in an uncle's phony school for aspiring young actors deriding people's hope for instant success. John Rechy's *City of Night* (1963) is a more scalding critique of sexual objectification. Though it is set in the world of gay hustlers rather than heterosexual liaisons, the problems are surprisingly similar: a premium is put on youth and beauty, each beautiful 'youngman' 'fears his inevitable aging; violence and competition abound, and money changes hands for sex or drugs. Names and faces fade into a sometimes pleasant, sometimes terrifying haze of sensation, which the hero begins to escape only when he meets a man who wants not just sex but love as well.

In a second group of bestsellers, sexuality represents not the centerpiece and symbol of the consumption ethos, but rather an attempt to transcend a social order in which the established forms of work and marriage have lost any intrinsic meaning, and to find a new identity through intimate connection. In such books, the wider world of institutionally defined identity and achievement represents anomie and despair, and its rejection gives the only hope for a new birth. Novelists affirm this rebirth, rather than any political or social regeneration, as the only cure for, or escape or shelter from, the malaise of the times. Elements of this formula resemble D. H. Lawrence's *Lady Chatterley's Lover*, which indeed became a hardcover bestseller in 1959, after a court decision defined it as literature, not pornography. Lawrence pitted the evils of industrial society against the fragile tenderness of individual passion, and envisioned fleshly intimacy engendering spiritual communion. Novels like Henry Sutton's *The Exhibitionist* (1967) and *The Chapman Report* by Irving Wallace not only borrow elements of the Lawrentian model, though deleting his critique of class divisions, but also make direct reference to his book in their own novels. Several other novels, from Grace Metalious's *Peyton Place* (1956) to Morris West's *The Tower of Babel* (1968), also incorporate the Lawrentian opposition between life-giving passion and a deadening social order. In the former book, sexual connectedness heals and frees the heroine and her mother, but demands rejection of social restrictions and

110

hypocritical respectability. In the latter, an Israeli agent who is disillusioned by modern politics turns to the intensely private consolation of a love affair with an Arab woman. Attempting to explain his actions to his superior, he says:

'To her Israel's just a name on a map. To me it's a place I love and can't live in. *I'm* her country. She's mine. What more do you want of us? The last stand of the Zealots at Masada?'[18]

The most eloquent examples of the formula, however, are John Updike's *Couples* (1968) and Elia Kazan's *The Arrangement* (1967).

Updike's book is set in an upper-middle-class suburb. Most of the men's occupations are routinized, interchangeable parts in a technocratic whole: they are brokers, dentists, engineers and scientists. Marriages are no less routine, and a group of couples begins a titillating and finally deadening round of sexual adventuring. Piet Hanema, who comes closest to being the protagonist of the book, has a skilled and fulfilling trade that is corrupted by the broader social context: he owns a small construction firm, and tries without success to maintain a craftsman's approach in an increasingly standardized business. Unlike the other men, Piet allows his affair with Foxy to escape his control, and this revitalizing passion shatters the established order of his life. His marriage dissolves as the town's Congregational church rather stagily catches fire, and in the ashes of the old order Piet and Foxy decide to marry and settle elsewhere. Although their love may have transfigured their personal lives and torn apart their small group of friends, Updike gives no indication that it can reshape the environing suburban *status quo*:

The Hanemas live in Lexington, where, gradually, among people like themselves, they have been accepted, as another couple.[19]

Kazan's *The Arrangement* is a similar, if more simple, version of this story. Eddie Anderson, upwardly mobile son of immigrants, successful advertizing writer, finds his established routine endangered by an affair with Gwen, a woman who first inspires animal passion, then respect for her integrity. Eddie is not eager to leave his wife, Florence, partly because he genuinely likes her, partly because she represents the 'tried and true forms' of civilization. But she aligns herself with a deadening security, the safe, dishonest way of life represented not only by his marriage, but by his work life as well. As she says, 'No one reaches their dream, baby; whoever has?'[20] Eddie finally does leave her, his job and his elegant house, because Gwen at least brings promise of the dream:

> Of course we had behaved like goddam fools, but the
> goddam fool part of us was the living part of us. And the
> sensible part of us was the dead.[21]

Having left, however, he is not ready to be with Gwen, because he has yet to find himself. 'All I ever did was think of someone besides myself,' he says about his prior life, 'That's what was wrong. I lost myself.'[22] He spends an interval of quiet introspection in a mental institution, then a longer period totally absorbed in writing about his past. Only then can he come together with Gwen, reconstituted.

In these bestsellers, the surge of passion signifies rebirth in the face of a debilitating institutional order that cannot itself generate life-giving values. The life that follows renewal is, however, itself constrained by the social order, so growth is almost entirely internal. Outwardly, the creative and passionate impulses lead back into a new social arrangement. As Eddie says:

> Have I satisfied my ambition? What was it? I have trouble
> remembering. I hope that's because I've satisfied it. I do
> write every morning. . . . But I do worry sometimes. Is this
> what all that drama, that great overthrow was for – this
> simple living and working, this day to day confluence?[23]

It is a quietistic and very private solution.

The two types of sexuality represented in bestsellers of this period are as remarkable for their similarities as for their ultimate differences in meaning. Sexuality both as a commodity and in the form that reconstitutes identity is invariably linked

112

to selfishness and gratification of impulse. In one case, self-gratification accommodates the established order; in the other, it provides the only avenue towards its transcendence and, despite inner renewal, leads back to conventional arrangements. Both types of sexuality also entail self-involvement, whether the simple self-delight of narcissism, or a more complex desire to discover the contours of the self and live the dream of *becoming*. Both celebrate sensation, either as an end in itself, or as the means to achieve deeper emotional involvement. And the element of exploration has been displaced from the entrepreneurial realm to very private interpersonal involvement.

Several novels published in this period reaffirm older values of marriage and the family, repudiating the open sexuality of the books discussed above. But three of these – written and probably read primarily by women – *Dearly Beloved* (1962) by Anne Morrow Lindbergh, Rumer Godden's *The Battle of Villa Fiorita* (1963), and Mary Ellen Chase's *The Lovely Ambition* (1960), are more than simple celebrations of domestic life. These authors offer a spiritualized domesticity as the source of individual and social salvation, the foundation of a healthy society. All three testify to the growing perception that success and love are not necessarily mutually reinforcing. In *Dearly Beloved*, for example, one character muses:

> The arid periods of life . . . were when he had been forced, by sheer busyness and distraction, to work outside the stream [of love and compassion] – the arid middle years, the years of success in the world.[24]

Moreover, the didacticism of these authors' hymns to domesticity suggests that the changes undermining the cultural importance of occupational success were also affecting the private sphere. Lindbergh's assertion that the 'endless small interplay' of housewifely tasks become 'the life everlasting' when spiritualized by self-sacrifice sounds all too much like a sermon directed at bored and restless housewives, or women threatened by changes in sexual mores. Similarly, *The Battle of Villa Fiorita* (1963) in which two lovers contemplate divorce but part, in the end, for the sake of their children, is a self-conscious defense of traditional marriages. In the very warmth of their partisanship, these authors imply that broad social changes may be undermining traditional domestic life. Yet, paradoxically, all claim that immersion in the family circle can bring collective regeneration. In *The Lovely Ambition* Chase certainly places her hope in families:

> As to our life as a family . . . I think it may hold some
> interest and perhaps even some value, at least for those who
> still believe that in the character of families lies our chief
> hope, or despair, for the redemption of this erring,
> perplexed, and overburdened world.[25]

This sense of a general social malaise marks a retreat from the optimism of the previous decade. And this new view of the family, as embattled, yet potentially redemptive, like the metaphors of sexuality as self-fulfillment, shows that the 'general malaise' was subtly influencing a reformulation not only of success but of private lives as well.

If some bestsellers of this period turn towards interpersonal intimacy, others turn towards the even more private realms of introspection, creativity and spirituality: these books formulate the renewal of innerness as a solution to social as well as individual anomie. Christian writers, for example, no longer link religious and entrepreneurial expansiveness, in part because they see material success as having led to spiritual emptiness for individuals and society as a whole. As Archbishop Carlin in Morris West's *The Shoes of the Fishermen* (1963) explains, even the established Catholic church may have become too involved with material success. He points to 'two reasons' for the church's spiritual problems:

> 'Prosperity and respectability. We're not persecuted any
> more. We pay our way. We can wear the Faith like a Rotary
> badge – and with as little social consequence. We collect our
> dues like a club, shout down the Communists, and make
> the biggest contribution in the whole world to Peter's Pence.
> But it isn't enough. There's no – no heart in it for many
> Catholics.'[26]

From Adela Rogers St. Johns to Morris West and Taylor Caldwell, these authors urge an enthusiastic reawakening of faith stripped of its doctrinal and bureaucratic rigidity, and founded instead in warmth, activism, and empathy – a religious humanism. In one novel, Taylor Caldwell calls Christ simply *The Listener* (1960). The heroine in Catherine Marshall's 1967 book *Christy* tests her faith by missionary work among the poor in Appalachia. And West's reformist Pope Kiril says:

> 'I want to lead you back to God, through men. . . . If we lose contact with men – suffering, sinful, lost confused men crying in the night, women agonizing, children weeping – then we, too, are lost because we shall be negligent shepherds who have done everything but the one thing necessary.'[27]

This humanist impulse draws these authors close to many other novelists of this period, whose books chronicle the search for a meaningful moral code in what they describe as a complex and troubled world.

In a more secular vein, Saul Bellow, J. D. Salinger, and Irving Stone also describe an internal search for meaning. Their religion is a creative humanism, and their novels celebrate an intensity of subjective experience not far removed from religious enthusiasm. The protagonists of their novels all stand at one remove from the materialism of business or professional life, and their internal processes of growth and emotional 'fineness' are elaborated in far more detail than their accomplishments in the public world of work or success. For example, Stone's book *The Agony and the Ecstasy* (1962) concentrates on Michelangelo's inner creative process. The book leaves the reader less aware of the artist's accomplishments than of the intensity and quality of his artistic feelings. Salinger's books, too, focus on experiential intensity suffused with Eastern mysticism. His characters preach a passionate detachment from ordinary life and worldly or conventional definitions of vocational achievements. In Salinger's novel *Raise High the Roof Beam, Carpenters and Seymour – An Introduction* Seymour, the 'enlightened man, the

God-knower' comments on his brother's writing career:

'You wrote down that you were a writer by *profession*. . . .
When was writing your profession? . . . It's never been
anything but your religion. Never. . . . Since it *is* your
religion, do you know what you will be asked when you
die? But let me tell you first what you won't be asked. You
won't be asked if you were working on a wonderful, moving
piece of writing when you died. You won't be asked if it was
long or short, sad or funny, published or unpublished. . . .
I'm so sure you'll get asked only two questions. *Were most of
your stars out*? Were you busy writing your heart out?'[28]

And Saul Bellow's *Herzog* (1964) describes an almost entirely
internal journey towards meaning or self-discovery. The hero
is a reflective and widely read academic humanist who has lost
confidence in his ability as a philosopher in part because of his
wife's betrayal. Herzog's personal crisis takes on overtones of a
general crisis in work and love, two strands of our collective
identities, as Herzog begins to address agonized imaginary
letters to the luminaries of Western culture. Bellow implies that
Herzog may be a touchstone for this collective crisis because he
represents the ideational and emotional side of his, and the
larger human, family:

But there's a strange division of functions that I sense, in
which I am the specialist in . . . spiritual self-awareness; or
emotionalism; or ideas; or nonsense. Perhaps of no real use
or relevance except to keep alive primordial feelings of a
certain sort.[29]

Herzog's conflict is lived out largely on this level. Though he
does dart out on impulsive trips to Martha's Vineyard and
Chicago, his quest is largely introspective. Through memories,
dreams, reflections, he touches the wellsprings of his life's
meaning. He emerges from an almost Laingian summer in
possession of an ineffable, perhaps meaningless experiential
truth that is his resting place:

I look at myself and see chest, thighs, feet – a head. This

116

strange organization, I know it will die. And inside –
something, happiness. . . . 'Thou movest me.' That leaves
me no choice. Something produces intensity, a holy feeling,
as oranges produce orange, as grass green, as birds
heat. . . . But this intensity, doesn't it mean anything? It is
an idiot joy that makes this animal, the most peculiar animal
of all, exclaim something? And he thinks this reaction a
sign, a proof, of eternity? And he has it in his breast? But I
have no arguments to make about it. 'Thou movest me.'[30]

All of these novels turn inward to find the wellsprings of
meaning, suggesting a withdrawal of involvement in the more
collective metaphors or structures of meaning most clearly
represented by success. The novelistic landscape of private life
and interiority grows in complexity as success loses its
transcendent meaning. The varieties of self-fulfillment become
compelling goals, and experiential intensity (sexual, religious,
creative) provides evidence of their achievement, and may,
some authors imply, point towards the possibility of social as
well as personal renewal.

The books of 1956–68 betoken a time of searching and some
confusion. The tone of the questioning and the mood of the
search, however, are not desperate. If the naive certainty in the
triumph of expansive American individualism has disappeared, its loss can be seen in part as another kind of
expansion: expansion through the admission of a more tolerant
and open morality, of a more finely shaded social, ethnic, and
cultural pluralism, of minority experiences into the hitherto
simplistic universe of these novels. Similarly, the critical
examination of success and the demand for personal fulfillment
can be affirmative in nature. From the questioning of received
opinions follows expression of desire for a social order that
permits freedom, joy, and spontaneity, and hence realizes the
implicit promises of industrialism. In their descriptions of a
complex, bureaucratized, alienating social world, however, the
novels point to some of the social constraints on personal
fulfillment and to the ways in which the social world not only
frustrates 'fulfillment' but also trivializes it.

5

Bestselling novels 1969–1975: the failure of success

The bestsellers of 1969–75 show a world-view in crisis. Not only has economic or vocational success lost congruence with personal happiness or moral worth in the world of bestsellers, but other definitions of personal fulfillment are also perceived as deeply problematic. In the previous period, affluence trivialized the goal of success and detached the individual from the collectivity, but the private search for sensation or a creative 'becoming' offered at least a sense of more personal modalities of 'achievement.' In bestsellers of the early 1970s, even this privatistic solution becomes dubious. Systemic issues come to the fore again, but this time in the context of doubt and a perceived possibility of individual and collective failure. Cultural assumptions about individual success and its rewards have now reached a critical and open-ended conjuncture.

The novels display several thematic symptoms of this cultural confusion. One of the most striking is the disappearance of moral sanctions and ideals. As an example of the former, sexual license becomes extreme, and often fades into interpersonal brutality. Four books make women the victims of titillating rapes, and *Deliverance* (1970) centers on a male rape at gunpoint. Brutalization in other forms, as well, is much more commonplace in novels of this period. Thrillers and books about the Mafia, for instance, feature frequent and graphic episodes of torture and murder. This represents an extreme form of the objectification which began to be a common feature

118

in books published during the previous decade. As sanctions disappear, so do models of 'the good.' Increasingly, novelists mock or deride traditional authorities, from college presidents and policemen to heroes of the American Revolution – or twists of the plot reveal them to be corrupt, evil, and unworthy of emulation. The naive sense of good and evil, heroes and villains, that characterized popular novels after World War II has evolved beyond openness and relativism to an arbitrary and destructive moral leveling. Novels also call the morality of success into question, and often characterize this traditional idealized value, like traditional heroes, as immoral or unenviable. Stories of 'success' show heroes contending with individual and systemic failure to a hitherto unprecedented extent, and grappling with complex inner conflicts that undermine their motivation towards achievement.

The elements of novelistic form also reveal dimensions of difficulty and doubt. The frequency of 'end of empire' settings in historical novels – usually described in a millenarial and pessimistic light – shows that the sense of an ending found contemporary resonance. A new tone is pervasive: on the one hand sophisticated and less obviously judgmental than in previous years; on the other hand, tending towards exhaustion, cynicism and despair. Characters, too, change during this period. The hero as vulnerable survivor, the alienated executive, the disaffected youth become novelistic commonplaces. Women characters' lives often illuminate the sexual aspects of social confusion; they are victims of sociopathic rapists and examplars of a voracious liberated sexuality. Often, too, bestseller plots are set in motion by an unbounded 'fictive crisis' that implicates many levels of society rather than an easily identifiable enemy or clearly demarcated group of villains. Happy endings become less common, indicating that the familiar formulaic resolutions may have lost plausibility. There is, in general, a loss of clear boundaries; divisions between past and present, fantasy and reality, life and death are increasingly blurred. This resembles the loss of moral distinctions mentioned above.

The novels as a whole appear to be confronting what is perceived as an increasingly difficult and unpalatable reality. Moreover, the guiding metaphor of individual success has not only been demystified by the realities of widespread affluence, but has also been attenuated by the failure of affluence to provide an orderly moral and social universe in any way resembling the American dream. The novels of this period bear witness to the imaginative disarray that arises when a central cultural metaphor loses plausibility.

There are three major modes of novelistic response to this perceived crisis. Those, like Heller and Updike, who write on a level of realism, are deeply critical of conventional business success and the world in which it is a measure of moral worth. Other novelists retreat into escapist realms, whether spiritualism, nostalgia, or pure romance. Many writers, however, use highly conventional plots and characters to contain and defuse disturbing elements of social reality. Genre books and formulaic stories permit exposure to the brutal aspects of contemporary life and allow expression of alienation and despair, but only to a certain point; then, a twist of the plot brings rigid solutions into play. Such conventions either make the unmentionable familiar and subject it to stereotypic moral judgments or allow a clichéd comprehension of the problem whereby it can be 'solved' and dismissed. Conventions of plot and character reveal themselves, thereby, as imaginative tools of great flexibility. At one point in time (the late 1940s and early 1950s) they helped formulate and enforce the American celebration; in a more tension-ridden period, they have acted to 'handle' what the novelists apparently perceive as a potentially disruptive social crisis. Hence, we find on the one hand the novelistic inclusion of hitherto censored parts of reality such as corrupt officials or organized crime, and on the other hand their dismissal through reduction to clichés. (For example, in *Wheels* Arthur Hailey blames the failure of automobile industry programs to help the hard-core unemployed of Detroit on cheating by low-level executives: a definition of a social problem that reduces it to manageable and nonthreatening terms.) The social function of popular literature thus varies over time.

Certain books, of course, seem not particularly affected by the general dismay. They represent a strand of connection with the previous decade. Such are Chaim Potok's *My Name is Asher Lev* (1973) and Dan Jenkins's *Semi-Tough* (1972). Both have characteristics of an earlier decade: a certain self-involved narcissism, a privatized vision of success on the one hand (Potok's hero is an artist), and a glamorized sense of the sexual rewards of entertainment and sports success on the other (Jenkins's hero is a professional football player, and much of the book is about his luxurious New York apartment and the parties it houses, not about the game itself). Even these books, however complacent, are touched by some of the marks of their time. Both, for instance, show some tension about ethnicity. However, these books do continue to purvey visions of achievement-oriented success, rewarded by worldly status and fame, and in *Semi-Tough* not only by sex, but by the love of a good woman as well. Their orientation gives them continuity with the previous period.

Michener's *Centennial* (1974), an epic about Colorado and Nebraska, represents an even older version of the story of success, one that links people to their region in a saga of progress and development. His understanding of progress is much more complex than Ferber's or Keyes's older regional celebrations, however, and the book's description of the past and present on the American plains takes on the quality of a call for the renewal of certain virtues which might otherwise have become lost or obscured. His book has a populist tone lacking in earlier sagas. All three of the 'success' stories which give continuity with the past are thus subtly but observably different from their earlier counterparts, although the differences are outweighed by the commonalities.

One of the most critical and self-conscious articulations of the problem of 'success' in this period is Joseph Heller's novel *Something Happened* (1974). It was recognized as emblematic of its times upon publication in a way reminiscent of *The Man in the Gray Flannel Suit* in the mid-fifties, and it expresses in more pointed fashion a message common to many books published during this period. Baldly stated, the picture is of work so routinized that process has completely eclipsed product, leaving only the struggle for money and position to motivate and satisfy, and of home life so isolated and intense that boredom, rage and smothering intimacy have eclipsed the possibilities of love. Given the conditions for 'success' as Heller outlines them, it is a minor miracle that anyone participates.

Something Happened maintains the corporate-suburban separation between work and leisure, the public realm and that of the family, which was established twenty years before in *The Man in the Gray Flannel Suit*. However, Slocum, the hero, is so alienated from both worlds that they lose independent reality in the process of translation into his single shriek of agony. If the separation of home life and work life is paradoxically dissolved in Slocum's alienation from both, the traditional relationship between the two spheres is also inverted. Work is no longer the sphere of rationality or productivity, but the location of Slocum's most intense emotional involvement. The work process has evolved towards such abstraction that only its bureaucratic aspects have reality (we never learn what Slocum's company makes, although Heller mentions specific departments and sketches in the hierarchy), and the void is filled by an overwhelming paranoia. Lacking any reference point outside the bureaucracy itself, competition gains in interpersonal intensity as it loses rationality. As Slocum says about his job:

I have a feeling that someone nearby is soon going to find out something about me that will mean the end, although I can't imagine what that something is.[1]

In this environment, success is terrifyingly subjective, since getting ahead depends less on achievements than on attitudes, deportment, personal style. Slocum's competitor Green will not make Vice President because he has underestimated the importance of the proper attitude. He cannot understand that those who succeed

work hard continuously and that they believe in the company, that they do well and meticulously whatever they are asked to do, that they do *everything* they are asked to do, and that they do *only* what they are asked to do – and that this is what the company wants.[2]

And Slocum's friend Kagle, who is eventually eased out in favor of Slocum, mistakenly believes that the proper attitude – working hard and believing in the company – is enough to assure success. He cannot see that *doing* has been altogether eclipsed by *being*. Like an entrepreneur from another era, Kagle

> really thinks that what he does is more important than what he is, but I know he's wrong and that the beautiful Countess Consuelo Crespi (if there is such a thing) will always matter more than Albert Einstein, Madame Curie, Thomas Alva Edison, Andy Kagle, and me.[3]

Slocum has it right. Consumption values have conquered those of production. Kagle is passed by for promotion because he lacks proper 'tone':

> His name is all wrong. (Half wrong. Andrew is all right, but Kagle?) So are his clothes. . . . He wears terrible brown shoes with *fleur-de-lis* perforations. He wears anklets (and I want to scream or kick him when I see his shin). . . . His manners are not good. He lacks wit (his wisecracks are bad, and so are the jokes he tells) and did not go to college, and he does not mix smoothly enough with people who did go to college.[4]

The elevation of style over substance is exemplified in the company façade of generalized 'niceness.' People are rarely fired, just pushed aside, the decor is pleasant, and there are many office parties. Yet 2.5 salesmen a year plunge to their deaths from office windows, and other workers simply go mad, like Martha the typist, whose removal by soft-spoken medical personnel closes the novel. The slickly humane organizational style masks a bureaucratic totalitarianism that swallows disputes and muffles rebellion through proper procedures culminating in dismissal and oblivion. And Slocum, despite his cynicism and essential disbelief in the company, is not a rebel. He wants success, if only because of the emotional intensity of work-based rivalry:

> I want the money. I want the prestige. I want the acclaim, and congratulations. And Kagle will care. And Green will care, and Johnny Brown will care so much he might punch me in the jaw as soon as he learns about it. . . .[5]

These emotions can compel Slocum towards success in part because the feelings associated with home life – the supposed source of warmth and love – have paradoxically turned to hatred or indifference. The only family member Slocum loves is the son he smothers to death with demands and warnings before he actually does smother him in an excess of panic and inappropriate care after a slight accident.[6] The suburban haven of the 1950s has turned into a shambles, a quagmire. At the beginning of the book, Slocum confesses:

> I can't face these long weekends anymore and don't know how I survive them. I may have to take up skiing.[7]

Work, even with its hypocrisies, is clearly easier to handle than the disaster of human closeness. Thus work becomes an escape from the home that heretofore has been seen as a shelter from the vicissitudes of labor.

Aside from his beloved elder son, Slocum's family consists of a young idiot child named Derek, a spoiled and discontented teenaged daughter, and his wife:

> My wife is unhappy. She is one of those married women who are very, very bored, and lonely. . . . I was with a married woman not long ago who told me she felt so lonely at times she turned ice cold and was literally afraid she was freezing to death from inside, and I believe I know what she meant. . . . My wife is a good person, really, or used to be, and sometimes I'm sorry for her. She drinks now during the day and flirts, or tries to, at parties we go to in the evening, although she really doesn't know how. (She is very bad at flirting – poor thing.)[8]

To them all (except his son) he responds with an almost structural indifference and isolation. His accounts of his wife's despair are not those of a cruel man; their marriage seems to have deteriorated because of common difficulties – suburban isolation, a man and woman with little in common, the routine stress of raising a family. Similarly, he would prefer not to betray his friend Kagle, but the corporate structure pulls him against his altruistic desires.

The most striking quality of Slocum's descriptions of relationships is the distance from which he speaks. All the characters outside his head suffer from a lack of individual definition. The shallowness is linked to the lack of feeling Slocum has for anyone else, since he can relate to them only from his own central void:

> Freud or not, I have never been able to figure out how I really did feel about my mother. . . . I think I felt nothing. I had the same feeling, or absence of feeling most of the time, toward the other members of my family and my best friend, with whom I am not on very friendly terms anymore. We grew tired of each other, and I am relieved. . . . I have never been sure I ever really cared for anyone in this whole world but myself and my little boy.[9]

Curiously, despite his apparent heartlessness, Slocum is not an unfeeling person. Throughout the book he describes his inner states in the most piteous terms:

> I feel tense, poor, bleak, listless, depressed. . . . I have judged, wracking inner conflicts filing, slicing, hacking, and sawing away inside me mercilessly like instruments of bone, stone, glass, or rusty, blunted iron butchering their own irreducible muscular mass. . . .[10]

But Slocum cannot translate this intensity of feeling into connection with the people he lives and works with. The family has borne too many strains and has cracked under the pressure, both as a whole and person by person. At work, you are closest to the man who will destroy you, or who you will, in turn, destroy. Interpersonal life is a desert. Isolation and despair are its prevailing emotional weather, and in time, they will erode personal relationships, personal integrity, and even personality.

One of the most compelling questions raised by Heller's book is that of motivation. If work and the family offer only anxiety, terror, heartache and numbed indifference as emotional rewards for participation in the struggle for achievement, participation in the search for success becomes problematic.

Slocum's own description of his ambitions makes it clear that the ideology that once unified internal drives and linked self-service to the greater social good has given way to a vacuum where the desire for power and prestige finds only the most cynical of justifications and the perceived lack of alternatives provides the most powerful reason for assent to the *status quo*. Given this development, it is understandable that the theme of adult disaffection and failure becomes a matter of central concern to novelists of this period, yet the dramatic nature of this thematic shift cannot be over-emphasized. For the first time, significant numbers of best-sellers are coming to grips with the consequences of the trivialization of a central American value, and critically examining problems of individuals disaffected from the goal of success.

In earlier decades heroes dropped out as a ruse – for instance, in John le Carré's *The Spy Who Came in from the Cold* (1964) – and people who did not follow traditional careers tended to be either ineffectual and marginal men, like the genteel failure of John O'Hara's *Elizabeth Appleton* (1963), or men caught up in extraordinary circumstances, like the father in Thornton Wilder's *The Eighth Day* (1967), who must flee town under a charge of murder. During the previous period, novelistic heroes sometimes retreated into private domestic or sexual preoccupations, or into introspection. However, in this period, 1969–75, eight books (as opposed to three in the previous, twelve-year period) are centered on very active, public, and vocationally oriented men who have either decided to leave the route towards mainstream success, or are increasingly caught up with other aspects of their lives and thus are more and more tenuously connected with their work. The institutions in which they work are often also in crisis, so that individual difficulties find an easy parallel in generalized problems.

In addition, all of these men have personal troubles. Bad marriages, inner difficulties caused by past relationships, complex problems with women or with sexuality, attest to a perception on the part of bestselling novelists that traditional expectations about life at home – as well as at work – are no longer being met in reality.

Certain novelists concentrate most explicitly on the social ills unsolved by affluence, others on the failure of success to 'deliver' personal happiness. For example, the hero of Harold Robbins's *The Inheritors* (1969) has dropped out of the TV world because of double-dealing at the high corporate level; and Adam Trenton, the hero of Arthur Hailey's *Wheels* (1971), is disenchanted with the auto industry because of its failure to address either poverty in Detroit or safety and ecology issues in car design. In both Jacqueline Susann's *The Love Machine* (1969) and Hailey's *The Moneychangers* (1975), however, the central figures are executives caught up in agonizing personal difficulties that attenuate their involvement with work. Susann's hero cannot 'feel,' more specifically, cannot link sex with love, partly because of his lurid, repressed childhood as the son of a German whore. Hailey's hero has an insane wife, and wants to marry his beloved mistress.

In the end, these disenchanted or preoccupied executives all resolve their difficulties and resume their duties. At least in bestselling social melodramas, heroes only experience limited alienation. Hailey's banker hero reaffirms his faith in bankiing and in himself by stopping a bank run singlehandedly: at work and in love, he weathers the crisis. Steve Gaunt of *The Inheritors* decides to come back when the executives promise him the chairmanship of a new amalgamated media empire: from this pinnacle, it is implied, he can make a real contribution. Hailey's *Wheels* promises reform of the auto industry. He shows the top executives responding to the criticism of a Nader-like consumer advocate by incorporating new technology and safety devices in automobiles, and by assuming a beneficent role in the community. They initiate a program to reach the hard-core unemployed, and sponsor a critical movie called 'Auto City', for example. The hero, Adam Trenton, decides not to drop out because the industry offers him not only a new and safer car to develop, but a renewed belief in corporate morality:

> As Adam saw it, a good deal was wrong with the auto
> industry, but there was a great deal more that, overwhelm-

ingly, was right. The miracle of the modern automobile was not that it sometimes failed, but that it mostly didn't; not that it was costly, but that – for the marvels of design and engineering it embodied – it cost so little; not that it cluttered highways and polluted the air, but that it gave free men and women what, through history, they had mostly craved – a personal mobility.

Nor for an executive to spend his working life, was there any more exciting milieu.[11]

In all these novels, the scenario of an executive's career at risk is resolved with a new determination, a declaration of faith and hope reborn, either through corporate reform or because of a more personal solution. A crisis is admitted, but contained by redefinition as a test of the individual and social fiber. The conventional recontainment becomes almost as hackneyed as politicians' rhetorical assertions that our problems are our challenge. It neatly packages, labels, and limits social tensions and individual discontents by asserting through plot and character development that, in the end, the hero can have it all without fundamentally modifying the social order. Such formulations are indicative not only of the problem of success in these years, but also of its tenacity as an ideal.

Despite novelistic conventions that act to contain problems associated with success, books of this period express a sense that both individuals and their social environment are in a state of fragility. Two thrillers of this period place historical figures at the center of threatening plots. Jack Higgins's book *The Eagle Has Landed* (1975) is about a World War II Nazi plot to kill or kidnap Churchill from an English country house, and Frederick Forsyth's *The Day of the Jackal* (1972) describes an assassination plot centered on de Gaulle. Both threats come within a hair's breadth of succeeding.

Two less formulaic books, John Updike's *Rabbit Redux* (1971) and Irwin Shaw's *Evening in Byzantium* (1973), explore individual and social vulnerability without arriving at easy answers. Their descriptions of the hero as survivor might, indeed, be seen as the beginnings of a new metaphor that takes fuller account of the problems inherent in older definitions of success. Updike's novel is the more literary of the two, but the novels have much in common. Both Updike's hero, Harry (Rabbit) Angstrom, and Shaw's Jesse Craig are 'middle-aged.' Craig is a burned-out movie producer at forty-eight, while Rabbit, a linotype operator, is going to fat at thirty-six. Both men have had a period, now past, of relative fame – Rabbit as a high-school athlete, Craig in the theatrical profession – and in the present both work in industries where rapid change has eroded the security and life-chances of old practitioners. Shaw's book opens with a lament for the good old days of the movie industry, when men were moguls and actresses screwed their way to the top:

> *Dinosauric, obsolete, functions and powers atrophied, dressed in sport shirts from Sulka and Cardin, they sat across from each other at small tables in airy rooms overlooking the changing sea and dealt and received cards just as they had done in the lush years in the rainfall forest of the West Coast. . . . Sometimes they talked of the preglacial era. 'I gave her her first job. Seventy-five a week. She was laying a dialogue coach in the Valley at the time.'. . . .*[12]

Rabbit works at an old-fashioned job at the Verity Press, as the operator of a flatbed letterpress. In describing Rabbit's relationship with his machine, Updike recalls a bygone era of industrialization with nostalgia and regret:

> The machine stands tall and warm above him, mothering, muttering, a temperamental thousand-parted survival from the golden age of machinery. The sorts tray is on his right hand; the Star Quadder and the mold disc and slug tray on his left; a green shaded light bulb at the level of his eyes. Above this sun the machine shoulders into shadow like a thunderhead, its matrix return rod spiralling idly, all these rustling, sighing tons of intricately keyed mass waiting for the feather-touch of his intelligence. . . . The machine is a baby; its demands, though inflexible, are few, and once these demands are met obedience automatically follows. There is no problem of fidelity.[13]

Though nineteenth-century Luddites saw such machines as a threat, Updike, who stands at another point in the trajectory of industrial development, sees man and machine in honest partnership. Rabbit knows his skills, and feels control, self-esteem, and even love, for his work – all of which are threatened by automation, as Updike explores the next step in industrial rationalization through Rabbit's career.

Both Rabbit and Craig are at a point of crisis in work and personal life. Craig, in the process of divorcing a compliant, extravagant, and deceitful wife, is without prospects in the Hollywood of new rules and new talent. Rabbit's wife, Janice, has left him to be with a Greek car salesman, and during the novel Rabbit is fired because of the introduction of automated offset-printing machinery. Both novels explicitly link the heroes' individual difficulties to a more generalized American crisis – Updike by small digressions about the Vietnam War, the moonshot, and racial unrest, Shaw by more obvious preaching:

> *At other places, in other meetings, men of science were predicting that within fifty years the sea that lapped on the beach in front of the terrace would be a dead body of water and there was a strong probability that this was the last generation to dine on lobster or be able to sow an uncontaminated seed.*[14]

Although differences in social class give each man's story a different coloration, and the plots take different turns, both men are demonstrably on the point of collapse. Both must come to terms with shattered lives in a threateningly changing world. And both do pull through the crisis, to wearily resume their responsibilities, and entertain the possibility, at least, of a more hopeful future. Jesse Craig's ace in the hole is a script that he finally sells after an exhausting stint at Cannes, during which his daughter runs away with an elderly writer who has long been his enemy, and Craig is himself seduced by a young journalist.[15] Returning to New York, Craig almost dies from an ulcer attack. But, though shaky and alone, he emerges from the hospital with a renewed commitment to writing:

> He was alone, alive, walking, each step stronger than the
> one before it, alone, with no address, drifting down a street
> in his native city, and no one in the whole world knew

where he was. . . . For this moment, at least, he had made a space for himself.

He passed a shop in which typewriters were on display.[16]

Rabbit lives out his crisis on the level of personal relationships rather than work. His involvement with a young hippie girl ends in her death as his house is destroyed by fire. Although he is still unemployed at the end of the novel, his wife returns and they find a weary peace in each other's arms:

He lets her breasts go, lets them float away, radiant debris. The space they are in, the motel room long and secret as a burrow, becomes all interior space. . . . His hand having let her breasts go comes upon the familiar dip of her waist, ribs to hip bone, where no bones are, soft as flight, fat's inward curve, slack, his babies from her belly. He finds this inward curve and slips along it, sleeps. He. She. Sleeps. O.K.?[17]

The stories of Craig and Rabbit are far from the youthful sagas of postwar expansion even from the more limited family-man success stories of the later 1950s and early 1960s, when personal fulfillment and the experiential rewards of success were central. Now survival itself is at stake, and the hero is past his prime and very vulnerable to the disquieting currents of social change. The heroes, insofar as they represent a typical American Everyman, seem to indicate the emergence of a new formula: the hero as fragile survivor. Like the more conventionalized books showing success reaffirmed through crisis, they point to difficulties in older conceptions of success, but unlike books such as *Wheels* or *The Love Machine*, they work through the crisis by affirmation of a weary, stoical integrity, by confirmation of the value of creativity or marriage despite a lack of optimism about individual happiness, social progress or success itself.

Novels of this period also describe youthful figures as vulnerable and disaffected. Young drifters, runaways, 'flower children' and affluent radicals become stock characters, sometimes marked as victims of a whole gamut of social ills, sometimes depicted as the cause of America's problems. Generally novelists look at the young from the perspective of

131

the older generation, as do Updike and Heller, or James Michener in *The Drifters* (1971), whose protagonists are young hippies, seen through the eyes of an avuncular narrator. This distance makes their stories less internally complex than those of adults who are disaffiliated from the corporation or the suburbs. Complexity enters when novelists identify causes and assign moral judgments, for like the parents of the young runaways and rebels, the novelists of this period find them hard to come to terms with. Heller and Updike, among the most sophisticated writers on the bestseller list, do not, in fact, attempt to explain. They are content to show their readers interactions between adults – as parents, as older lovers – and the young, to detail the limited ways in which young people can be known, and to point out the mysterious dimensions of youthful existence that lie beyond their ken.

John Fowles's book *The French Lieutenant's Woman* (1970) and Gwen Bristow's *Calico Palace* (1970), though far apart in literacy and sophistication, both center on young women breaking free from the constraints of sexual conventions. Each is set in Victorian times, and each has a modern resonance: Bristow reveals the underside of the Gold Rush days in San Francisco, and Fowles the communal and bohemian lifestyle which was an inspiration for and precursor to the twentieth-century communal movement. In both these books the young women manage to build quite happy endings for themselves, whereas in novels from the previous period like Henry Sutton's *The Exhibitionist* (1967), the girl is a passive and unhappy victim of liberalized sexuality. A counterexample would be Judith Rossner's *Looking for Mr. Goodbar* (1975) but, in this period, harsh moral judgments are not always levelled at sexually active young women.

Susann's *Once Is Not Enough* (1973) and *Burr* (1973) by Gore Vidal discuss young people whose lives have been blighted because a dynamic father has explored and enlarged the world, leaving his child with little left to accomplish, and the sense of a life diminished before it has properly begun. This concern is echoed in the portrait of the young son in *Something Happened*: neither the boy nor his father can imagine a future for him. Whether playfully or seriously, both Vidal and Heller ask where the next generation can go, though only Heller shows the source of the dilemma in a social system that has reached such a cynical cul de sac that no father would want to imagine his son's adulthood, and such a level of bureaucratic abstraction that the son cannot envision it. Two ambitious writers are pointing to one symptom of general social confusion: the younger generation's inability to find productive ways of gearing into the public world, and consequent inability to construct individual futures which can meld with more generalized forces of social progress.

Several books published during this period explicitly describe the disaffection of American youth as a central feature of a social crisis, though the young are not usually the protagonists of bestsellers, but rather the target of novelistic moralizing. Judgments about them run the gamut from Helen MacInnes's contempt, in her *Message from Malaga* (1971), through the liberal evenhandedness of Joseph Wambaugh's *The Choirboys* (1975) and Robert Ludlum's *The Matlock Paper* (1973).

Ludlum, for example, does not approve of the vigilante violence of a group of student revolutionaries who want to kill their college president, having discovered that he is the leader of a huge New England narcotics ring. Nonetheless, he admires their courage and mourns their deaths. If authorities have become corrupt, direct action against them cannot be too harshly judged even if it is outside the law. In his novel, the president and his hoodlums and the young revolutionaries destroy each other, neatly leaving the field to a liberal young professor.

At the other end of the spectrum are books like Michener's *The Drifters* (1971) and Judith Rossner's *Looking for Mr. Goodbar* (1975), which are openly sympathetic to the plight of the young, and tell their stories from a narrative viewpoint which allows some access to their interior lives. Michener's book even enumerates the social ills that his young drifters are seeking to escape. For example, Joe, an average American college student, searches his conscience about the war in Vietnam, and decides to leave the country. Britta flees a tiny town in Norway: its constraints make little sense when advertisements offer a glamorous wider world. And Cato is a brilliant young black American who has become a militant radical after his friend dies in a random incident of ghetto violence. The book is in some ways a representation of the case young people are making against their parents and their society.

In all these books, novelists perceive the crisis that alienates both the young and their elders as an integral part of the American way of life. No writer sees this crisis as easily comprehensible, but each shows that it cannot be explained away solely by reference to the machinations of some external government or foreign power. Perhaps more important than any cause the novelists enumerate (and these range from corporate or official corruption, the world financial crisis, the Vietnam War, and overmaterialism, to unloved childhoods, and even the Mafia) is their strong sense that people of all ages are having difficulty giving allegiance to traditional ideals and institutions. Lives are in crisis, the villains are not outside, and there is no easy solution to the problems that may be the one thing the generations have in common.

The formula that shows heroes rebounding from such problems – either with renewed protestations of loyalty (*The Moneychangers*, *Wheels*), or through a more limited acceptance and quiet resumptions of duties – seems almost too weak to contain this discontent. The pull of the happy ending is always strong in popular literature; it bespeaks resolution of tension and a renewal of the moral ordering of the world. If these novels represent the 'best' of imaginable happy endings – where 'best' stands for some combination of believable and satisfying – then they provide evidence of a crisis of serious social and moral dimensions.

In this period, traditional ideals of social progress and an inherently meaningful calling are upheld by books that translate these themes to a nonhuman realm, such as Richard Adams's *Watership Down* (1974) and Richard Bach's *Jonathan Livingston Seagull* (1970). This convention permits avoidance of the complexities of human social arrangements, even sexuality (females are marginal or stultifyingly silly or conservative). The band of rabbits who strike out for a new burrow in *Watership Down*, for example, resembles every group of frontier heroes portrayed in the popular arts: Hazel, the all-round leader; Fiver, the delicate visionary; and two strong, loyal fighters. These rabbits are fierce, too, although it is interesting that a species-identification is now being formed with the rabbit, when lions and other predators have been the traditional heroes of adult animal stories.[18] It is also unclear how their quest could be translated into human terms. The two rabbit burrows or 'societies' rejected by Hazel and his band of explorers represent an authoritarian, regimented totalitarianism and a modern bureaucracy. For example, in the second burrow rabbits are enslaved to shadowy masters (the rabbits' master is a farmer who feeds them, but the metaphoric equivalent for human society is not clear), have forgotten their true natures, and spend their time creating agonized pieces of sculpture and poetry in the modern style. Both rabbit burrows resemble facets of contemporary life. But the burrow on Watership Down, the vision of 'the good society' – loose and democratic yet highly patriarchal, free and innovative, but close to the good old traditions – seems an exercise in nostalgia, a depiction of an idealized world we have lost.

This nostalgic conservatism pervades Adams's treatment of females as well. One reviewer, in fact, objected to his distortion of the relationship between male and female rabbits.[19] When Adams mentions females at all, they are merely breeders, or singers of conservative and mindless myths to the young. *Jonathan Livingston Seagull* repeats this lacuna in its portrait of seagull society. I would speculate that this avoidance points to a certain tension between the sexes in present-day society, which means that novelists must revise or excise male–female relationships when constructing animal parables of idealized human groups.

Jonathan Livingston Seagull (1970) shows the uttermost spiritual transmogrification of the individual calling. It reaffirms idealistic individualism not only by transcending the human – since the book is about a seagull – but also by transcending the material world itself. Over half the book takes place after Jonathan's death and assumption into a higher realm. He can only become perfect by denying material reality altogether:

> He knew with practiced ease that he was not bone and
> feather, but a perfect idea of freedom and flight, limited by
> nothing at all.[20]

The lesson he preaches upon his return to the ordinary, earthbound seagulls (the author, by the way, claims to have written the book under divine inspiration) is that each of us has *within* ourselves an essential devotion to freedom and the capacity to achieve the limitless ideals inherent in our natures. Yet these capacities are discussed on an extremely internal, inhuman and transcendent level. Even for a gull, precison flying is removed from the grubby 'work' of living. When Jonathan, the lonely daring individual devoted to a higher calling, begins to respond to the intrinsic freedom and delight of flight in and for itself, his father sums up the materialist perspective on life:

> 'See here, Jonathan,' said his father, not unkindly. . . . 'If you must study, then study food, and how to get it. This flying business is all very well, but you can't eat a glide, you know. Don't you forget that the reason you fly is to eat.'[21]

Jonathan transcends the mundane conformity of the flock by denying the constraints of material reality altogether, though Bach describes him as taking in 'new ideas like a streamlined feathered computer,'[22] thus blending high-tech metaphors with a quietistic message about detachment from the world. Similarly, Bach amalgamates Western notions of progress and a very Eastern idea of reincarnation, retaining elements of optimistic individualism in recombination with convenient snippets of a word-denying mysticism. As another gull says to the born-again Jonathan:

> 'Most of us came along ever so slowly . . . forgetting right away where we had come from, not caring where we were headed, living for the moment. Do you have any idea how many lives we must have gone through before we even got the first idea that there is more to life than eating, or fighting, or power in the Flock? A thousand lives, Jon, ten thousand! And then another hundred lives until we began to learn that there is such a thing as perfection. . . . The same rule holds for us now, of course: we choose our next world through what we learn in this one, all the same limitations and lead weights to overcome.'[23]

One can, clearly, only *improve*. The wheel of *maya*, in its American version, does not permit rebirth on a lower level; one must progress, even if it takes a thousand lifetimes. Yet this progress, and this lofty individual calling, are achieved in a world far removed from human life on earth.

Books about private experience and internal belief, rather than about success or failure or parables about an idealized calling, focus on some of the inner consequences of the processes of disenchantment with success as a central social ideal, and point to particular areas of strain and uncertainty in the social landscape of affluence. They can also be read as indicators of different modes of adaptation to a world without a center. Although these 'responses' are widely divergent, ranging from a retreat into sensual gratification to a spiritual millenarianism, many show the desire for a solution – some simple answer that can provide a moral ordering principle that the fable of success no longer offers.

Sexuality and love provide one such substitute reward system. Novels like *Love Story* by Erich Segal (1970) and Jacqueline Susann's *The Love Machine* (1969) or *Once Is Not Enough* (1973) tout the importance of romantic rewards over external gratifications, such as wealth, power, or fame. This theme, of course, far antedates the period under study, yet such books seem colored by their time in subtle ways. The hero of *Love Story*, for example, is insecure because of his accomplished super-WASP family, and only the heroine's Italian working-class vibrancy and brilliance enable him to break with the older generation and strike out on his own. The heroine of *Once Is Not Enough* is also weighed down by the accomplishments of her father, and her love has an other-worldly narcissism that links it to other escapist books of this period. She finally finds happiness with a being from outer space, who can shape himself (itself?) to the lineaments of her desires. She is taken with him into life beyond earth: the happy ending veers sharply away from realism.

Other novelists celebrate the infinite variety of sexual pleasures, as if sensation were the only surviving realm of significant acts. Harold Robbins's *The Pirate* (1974) is characteristic of such books in its inflated and exotic descriptions of bizarre sexuality. Drugs permeate all social occasions, and

Robbins's descriptions of sexual encounters incorporate elements of perversion and sadism. For instance, in his earlier novel *The Adventurers*, rape is rape, but in *The Pirate*, Badyr (the hero) maneuvers two girls into sexual coupling with each other, then seizes one from behind and penetrates her anally without any warning:

> The girl froze for a moment at the unexpected assault, then opened her mouth to scream. As she sucked in her breath for air, he broke two capsules [of amyl nitrite] under her face. Instead of screaming she climaxed in a frenzied spastic orgasm. A second later, he cracked an amie for himself and exploded in an orgasm he thought would never end.[24]

Sensation appears devalued by virtue of its easy access, and the horizon of transcendent sexual intensity is constantly receding.

Irving Wallace's *The Fan Club* (1974) shows some uneasiness about sexuality as anodyne or alternative source of self-esteem. It is the story of a kidnapping, sexual abuse, and eventual escape of a beautiful Hollywood sex goddess. The abduction of Sharon Fields, the brilliantly successful movie actress, is, in part, an expression of generalized resentment by those who have not achieved success towards those who have, a particularly powerful combination of sheer lust, lust for wealth and fame, and hatred of the rich and fortunate that is sexually vented on the body of a woman. Moreover, Wallace connects her fate to her development of personal integrity and self-sufficiency as a woman in a very disquieting way. She is not just a Marilyn Monroe type, victimized by the processes that helped create her success. Rather, she has been able to come to terms with her own peculiar social and symbolic position through self-discovery. As she says:

> 'It's something, discovery of self. Like planting a flag on a new territory. I don't have to be approved by everyone, loved by everyone, anymore. What a relief. I just have to know that I love myself, what I am, how I feel, what I truly can be, as a person, not an actress, just a person.'[25]

Barely two days later, she is forcibly kidnapped, tied to a bed, raped repeatedly (with great attention to detail), and almost killed. Wallace shows some critical understanding of the role that sex-ploitation and image creation have played in her plight, but it is more than ironic that her hard-won sense of self should be thus rudely shattered. She does survive – by manipulation, flattery, play acting, and the usual battery of female tricks. But at the end of the book, she is characterized as a 'tough, surviving bitch,' and she has declined as a character into the classical hardened-whore-as-star, all traces of a new womanhood knocked out of her by the assault.

The four men who are responsible – a pallid accountant, a bitter mechanic, a two-bit insurance salesman who has not been able to capitalize on his moment of glory as a football player, and a failed writer – are characterized as both titillated and frustrated by the promises of an affluent society that has failed to give them either success or 'fun.' As the accountant says, the 'girls, that good life out there' remained the prerogative of 'real people, the achievers,' unavailable to a 'total nobody' like him.

> And it was not right, simply not right, because there was so much inside of him. . . . He was a person who deserved something, who deserved better.[26]

The extremity of the crimes these very commonplace men commit illuminates the demeaning nature of ordinary life, the paucity of social rewards for people who behave like responsible adults, and the distance between what is and what is promised by advertisements, television, and the other purveyors of hedonism and immediate gratification.

Other novelists both indulge in sexual titillation and express some fear of the consequences of 'liberated' sex. In *Looking for Mr. Goodbar* by Judith Rossner (1975), the heroine is a victim of the freedom of single bars and anonymous urban sex, while in *Naked Came the Stranger* by 'Penelope Ashe' (1970) a career woman betrayed by her husband devastates the entire male population of a Long Island suburb when she goes on a vengeful sexual rampage. Both show some concern about the unsettling of traditional roles for women. In Rossner's book, for example, the heroine, Theresa, cannot find a useful model for her own life, for one of her sisters has fled into a stultifying domesticity and the other carries her narcissism intact from one marriage to another. Rossner cites many reasons for Theresa's own anomic inability to love: her rigid and unhappy background, urban loneliness, and the easy availability of inconsequential sex. But finally she focuses on Theresa's own self-destructiveness, leaving the reader with a portrait of the self-created victim and a fear of easy sex and singles bars. The heroine of *Naked Came the Sranger* refuses to be victimized, but instead assumes the role of voracious sexual aggressor. Her story, though humorous, betrays some nervousness about women's increased independence and what female liberation might entail for masculine sexual identity. Such books express great uncertainty about relationships between men and women – implying as does Heller's book that the privatistic haven of the late 1950s has, like success, become problematic itself.

In fact, the question of appropriate sources of manhood arises in several books of this period, influenced, I would surmise, by developments both within and beyond the sphere of sexuality itself. Liberated sexuality implies loss of male mastery to an ideology of pleasure for all. Moreover, in the absence of an ideology of success that can suffuse the mundanity of corporate or bureaucratic work with heroism, other models of manhood appear to have gained appeal. For example, James Dickey's *Deliverance* (1970) looks back to the ancient combat between man and nature, and the direct, life-or-death, man-against-man struggle in the wilderness. A canoe trip becomes paradigmatic of a quest that can provide meaningful manhood at least partially because of deliverance from the daily office routine. The hero's reflections on his river journey show quite clearly that his everyday achievements have lost their transformative aura and that he, at least, seeks transcendence elsewhere:

> The river and everything I remembered about it became a possession to me, a personal, private possession, as nothing else in my life ever had . . . I could feel it – I can feel it – on

different places on my body. It pleases me in some curious way that the river does not exist [it has been dammed] and that I have it. In me it still is, and will be until I die, green, rocky, deep, fast, slow, and beautiful beyond reality. I had a friend there who in a way had died for me, and my enemy was there.

The river underlies, in one way or another, everything I do. It is always finding a way to serve me, from my archery to some of my recent ads and to the new collages I have been attempting for my friends.[27]

In two books about the Mafia, Puzo's *The Godfather* (1969) and Jimmy Breslin's *The Gang that Couldn't Shoot Straight* (1970), the old-fashioned ties of kinship and blood feud provide challenges to and confirmations of manhood that are transparent and highly personalistic, harking back to an older epoch. Nothing could be further from the abstract bureaucratic roles and the complex white-collar hierarchies of the corporate order. In the Mafia's world, dominance comes from strength and cunning, and women exist to feed and support their men, to bear them sons, and to nourish their understanding of the historic debts of loyalty and revenge that are the source of each man's duties and mission. These books are at once sharply cynical about the liberal state and the established mainstream of society, and suffused with an almost mythic nostalgia for face-to-face combat and direct confrontation.

A further indication of the erosion of the sources of masculine self-esteem is the increasing number of depictions of brutalized relationships with women. Novelists show women being raped or, as in *The Matlock Paper* (1973) and *Message from Malaga* (1971), simply tortured. Sex and love clearly manifest the strains of a more generalized cultural crisis. Whether nostalgic, glamorized or plainly sadistic, these relationships seem to offer, finally, no escape. The disintegration, isolation and pessimism of the world at large have entered the private sphere with full force, chilling evidence of a culture without a center.

This same sense of crisis appears in books with a religious perspective. They manifest a continued attenuation of the confident 'progressive' religiosity that in the earlier periods was the spiritual prop of entrepreneurial individualism. In this period, the incursion of satanic elements or bizarre pre- or post-Christian varieties of spiritualism is a particularly striking development. This began with *Rosemary's Baby* (1967), by Ira Levin, in which a New York actor sells his soul to the Devil, in return for success. The Devil then impregnates his young wife, Rosemary, who, alone in the big city, cannot save either herself or her baby from the fiendish coven of Satan-worshippers. Disturbingly, Evil totally overwhelms both God and the good. More disturbing yet is the manipulation of the realistic underpinnings of the fiction to maintain belief in the plot. Commonplace themes of everyday life – urban isolation, the proliferation of mystical subcultures, the loss of traditional faith, the onset of sexual openness – substantiate the surrealistic elements of the story. A sense of general crisis, bewilderment and nervousness about where individuals and social relationships are heading sustains the fiction. Without that pre-existing tension, the book would lose its power to disquiet its readers.

Books like Blatty's *The Exorcist* (1971) continue this fascination with the power of evil. Though in Blatty's novel the child is finally delivered from her incubus, two priests die to save her, and never during the course of the book are God and faith in God concretized with the kind of power and detail that is given the demon and the effects of his possession. One feels the strength of evil, and its spiritual force; against it stands a very abstract faith in God, and two frail men.

Other novelists, from Jacqueline Susann in *Once Is Not Enough* (1973) to Saul Bellow in *Humboldt's Gift* (1975), dabble in a more transcendent spiritualism. Though very different, both discuss magical solutions to earthly limitations. The heroes of Mary Stewart's historical novels about Merlyn, *The Crystal Cave* (1970) and *The Hollow Hills* (1973), and of Daphne du Maurier's *The House on the Strand* (1969), also display a fascination with the fey and the magical. Stewart's Merlyn is both the only civilized man left in the ruins of Roman Britain, and a shaman of supernatural powers. The disjunction between his urbane sophistication and his wizardry generates a disquieting sense of the irrationality underlying civilized forms. Stewart's novels are also remarkable for their concern with the decline of civilization, a characteristic that in Taylor Caldwell's novel about St. Paul, *Great Lion of God* (1970), becomes an explicitly articulated sense of millenarial doom. She announces her sense of historical parallel in the Foreword to her book:

> The Roman empire was declining in the days of Saul of Tarshish as the American Republic is declining today – and for the very same reasons: Permissiveness in society, immorality, the Welfare State, endless wars, confiscatory taxation, the brutal destruction of the middle-class . . . and, above all, the philosophy that 'god is dead,' and that man is supreme.[28]

Her solution is a regeneration of Christianity; the other authors abandon traditional faith for more magical sources of belief and certainty. All find otherworldly answers compelling.

Another religious response to the times incorporates a more humanistic openness. Novels like *Two from Galilee* (1972) by Marjorie Holmes and *I Heard the Owl Call My Name* by Margaret Craven (1974) confront life among the poor, and the Christianity they embrace is both populist and antimaterialist: a regeneration of faith through its disassociation from the affluent and from material success. Clearly, the earlier comfortable faith in God, which was coextensive with an equally comfortable assurance about progress, success, and the American way, has been significantly eroded in the world of bestsellers. The sense of crisis that began to permeate religious books during the preceding period has deepened and intensified. Even religious books that are more positive express an optimism forged from new elements of religious belief that are as distant from the postwar entrepreneurial confidence as from the more despairing voices of this period.

Genre books – especially thrillers and historical novels – show a sharp quantitative increase in proportion to other novels in this period, perhaps indicating an increased appetite for escapism. Qualitatively, they are of a piece with the other books of the time, expressing disenchantment with easy definitions of progress, a pervasive sense of systemic crisis and liberal exhaustion.[29] Social melodramas, as discussed above, usually resolve the crisis through reform or a renewal of

143

personal mission. The one exception, Joseph Wambaugh's *The Choirboys* (1975), is a portrait of an urban police force that describes a group of young policemen – already shell-shocked by Vietnam – as the front line troops in the domestic battle against social chaos. The random urban brutality they confront every day erodes their reserves for hope and idealism, and finally, their sanity.

Thrillers are more complex. They show an escalation of sensationalism (Frederick Forsyth is the master of a particularly brutal style, and Harold Robbins's obsession with sex and drugs becomes accentuated), and an increasing cynicism about the Western imperialist adventure, indeed all aspects of state bureaucracy.

Forsyth's *The Dogs of War* (1974), for example, reduces all of African politics to questions of greed and manipulative self-interest, whether on the part of the Africans themselves, multinational corporations, or nations. Only the paid mercenaries are pure, because they hide behind no overblown causes or ideals, but admit their motives and their role, and feel at least the elements of community in the blood brotherhood of battle. Graham Greene's *The Honorary Consul* (1973) pays lip service to the ideology of self-determination for Latin American nations, but the plot shows an incompetent terrorist band kidnapping the wrong American to achieve its goals, and causing the death of the last – admittedly jaded and hopeless – European liberal in the city.

Similarly, the problems that provide the basis for plots in thrillers with American settings implicate every level of society. In Robert Ludlum's *The Matlock Paper* (1973) the financial difficulties of New England colleges and the unwillingness of government or business to help them impells the college presidents to become wholesale dealers in illicit drugs. Paul Erdman's *The Billion Dollar Sure Thing* (1973) shows the American dollar and the world commercial system about to buckle – through no individual's fault, though evil men try to benefit from the situation. Scientists, greedy officials, alienated youth and big business are among the groups at fault in other novels, and at least three of the eleven thrillers have abandoned the standardized happy ending common in the genre: no simplistic moral resolution of such

144

generalized disorder appears plausible.

The uses of history in novels of this period are several. John Fowles's *The French Lieutenant's Woman* (1970) and E. L. Doctorow's *Ragtime* (1974) combine nostalgia with an almost scholarly passion to revive the past on its own terms. In some cases, their essayistic descriptions of the past seem to hold forth a vision of alternative ways of life, a look backwards for possibilities of rethinking the present. For example, Fowles's 'lecture' on the Victorian middle-class experience of time could unsettle our tendency to rush through life at top speed:

> Though Charles liked to think of himself as a scientific young man and would probably not have been too surprised had news reached him out of the future of the aeroplane, the jet engine, television, radar: what *would* have astounded him was the changed attitude to time itself. The supposed great misery of our century is the lack of time; our sense of that, *not* a disinterested love of science, and certainly not wisdom, is why we devote such a huge proportion of the ingenuity and income of our societies to finding faster ways of doing things. . . . But for Charles, and for almost all his contemporaries and social peers, the time-signature over existence was firmly *adagio*. The problem was not fitting in all that one wanted to do, but spinning out what one did to occupy the vast colonnades of leisure available.[30]

Other novelists refer back to the golden age of capitalism. R. F. Delderfield's *God Is an Englishman* (1970), for instance, delivers a cheeerful expansionist portrait of Victorian England and of an enterprising couple's rise to great success, a narrative that is reminiscent of Costain's exuberance. Gwen Bristow's *Calico Palace* (1970), set in gold-rush San Francisco, and *The Vines of Yarrabee* by Dorothy Eden (1969), set in early nineteenth-century Australia, also enjoy an optimistic and expansionistic sense of the historical universe, but they are marked by a moral acceptance of open female sexuality that is rather different from the view of women that prevailed in novels like *Forever Amber* (1945).

In Daphne du Maurier's *The House on the Strand* (1969), the nostalgic pull of the past has become a deadly force. A young man unsure about what to do with his career takes a hallucinogenic drug that gives him access to the life of a fourteenth-century squire. He becomes so absorbed in the past that, despite the warnings of his family, his doctor and the scientist who first gave him the drug, he takes an overdose that leaves him paralyzed. Her book seems to be a warning against the misuse of the past as a 'solution' to the complexities of the present.

The sense of the end of an era is strong in historical novels of this period, sometimes regretful and sometimes foreboding. For example, Gore Vidal's 1973 novel *Burr* looks back to the glorious days of the American Revolution, while revealing the pettiness of its heroes. Taylor Caldwell's and Mary Stewart's historical novels, on the other hand, show concern about faith and scholarship in eras when civilization itself is threatened with a rising tide of savagery. No longer is the past a mirror of the smug and optimistic present. Indeed, it provides escape from, or warning parallels to, a time of perceived uncertainty, a resource for a more complex confrontation with a demystified world.

The bestsellers of the years from 1969 to 1975 delineate a crisis in cultural legitimation which, on the level of novelistic content, calls into question the most private sources of character and aspiration, and almost every institution – familial, occupational, educational, religious – that constitutes the wider social realm. The crisis is played out along several dimensions of what one might call the literary order. The novelistic mood is cynical, nostalgic, often brutally hedonistic, newly mystical and millenarial, embattled, or despairing. Settings emphasize the tendency towards nostalgia and apocalyptic visions. Heroes embody failure and alienation; heroines bear the sexual fallout of despair; and the young are more and more disconnected from society. Plots increasingly turn on fictional crises that implicate the whole established order. Villains are no longer 'foreign' in any respect; instead they are ordinary people, or institutions that are integral to our way of life.

The books of this era return to preoccupations with the public realm, in part because the private realm that was a haven in the previous period is itself disintegrating. But

146

whereas once the individual and society were both secure and dedicated to progress – giving the individual's economic success the legitimation of synchrony with an expansive and moral world order – now both individual and collectivity are exhausted, fragmented, and at bay.

Even though the books of this period are marked in various ways by the exhaustion of a certain conception of individual material success, they manifest a cultural open-endedness that is not without hope. In the midst of the confusion and disarray is at the very least a sense that traditional verities are too simple to handle the complexities of modern times. Attenuation of the metaphor of material success leaves the way open not only for nostalgia and brutalization, but also for a multidimensional exploration of other values, other times, and other rewards. Although many of the novels seem to be in search of a single moral ordering principle to replace that of success, the very variety of solutions they advance speaks to the possibility of a new flexibility and relativism in the American popular imagination.

6

The social critics

Until now I have been describing American popular novels of 1945 to 1975. Chapter 2 discussed the social context of their production, dissemination, and reception.

Chapters 3, 4 and 5 analyzed the strands of novelistic content that had particular relevance to the American Dream: novelists' definitions of success and the good life, and their assumptions about individual motivation and the social order within which characters dream, desire, act, and suffer the consequences of their actions. In this chapter, I will examine how two 'generations' of American social critics have surveyed the same social landscape that gave popular novelists their points of view and taken-for-granted assumptions about the world, even when they were not writing about present-day America.

As the preceding chapters have demonstrated, the content and tone of popular novels have changed strikingly over this thirty-year period, but not in any simple or automatic fashion. For instance, novels whose heroes successfully pursued entrepreneurial quests that developed their character, and brought them material and emotional rewards, while simultaneously contributing to more general social progress, gradually disappeared from the bestseller lists.

In the wake of this fictional synthesis, some novelists examined occupational and material success quite critically, but others continued to celebrate entrepreneurial behavior. Yet, twenty-five years after World War II, even such novels depicted heroes and their institutions in some disarray, grappling with crises that ranged from systemic breakdowns to personal troubles that undermined effective participation in the public world. Although, from the late 1950s on, novelists were no longer portraying this public world as a simple backdrop for entrepreneurial conquest, they showed protagonists responding to its difficulties in a variety of ways: some retreating towards existential, spiritual, or experiential quests, some surrendering to the blandishments of immediate gratification, some reasserting traditional commitments to family or religion, and some continuing their tasks with weary stoicism.

This chapter will show that the social critics writing during this same period have failed to grasp the complexity of the cultural developments that bestselling novels reveal, because they have tended to categorize individuals and their culture as unreflective objects of institutional change. At the end of this chapter I will argue that this view arises from the unexamined nature of the critics' relationship to their own social context. They do not study American culture carefully, because their very membership in it seems to lead them to believe they can understand it intuitively. This means that their intuitions have too little empirical ballast. Conversely, their position as intellectuals seems to encourage them to assume that other people have little critical distance from their culture. This, too, makes it difficult for social critics to attend to other voices of cultural reinterpretation. Moreover, by virtue of membership in the intellectual community, modern social critics have inherited intellectual conventions or traditional methods for understanding the world. Although, by the end of this period they, much like popular novelists, have begun to abandon certain traditions, they maintain the conventional method of describing change by abstracting Past and Present and then contrasting these abstract categories – a convention that impedes their efforts to understand the process and content of cultural change.

Nonetheless, the social critics provide an important counterpoint to the novelists not only despite this problem but because of it. First, they write with great insight into the social causes of what the novelists portray as individually experienced

dilemmas and constraints. Their perspective not only comple-
ments the novelistic vision, but enriches the social dimension
of any attempt to understand modern America. Second, and
more paradoxically, the social critics' portrayals of American
culture are valuable precisely because of their flaws, since what
makes them problematic as empirical descriptions makes them
useful as projective or expressive documents. Insofar as these
thinkers do not draw their descriptions of American culture
from a careful consideration of cultural evidence, their accounts
are based on the same kind of unspoken convictions,
assumptions, and hunches about the environing culture that
novelists implicitly express in their work. Thus, like popular
novels, the social-critical accounts are a fruitful source of
evidence about cultural change.

This chapter, then, has three somewhat different purposes.
The first is to outline the social critics' general endeavor in
order to suggest how their insights can augment other
perspectives that are attuned primarily to individuals. Second,
while reviewing their work, I will indicate how it can be
reframed as an important cultural artifact that betokens some
of the same cultural developments displayed by bestselling
novels. Like the novelists, these social critics are guided by
powerful metaphors and by emotional as well as analytic
responses to their times. And like the novels, during this
period their accounts evince increasing concern with areas of
life beyond the public world of work, increasing pessimism,
increasing fascination with inner experience, and increasing
desire for some moral ordering principle that can provide
coherence for a world they perceive as being in disarray. Third,
at the end of the chapter, I will point out some problems
inherent in these social thinkers' formulations of the task and
method of sociocultural criticism.

Examining the social landscape after World War II, social critics
like David Riesman, C. Wright Mills, and William H. Whyte
were struck by the difference between mid-twentieth-century
America and the industrializing nation of the nineteenth
century. It seemed to them a 'new age,' marked by social
transformations that had left no aspect of life untouched, from
the institutional structures of labor and leisure to the inmost

dynamics of personality formation. Defining the nature of this sharply felt break with the past was, for them, an essential part of coming to grips with the present. In turn, this project led them to explore new themes, such as power, affluence, leisure, and the mass society, that gave their analyses a very different tone from those of prewar social critics, who had grappled with issues like social class and the future prospects of capitalism.[1]

All three of these thinkers identified the distinguishing characteristic of this new age as the domination of economy and society by large-scale bureaucratic organizations. Even the remarkable affluence of the 1950s seemed less important than the deleterious effects of bureaucratic specialization and concentration, which they felt were eroding every foundation for individual freedom. The organizational leviathan had swallowed up independent entrepreneurship; America was increasingly becoming a nation of dependent employees.

As described by C. Wright Mills in *White Collar* (1951), David Riesman in *The Lonely Crowd* (1950), and William H. Whyte in *The Organization Man* (1956), this process profoundly altered mobility, personal aspirations, and social stratification, and affected almost everyone except a few small businessmen and farmers driven to the less profitable margins of the economy. At the top, corporate managers replaced captains of industry, and corporate or quasi-corporate organizations captured 'free professionals' like doctors and lawyers. Mid-level employees could no longer hope for independent ownership, but instead looked forward to climbing career ladders within the organization; while technologically sophisticated production methods like the assembly line usurped the artisan skills of erstwhile master craftsmen. And, overall, the rapid proliferation of white-collar hierarchies made the nineteenth-century Marxist vision of a sharp dichotomy between capitalists and proletariat seem like an old-fashioned Victorian mezzotint. Mills felt that this organizational absorption of individual skills, expertise and authority meant that even those near the the apex of the 'managerial demiurge' were becoming only well-paid cogs, marking places in impersonal chains of command that would outlast them, as the bureaucracy lumbered into the future under its own mysterious imperatives.[2]

Dependence on large organizations had several consequences for the individual, according to Riesman, Whyte, and Mills. Whyte felt that the new employees were 'deeply beholden' to the organization in an almost feudal sense: it claimed their total loyalty and obedience.[3] Thus, his title *The Organization Man*. Large-scale organizations also required a new level of interpersonal coordination, and Whyte felt that this could lead to increasingly manipulative and intrusive demands on the individual:

> The skills of human relations can easily tempt the new administrator into the practice of a tyranny more subtle and more pervasive than that which he means to supplant. No one wants to see the old authoritarian return, but at least it could be said of him that what he wanted primarily of you was your sweat. The new man wants your soul.[4]

Mills underscored the personal vulnerability and political ineffectiveness that he thought were concomitants of the loss of middle-class control over the means of production. He contended that the new white-collar hierarchies had broken the linkage between 'property and work as a basis of man's essential freedom.'[5] Propertylessness and the fear of unemployment contributed to a pervasive sense of insecurity – an important component of a vague, all-pervasive anxiety that he felt was emblematic of modern times. Coupled with a specialized division of labor, white-collar dependency had resulted, in his analysis, in a new social formation: new middle classes that were internally 'split, fragmented,' and externally 'dependent on larger forces,' thus both personally and politically powerless.[6]

In part due to this dependency, individuals could no longer even 'possess' or develop their own special goals or visions of accomplishment, in Riesman's view. He felt that large organizations were molding the modern world for their own purposes, making parents too insecure about a future beyond their control to instill in their children goals that might be obsolete in a few years. Anxious parents, the mass media and 'new style' teachers were, as he described it, weaning children from an inner-directed sense of work as a self-generated vocation. Instead, these agents of socialization were inculcating children with an 'other-directed' interpersonal flexibility suited to a managerial society that needed workers whose only goal was to win approval from whatever peer group they were part of at the moment.[7] Whyte, too, felt that organizational dependency deprived people of work as a personal vocation. In his description, even if certain individuals escaped into adulthood with capabilities for initiative and entrepreneurial drive, the organization would stifle their creativity, indenturing them to group-think committees, or forcing them to give up their concrete scientific or technical skills if they wanted organizational success.[8]

As the social critics saw it, bureaucratization had altered the very character of work itself. A newly complex division of labor made it increasingly routinized, abstract, and meaningless. In Riesman's analysis, work was no longer worth a substantial investment of the self. His book was written, in part, to persuade people to look elsewhere, towards leisure for example, for opportunities for self-development and autonomy.[9]

He, Whyte, and Mills noted that, with the rise of large bureaucratic organizations, occupations centered on the processing and coordination of information and the management of people were supplanting classically industrial jobs that centered on the production of things. And all three felt that this new kind of work encouraged subtle skills of manipulation, covert rather than honest competitiveness, and self-alienation on the 'personality market.' Mills eloquently described how this process degraded the traditional integrity of such skilled workers as the foreman. According to Mills, the foreman had once been a lynch-pin in factory production because of his knowledge of a specific craft, but was now merely an agent of interpersonal manipulation. In modern plants, the foreman's task was that of instilling proper motivation in his subordinates to accomplish essentially mindless work. To do so, he had to use his detailed knowledge of informal work groups on the shop floor to manipulate behavior: preventing the self-organization by which workers limited productivity and eliciting an artificial enthusiasm and dedication in the service of high performance.[10]

Riesman and Whyte concentrated primarily on the managerial level of the corporation. Whyte mourned the decline of an older reward system based on open, if harsh, competition for profit, and criticized its replacement by a more shadowy but no less competitive struggle for interpersonal domination within the corporation. Riesman called this concealed competition 'antagonistic cooperation.'[11] Whyte felt that this new path towards a new kind of success was legitimized by a conformist psychology, and enforced by personality testing, and that the entrepreneurial young executive's only hope for 'honest' success was to understand the system and manipulate it for his own purposes.[12] Riesman, though less nostalgic for the old order, also felt that these new conditions undermined the entrepreneurial character because modern success depended 'less on what one is and what one does than on what others think of one – and how competent one is in manipulating others and being oneself manipulated.'[13] Work, in other words, no longer seemed to offer a field for the development of individual initiative, discipline, and self-sufficiency, but bred personal insecurity, and pressured workers towards an anxious conformism.

In fact, Riesman, Whyte, and Mills all thought that the organization itself had appropriated the entrepreneurial virtues. Riesman characterized bureaucratic institutions as the repositories of long-term goals that had once been the provenance of individual planning and investment on the nineteenth-century frontier of production.[14] Mills claimed, in more Weberian terms, that large organizations

> by their bureaucratic planning and mathematical foresight
> usurp both freedom and rationality from the little individual
> men caught in them. The calculating hierarchies of depart-
> ment store and industrial corporation, of rationalized office
> and government bureau, lay out the gray ways of work and
> stereotype the permitted initiatives.[15]

Mills dreaded a future molded by bureaucracies because he was sure they expressed in new guise the old capitalist imperatives of exploitation and expansion, which functioned at the expense of the individual. Whyte, on the other hand, felt that once people defined their individual self-interest as comfort within the organization, a new paternalism would not only crush individuals but also halt the march of social progress, for 'the Organization of itself has no dynamic.'[16] He worried about the security-minded passivity of college students who chose corporate careers, and the present-oriented materialism of installment-plan suburban living not only because of what the loss of thrift and independence would mean for individuals, but also because he feared for the future of society as a whole.

However their analyses differed in detail, all of these critics agreed that the transformation of a relatively decentralized economy into a centralized and interdependent set of interlocking bureaucratic hierarchies had left little room for the entrepreneurial endeavor, style, or character. Perhaps this is why, in striking contrast to our images of the affluent 1950s, Mills, Riesman, and Whyte all described an end to expansion. All three claimed that metaphors of America as an open society, where every man could pull up his stakes and light out for the territory, were outmoded myths that distorted modern reality. All three did admit that the middle classes had expanded, but could not see this as evidence of social amelioration. They focused instead on evidence pointing to the loss of conditions favorable to genuine opportunity, solid independence, or even individuation itself. Riesman was the most openly nostalgic about the loss of sheer physical expansion. Indeed, his book differentiated between the inner-directed, individualistic nineteenth century and other-directed modernity on the basis of demographic trends: inner direction corresponded to a time of population expansion, but other-directed moderns were living in a phase of 'incipient population decline,' when the world was becoming 'shrunken and agitated by . . . contact.'[17] Inner-directed man conquered the frontiers of production, colonization, and intellectual discovery, and in America assembled our 'expanding capital plant' with zeal and ruthlessness. But beginning in about 1890 when 'the "no help wanted" sign was posted on the frontier,' the era of conquest was over, and the sphere of production no longer seemed a jungle or a wilderness that tested courage, ingenuity, determination or self-discipline.[18]

Even David Riesman, however, used the loss of the physical

155

frontier mainly as a metaphor for the passing of a certain social order. In common with Mills and Whyte, he described the gradual disappearance of a 'loose-jointed and impersonal' economy, and its replacement by a more tightly integrated corporate society, which in turn produced Riesman's 'glad-handers,' Mills's 'little men,' and Whyte's 'organization men.'[19] Each claimed, in other words, that this new social order was destroying true individualism, and giving rise to a herd of petty, manipulative people – all marginally differentiated according to personal style very much like the brand-name consumer durables that flooded the market in the 1950s.

Mills best described what all three thought was happening to the entrepreneurial spirit under these conditions. In *White Collar*, he discussed the remnants of older entrepreneurial groups, but only to make clear that large-scale bureaucracies were superseding their ways and world. In contrast to his predecessors 'who operated in a world opening up like a row of oysters under steam,' the new entrepreneur faced an essentially closed world 'in which all the pearls have already been grabbed up and are carefully guarded.'[20] Mills felt that the new entrepreneur's only possible route to 'independent' success was in 'a zig-zag pattern upward within and between established bureaucracies,'[21] often working in industries like public relations or advertising, that sold intangible services and inevitably justified the *status quo*. Although he might display great initiative, the new entrepreneur was of necessity an operator, a fixer, using deceit and cunning to maintain his tenuous position 'on the guileful edges of the several bureaucracies.' To Mills, he represented the moral corruption of the spirit of free competition, for his rise was predicated on the shady deal, the organizational secret betrayed. 'In an expanding system,' as Mills pointed out,

> profits seem to coincide with the welfare of all; in a system already closed, profits are made by doing somebody in. The line between the legitimate and the illegitimate is difficult to draw because no one has set up the rules for the new situation.[22]

As monopoly perverted free competition, the invisible hand

that once sorted out the gifted and hardworking from the unworthy, was becoming less like the hand of a Calvinist God than like the pimp's bejeweled and beckoning finger. To these critics, the disappearance of an older form of competition made the new society seem both closed and incapable of generating a vision of moral transcendence. This was the new situation in Mills's view, and his book promised little in the way of individual salvation within it.

For all three social critics, the increasing affluence many Americans experienced during the 1950s, and their achievement of heretofore middle-class standards of education and comfort, were much less important features of the social landscape than the erosion of opportunity for ownership of the means to earn a livelihood without dependence on anything but impersonal market mechanisms. The erosion of middle-class independence by large organizations seemed to them to mark the end of meaningful social and economic expansion. They also thought it presaged the disappearance of certain inherently valuable character traits – hard work, thrift, initiative, rational planning, competitiveness, and self-reliance – essential to independent individuals and even to the formation of individuals *per se*. This belief makes their overwhelming fear of conformity or mere 'marginal differentiation' among the populace more comprehensible.

Of course, the technical efficiency of centralization and specialization fueled an economy that could offer not only more affluence but also more leisure than ever before. But perhaps because they regarded work as the only stable foundation of individual identity, Whyte, Riesman, and Mills thought that increased leisure offered no real possibility for freedom, but only the shallow joys of the consumer. Riesman, for example, claimed that the modern era opened up 'new possibilities of being and becoming' as the frontier shifted from production to consumption.[23] Yet in the latter part of *The Lonely Crowd*, he explored the obstacles to individual autonomy that he thought were lurking beneath the tolerant permissiveness of the postwar years. In his analysis, the influence of the mass media and the peer group, and the reduction of previous arenas of rebellion, such as sexuality and bohemia, to a range of consumeristic lifestyle choices, represented 'shadowy entanglements' that incorporated people more tightly than ever before into the *status quo*.[24] Leisure, then, brought the tyranny of overadjustment, which was the more effective because of its seeming beneficence. More bleakly, C. Wright Mills said, 'Every day men sell little pieces of themselves in order to try to buy them back each night and week end with the coin of fun.'[25]

Looking out over the American social scene, these critics were preoccupied by the loss of older forms of community, of established traditions and values. In the 1950s, Mills's, Riesman's, and Whyte's worries about other-direction and conformity revealed their conviction that smaller collectivities, from the small town to the owner-managed business, were disappearing. Like conservative mass-culture theorists, such as Ortega y Gasset or T. S. Eliot, they thought the geographic and social mobility associated with the rise of nationally oriented organizations were shattering people's ties to primary groups such as the nuclear family or stable local neighborhoods, and severing people's adherence to longstanding traditions nurtured by these groups and enforced by local elites. The disappearance of such traditional wellsprings of individual values would, in this analysis, leave individuals isolated and vulnerable to the capricious imperatives of increasingly powerful institutions. In Mills's words, a society of 'widely scattered little powers' was becoming a mass society, in which individuals, unanchored by traditions and traditional ties to kinship and community 'as ways of "fixing men into society",' were increasingly helpless to counteract 'monopoly control from powerful centers, which, being partially hidden, are centers of manipulation as well as of authority.'[26] Leisure and affluence, then, failed to engender freedom because they were part of the social process that had unsettled older communities and left only a 'lonely crowd.'

In this formulation, kinship and community stood for mediation, a middle level of social organization interposed between its largest and smallest units – Organization and Individual – and providing a protective enclave within which the individual could develop his or her own idiosyncratic character. Without these mediating structures, the social critics felt that the possibility for individuation as such was problematic. The individual would be exposed to the full strength of influence from the powers-that-be, such as the mass media, which the critics thought were both more inaccessible and more intrusive than ever before. They claimed that all intermediate levels of society, 'the complex of geographical and family ties that has historically knitted Americans to local society,' and the class and status lines that gave order to local society, were disappearing, widening the gap between what they saw as 'atomized and submissive masses' and the institutionalized machinery of social and cultural manipulation.[27] Unlike the seventeenth-century observers of the English Revolution who saw a world turned upside down, these observers analyzed America in the 1950s as a world without a middle.

Riesman, Whyte, and Mills interpreted the enormous economic expansion of the 1950s as the end of expansion because they feared the loss of entrepeneurial independence. Similarly, they interpreted the enormous expansion of middle-class styles of leisure and consumption as the reduction of Americans to an atomized and conformist herd because they concentrated on the loss of older communities and standards. Without such contexts and guidelines, the lower orders would still remain the masses, no matter how rich they became.

The critics also described the rise of new and more manipulative institutions and groups – such as the mass media and the peer group – which they thought were undermining the very freedom an affluent leisure might permit. In the social vacuum of the suburbs or the anonymity of the metropolis, the mass media were the wholesalers and the peer group the retailers, in Riesman's analogy, for a process that degraded culture and leveled individual differences. In leisure, as in work, these critics saw only increased dependence, increased conformity.

C. Wright Mills, in both *White Collar* and *The Power Elite*, argued that metropolitan man was most vulnerable to the manipulation of the mass media, for the city-dweller's experience was fragmented, his social relationships were short-lived and superficial and his own status was ambiguous, 'revealed only in the fast-changing appearances of his mobile, anonymous existence.'[28] In such conditions, people must depend on the media for connectedness to the world. 'Mass communications replace tradition as a framework for life. . . . The metropolitan man finds a new anchorage in the spectator sports, the idols of the mass media, and other machineries of amusement.'[29]

The media, according to Mills, were beginning to mold the very foundation of personality by providing banal and stereotypic models that organized individual perceptions and aspirations. This ensured external conformity, by insinuating motivations and desires in the audience. But this also alienated people from their own personal experience and stunted their capacity for critical self-reflection.[30]

Like Mills, Riesman highlighted the totalitarian nature of the way mass communications mediated between individual and society. He claimed that an onslaught of compelling media images prevented individuals from escaping into the free play of their own imagination, so the audience passively absorbed the media's training in group adjustment and proper habits of consumption.[31] Riesman also argued that media stars were often such intimidating models that they blighted the audience's own aspirations to develop their talents, thus encouraging another kind of passivity. He felt that the media were disrupting even the privacy and authority of the family, for not only did parents look to the media for reassurance, but their children could independently learn the norms of parental behavior through the media – and hold their parents accountable for deviating from stereotypic roles. In sum, the media caused parents to surrender their self-reliance, and made all family members anxious to imitate the abstracted 'others' crystalized in media interpretations of the world.[32]

Since, in Mills's view, modern society pitted the centralized forces of manipulation against disorganized white-collar masses, he thought the mass media had gained tremendous power over individuals. Like most social scientists of the day, however, Riesman thought that even though social change had dissolved traditional communities, it had given rise to an intermediate social group – the peer group – that could moderate the influence of large-scale organizations on individuals. Empirically, the notion of the peer group had grown from several kinds of social research. Field studies of new suburbs had laid bare intricate structures of sociability that belied the suburban appearance of uniformity. Sociometric analyses of friendship and loyalty among gangs, college students, and industrial workers showed not only the elaborate patterning of peer interactions, but also the strength of group influence over individual members. Communications and propaganda research spurred by the war effort, moreover, revealed that people did not take their opinions directly from the media, but filtered them through local opinion leaders and small groups of friends.

Social critics like Riesman and Whyte used the concept of the peer group to add theoretical complexity to their descriptions of modern society. They thought the model of a sharp dichotomy between powerless masses and manipulative organizations inaccurate. The peer group, at least potentially, could mediate between center and periphery, thus adding flexibility and diversity to an increasingly centralized society by adapting media messages to particular local situations, and in some cases generating ideas that could influence the media. Riesman emphasized that 'feedback' from peer group to media might give individuals some autonomy. 'The flow,' he said, 'is not all one way.'[33] And Whyte pointed to the peer group as evidence that America was *not* a mass society:

> On the surface the new suburbia does look like a vast sea of homogeneity, but actually it is a congregation of small neighborly cells – and they make the national trends as much as they reflect them. The groups are temporary, in a sense, for the cast of characters is always shifting. Their patterns of behavior, however, have an extraordinary permanence, and these patterns have an influence on the individual quite as powerful as the traditional group, and in many respects more so.[34]

As the latter part of Whyte's statement suggests, however, both he and Riesman felt that, despite its potential, the peer group actually worked against the autonomy of individual members. Like affluence itself, the peer group promised freedom, but delivered only more insidious constraints. Whyte, for example, thought that affluence presented people

161

with such a bewildering number of consumer choices that, in the absence of established cultural standards, people would be driven to conform with their peers in matters of taste.[35] The peer group, then, functioned as an important carrier of conformity. And even if the peer group gave people new values in a new status system that appeared to be increasingly based on criteria of taste and consumption, Riesman and Whyte characterized these new values as pernicious, betokening a destructive social leveling. They thought, for example, that the peer group invaded individual privacy to an unprecedented degree. Whyte described the young executive and his wife subjected to a continuous barrage of suburban sociability, whose insistent friendliness would gradually wear down all traces of eccentricity.[36] Riesman felt that the distant courtesies of etiquette, which had been appropriate for a 'graded society,' were being replaced in suburban peer groups by a 'continual sniffing out of others' tastes, often a far more intrusive process.'[37] Moreover, in Whyte's account, the seeming tolerance of the peer group did not extend upwards to embrace elite culture, so people who enjoyed reading Plato either had to do it in secret, or submit to being melted down in the suburban pot.[38] Though these critics claimed to be concerned that the peer group would eliminate 'all knobby or idiosyncratic qualities and vices,' textual evidence indicates they worried most that it was enforcing lowered standards and the herd-instinct of an undifferentiated and uneducated mass.[39] The peer group, then, could neither truly protect the individual from the incursions of a manipulative media, nor provide a context for the nurturance of independent values and lifeways. Instead, like the media, the peer group seemed to foster a frenetic materialism instead of real freedom.

Concurrently with these institutional changes that had transformed labor and leisure so that affluence paradoxically worked against individual autonomy, the social critics of the 1950s identified a deep change in the environing culture. They contended that a new American ethos had emerged – an ideational reflex of the new institutional order that had exacerbated its social-structural pressures towards conformity. William Whyte discussed this 'major shift in American ideology' most straightforwardly and simplistically. He felt that the increasing bureaucratization of society was undermining even official adherence to the Protestant Ethic, and leading to the formulation of a new 'Social Ethic' that 'makes morally legitimate the pressure of society against the individual.' He traced the sources of this ideology to the social determinism of pragmatists like James and Dewey, and discussed three modern groups who propounded its main tenets. Social scientists searching for predictability and control over human beings were responsible for 'scientism.' The human relations school of management, who wanted each person to be totally integrated into a stable, conflict-free group, were advocating 'belongingness.' And bureaucrats, who emphasized group endeavor and the committee way of organizational leadership, were enforcing 'togetherness.' All, in his analysis, had gone too far in hobbling individual creativity and initiative. While he felt that the simple individualism of the work ethic might not suit an age of large organizations and affluent living, he called for some reconstitution of its central ideas to keep alive the tension between individual and collectivity, which he felt had been fruitful for both.[40]

Riesman claimed that modern America was witnessing not merely a new ideology, but a shift in 'modes of conformity,' or personality formation, as fundamental as the shift from traditionalism to the 'spirit of capitalism' discussed by Max Weber in his original formulation of the Protestant Ethic. In his typology of social character, Riesman contrasted the rigid, conscience-driven, enterprising, inner-directed men who characterized the epoch of capital accumulation and industrialization – the men of the Protestant Ethic – with what he called the 'other-directed' men spawned by the affluent bureaucratic society of the present.[41] New agents of socialization, not only the mass media, but comic books, magazines, the peer group and progressive educators, were purveying cultural messages that encouraged other-directed moderns above all to be sensitive to cues from whatever social groups their mobile and cosmopolitan lives presented them with. A diffuse and rapidly adaptive 'radar' of moment-to-moment anxiety about the opinion of these relevant 'others' had supplanted the internal gyroscope of guilt or conscience. So, despite its apparent flexibility, the culture of 'other-direction,' like Whyte's Social

163

Ethic, left the individual unprotected from the shifting tides of social pressure.[42]

Like Riesman and Whyte, Mills was sometimes nostalgic for the entrepreneurial world-view. Yet one of the major thrusts of *White Collar* was to undermine the ideology of independent entrepreneurship, an image of the American way of life that he thought had distorted modern social reality and obscured the main drift of the times. To make rational choices about where they and their society should go, white-collar people had to cast aside their sense of themselves as 'go-getting, claim-jumping, cattle-rustling pioneers of frontier mythlogy' and 'become aware of themselves as members of new strata practicing new modes of work and life in modern America.'[43] Insofar as he admitted that any new certainties were displacing this mythology of frontier individualism, Mills characterized them as simple refractions of the emerging bureaucratic order. For example, he thought that modern success manuals urged people to adopt 'the style of efficient executive,' explained success as a matter of accident, circumstances, and a smoothly polished personality, and stressed a purely instrumental view of success: indications that the new ideology had abandoned the claim that individual success served a higher moral purpose.[44] Mills also examined modern popular novels, and thought they preached the 'internal virtues' of resignation and peace of mind, 'in line with a relaxed consumer's life rather than a tense producer's.'[45] He talked about a contradiction in American culture: the entrepreneurial ethos was hanging on beyond its time, like the decrepit patriarch of a family farm holding the present in thrall to the past. In the shadow of the old order, there existed both 'compulsions to amount to something' and 'a poverty of desire,' but no transcendent purpose to link the individual to the larger collectivity. Reading *White Collar*, it is in fact unclear whether Mills, himself very much the iconoclastic individual, could envision any transcendent or heroic virtues appropriate for a world of clerks. Dependent moving parts in a great bureaucratic machine, their best hope in Mills's analysis appeared to be the choice not to let their status anxieties lead them to neo-fascism, but instead to cast their lot in with the blue-collar workers whose situation, he reiterated again and again, was the most like their own.

The turbulent 1960s drew sociologists to the study of power, inequality, race, ethnicity, and social change – from reform to revolution. Cultural studies tended to focus on the counter-culture or ethnic subcultures. Some social thinkers, such as Herbert Marcuse and Philip Slater, did discuss American values, but from an *a priori* assumption that they were well-nigh pathological. In general, though, it was not until the cultural turmoil of a decade's social unrest had begun to subside that social critics began once again to discuss the main drift of American society and its relation to middle-class culture.

Daniel Bell, Christopher Lasch, and Richard Sennett were the most influential spokesmen for this renewed tradition of sociocultural analysis. Like critics of the 1950s, they were preoccupied with the relationship between the individual and the larger collectivity and with the meaning of affluence for human freedom. But events of the 1960s had altered the social landscape and made many of the insights and fears of the earlier social critics seem somewhat dated. Riesman, Whyte, and Mills perceived the postwar era as a time of alarmingly bland cultural conformity. They were concerned about the effects of new and perhaps more manipulative forces of social integration that belied the promise of freedom through material well-being. After the tumultuous 1960s, when the bland surface of a seemingly conformist society fractured along racial, ethnic, class, sexual, and generational lines, Bell, Lasch, and Sennett became alarmed by the specter of social disintegration. They felt that more organic forms of social bonding had all but vanished, leaving Americans united only by their dependency on bureaucracies. In *The Culture of Narcissism*, for example, Lasch repeatedly referred to American social life as 'the war of all against all,' while Sennett's *The Fall of Public Man* drew an explicit parallel between modern America and the fall of ancient Rome. Daniel Bell voiced the same sentiment in more measured tones. 'Society,' he claimed in *The Cultural Contradictions of Capitalism*, 'is not integral, but disjunctive.'[46] The metaphor of social disintegration was so compelling for social critics of the 1970s that some of the very same phenomena their predecessors had identified as causes of conformism appeared from their perspective to be responsible for the centrifugal tug towards social dissolution. For instance, in the 1950s social critics categorized large-scale bureaucratic organizations as enforcers of conformity because they mystified competition on the job and manipulated consumer insecurities. Daniel Bell, writing in the 1970s, said that the technical rationality of these same organizations contributed, paradoxically, to the cultural contradiction that he saw at the center of contemporary life: a disjuncture between an economy based on efficiency and a culture based on hedonism and self-indulgence. According to him, this disjuncture had disrupted a pre-existing sociocultural unity, evident in nineteenth-century metaphors of the 'web of society.' The split between economy and culture also created conflicts within the individual, because large organizations taught very different standards of behavior, almost different personalities, for work and leisure:

> On the one hand, the business corporation wants an individual to work hard, pursue a career, accept delayed gratification – to be, in the crude sense, an organization man. And yet, in its products and its advertisements, the corporation promotes pleasure, instant joy, relaxing and letting go. One is to be 'straight' by day and a 'swinger' by night. This is self-fulfillment and self-realization![47]

The inner logic of capitalism – efficiency, economies of scale – gave rise to the large corporation, which then, through mass production, advertising, and installment buying, fueled a consumer culture that urged people to attain the pleasures of self-realization by leisure-time spending. This anarchistic culture of personal development through self-indulgence was by now, in Bell's analysis, in conflict with values, such as hard work and delayed gratification, that he felt were necessary not only for capitalism, but for civilization itself.

As Bell's analysis implies, the critics of the 1970s were not only convinced that society was disintegrating, but saw this process reflected in individual personalities as well. Earlier critics thought that dependence on large organizations had left individuals isolated and vulnerable to organizational manipulation; twenty years later, critics thought the same process was leading to the dissolution of the adult self at its very core. In *The Lonely Crowd*, for example, Riesman argued that parental authority was declining in part because parents felt insecure about preparing their children for a future whose direction was controlled by large organizations. In his opinion, this heightened social influences toward conformity, since the mass media and the peer group would shatter the inner-directed individualism once nurtured in the nuclear family. Twenty-eight years later, Christopher Lasch argued in *The Culture of Narcissism* that experts in public and private bureaucracies were appropriating parental authority, and that this contributed to the diffusion of narcissistic character traits in the next generation.[48] This worked in the following fashion. Even well-meaning experts on child-rearing undermined parents' (especially mothers') sense of self-confidence. Because of this, as well as father-absence and the decline of parental authority due to people's general dependence on bureaucracy, Lasch felt that parents would either pass on to their children their habits of anxious self-scrutiny, or retreat from any authority out of fear of doing something wrong. Such parents would be capable of showing their children only the false empathy of narcissism – in which the parent sees the child only as an extension of him- or herself – instead of true attention to the child's needs. According to Lasch, this would make parents both suffocating and distant, causing deep-seated psychic disturbance in their infants. Pre-Oedipal rage and fear caused by inappropriate parental response would lead to an impulse-ridden and chaotic adult personality, who would be unable to form deep and lasting relationships with others, and incapable of deferring or sublimating any impulsive desires, or identifying with and planning for posterity. Since Lasch argued that the industries of mass consumption were also encouraging parents to be self-oriented – exacerbating their inappropriate behavior towards their children – he thought large organizations were 'producing' narcissists in a second fashion as well. Such people, unable to connect with others, or with the warring fragments of their inner selves, would in turn contribute to a 'weakening of social ties' that could be further exploited by paternalistic bureaucracies of work, welfare, and leisure.[49]

That the same features of the social landscape could be so

differently interpreted after such a relatively short interval points up the power of metaphors of conflict and disintegration over the 'sociological imagination' of the 1970s. Even in the 1950s, social critics had mourned the passing of a social totality in which cultural ideals and institutional realities, individual aspirations, and collective purpose found relatively harmonious resolution. As we have seen above, they referred back to the days of the Protestant Ethic and entrepreneurial capitalism with some nostalgia, and regretted the transformation of traditional social relationships and cultural standards. By the 1970s, social critics had begun to display a much more acute sense that the boundaries, standards, and traditions crucial for structuring both the individual personality and civilized social life were dissolving. They interpreted the media marketplace of glamorous personalities, the therapist's siren call of self-awareness and personal growth, even the goal of a self untrammeled by conventions and traditions that has been so central to modernist culture, as part of a process that encouraged unrestrained self-involvement, hedonism, and narcissism.

For example, in *The Fall of Public Man*, Sennett argued that the proper boundary between public and private life had eroded, to the impoverishment of both. In the late eighteenth century, impersonal conventions gave public behavior the civility and security of self-distance. People looked for intimacy in the family, which they characterized as the realm of 'nature,' a part of life equally important as the public sphere, but fundamentally different. During the nineteenth century, in his account, the convulsions of industrialization made life in public overwhelming for people for all classes. As immigration and population growth flooded the cities with mobile and anonymous strangers, people retreated into the family and assigned it moral superiority over the public realm. They began to judge public behavior by intimate standards, such as the Romantic ideals of authenticity and self-revelation. By the mid-twentieth century, the ideology of intimacy, fueled by pop psychology and the media's obsession with glamorous personalities, had begun to pervade both public and private life. Consequently, Americans were letting the public places of city life fall into disrepair, not realizing they provided a rich territory for the delights of impersonal encounters with unknown others. Political life was withering as well, for people were judging politicians according to personal appeal, rather than public effectiveness. According to Sennett, this could easily lead to the irrationalities of charismatic demagoguery. The almost consumeristic search for intimacy was also degrading private life, for in and of themselves personal relationships could not give people the sense of meaning they so voraciously and fruitlessly sought. Without the balance of some collective involvement, personal life, too, was becoming trivial and inconsequential.[50]

Lasch and Bell, as well, were preoccupied with the question of the unrestrained, anarchic self that they saw springing up in the absence of countervailing standards and traditions. Even more than their predecessors, they seemed to yearn for the revival of an idealized past. Lasch, in *The Culture of Narcissism*, for example, not only excoriated the cult of consumption, the media star system, and the nature of modern work for encouraging narcissism, but also regretted the passing of masculine standards of chivalry under the onslaught of feminism. Without such codes, he feared that relations between the sexes would degenerate into an all-out war. Though he claimed to be critical of capitalism, he also spoke nostalgically of the old, propertied elite for preserving the virtues of 'discipline, courage, persistence, and self-possession,' and maintained that the new elite of bureaucrats and therapeutically inclined professionals was failing because it identified 'not with the work ethic and the responsibilities of wealth, but with an ethic of leisure, hedonism, and self-fulfillment.'[51]

Perhaps because his own work once expressed the limited optimism of the 1950s, Daniel Bell, by the 1970s, was arguing even more elaborately than Lasch that loss of traditions would bring cultural impoverishment, and calling with passionate anguish for a reconstitution of traditional modalities of sociocultural cohesion. Though he titled his book *The Cultural Contradiction of Capitalism*, and in it explored the disjunction, mentioned above, between economic rationality and cultural hedonism, much of his discussion was directed to questions of a predominantly religious nature. 'The real problem of *modernity,'* he wrote, 'is the problem of belief. . . . It is a spiritual crisis, since the new anchorages have proved illusory, and the old ones have become submerged.'[52]

According to Bell, the Protestant Ethic for a time provided a holistic and transcendent framework within which the energy of capitalism flourished, but once unleashed, that energy finally undermined religious authority. By the mid-nineteenth century, belief in reason and progress had already shrunk the sea of faith, and people began to look to culture for ultimate meanings. But modern culture could never generate the 'kinds of meanings that sustain a society' – in part because modernist art and thought always opposed bourgeois society, its economy, and its values, thus divorcing the territory of ultimate meanings from a central part of life.[53]

More significantly, in Bell's analysis, modernist culture, from its inception, had repudiated the central function of all religions: the restraint of the self in the service of some transcendent moral order. Instead, since the nineteenth century, the modernist avant-garde had pursued 'the idolatry of the self,' breaking with artistic and moral conventions from the past, elevating feeling and instinct above reason, and justifying any impulse, however 'demonic,' in the name of self-realization. Bell contended that this cultural impulse, though responsible for an exciting efflorescence of formal and stylistic experimentation in the arts, had led to an existential dead end. In the cold light of the mid-twentieth century, the trajectory of modernism had played itself out. What had begun as an 'adversary culture' now dominated the cultural establishment, and having succeeded all too well in its sustained Oedipal revolt against the past, remained to pick over the rotting corpse of Western culture. 'There is no longer an avant-garde because no one in our post-modern culture is on the side of order or tradition.'[54]

Moreover, Bell felt that the machinery of commercialized hedonism had diffused the cult of the 'imperial self' among the populace, with disastrous results. The seeming 'democratization of culture in which a radical egalitarianism of feeling superseded the older hierarchy of mind' had brought an emphasis on immediacy, impact, sensation. This led in the 1960s to the celebration of violence, perversity, and irrationality

170

not only among experimental artists and young radicals but also among television programmers, fashion designers, advertisers, pop psychologists and their audiences, consumers of the new self-oriented lifestyle.[55]

Bell turned to religion, then, in the hope that it would reawaken our 'collective conscience.'[56] By religion he meant the values that could hold societies together:

> If religion is declining, it is because . . . the shared sentiments and affective ties between men have become diffuse and weak. The primordial elements that provide men with common identification and affective reciprocity – family, synagogue and church, community – have become attenuated, and people have lost the capacity to maintain sustained relations with each other in both time and place. To say, then, that 'God is dead' is, in effect, to say that the social bonds have snapped and that society is dead.[57]

By the same token, reinvigorating religion signified hewing to a transcendent ideal of collectivity. More specifically, Bell urged submission to tradition, and to a traditional social and moral hierarchy. He called for the reconstitution of an authoritative elite culture, of a sharp mind/body dualism, with mind having clear precedence, and of a patriarchial chain of authority that could bring 'the mutual redemption of fathers and sons.'[58] The almost unmitigated conservatism of this vision of collective life reveals the depths of Bell's despair as he confronted what he saw as a society pulled asunder in the name of the false god of personal liberation.

So, like Lasch and Sennett, Bell thought that the affluence attained by postwar Americans was shattering all forces of social cohesion. It had not only destroyed the necessity for self-restraint and delayed gratification, but had celebrated that destruction in the name of self-realization. By obviating the necessity of personal submission to a larger collectivity or moral principle, this process was unleashing people's most primitive appetites and instincts, appetites which had been successfully harnessed by reducing individuals to the character structure of spoiled children. The organizational order that had already stripped us of meaningful adulthood at work with one

171

hand, was with the other giving us the toys to while away our trivial private lives in childish play.

Clearly, there are differences in the analyses of social critics writing in the 1950s and the 1970s. In the 1950s, it seemed that affluence had uprooted individuals and exposed them to the crushing forces of social conformity, while in the 1970s affluence seemed to have encouraged individual appetite and self-interest to the point that all sources of social solidarity were being corroded. The former position held that society exacted too much from the individual; the chains of society were judged to be too heavy. Twenty years later, social critics saw society allowing, even urging, individuals to be unabashedly dedicated to themselves; society had set its members loose to pursue the false freedom of release. The earlier fear of social pressure gave way in the 1970s to a terror of social license.[59]

The fundamental shift in the characterization of the 'main drift' of contemporary society was accompanied by equally striking differences in the way social critics of the 1970s defined the idealized past of the 'Protestant Ethic' and the ideology or culture they felt had replaced it. In their characterizations of the momentous changes they felt American society had undergone since the early decades of industrialization, Riesman, Whyte, and Mills looked back to a Protestant Ethic of independence, self-reliance, self-sufficiency, and clear-cut competition they thought had disappeared by the middle of the twentieth century. They felt true individualism had been undermined by passivity and conformism. In the 1970s, social critics redefined the central tenets of a past cultural ethos to accord with their very different sense of what had vanished from contemporary social relationships and personality structure. Again referring, sometimes only implicitly, to the Protestant Ethic as a shorthand for what had been lost, they mourned the passing of thrift, delayed gratification, restraint, and self-discipline. Bell, for instance, claimed that 'restraint in gratification' characterized the Puritan temper, and that 'saving – or abstinence – is the heart of the Protestant Ethic.'[60] Similarly Lasch noted that the 'new narcissist,' though 'acquisitive in the sense that his cravings have no limits . . . does not accumulate goods and provisions against the future, in the manner of the acquisitive individualist of nineteenth-

century political economy, but demands immediate gratification and lives in a state of restless, perpetually unsatisfied
desire.'[61]

Sennett argued more subtly that modern self-involvement
was not the erosion but the perversion of the Protestant Ethic –
a reawakening of its most destructive elements in a culture
lacking the restraint of religion or a 'moral' materialism. In his
analysis, the Puritans, like modern Americans, were preoccupied with self-justification, but achieved it through self-
denial. Paradoxically, even this moralistic self-denial, Weber's
'worldly asceticism,' led to an intense and anxious self-
scrutiny, which Sennett identified as an early psychological
symptom of secularism and capitalism. Modern 'liberated'
Americans showed their Puritan ancestry in their inability to
genuinely enjoy their hedonism. They were still enmeshed in
intense self-examination, which put a screen of narcissistic
anxiety between self and experience of the world or of other
people, so the self was still denying the self pleasure. An
appetitive asceticism, perverse indeed. Yet despite Sennett's
inclusion of the Protestant Ethic within the trajectory leading to
the fall of public man, he did, like Bell and Lasch, praise
nineteenth-century bourgeois life for the 'essential dignity' of
its moral seriousness and self-restraint.[62]

In these latter-day views, then, the Protestant Ethic signified
a lost culture not of independence, but of restraint: of the
present by obligations to past and future generations, of
appetites by moral and social codes, of individuals by society.
By the same token, Bell, Lasch, and Sennett defined the new
'culture' or ethos that had supplanted the Protestant Ethic as a
false doctrine of freedom, an ideology that encouraged what
they saw as an obsessional, anarchic, and ultimately unful-
filling quest for self-gratification. The thrust of sociological
characterizations of the American ethos in the 1950s, such as
other-direction or the Social Ethic, was to show that the
apparent freedom of affluence was illusory, since strong
ideological and social pressures had begun to jeopardize
individual independence. In the 1970s, social critics identified
the apparent freedom of hedonism, immediate gratification,
and instinctual liberation – their new reading of the ethos that
had replaced the Protestant Ethic – as an even more dangerous

illusion because of its perversion of the ideal of freedom. The earlier formulation at least allowed social critics to hope that once the subtle constraints of affluence had been pointed out, Americans might realize 'true' freedom and, in Riesman's words 'explore new possibilities of being and becoming.' But twenty years later, critics felt that the new culture of the 'self' had transmuted freedom itself, one of the central tenets of individualism, into an ideological prop for a voracious material-ism that threatened literally to destroy individuals and the social order.

It appeared as if the critics of the 1970s were trying to grasp another level of manipulation by increasingly mystified struc-tures of domination. A generation before, social critics regretted the subsumption of older, more 'transparent' author-ity relations, within the small business and the family, for instance, by large organizations. They thought these organiza-tions possessed hitherto unknown powers of mass persuasion and used them to broadcast an ethos that encouraged dependency on the bureaucratic routines of work and consumer-oriented leisure. Bell, Lasch, and Sennett thought the culture of narcissistic hedonism a far more destructive ideology, and seemed to think that the forces of domination it served had escaped the control of any authority. Lasch, it is true, identified these forces rather clearly as a new elite of professional/therapeutic/bureaucratic experts. Sennett and Bell were much less clear about who, other than The Bureaucracy and its managers, were profiting from the situation. And all three felt that even those in social ascendence were victimized by the new ethos as individuals. Their sense that all of American society was standing on the brink of a cultural abyss, blind to its dangers because the modern ethos had promised them wings of freedom, gave their descriptions of the new culture of the 'self' an edge of despair and pessimism only faintly presaged in the writings of social critics twenty years before.

Certainly the thinkers of the 1970s thought that the modern ethos cut much more deeply into the foundations of individual character. Riesman and Whyte, for instance, described other-direction and the Social Ethos subtly molding a more impres-sionable American character. They thought individuals were becoming more flexible, more sensitive to cues from others, and more responsive to the 'radar' of anxiety about not fitting in. In their view, affluent Americans had almost literally gone soft. According to Christopher Lasch, on the other hand, the 'culture of narcissism' was far more corrosive. It had dissolved the possibility of achieving a coherent or integrated self:

> Archaic elements increasingly dominate personality struc-
> ture, and 'the self shrinks back,' in the words of Morris
> Dickstein, 'toward a passive and primeval state in which the
> world remains uncreated, unformed.' The egomaniacal,
> experience-devouring imperial self regresses into a grand-
> iose, narcissistic, infantile, empty self.[63]

The metaphor was one of infantilization, inherently frustrating appetite, and a chaotic inner void. In Lasch's and Sennett's accounts, the contemporary narcissistic ethos had not merely reshaped individual character but destroyed the structure of personality altogether. Of those writing in the 1950s, only Mills acknowledged that the environing culture, through the mass media, could so profoundly alter perception and desire, and even he thought in terms of the imposition of stereotypes rather than the perversion of basic drives and impulses that Lasch, Bell, and Sennett thought had accompanied the perversion of a central cultural ideal.

These critics despaired of any escape from the prevailing ethos because they felt that the desire for emancipation itself – the goal of freedom, independence, and autonomy that Mills, Riesman, and Whyte tried to revive during the 1950s – had become integrated into the very language and ideology of domination. For example, at the end of The Lonely Crowd Riesman urged modern Americans to embrace autonomy by 'choosing oneself' despite the pressure to become what Others (the media, other people, and large organizations) wanted. This was the goal of freedom for other-directed moderns.[64] Sennett, who said in The Fall of Public Man that he was turning Riesman's argument around because Americans were actually much too inward-directed, described the dangers of autonomy in his next book, Authority. According to him, the ideal of autonomy represented an impoverished understanding of people as entirely self-possessed and self-developed. This was only a partial truth, for it denied the social dimensions of our being: in fact, we were nurtured as children within the social web of the family, and we continued to develop as adults because of the relationships that made us part of the larger social world. Moreover, the ideal of autonomy was ideological because it served to legitimate modern bureaucratic hierarchies. Managers drew on their personal sense and institutional position of autonomy to evoke fear and awe and gain authority over subordinates, while workers blamed their powerlessness on their personal incapacity to become autonomous and 'together' people. Insofar as Americans espoused the individual goal of autonomy, dire political and psychological consequences would ensue, in Sennett's analysis. Politically, people would take a defensive posture against intrusions on their autonomy from the collectivity, so they would trade off legal rights to the state in order to preserve a diminishing sphere of intimate freedom. Perhaps more tragically, the search for autonomy would lead people to see personal relationships not as avenues to fulfillment but as obstacles in its path, 'as though the self were like a vast warehouse of gratification that one's social relations had kept one from exploring.' Isolation, restlessness, and 'a terrible anxiety' were the only rewards of the search for 'freedom through autonomy.'[65]

This new understanding of the contemporary ethos as a perversion of the ideal of freedom by newly abstract and manipulative forces of domination had three important consequences for the work of Sennett, Lasch, and Bell. First, in their efforts to locate a point in history before the seeds of a corrupt present had taken root, they became more backward-looking than the social critics of the 1950s. Critics of the 1950s also referred to an idealized past: Mills to the age of decentralized entrepreneurship and skilled craftsmanship, Whyte to the days of perfect competition. Lasch resembled them in their nostalgia for the nineteenth century, for he felt that new kinds of professional authorities had seized social power during the Progressive Era, and from the turn of the century had begun to legitimate their new status by formulating an ideology of bureaucratic dependence and narcissism.[66]

Sennett and Bell, however, having identified a culture of privatized self-fulfillment as the problem, and as part of their effort to reconstitute the social bonds that could, perhaps, nurture true fulfillment, turned back to the time before Romanticism first celebrated the limitless self. Sennett described an idealized past antedating industrial civilization. Though denying that the pre-industrial world was a utopia, he claimed that public and private life last found harmonious balance in the eighteenth century.[67] And his discussion of the Protestant Ethic implied that Americans needed to look even further back in history, before the anxious self-scrutiny that came with Calvin, to find a valid guidepost for reshaping the present. Bell, as we have seen, not only harked back to a time before Romanticism laid the foundations of a self-oriented culture, but seemed to wish that the entire process of secularization could be reversed.[68] Their deepening sense that individualism was in crisis penetrated more deeply into their sense of historical time, causing them to call into question many of our received notions about past traditions, like freedom, for instance, that could serve as beacons for the future. Bell and Sennett proffered a utopian retrospect that eschewed not only modern times, but almost the entire course of industrialism.

Second, and more paradoxically, the attempts of social thinkers to come to grips with the contemporary 'obsession with the self,' as Sennett calls it, made their own work more interiorized, as if exposure to the problematic of interiority had transmitted the disease. Since all three thought the ethos of self-gratification had corrupted individual goals and desires, and indeed the very categories by which the self experienced itself, their analysis of that process necessarily led them towards the inmost recesses of experience to discover what had gone wrong. But this turned their own work inward, too, making it an expression of the same process they sought to describe.

Daniel Bell, for instance, declaring that for modern Americans 'experience, rather than tradition, authority, revealed utterance, or even reason, has become the source of understanding and identity,' launched an exploration of how our 'modes of experience' – quasi-Kantian categories of time, space, self-consciousness – had evolved over the past two hundred years. In so doing, he was departing quite self-consciously from the conventions of social science, which has traditionally studied, in his words, 'formal organizations or social processes.'[69] Similarly, in his *The Culture of Narcissism*, Lasch was essentially discussing the life of the emotions in modern society. He wanted to show precisely how people's felt experience, even their fantasies, had become numbed and distorted by modern institutions and ideologies. Sennett's *The Fall of Public Man* analyzed the experiential meaning of 'images of the body' and patterns of speech as constitutive factors in the categories of public and private.[70] And he announced that his next book, *Authority*, was 'the first of four related essays on the emotional bonds of modern society. I want to understand how people make emotional commitments to one another, what happens when these commitments are broken or absent, and the social forms these bonds take.'[71]

Third, at the same time as these critics turned towards the inner world of emotion and experience in order to understand the dissolution of individualism into self-involvement, they also tended to abandon traditional canons of evidence and proofs of certainty or causality. Sennett did not wish to explain what had caused the fall of public man, for example, but to give a plausible account of certain 'affinities' between social conditions and cultural categories.[72] In *The Culture of Narcissism*, Lasch moved easily from clinical accounts of narcissistic patients to generalizations about the American population, from a description of the goals of therapeutic experts to an assumption that they had achieved their goals, from an indictment of the public school system to the supposition that its problems were due to the culture of narcissism.[73] I do not mention this to defend traditional definitions of what social science or social history should be, but to point out that the difficulties these thinkers encountered with the conceptual category of 'individualism' seemed to be serious enough to challenge many intellectual conventions that were part of the traditional social-scientific legacy from the nineteenth and early twentieth centuries. The experiential crisis of the early 1970s that led bestselling novelists of the time to abandon fictional conventions like the happy ending, also appears to have led intellectuals to question their conventions for understanding the world. Moreover, the symptoms of this 'crisis of knowing' in the work of Bell, Lasch, and Sennett – increasing interiority and the rupture of traditional conventions – replicated on an intellectual or conceptual level the symptoms of social dissolution each thinker was experiencing and trying to analyze.

The social critics of the 1970s differ from their predecessors, then, not only in their reformulation of the main drift of contemporary society and culture, and in their reinterpretations of the idealized past, but also because their own work embodies an overwhelming anguish at the plight of modern Americans. Their writing expresses the effects of what they define as deepening social and cultural problems. Like certain novelists of 1969–75, they despair of encompassing social reality within a conventional framework, and again like some novelists, their pessimism drives them to search for a viable ordering principle, or some transcendent source of collective meaning.

Yet the differences between these two generations of social critics, however important, should not obscure the underlying unity in their interpretations of modern America. From Riesman to Lasch, all depict the disappearance of an entrepreneurial order and ethos, and the consequent distortion of a satisfactory relationship between individual and collectivity. In their view, the postwar institutional order is pernicious. The superficial sheen of its affluence symptomatizes a deep-rooted malignancy rather than social or personal wellbeing. This disorder is difficult for them to conceptualize – it is historically unprecedented, after all – but they itemize its debilitating effects on work, love, private and public life, and characterize it above all as a problem of meaning, of human values.

Moreover, these critics have little hope that contemporary individuals can grapple with this problem, because they presume that America is in the grip of a new cultural ethos that is a simple ideational reflex of the inimical social order they describe, an ideological servant of new structures of domination. Lasch, for example, describes a new therapeutic ethic – an important constituent of his culture of narcissism – which he thinks benefits the new professional elite of doctors, welfare workers, and civil servants, and also 'serves the interests of monopoly capitalism as a whole.'[74] In like wise, Mills feels that the ethos of 'resignation and peace of mind' he describes in *White Collar* has legitimized a new social structure burdened by a new power elite and a perpetual war economy.[75] Bell relates the ideology of commercialized hedonism to mass production and the industries of mass consumption: 'fashion, photography, advertising, television, travel.'[76] And, in their critiques of modern bureaucracy, both Whyte and Sennett contend that a new ethos is reinforcing bureaucratic authority, although Sennett thinks managers have mobilized narcissistic anxieties, while Whyte identifies corporate chieftains as both spokesmen and victims of the conformist Social Ethic.[77]

Third, the cultural ethos these critics describe is firmly grounded in the middle and upper-middle classes – a social universe similar to that of the authors, publishers, and audiences for bestselling novels. Riesman speaks about other-direction in relation to the upper social stratum, particularly what he calls the new middle class of salaried professionals and managers who are at home in cosmopolitan urban centers. Whyte's 'organization man' is a purposely vague category encompassing junior executives, team-oriented scientists, clinic doctors, and federal administrators. Mills ranges from the top to the bottom of the white-collar hierarchies, but one of his major concerns through the book is to trace what has become of the old middle class. Bell speaks rather grandly of 'the culture,' as if one did not need to concretize the term, but his description of cultural modernism and its relationship to the work ethic implicitly devolves around a cast of social actors from the middle and upper-middle levels of society.

Lasch and Sennett, influenced in a complex and self-conscious fashion by radical currents of the sixties, both write with, as it were, occasional glances over their shoulders at the working class. For example, Lasch speaks in the preface of *The Culture of Narcissism* about 'solutions from below' that constitute 'signs of a new life' in the midst of the dying culture of competitive individualism, and in the concluding chapter about the need for ordinary citizens to fight the new elite by creating new 'communities of competence.'[78] Sennett expands his discussion of new ideologies of domination and their effect on working people in his book *Authority*. However, both Lasch and Sennett concentrate on middle-class people and 'their' novelists or journalists when they describe cultural developments. In Lasch's analysis, radicals, feminists, new corporate managers, pop psychologists, and confessional journalists embody 'the culture of narcissism.' Moreover, the culture of narcissism has social significance in part because it marks an incursion into the middle classes of lifeways and worldviews from the lower class:

> The poor have always had to live for the present, but now a desperate concern for personal survival, sometimes disguised as hedonism, engulfs the middle class as well. Today everyone lives in a dangerous world from which there is little escape.[79]

In much the same way, the categories of public and private that Sennett analyzes in *The Fall of Public Man* are firmly anchored in middle-class life: the book describes the rise and decay of bourgeois civilization, and, especially in its discussion of the family and emotional life, harks back to bourgeois forms.[80] Sennett, Lasch, and Mills, in particular, show by their attention to low-level clerks, factory workers, and minor technicians that they are sensitive to the issues of social inequality, yet like Whyte, Riesman, and Bell, when they define a new cultural ethos they are speaking primarily about the lives and dilemmas of the middle class.

Yet, the preceding three chapters have shown that the sociological characterizations of even middle-class American culture are inadequate. They ignore the considerable complexity of popular novels' responses to institutional change, a cultural complexity that could no doubt also be revealed by the systematic analysis of other kinds of cultural products. While it is clear that the novels express some of the very difficulties the social critics discuss – the problem of meaningful work, the unease of modern family life – they do so with varying degrees of critical insight, a range of reflectiveness the social critics' view of culture cannot account for. Certainly some bestsellers purvey a shallow hedonism, for instance, but others describe a sincere search for connection in work, love, and even public life.

Why have these social critics, whose serious attention to cultural issues makes them more attuned to the 'innerness' of our society than the great majority of social thinkers, been unable to see with more accuracy the very culture they are attempting to grasp? To ask the same question more methodologically, how has the way they approach culture inhibited them from using cultural evidence to better ground their generalizations about modern American society and how its culture is changing? Two components of the sociological perspective – the unexamined relationship between critics and their culture, and the tendency of social thinkers to describe change by making abstract comparisons between Past and Present – severely constrain the ability of social thinkers to understand the processes of cultural change.

The relationship between critics and their culture is itself complex, for on the one hand these social critics apparently feel that they can easily understand middle-class American culture because they are a part of it, while on the other hand they seem to assume that their professional training gives them a reflective distance from society not shared by other people. Of course, social critics *are* both a part of and apart from the culture they describe, but a lack of attention to this issue, and a lack of recognition that other people are in a similar position, impedes their analytic efforts.

Their sense that they understand American culture because they belong to it leads these social critics to treat cultural evidence quite casually, as if they could intuitively grasp the cultural ethos of the society whose lifeways they share. Certainly, the offhand way they select examples from popular culture and integrate them into their arguments about the American ethos seems to disclose the belief that cultural developments are self-evident rather than requiring the same analytic attention they accord institutional developments. Each of these critics deploys cultural evidence in a similar fashion, idiosyncratically choosing certain novels, magazine articles, movies, or children's books and using these materials as anecdotal illustrations for what each has already concluded the 'main drift' of American culture to be. William Whyte, for example cites *The Caine Mutiny* as evidence of a new need to conform at any price, *The Man in the Gray Flannel Suit* as proof of the decline in creative tension between the individual and society, and an assortment of nonfiction books and magazine articles as testimony to the fact that in the era of big organizations, society, not the individual, is the hero. He claims that these books and articles serve as a prop for the Social Ethic, but they also serve as an important prop for his contention that such an ethic exists.[81]

When Mills uses a few contemporary plays and novels to show that older images of success are 'tarnished' and that a new 'literature of resignation, of the peace of the inner man,' has replaced the traditional ideal of vocational success, his method is very similar to Whyte's and shows some of its dangers. His description contradicts both the main sense of *White Collar*, which is that the new social order lacks a coherent belief system, and other conclusions about success more empirically grounded in an examination of twenty inspirational success manuals published between 1856 and 1947.[82]

Riesman and Lasch draw on cultural products with a similar disregard of criteria for selection, the first picking a few novels and some journalism as evidence for a conformist 'other-directed' America, the second using the same strategy to demonstrate that we are in the grip of a 'culture of narcissism.' For example, to show that modern society demands a constricting conformity, Riesman analyzes a single children's book about a little engine who was pressured into staying on the track. His discussion of how magazine fiction disseminates values like self-manipulation and group adjustment among other-directed parents is vitiated by the same haphazard selection. A further irony in this case is that the selection he picks is directed towards women, for whom 'manipulating the self in order to manipulate others, primarily for the attainment of intangible assets such as affection' has been a strategy for survival that considerably antedates the twentieth century.[83]

Unlike Riesman, Lasch bases his analyses almost entirely on secondary sources, which gives his book a curiously divided quality. On the one hand he speaks with passionate conviction about the evils of our time, while on the other hand he relies on other voices to give his narrative the authority of doubled distance from social reality. Yet even his representation of these authoritative voices is often partial. He bases his portrait of the new narcissist on Kernberg and Kohut's psychoanalytic decriptions of narcissistic patients, without mentioning Kohut's discussion of the higher functions of narcissism. And when Lasch quotes directly from novels or journalistic accounts as evidence of narcissism, his selection suffers from the same lack of systematization as does Riesman's.[84] Yet if the evidence to support the contention that a new American ethos or character type exists is, to a significant degree, drawn from literary or other popular cultural sources, misuse of these sources must call into question any conclusions about the nature – and very existence – of that ethos.

Aside from raising doubts about the adequacy of these representations of modern American culture, a lack of systematic selection of cultural evidence also reveals an implicit assumption that America has only one relatively homogeneous culture. I am sure none of these thinkers, all of whom are sensitive to issues of social stratification and inequality, would explicitly claim that such is the case, but in making an idiosyncratic selection of cultural materials, they operate as if all of culture were more or less the same. If the context of production, dissemination and reception is ignored and if one novel or article 'stands for' all the rest, this means that culture is conceived of as being above and beyond context, floating somewhere outside the divisions that characterize social reality. Thinkers who equate high culture with all culture often hold this conception of culture – and indeed both Daniel Bell's and Richard Sennett's analyses manifest this tendency.

Most of the cultural artifacts, such as paintings or novels, that Bell interprets in his *The Cultural Contradictions of Capitalism* as exemplars of modernism and post-modernism come from the realm of 'high' culture. He tends to elide the sensibility of small cosmopolitan elites with a general cultural ethos, assuming that modernism has trickled down in popular and vulgarized forms from the peaks of artistic achievement. This in spite of the fact that he asks whether culture might not be increasingly bound to particular groups or classes of people in an increasingly differentiated and specialized society.[85] Sennett's book *The Fall of Public Man* shows a similar, though less marked, disregard of popular culture. The publics he describes – theater audiences, urban pedestrians, coffeehouse gatherings – are not entirely bourgeois, but it is in the main bourgeois diarists, journalists, and novelists whose descriptions of the public world he cites. He also peppers his book with references to high cultural figures, from Brancusi to Satie, Toscanini, and Vermeer, often just to illustrate a point. Although this gives his books an appealing aura of civility, the world of the 'we' he often uses, especially in his book *Authority*, is the world of those at home with Duse and Delacroix.[86]

The social critics appear to assume not only that American culture is univocal, but also that it is relatively transparent. This leads them to impute meanings to cultural products and processes in a relatively careless fashion. To take a commonly discussed example, Riesman thinks television sets high standards of performance, thus inhibiting individual creativity, Sennett thinks it encourages passivity and a compulsive interest in personality, and Lasch thinks it intensifies narcissistic dreams of fame, encouraging the common man to identify himself with the stars and to hate the 'herd,' and making it 'more and more difficult for him to accept the banality of everyday existence.'[87] This kind of statement shows a disregard for the complexities of interpretation involved in discovering the meaning of any cultural artifact for individuals within a culture, broadly defined. But this attitude hardly seems intentional; it reveals nothing worse than the certainty that comes from familiarity. And although this sense of familiarity leads to problematic claims and contentions, examining it, and thereby shattering its hold, would clearly deepen the sociological understanding of American culture.

If the social critics' casual use of cultural evidence is related to a sense that their membership in American culture enables them to comprehend it intuitively, their attitude towards other people's capacity to understand the social order appears to be similarly related to their situation as intellectuals. These thinkers implicitly assume that the role of social critic gives them both a certain distance from American culture and a special ability to interpret cultural trends that other people do not have. All the critics write as if the Americans they describe and address are confronting a society of such complexity and abstraction that it is becoming impossible for people to

185

understand. Thus, they depict Americans as bewildered casualties of social change, as victims of a dual determinism, constrained by the conditions of material life to become, willy-nilly, new sorts of personalities and lulled into acquiescence by emergent belief systems, whether the conformist 'other-direction' or the hedonistic 'culture of narcissism.' From this state, the social critics propose to awaken their audience by insights into social trends that cannot be grasped by laymen and by exhortations to cast off the fetters of the mystifying ideology.

This formulation is paradoxical at several levels. To draw out just one of its implications: if people are so easily duped, their capacity for reason must be negligible, thus it seems a fragile hope that the liberating insights offered by social critics can or will be heeded. Yet this, and other self-contradictions, lie at the heart of the social-scientific endeavor. It was only when nineteenth-century social life attained a certain level of complexity that the abstract category of 'society' emerged as a conceptual marker for the experiential process that also gave birth to the profession of sociology. People's recognition that society had become complex helped the profession establish the legitimacy of its claims to esoteric knowledge and expertise.[88] So, one might say that from its beginning the profession has had a stake in maintaining that society is truly difficult to understand. But in mid-twentieth-century America, social critics do not celebrate social complexity. Quite the contrary – all write with a sense of urgency. People must be made to understand what is going on in American society before it leaves their control altogether. Clearly, the very act of writing shows some faith that people will understand. Equally clearly, they write out of a conviction that the sociologist's task is to generate such understanding. Joseph Gusfield's discussion of the task of the social scientist exemplifies this attitude. He feels that the most important function of recent sociological work has been to interpret America to itself, since no one in a highly segmented society can personally experience the totality of social relationships.[89] In this conception of understanding, laymen can experience, but someone must bring in interpretive and theoretical sophistication from the outside for true comprehension to take place. This places rationality firmly outside the grasp of anyone other than the social scientist, and presumes that only the possession of specialized knowledge allows a person to reflect critically on the social order and his or her place within it.

Such a perspective leads, of course, to two closely related problems. Social scientists can easily forget that they, too, are 'inside' society and that every human being is, to a greater or lesser degree, capable of reflection. Both lead to a form of hubris that makes it hard for social critics to recognize that there may be others who are independently thinking about or interpreting their culture, or to see social change as an ongoing process of cultural reformulation in which social-scientific voices are only part of a larger chorus. Implicitly, of course, contemporary social critics recognize the power of other voices – in particular those of various forms of popular culture. But the important social critics of postwar America tend to classify other contenders for interpretive legitimacy among the voices of unreason, as part of the apparatus of mindlessness. It is clear that social scientists have been crucially important in the American project of self-understanding, and equally clear that popular culture is not always reflective. But a perspective such as the one outlined above makes it hard to be judicious about the content of popular culture or even open to the possibility that other people, too, are thinking subjects as well as objects of social and historical determinism. Further, only by entertaining the possibility that they are as human as other people – that is to say, as bound by their own situation in time and culture – and only by realizing that other people are as human as they are – as capable of reflecting about their situation – will social scientists be able to understand the process of cultural change.

A second methodological habit augments the problems these social critics have in using cultural evidence to understand change, a habit that has been the hallmark of the sociological thrust towards abstract generalization as a mode of comprehension. In trying to distinguish industrial from pre-industrial society, and at the same time to establish scientific laws of social change, sociologists from the time of Max Weber have typified the characteristics of Past and Present at a very abstract level and then contrasted these dichotomous categories. Contemporary social critics have followed much the same methodological strategy to understand modern America. They formulate as the baseline for comparison a secularized version of what Weber called the Protestant Ethic: a cultural ethos emphasizing thrift, rigidly internalized self-discipline, and denial of present pleasures in the service of accumulation for the future. They then use the category, which represents their summary of nineteenth-century social relations and cultural values, to draw implicit or explicit contrasts with modern culture.

Leaving aside questions of the validity of the work ethic as a conceptual summary of earlier American attitudes, its use as one term in this kind of analytic comparison leads the critics discussed above into two opposite but related difficulties. First, it hypostatizes the past and tends to make processes of change appear excessively disjunctive. This problem might be lessened if the critics employed a more complex empirical reading of either past or present, or if they were dealing with a more epochal historical transformation. As it is, the brush strokes are too broad to capture transformations from the nineteeneeth-century past to the twentieth-century present with accuracy.

Second, as we have seen, the critics' definition of the essential features of the Protestant Ethic changes in relation to the changed definition of what is problematic about the present. In the 1950s, when Whyte, Riesman, and Mills feared contemporary tendencies towards passive conformism, they emphasized the independence, self-reliance, and open competition of an idealized nineteenth-century past. Twenty years later, when Bell, Lasch, and Sennett were appalled at Americans' hedonistic materialism and privatized self-involvement they focused on a lost ethos of thrift, delayed gratification, restraint, and self-discipline. So the hypostatized past has a curious malleability. Theorists of history and sociologists of knowledge have long understood that characterizations of the past shift in relation to the questions of 'projects' of the present.[90] But in this case the typological shorthand for the past – the Protestant Ethic – remains the same. Its use as an unexamined term in a schematic cultural comparison obscures both the considerable fluidity of what the category encodes and the way the category, the idealized past, functions as a repository for all the values modern social critics feel are missing from their world.

The conceptual strategy of typological contrast also subtly distorts contemporary sociocultural processes because it tends to demand an equally coherent categorization of the recent past and present. Often social scientists are tempted to define the present in the retrospective mode. This suppresses theoretical consideration of their own embeddedness in the present and in present-day social milieux and institutions. It also obscures the need to challenge the limitations that come with any one perspective, any one set of experiences, by a more careful consideration of a culture that, precisely because the critics are a part of it, is less intuitively knowable than it may seem.

When they contrast the present with an abstract past, social critics also tend to envision the present as standing in relatively simple opposition to what they think has gone before. Thus, Riesman substitutes 'other direction' for 'inner direction,' William H. Whyte speaks of a Social Ethic that has replaced the individualistic Protestant Ethic, and Lasch and Bell maintain that hedonistic self-involvement has supplanted self-denial. This approach both suppresses the multiplicity of cultural cross-currents that are the stuff of social change, and simplifies social change by limiting it analytically to the antithesis of the past. Since these same thinkers constitute the category of 'the past' as an idealized foil for the problematic present, this method makes it hard for them to confront empirically their own pre-given notions about modern America.

In sum, the social critics' approach to modern American culture is problematic. Yet they have confronted the difficult questions of our time, and illuminated the social dimensions of contemporary cultural dilemmas; and their work is a powerful expression of the discontents experienced by many Americans. Their work is also valuable because it is rooted in a genuine concern with the vicissitudes of subjectivity in modern life. If their accounts of American culture sometimes resound with the prophetic doom of Jeremiads, it is due in large part to their dismay at the ways in which modern society, despite its affluence, has stunted the human spirit and thwarted people's desires for moral action, human connectedness, and a meaningful life. In an age when the marvels of technique have overshadowed consideration of the ends that our elaborate means should serve, and the apparatus of mass consumption proffers false promises and shallow solutions, these thinkers have kept critical inquiry articulate and alive. I have been critical of their work, but only because I share their purpose.

7

Conclusion

The preceding chapters have presented evidence about the American Dream in the years after World War II from two different sources: bestselling novelists and social critics. At the end of the Introduction, I suggested that counterposing these two groups would generate a new reading of American culture, further the analysis of short-term cultural change, and help to redefine the project of social and cultural criticism. This chapter addresses these issues.

The reality of the successful life has always been in tension with the transcendent metaphor of individual enterprise, but rarely has the disparity been perceived by any but the privileged few. During the first thirty years of the postwar era, the unprecedented affluence that transformed America inevitably loosed the hold of the entrepreneurial ethos on the popular imagination. Both bestselling novelists and social critics chronicle this dramatic cultural transformation. In its large outlines, of course, this development is not news to anyone who has lived through the aftermath of affluence. Yet, in describing some of the structural determinants that enabled affluence to be so widely attained, both novelists and sociologists indicate institutional reasons for the failure of affluence to engender individual happiness. Americans are not simply spoiled children. Large-scale impersonal bureaucracies, meaningless corporate work, stereotypic suburban family roles, the commodification of leisure, sexuality, and even 'meaning-

191

ful experience' – all are social contributions to the individually experienced malaise that increasingly pervades bestselling novels and sociological descriptions of modern America.

The novels discussed here are particularly important cultural artifacts, however, because they provide evidence that not only supports but enriches social-scientific categorization of American culture, broadly defined. First, the findings of this study show that the entrepreneurial ideal is not dead. Despite the critical note struck by Steinbeck, Weidman, and Heller, heroes of many novels continue to give their allegiance to this ideal throughout the period under study. But it has lost its certain connection to broader moral and social progress. The cultural synthesis that fused individual self-interest with social amelioration has lost plausibility even among the middle classes, its natural constituency. Both novelists and social scientists bear witness to this rupture. And in the aftermath of the once triumphant entrepreneurial synthesis, the novelists describe changing features of the heretofore entrepreneurial world that can be seen as both cause and consequence of its demise.

For instance, novels published between 1945 and 1955 described a social world that, while not a *tabula rasa*, provided an arena well suited to the exercise of entrepreneurial drive. It was expansive, and set few limits on heroic accomplishment. It was simple – unmarred by alternative value-systems, or social, racial, ethnic, or religious complexity. And it was unconflictual. Entrepreneurial heroes faced no contradictory demands and received love, glory, and status as rewards for their success. By the late 1950s, this simplistic milieu had begun to disappear from bestselling novels. Tom Rath, the protagonist of *The Man in the Gray Flannel Suit*, faced a fragmented world, where opportunity was constrained by the corporate hierarchy and great success could be achieved only by a commensurate sacrifice of family life and leisure. Soon novelists began to portray disparate ethnic groups, to reward nonentrepreneurial values, and to question easy assumptions of social progress in their descriptions of powerful bureaucracies, social unrest, and the possibilities of a technological *Götterdammerung*. By 1975, the end of this thirty-year period, the social worlds of bestselling novelists were often characterized by a loss of all traditional sanctions, ideals, and authorities. Such worlds were not only complex, but frighteningly chaotic and beyond control – surely an inhospitable environment for the entrepreneurial spirit.

Popular novelists' understanding of motivation also evinces the breakdown of this entrepreneurial synthesis. In early bestsellers, the entrepreneur, like his world, was naturally expansive and unconflicted. His motives were simply explained and, because his world provided challenges but no mutually exclusive choices, he stood above and beyond the fetters of any social context of constraint. Only successful heroines, in the early postwar years, gave some indication of the inner doubts and turmoil that would, in time, be visited on heroes of bestsellers.

By the late 1950s and 1960s, heroes were forced to justify their strivings for success as its moral content and social value became more dubious. Self-examination replaced the transparency of earlier motives, or the practitioners of success lost all claim to moral agency, becoming amoral representatives of the glamorous world of commodities and packaged experience. Later yet, heroes faced failure, or delved deeply into their past experience in order to confront their temptations to drop out altogether, and some heroes could only justify success in the most cynical terms.

The growing complexity of both self and society in bestselling novels can be interpreted both as a reason for the decline of the entrepreneurial synthesis, and as a consequence of it. An observably fragmented world with uncertain forward momentum calls into question the link between individual accomplishment and social progress; but at the same time, once people begin to doubt that individual self-interest and social amelioration are synonymous, the meaning of individual motives and social phenomena are themselves no longer clear. Certainly, as this central cultural formula began to lose coherence, previously suppressed or unseen aspects of reality attracted the attention of bestselling novelists, and their fictional worlds grew in complexity, as well as in cynicism and despair.

Despite the loss of entrepreneurial innocence in the bestselling novels of this period – a loss that is much more gradual

193

than indicated by the social critics – it must be stressed that popular novelists resolutely adhere to certain core components of the entrepreneurial dream, even while subtly redefining them. Heroes as different as Tom Rath and Jonathan Livingston Seagull, for example, continue to reaffirm the value of individual independence, although Tom's act of independence consists in the repudiation of entrepreneurial behavior, and Jonathan's spiritual and esthetic quest for perfect flight is placed in opposition to the instrumentalism of mere survival that prevails among the other gulls.

Similarly, the ideal of a calling does not disappear from bestsellers during this period, though it becomes more internal, more spiritual, and less related to instrumental success in the workaday world. Characters in bestselling novels can apparently no longer easily find (or invest) supramundane purpose in demystified work. Rather, they seek it in the act of artistic creation, the process of creative self-reflection, and the passionate exploration of intimate relationships, and it is reaffirmed by translation into the nonhuman realm. Experiential transcendence of mundane routines, even if it is always in the shadow of consumerism, may not fill the void left by the departure of the transcendent Calvinist God, but perhaps the idea of the calling, lingering on even in dissociation from the compulsion of work and the blandishments of material success, will rattle the bars of what Max Weber called the 'iron cage' of bureaucratic rationality.

Many bestselling novels also still cling to a rather traditional delineation of character. True, the world confronted by heroes of bestsellers tends to become more unmanageable, even inimical, during the thirty years under consideration; heroes cannot stand in splendid isolation, but are weighed down by cares, crises, and complex moral conundrums. In some novels at the end of the period, character is forged through failure instead of success. Nonetheless, a significant proportion of bestselling novelists remain unwilling to abandon the notion that people have coherent personalities, follow a comprehensible course of development, and demonstrate a moral dimension in their actions. Lasch and his peers may have overestimated the power of our institutions to destroy the reality, or at least the ideal, of self-discipline, resolution, seriousness of purpose, and personal integrity. And in general, social critics have underestimated the strength of the entrepreneurial ideal.

Until now I have been speaking of the decline of the entrepreneurial synthesis that links individual achievement to social progress, and of the remarkable persistence of ideals of vocational purpose, individual independence, and 'character,' however redefined, into the present. This persistence alone calls into question characterizations of America under the sway of a full-blown new sociocultural order that is the antithesis of what went before. Furthermore, the bestsellers show a striking multiplicity of explicitly innovative response to social-structural change. For example, as entrepreneurial success begins to require justification by the standard of personal fulfillment, novelists express quite different models of what fulfillment should be. Some books show heroes engaged in moral reflection about self and society and finding legitimation for their success in the comfort it can provide their families, while others legitimate achievement by the fact that it can provide access to the delights of consumerism and the fabulous experiences of the privileged. Still other bestsellers locate the excitement and creativity that used to belong to entrepreneurial work in the sphere of artistic creativity or spiritual development.

Novels published later often express even more disaffection from the entrepreneurial life, and display an even wider range of response. After an interval of exhaustion, some heroes renew their determination to reform 'the system,' or to reaffirm their personal mission. Less hopeful narratives make their central characters vulnerable survivors, stoically resuming their traditional duties and commitments. Sometimes, in the absence of a cultural definition of morally significant work, novels elaborate a substitute reward system, such as sexuality, romance, or a vision of heroic manhood, tested against nature or other men.

By the same token, novels centered on private life rather than the quest for success not only articulate the stresses of contemporary love and marriage, but describe various ways of living out the dilemmas of modern relationships. From a reaffirmation of older definitions of love to a celebration of hedonistic release, or the portrayal of sexuality as the location

195

for self-discovery and intimate connection with another, novels express a gamut of strategies and rewards.

As the central cultural metaphor of entrepreneurial achievement loses coherence, calling into question received notions about private as well as public life, some narratives display a disturbing erosion of moral sanctions and ideals, but others still embody the search for some moral ordering principle. Thus, books describing religious cynicism or even the bizarre mysteries of satanism achieve popularity at the same time as novels depicting religious millenarianism or an empathic and tolerant religious humanism. Such diversity demonstrates the need to comprehend the present in the flux of construction and the need to recognize subjective perceptions of social reality as part of that process. It calls into question, as well, the adequacy of sociological characterizations of individuals as passive flotsam and jetsam borne along by waves of social change. In showing individuals choosing various pathways through their worlds, with greater or lesser degrees of self-reflection, popular literature urges both theoretical consideration of individuals as more than reflections of large-scale institutional patterns and empirical analysis of the various ways individuals surrender to, but also rework or resist, the institutional constraints on their lives.

Both the tenacity of the entrepreneurial ideal and the multiplicity of responses to its gradual erosion challenge the social critics' readings of American culture. The novels demonstrate that the entrepreneurial ethos has been losing ground only gradually, despite the disjuncture between individual achievement and moral or social progress apparent in bestselling novels from the mid-1950s on. The diversity of novelistic responses to this disjuncture also indicates that no new cultural ethos has emerged, as the social critics have claimed, to replace the entrepreneurial dream of success. Indeed, evidence from these critics, as well as from popular novels, seems to show that we are still in a period of searching and confusion. The times have unsettled widely held conceptual and emotional assumptions, and called into question traditional sources of meaning and authority, but have not yet permitted people to find secure answers. Americans show reluctance to abandon their older values, but at the same time they feel a widespread desire to find some new foundations for certainty, some new hierarchy of values that can command allegiance.

Social critics and popular novelists alike express the difficulty of this cultural dilemma in the breakdown of their traditional conventions – social-scientific categories and strategies for structuring knowledge on the one hand and narrative structures and strategies on the other. In the 1950s, both novelists and social critics attempted a form of compromise with a markedly new reality. In making his 'corporate-suburban' compromise, for example, Tom Rath departed from the classic path towards entrepreneurial success, yet Sloan Wilson, his creator, deployed old standards of independence and integrity to validate Tom's new choices. The social critics of that time also recognized great changes in work and leisure and adopted new categories of analysis, such as 'conformity' or 'the mass society,' in the place of categories like 'social class,' that seemed more appropriate to industrializing societies. Yet social critics also hoped for a compromise with the new realities that would not vitiate old ideals, whether that meant for Whyte that organization men should struggle for independence at work, or for Riesman that other-directed moderns should seek integrity and seriousness of purpose in their leisure hours.

The compromise of the 1950s was short-lived, however. By the 1970s social critics began to question their most basic analytic conventions. Daniel Bell abandons the traditional subjects of research for a discussion of cultural 'modes of experience.' This signifies both that, at least in his view, the fundamental categories of social thought are exhausted, and that he must question the very assumptions on which they rest in order to begin the work of categorial reconstruction. Lasch and Sennett, like Bell, not only manifest discontent with traditional forms of analysis, but also question deeply held cultural ideals. According to them, the entire moral framework that undergirds America must be dismantled and built anew. Confronting this extremity, their tone verges on despair.

Bestselling novels of the late 1960s and early 1970s also show symptoms of cultural volatility and open-endedness, but manifested as a breakdown of imaginative rather than analytic

197

conventions. Fictional worlds where brutality ranges unchecked and happy endings are hard to find, where fictive crises implicate even traditional authorities in widespread webs of evil or incompetence, suggest that novelists, too, are finding their most fundamental assumptions in disarray. Like the social critics, novelists often describe alienation, disaffection, and individual or systemic failure, and speak in tones of exhaustion or bitter cynicism. Novels express a sense that the world has lost its moral center, while social criticism searches for the conceptual apparatus to uncover the inner dynamics of the process. But the correspondences between these different cultural artifacts imply that the dissolution of the entrepreneurial ethos has shattered our cultural conventions for both knowing and feeling – engendering a predicament that is not only intellectual, but also emotional or spiritual, since both the ideational and moral maps that have guided our pathways through the social world are out of kilter with the experiential landscape.

Certain characteristics of this cultural quandary may also be indications of a search for materials with which to reformulate a set of beliefs that can once again give coherence to individuals' private and collective endeavors. Certainly there is evidence in popular novels from the latter part of the period of such a search for fundamentals. These novels express not only skepticism or despair, but also an increased attention to inner experience and to history, defined as something other than a mirror of the present.

Both strategies, of course, are problematic. The inner voyage that heroes of bestsellers take to reevaluate their past experiences, their goals, or their relationships can be decried as a retreat into the self. Certainly in bestsellers, it rarely culminates in a disruption of the *status quo*, for even if heroes cut loose from conventional 'arrangements' to reconstitute a more meaningful life, they return to a conventional world. From another perspective, this strategy can be construed as an attempt to find a solution to the painful incongruity between worldly achievement and personal contentment. If so, it is significant that what these heroes seek is a renewed connection with their past or with other people, a source of certainty, whether in God or in a gut-level experiential 'truth,' or some

198

grounds for the exercise of creativity. Similarly, bestselling novelists from the late 1960s on use history for prophetic parallels, millenarial warnings, and exercises in nostalgia. History can be distorted by these purposes yet, again, the novelists' recognition that other times are profoundly different from our own can give them and their readers distance from, or alternatives to, the present.

Much the same ambiguity attends the very similar strategies employed by social thinkers of the 1970s. They, too, look backwards with nostalgia and regret. Sennett draws a disturbing historical parallel between present-day America and a decadent Rome awaiting her fall. Although the first backward-looking strategy may generate an inward-turned conceptual paralysis, and Sennett's may misuse history, both embody a search for fundamentals with which to rebuild a viable culture. When Bell urges restoration of the sacred, for example, he reveals his desire for a source of certain authority that can bind individuals to each other and nurture the best parts of themselves. Sennett and Lasch also seek new modes of connection between people, new outlets for human creativity, though Lasch refers to local initiatives and 'communities of competence,' while Sennett calls for restructuring, in meaning and in reality, both public and private life.

One reason why these social critics have not recognized concerns similar to their own in products of the environing culture like bestselling novels, is that they are too easily convinced that modern ideology – the culture of narcissism or of conformity – is totally hegemonic. If our society were in the grip of such a totalizing force, popular culture would merit little serious attention, for its function would be simple: to accommodate people to the prevailing structures of domination, and solicit their unthinking assent to an unpalatable *status quo*. As the previous chapter hinted, this conviction itself can be construed as accommodationist, in that it confirms the distinction between the few who think and the many who cannot – a distinction that tends to follow class lines, and engenders pessimism about the very possibility of collective resistance, even on the level of culture. But the findings presented here show that this is far too simple a rendering of popular culture. Accommodation and resistance intertwine in bestselling novels – and, despite their oppositional stance, in the work of social critics as well. This study points to the need for a fuller understanding of this double-edged cultural process; and new work in sociocultural analysis has begun to map it out, and explore its relationship to social change.

This new, or at least revised, 'reading' of American culture has emerged from a new method of investigating cultural change that suggests, by its limitations as well as its strengths, new horizons for further inquiry. Certainly the method of this study calls into question accounts of cultural change based on unitary, normative statements about American culture made without systematic attention to cultural evidence. This work also shows that popular literary texts are richly expressive or projective screens. They may be more accurate sources of evidence about 'the main drift' of American culture than are literary masterpieces, if only because of their more secure relationship to a wide audience. If so, this may help to unseat the disproportionate attention cultural analysts have given to 'high culture' texts, or encourage even those examining the cultural meaning of unabashedly literary texts to consider the relationship of these books to the social context of their production, dissemination, evaluation, and reception.

I have searched the books under study for what they could reveal of their authors' and readers' assumptions about the American Dream, or in other words about success, the good life, getting ahead, motivation, social mobility, and social progress. Such a 'checklist' would naturally vary according to the kinds of attitudes or assumptions under study. To find evidence related to these general categories, I looked at the ways novels communicate through characters, narrative structures, patterns of reward, tone, and perspectives on the social world. This holistic strategy seemed appropriate, but I am sure that other, more systematic interpretive frames would also be very fruitful. Again, such work is already underway in various branches of interpretive cultural studies, such as semiology, the sociology of culture, and cultural anthropology.

Whether bestselling novels or works of social criticism, books provided my evidence about more general cultural developments. Obviously, we also need studies based on other kinds of cultural artifacts, like music, movies, and television, that may reach different audiences. Perhaps less obviously, we need to know much more about how people integrate cultural products like books into their own ongoing lives and to what degree they psychologically appropriate their contents. As I indicated in Chapter 2, it is likely that bestselling novels mesh easily with their readers' values, as evidenced by their popularity. Yet responses to novels vary. Especially in cases where cultural products are mass-produced, constraining people's choices about what to read, listen to, or watch – for instance, television, movies, advertising, popular music, and mass market literature – we need to know much more about what meanings people forge from the prepackaged signs and symbols they receive in order to extend discussions of cultural artifacts to generalizations about people's values and implicit assumptions. This kind of investigation, already adumbrated, for example, by reader response theory, is crucial for elucidating broad issues like those of ideological hegemony and cultural resistance.

This study has been limited to books and has also, like the bestsellers themselves, stayed within the limits of the middle class. Middle- and upper-middle-class people wrote, disseminated, and read these novels, which in turn provide a remarkable mode of access into the shifting cultural values and ideas of the middle classes over a thirty-year period of great significance. The social critics, too, are firmly middle-class – though Daniel Bell came to Harvard from New York's Lower East Side – and have written for an even more narrowly middle- and upper-middle-class audience. This study of bestsellers is valuable because it explores the complexity of American middle-class culture, which has been curiously taken for granted in discussions of American society, despite the social-scientific tendency to describe Everyman as a middle-class American.

But America is not a homogenized society, even if this component of the American Dream still lingers on in cultural myths. The effort to understand American culture as a whole must put the myths in perspective by analyzing cultural products of other classes and groups and their interaction with the pervasive middle-classness that has been America's cultural hallmark.

Such a research agenda urges that social and cultural critics redefine their task. Indeed, one of the main thrusts of my argument has been to demonstrate that social critics have no monopoly on critical thought; people are continually remaking their culture, and in so doing redefining the past, reconstituting the present, and reconceptualizing what they desire from the future. This active involvement in making sense of the world may be particularly pressing during times, like our own, when conventional answers no longer satisfy. Now, especially, critics must understand social and cultural change as a recursive process.

Recent developments also suggest that American culture may be becoming more democratic; certainly interpretive voices from beyond the academy are strikingly evident in contemporary America. Social critics appear to be objectively in a less privileged cultural position than in the past; the partial breakdown of the cultural hierarchy of interpretive privilege may be one reason for their pervasive pessimism. Because of this, any critic who wishes to assert a view of the whole of American culture, rather than using a few texts or trying to grasp the whole intuitively, must attend to the range of other voices in the complex cultural discourse that is one constituent of social change; must survey their social locations; and must try to discover, as well, what people are making of the interpretive models that various cultural interpreters and analysts offer them.

In suggesting this strategy, I am urging a revival of empiricism as a disciplined way of looking out into the world that offers at least the possibility of loosing the grip of the researcher's own preconceptions. A serious examination of cultural evidence may not generate an entirely objective or context-free interpretation, but it promises the inclusion of a wider spectrum of subjectivities and contexts than has heretofore been the case. This 'intersubjective empiricism' also implies the necessity of examining the relationship between researcher and his or her own social context, which includes, for the intellectual, taking a long look at the received ideas of the scholarly tradition. Social thinkers have made a genuine contribution to the search for new values and choices that is already underway in American society. Dissatisfaction with the

202

status quo is often formulated shallowly and personalistically – as in some popular novels – because many individuals do not understand anything about the collective or institutional world beyond what is necessary to survive within it. In elucidating the interaction between social structure and human agency, social thinkers make the search for alternatives to the *status quo* more fruitful. But they can enrich the individual and social process of self-reflection still further if they recognize, theoretically and empirically, that they are just one among many groups of participants in the discourse on social and cultural change.

This book has explored some of the central cultural categories by which Americans have understood themselves and have attempted to come to terms with the changed circumstances of their lives. These categories are important, for what people mean by success or the American Dream embodies fundamental assumptions about moral action on the public as well as the individual level. Yet tragically, there is almost no place in American public life where these issues can be discussed. The absence of such a public forum is especially disquieting because the popularity of these novels and works of social criticism indicates that people are open to questioning the cultural ground of their lives. It is important to bring such questions out of the web of implicit novelistic assumptions, out of the shelter of academic debate, and grant them the attention they obviously merit. Only then will Americans have public purchase on how to enact new definitions of success, the good life, and the American Dream that may restore a broader sense of purpose to our individual endeavors.

Notes

1 Introduction

1 Obviously the cinema, and even some television programs and magazine fiction, also achieve a level of great expressive, symbolic, and cognitive sophistication. In fact, two pragmatic considerations led me to novels. First, novels are more accessible to the researcher. Second, having worked in publishing, I am personally familiar with the institutional foundation of American book publishing.

2 The reference is to Rabinowitz's 'Assertion and Assumption: Fictional Patterns and the External World', *PMLA: Publications of the Modern Language Association of America*, vol. 96, no. 3, May 1981, pp. 408–19; see especially pp. 409–14. This discussion is necessarily very compressed. Obviously, realism is itself a complex construction, sustained by a variety of literary devices, and operating on a variety of levels. Analysts of the differences between popular and 'high' literature have, for instance, differentiated between 'realism of detail' and 'realism of structure' (David Chaney, *Fictions and Ceremonies*, New York, St. Martin's Press, 1979, p. 77) or have referred to the 'elementary' realism of formulaic fiction. Umberto Eco's discussion of the 'technique of the aimless glance' (*The Role of the Reader*, Bloomington, Ind., Indiana University Press, 1979, p.166) is an effort to pin down the novelistic strategies for maintaining a sense of realism or 'believability.' And Rabinowitz's essay deals with modern and postmodern literature, which often violates the traditions of realism. In it, he develops a remarkably lucid theoretical framework for understanding the similarities and differences between realism in realistic and nonrealistic novels. For discussions of the community implied by text, see the work of Raymond Williams, especially his *The Country and the City*, London, Chatto & Windus, 1973, and Stanley Fish, in particular his *Is There a Text in This Class?*, Cambridge, Mass., Harvard

University Press, 1980.

3 It is because I have studied the concept of ideology extensively that I have been wary of using it. It is a remarkably complex conceptual category, implying certain relationships between ideas and social class, between subjective views and objective knowledge. At worst, it is a conceptual shorthand that glosses over precisely these relationships between ideas, beliefs, or cultural assumptions and the social order that this study attempts to elucidate.

4 There are two reasons why I chose to examine hardcover rather than paperback bestselling novels. First, the beginning of the period under analysis falls in the early years of the 'third paperback revolution.' This modern transformation of inexpensive book publishing, begun in the late 1930s and hampered by the exigencies of World War II, took off in the late 1940s and gathered strength in ensuing decades, with the introduction of high-quality paperbacks in the late 1950s, increased publication of formulaic novels such as romances in the 1970s, and a growing emphasis on paperback originals. Mass market advertising and distribution have also been major innovations. In all, this revolution changed the shape of paperback publishing so profoundly in thirty years that a comparison of paperback bestsellers at the beginning and end of my period would be a comparison between two rather different cultural phenomena. While, as we shall see in Chapter 2, hardcover bestsellerdom has been influenced by some of the same factors at work in paperback publishing, it has remained more nearly the same endeavor that it was in 1945.

Second, the focus on hardcover bestsellers arose from consideration of the probable audience. Though audience research on novels is fragmentary (again, see Chapter 2), hardcover novels probably appeal to a relatively more affluent readership than do paperbacks. Thus, insofar as one can generalize from texts to social world, this study addresses primarily the world of the middle and upper-middle classes. (Libraries and media 'spin-offs' of novels, of course, assure that these books have an impact beyond the numbers of copies sold.) These are precisely the social strata discussed by the social critics of modern American culture whose work I address in the next section of this introductory chapter – and their primary audience, as well.

5 There are, of course, certain problems inherent in using this kind of instrument mechanically to define the sample of bestsellers under study. For example, the lists exclude influential books that sell slowly and steadily over several years. Although the lists are compiled on the basis of sales for books published during the past two years, several important popular novels published during this period are not listed – for example Joseph Heller's *Catch-22* or J. D. Salinger's *Catcher in the Rye*. In most cases, authors of such books do achieve immense popularity with the next novel they publish, and usually those books continue to deal with similar themes. But clearly, the relationship between books and audience is complex, and using the *Bowker Annual* lists marks a compromise. The lists also exclude books appealing to

special subgroups within the reading public (e.g. feminist or religious novels). This is a symptom of the fragmentation of modern life and thus of the audience for fiction. However, if such special-interest books become more generally popular – whether because of compelling presentation of certain themes – or because of a more generalized social awareness of certain issues – they do appear as bestsellers. The *Bowker Annual* lists represent, again, a compromise: between cultural diversity and an equally pervasive homogeneity, which is also a hallmark of American culture.

6 I have chosen to discuss these social thinkers both because they have written about values, attitudes, and beliefs, and because they have been influential beyond the groves of academe. They have been recognized by the profession for substantive and theoretical contributions, and they have spoken to a wider audience as well. More than many social thinkers, they have played an important part in the process of American self-reflection. Whyte, Riesman, and Mills wrote their most influential books of cultural analysis in the 1950s; Lasch, Sennett, and Bell in the 1970s, though all three were active before that decade. In the 1960s, most sociologists concentrated on issues related to the turbulence of those years. Studies of power, conflict, and social change stood at the center of the discipline. There is a hiatus in sociological thinking about middle-class culture, the result of social developments that made it seem beside the point, for a while. Social thinkers who did discuss middle-class American values took an overwhelmingly critical stance that makes their discussions about the relationship of culture to society less than satisfactory, the critical judgment short-circuiting analysis.

7 Lasch is, of course, a social historian, not a sociologist. But his book *The Culture of Narcissism* is a general analysis of American culture and as such can fairly be called a sociological statement.

2 Success in bestselling novels: the social context of thematic content

1 L. Lowenthal, *Literature, Popular Culture, and Society*, Palo Alto, Cal., Pacific Books, 1961. Also see his book *Literature and the Image of Man: Sociolgoical Studies of the European Drama and Novel, 1600–1900*, Boston, Beacon Press, 1957.

2 R. Williams, *The Country and the City*, New York, Oxford University Press, 1973. See especially chapters 1, 2, and 25.

3 R. Escarpit, *The Book Revolution: Books and the World Today*, London, Toronto, Wellington, Sydney, and UNESCO Paris, George Harrap, 1966, pp. 42, 46, 47.

4 R. Williams, *Culture and Society: 1780–1950*, London, Chatto & Windus, 1959, p. xiii.

5 Other bestselling authors of the 1940s and 1950s were considered serious writers by their contemporaries as well. I have set

off the word in the text to highlight the fact that reputations do change. One can account for this by exclaiming how strange or quaint it is that our predecessors could not distinguish true greatness, or by recognizing that literary canonization is a social process.

6 The *New York Times* said of Douglas's *The Big Fisherman*: 'His Spenglerian Roman Mencius, his clumsy attempts to write the sophisticated dialogue of the palace set, his painted backdrops – none of this will prevent "The Big Fisherman" from netting one of the largest readership hauls of the year.' (Excerpted from a review in the *New York Times*, November 21, 1948, p. 6, in M. M. James and D. Brown (eds.), *The Book Review Digest*, New York, H. W. Wilson, 1949, p. 225.) Frank Yerby's *The Foxes of Harrow* received equally stinging comments. The *New Yorker* said: 'Mr. Yerby has packed everything in – passion, politics, Creole society, sex, the clash of races, and war – but he never captures the faintest flutter of the breath of life.' And N. L. Rothman wrote in the *Saturday Review of Literature*: 'It is not a historical novel – for that must have some reality in it – but it is a good example of the technicolored fantasies that have been passing as such of late.' (Excerpted from the *New Yorker*, February 9, 1946, p. 96, and from the *Saturday Review of Literature*, February 23, 1946, in M. M. James and D. Brown (eds.), *The Book Review Digest*, New York, H. W. Wilson, 1947, p. 914.) A. W., writing in the *Atlantic* in September 1947, characterized Costain's *The Moneyman* as 'A kind of "hindsight" historical novel. The present is always with us, looking down its nose at the past. . . . This happy position makes the book easy to understand: we like the swordplay and the action and the suspense, and we are pleasantly aware of our own superiority to the misguided creatures who caper and prance before our eyes. . . . It is hard to write from that standpoint and produce a work of art.' Clavell's *Shogun* aroused the *New Yorker* to the same pitch of irritation as did Yerby's book almost twenty years before: 'A slick, ambitious, eight-hundred-and-two-page popular novel about seventeenth-century Japan which disadvantageously combines the worst qualities of the fact-crammed historical novel with the sort of flashy Hollywood dialogue and derring-do that haven't been around since the heyday of the Errol Flynn movie.' (Excerpted from the *New Yorker*, July 28, 1975, p. 80, in J. Samudio (ed.), *The Book Review Digest*, New York, H. W. Wilson, 1976, p. 237.) Susann's *Valley of the Dolls* called forth this comment from Gloria Steinem: 'For the reader who has put away comic books but isn't yet ready for editorials in the *Daily News*, *Valley of the Dolls* may bridge an awkward gap.' (Excerpted from *Book Week*, April 24, 1966, p. 11, in J. Samudio (ed.), *The Book Review Digest*, New York, H. W. Wilson, 1967, p. 1175.)

7 By imprint (and one can argue, for example, that Knopf is editorially independent of Random House, its parent company), the figures are even closer. Twenty-two publishing entities account for the fifty-six titles, nine for forty-one of them (or 73 percent), and five for thirty of the novels (or 53.6 percent). These figures are strikingly

similar to those from 1945 to 1950.

8 See Thomas Whiteside's book *The Blockbuster Complex: Conglomerates, Show Business, and Book Publishing,* Middletown, Conn., Wesleyan University Press, 1981. His interviews with spokesmen and spokeswomen from the industry reveal concern in many sectors of the publishing world.

9 B. M. Compaine, *Who Owns the Media: Concentration of Ownership in the Mass Communications Industry,* White Plains, N.Y., Knowledge Industry Publications, 1979, pp. 260–1. The section on books, pp. 251–91, contains a very thoughtful discussion of economic concentration in publishing.

10 Whiteside, *op. cit.,* pp. 13–15, and chapters 12–14 (pp. 139–93). The effects of mergers are also discussed in L. Coser, C. Kadushin, and W. Powell, *Books: The Culture and Commerce of Publishing,* New York, Basic Books, 1982, pp. 8, 41–61, 127–43, 175–84.

11 Coser, Kadushin, and Powell, *op. cit.,* pp. 26–33. And John P. Dessauer, personal communication. The economic boom of the 1960s was probably an even more important impetus for the growth in numbers of titles. Similarly, as the boom faded, publishers would try to find ways of assuring profits. Cutting back titles and turning to 'certain' sellers is one such strategy.

12 Coser, Kadushin, and Powell, *op. cit.,* p. 8.

13 Whiteside, *op. cit.,* pp. 49–88. Whiteside says on p. 72 that he has heard this process referred to as 'the spontaneous generation of a literary property.'

14 Coser, Kadushin, and Powell, *op. cit.,* pp. 29, 35.

15 Whiteside, *op. cit.,* p. 41, and John P. Dessauer, personal communication.

16 Whiteside, *op. cit.,* pp. 45–7. A development in tax law – an I.R.S. ruling based on a Supreme Court decision about the Thor Power Tool Company – makes it impossible for publishers to write off inventories of unsold books. This also tends to shorten the life of books that do not sell quickly, since there is a marked disincentive for publishers to keep them in print for long periods. Whiteside discusses this on pp. 112–13; Coser, Kadushin, and Powell, *op. cit.,* on pp. 370–1.

17 The discussion of publishing in Coser, Kadushin, and Powell, *op. cit.,* especially pp. 3–35, is a fine example of a historically grounded perspective on modern developments in the industry. Charles A. Madison's *Book Publishing in America,* New York, McGraw-Hill, 1966, is an excellent general exposition. His *Irving to Irving: Author Publisher Relations 1800–1974,* New York and London, R. R. Bowker, 1974, concentrates on certain changes in the interrelationships between authors and publishers. Frank L. Mott, *Golden Multitudes: The Story of Best Sellers in the United States,* New York, R. R. Bowker, 1947, remains a valuable resource for research on popular novels, as does James D. Hart's *The Popular Book,* New York, Oxford University Press, 1950. Also important is John Tebbel's *A History of*

Book Publishing in the United States, a four-volume chronicle spanning the years 1630 to 1980. It was published by the R. R. Bowker Co., New York, between 1972 and 1981. All of these sources speak to the point, though Coser, Kadushin, and Powell, *op. cit.*, put it most succinctly on p. 16: 'Trade publishing in this country has almost always been oriented toward the mass market.'

18 See C. A. Madison's *Book Publishing in America*, p. 559. Also Caser, Kadushin, and Powell, *op. cit.*, on p. 20, and Compaine, *op. cit.*, p. 254.

19 See Compaine, *op. cit.*, pp. 254–6, Coser, Kadushin, and Powell, *op. cit.*, pp. 21–3, 176, and Mott, *op. cit.*, pp. 78–9.

20 Coser, Kadushin, and Powell, *op. cit.*, p. 21.

21 *Ibid.*, p. 286. Also C. A. Madison, *Irving to Irving*, pp. 255–6. At the same time, other publishers objected to the emphasis on profits over literary quality, and to large retailers selling 'big books' at a discount. See Compaine, *op. cit.*, pp. 257–8.

22 Compaine, *op. cit.*, pp. 258–9, citing a table from Cheney. He also cites figures from later Bureau of the Census surveys that show, if one compares Cheney's concentration ratios based on titles with Census ratios based on 'Percent of Shipments Accounted for' (units that are not strictly comparable), the largest companies did not have a much greater market dominance in 1972 than in 1925–30. In 1972, the four largest companies accounted for 16 percent of shipments, and the largest twenty for 52 percent.

23 See William Miller, *The Book Industry: A Report of the Public Library Inquiry*, New York, Columbia University Press, 1949, p. 19.

24 *Ibid.*, p. 51. I have relied heavily on Miller's study of publishing in the late 1940s in my discussion of that period.

25 *Ibid.*, pp. 20, 43–60.

26 *Ibid.*, pp. 13–14. For a fascinating account of the promotional tours that bestselling authors made in the late 1940s, see Kathleen Winsor's next bestselling novel, *Star Money*, New York, Appleton-Century-Crofts, 1950.

27 On book departments of large department stores, see W. Miller, *The Book Industry*, p. 100. On production and warehousing costs, see *ibid.*, pp. 65–73. These market factors appear to have pressured publishers in much the same way as the recent tax ruling on inventories discussed in n. 16. (Printers had been happy to store plates, pages, and even bound books during the Depression, but this ended with World War II, when plates were melted for metal and printers were working overtime. This pressured publishers not to publish small-run books and not to keep slowly selling titles in print for long.) Miller discusses the break-even point and its effects on editorial decisions on pp. 73–4. Coser, Kadushin, and Powell, *op. cit.*, say on p. 147 that the lowest break-even point trade editors mentioned in interviews during the late 1970s was 6,000 copies, but that 70 percent put the figure somewhere between 10,000 and 50,000 copies. Of course, the American population has also increased

dramatically since 1949, as has the number of titles published, so a rise in break-even points does not automatically imply the end of cultural diversity or consumer choice.

28 Charles S. Steinberg (ed.), *Mass Media and Communication*, New York, Hastings House, 1966, pp. 321–2. (Reprinted from *American Scholar*, vol. 23, no. 2, Spring 1954.)

29 See J. Tebbel, *A History of Book Publishing in the United States*, vol. IV, *The Great Change, 1940–1980*, New York and London, R. R. Bowker, 1981, p. 724.

30 Coser, Kadushin, and Powell, *op. cit.*, discuss several ways of conceptualizing what is going on in publishing within the broad context of modern industrial society. On p. 373, they say: 'While publishers may believe their problems are unique, they are in fact endemic in modern industrial societies, which are plagued with a basic contradiction: while the logic of mass production homogenizes tastes, the relative affluence of the society and the complex division of labor gives rise to specialization and differentiated tastes.' Elsewhere in the book, especially pp. 41–54, they say that publishing itself is shaped by these two tendencies which lead to a dual market. They describe one sector of publishing, what they call the mass-oriented 'core,' as distributor-oriented and closely linked to other mass media. Such houses may also operate with a shorter time perspective and produce books that will meet an existing demand. Other houses, in their words, the 'periphery,' tend to be producer-oriented and are less interested in rapid profits than in the accumulation of what Pierre Bourdieu calls 'symbolic capital.' This seems a much more promising approach than the massification model, yet more research is needed to confirm its adequacy.

31 For a good discussion of the available statistics, see Compaine, *op. cit.*

32 *Ibid.*, p. 261. The 1977 U.S. Census of Manufacturers revealed, according to J. Tebbel, *op. cit.*, p. 725, that 'a large number of small, new publishing ventures had made a substantial impact on industry sales.' Townsend Hoopes's quote in T. Whiteside, *op. cit.*, pp. 11–12, shows an optimism about the structure of the industry and the variety of its offerings that is based on these figures. In personal communication, John P. Dessauer, a noted industry analyst, suggested that the numbers of small houses are probably even larger than the Census indicates.

33 Coser, Kadushin, and Powell, *op. cit.*, pp. 25, 47–9.

34 *Ibid.*, p. 53.

35 Compaine, *op. cit.*, p. 264. Even within the paperback industry, specialization coexists with massification. With the growth of 'quality paperback' lines like Mentor and Anchor, already established in the 1950s when Harold Guinzberg was worried about lowest-common-denominator publishing, paperbacks began to reach a growing audience of college-educated readers.

36 T. Whiteside, *op. cit.*, p. 47.

37 Specialized book clubs are also proliferating (J. Tebbel, *op. cit.*, p. 740). They enable even people far from large bookstores to have access to a wide range of titles.

38 John P. Dessauer, personal communication.

39 Compaine, *op. cit.*, p. 276.

40 Faith Sale, personal communication.

41 A famous example of the latter is Rod McKuen's poems. They were underground bestsellers and were only discovered by Random House when a publisher's representative asked the manager of a college bookstore what was selling well. *Our Bodies Ourselves* also began as an underground bestseller.

42 The line between the two is sometimes difficult to discover. Janice Radway's research on romance publishing shows that one reason why the genre has had such a great recent success is that publisher-sponsored market research made possible accurate identification of what romance readers want. Yet this information has been codified into formulas by romance publishers, and aspiring authors must often write to formula to be published. Since many romance authors come from the ranks of romance readers, such restrictions may inhibit the genre from developing in the directions its audience and authors desire. See Janice Radway, *Reading the Romance*, Chapel Hill, University of North Carolina Press, 1984.

43 Coser, Kadushin, and Powell, *op. cit.*, pp. 106, 112–15. They also tend to be Protestant and white.

44 Thus, major New York houses publish few of the ever-popular religious books. And Rod McKuen's poems (see n. 41) were rejected by major publishers at first because they were not seen as legitimate poetry.

45 See R. Williams, *Culture and Society: 1780–1950*. Also A. B. Harbage, *A Kind of Power: The Shakespeare–Dickens Analogy*, Philadelphia, American Philosophical Society, 1975, and his *Shakespeare's Audience*, New York, Columbia University Press, 1941.

46 I would like to thank Amé Battle, Sylvia Wang, Laurie Kyle, Mike McKinney, Mark Fowler, and Alicia Mikula for their help at various stages of the search for data for this section. Many sources were consulted but the most fruitful were *Contemporary Authors: A Bio-Bibliographical Guide to Current Authors and Their Work*, First Revision, vols. 1–108, and New Revision Series, vols. 1–9, published between 1962 and 1983, Detroit, Mich., Gale Research Company; *Contemporary Literarary Criticism*, vols. 1–25, Detroit, Mich., Gale Research Co., published between 1973 and 1983; J. Wakeman (ed.), *World Authors 1950–1970*, New York, H. W. Wilson, 1975; S. J. Kunitz and H. Haycroft (eds.), *Twentieth Century Authors: A Biographical Dictionary of Modern Literature*, New York, H. W. Wilson, 1942; S. J. Kunitz (ed.), *Twentieth Century Authors, First Supplement*, New York, H. W. Wilson, 1955; B. Nykouck (ed.), *Authors in the News*, vols. 1 and 2, Detroit, Mich., Gale Research Co., 1976; L. Mainiero (ed.), *American Women Writers: A Critical Reference Guide from Colonial Times to the Present*, vols.

1–4, New York, Frederick Unger, 1979–82.

47 The first period is five years longer than the rest to include Lloyd Douglas, the one author born before 1880. Only three authors of bestselling novels published by 1975 were born in the last period, so I also gathered data on authors from that period who had published bestsellers between 1976 and 1980. This brings the total number to eight, which is still far too small to support generalizations, but is suggestive, perhaps, of certain patterns.

48 Even if all the authors who cannot be easily placed are counted among the non-middle-class group, the proportion never exceeds one-fourth.

49 In the 1875–1900 period, at least eighteen of the thirty-six authors (50 percent) came from professional families. In the following period at least 29 percent, and in the 1921–40 period at least 39 percent came from professional families. Over 35 percent of those professionals were literary, academic or artistic in the periods between 1875–1900 and 1921–40. The percentage is lower (25 percent) in the 1901–20 period.

50 Twenty-two of the thirty-six authors born between 1875 and 1900 whose novels were on the bestseller lists between 1945 and 1975 were American, fourteen were foreign-born, and of those nine came from Great Britain or 'Commonwealth' countries. Forty-eight of the seventy authors on the bestseller lists between 1945 and 1975 who were born between 1901 and 1920 were American, twenty-two were born and raised in other countries, and of those fourteen came from Great Britain or Commonwealth countries. In the next period (1921–40), thirty-four of the forty-two authors were American, and eight were born and raised in other countries, while among them six came from Great Britain or Commonwealth countries. All three of the authors born between 1941 and 1960 who published bestselling novels between 1945 and 1975 were American. Authors born during this period who published bestselling novels between 1976 and 1980 were combined with those three. Of this group of eight, there was only one who was not American, and he was British.

51 For 1875–1900, three writers could not be identified by region. Four came from New England, the South, and New York City, five from the Midwest, two from the Mid-Atlantic states. For 1901-20, three writers could again not be identified by region. Thirteen came from New York City, seventeen from the Midwest, including four from Chicago. Four came from the West, six from the South, and three from both New England and the Mid-Atlantic states. For 1921–40, eleven of the thirty-three American bestselling authors came from New York City. Seven came from the Mid-Atlantic states, including four from the areas in New York's cultural orbit. Five came from the Midwest, and five from the South; four came from New England, and one from the West. Two of the three writers born between 1941 and 1960 came from New York City; the other was born in Chicago and raised in New York. If one also considers authors born

in this period whose novels appeared on the bestseller lists between 1976 and 1980, a total of four came from New York, two from New England, and one from the Midwest.

52 For 1875–1900, twelve American-raised authors came from rural or small-town backgrounds, seven from large cities, and three from 'cosmopolitan' backgrounds spanning different regions or countries. For 1901–20, not enough is known about four authors to place them on the rural–urban axis. Sixteen, or 33 percent, came from rural or small-town settings, twenty-seven, or 56 percent, from large cities. This almost reverses the proportions from the previous period. One writer has a 'cosmopolitan' background. For 1921–40, one writer cannot be placed, and one was a hoax. Of the forty-one American-raised authors, seven, or 21 percent, came from rural or small-town backgrounds, twenty, or 61 percent, from large cities, and five, or 15 percent, appear to have come from suburbs. All of the three authors born between 1941 and 1960 came from large cities. Adding authors born during this period who wrote bestselling novels published between 1976 and 1980, six of the seven American authors came from large cities.

53 *1875–1900*: Ten (or 43 percent) of the twenty-three writers educated in the United States attended Ivy League schools, two attended non-elite private colleges, and one attended four colleges, including two Ivy League schools. Two attended unnamed universities, two completed degrees at state colleges, and two attended state colleges for short periods. The latter two, and four others, apparently had little formal education. *1901–20*: Fifty authors were educated beyond secondary school. Twelve (or 24 percent) attended Ivy League colleges, and four went from other schools to do graduate work at Ivy League schools, so 32 percent passed through these institutions. Sixteen attended other elite private undergraduate institutions (three dropped out after two years), one attended Oxford, and another was a Rhodes Scholar there. Four authors attended less prestigious private colleges, and ten attended state colleges or universities. One attended a small unidentified college. Three dropped out of school before college, and there is no information about three. *1921–40*: There is no information about four of the thirty-five authors educated in the United States. Eleven authors, or 31 percent, attended Ivy League schools, and two more did graduate work at these universities. Five other authors attended elite private colleges or universities (one going on to an Ivy League school), so almost 49 percent passed through prestigious private institutions. This is a lower percentage than in the previous period. Six authors attended less prestigious private colleges, and five went to state colleges, so 31 percent of the authors did not attend elite schools. Though the data is not entirely clear, it appears that fifteen (or 43 percent) of the authors attended graduate school. Three authors, on the other hand, had no college, and one finished only one year. *1941–60*: Of the three American authors, one attended a state school, and two went to Harvard. Considering authors born

during this period who published bestselling novels through 1980, of the total of seven, two attended Harvard, two attended elite private colleges and did graduate work at Ivy League schools. The three others attended state universities.

54 The figures for writers of bestselling novels on the American lists who were born and educated abroad are even harder to interpret because the numbers are so small.

55 *1875–1900*: Of the thirty-six authors, five lived almost entirely by writing fiction, fourteen (39 percent) wrote for newspapers, magazines, or advertising, eight (22 percent) worked in publishing or academic life (seven of the eight), and eight (22 percent) in other professions or jobs (six of the eight were professionals). *1901–20*: Of the seventy writers, nine (13 percent) lived by writing fiction, twenty-two (31 percent) also wrote for or edited newspapers or magazines, sixteen (23 percent) worked in academic life, publishing or as translators (fourteen of these were academics, but six worked in journalism or entertainment media as well), eleven (16 percent) worked in other entertainment media (but four of these also taught or wrote for magazines or newspapers), and eleven worked in other unrelated professions or jobs. *1921–40*: Of the forty writers for whom there is information, eight, (20 percent) lived by writing fiction, six (15 percent) also wrote for or edited newspapers or magazines, eight (20 percent) worked for nonprint media (but three of these were also journalists or academics), nine (22.5 percent) were academics (but three also wrote ads or journalism), one worked in publishing, and nine worked in other professions (but four also taught or wrote for magazines). *1941–60*: The three authors born during this period were all involved with other entertainment media, though one also was a speech writer and news reporter. The five authors born during this period who published bestselling novels between 1976 and 1980 all worked in academic settings as well as writing fiction.

56 Yankelovich, Skelly & White, *Consumer Research Study on Reading and Book Purchasing*, BISG Report No. 6, Book Industry Study Group, October, 1978, p. 46. B. Berelson, with the assistance of L. Asheim, *The Library's Public: A Report of the Public Library Inquiry*, New York, Columbia University Press, 1949, p. 7. Philip H. Ennis reports that a 1965 NORC survey showed 49 percent of the sample had read a book within the past six months. (See P. H. Ennis, *Adult Book Reading in the United States: A Preliminary Report*, National Opinion Research Center Report No. 105, Chicago, National Opinion Research Center, 1965, p. 34.) Jan Hajda's 1962 study of readers in Baltimore found that 52 percent of the sample had read a book within a year. And Gallup polls of 1971 show a slightly higher percentage (46 percent) of occasional readers than earlier polls. (See V. H. Mathews, 'Adult Reading Studies: Their Implications for Private, Professional and Public Policy,' *Library Trends*, vol. 22, no. 2, October 1973, p. 153.)

57 See Berelson, *op. cit.*, p. 6; Ennis, *op. cit.*, pp. 42–3; Mathews, *op. cit.*, p. 153. Although the audience, as reported in these studies,

has grown slightly during this period, the number of books sold has trebled. These are problematic findings, especially since, according to Ennis (*op. cit.*, p. 43), the serious readers do not appear to be reading more books than they did in the late 1940s. Yet Ennis shows people often report fewer books than were actually read (*op. cit.*, p. 41). This flies in the face of accepted wisdom that people overreport their reading, since our culture values reading positively, but accords well with some data that suggests Americans underestimate reading in comparison with Europeans. (See Mathews, *op. cit.*, pp. 151–2.)

58 Yankelovich, Skelly & White, *op. cit.*, pp. 26, 50–3. See also Berelson, *op. cit.*, pp. 19–40; Mathews, *op. cit.*, pp. 152–3; Ennis, *op. cit.*, pp. 33–57. See also P. H. Ennis, 'Who Reads?', in R. W. Conant and K. Molz, *The Metropolitan Library*, Cambridge, Mass., and London, MIT Press, 1972, pp. 52–4.

59 Yankelovich, Skelly & White, *op. cit.*, pp. 51–60. P. H. Ennis, *Adult Book Reading in the United States*, pp. 22–4. B. Berelson, *op. cit.*, pp. 41–6.

60 B. Berelson, *op. cit.*, pp. 3–18.

61 Yankelovich, Skelly & White, *op. cit.*, pp. 56, 61–9.

62 V. Mathews, *op. cit.*, p. 157. E. W. McElroy, 'Subject Variety in Adult Reading: I. Factors Related to Variety in Reading,' *Library Quarterly*, vol. 38, no. 2, April 1968, pp. 164–6.

63 Yankelovich, Skelly & White, *op. cit.*, pp. 122, 155, 156.

64 *Ibid.*, pp. 20, 36, 140, 143, 145, 165. E. W. McElroy, *op. cit.*, pp. 157–8.

65 Yankelovich, Skelly & White, *op. cit.*, pp. 164–72. Only 12 percent of the last nonfiction books read are bestsellers, but 44 percent of the last novels read are bestsellers, according to this study.

66 P. E. Ennis, 'Who Reads?', p. 48.

67 *Ibid.*, p. 48. *Literary Market Place: The Directory of American Book Publishing*, New York and London, R. R. Bowker, 1982.

68 See R. Strang, *Exploration in Reading Patterns*, Chicago, University of Chicago Press, 1942. Strang's study was inspired by sociological interest in communications that developed in the late 1930s. Also, see P. H. Ennis, *Adult Book Reading in the United States*, pp. 1–32. And E. W. McElroy, *op. cit.*, and 'Subject Variety in Adult Reading: II. Characteristics of Readers of Ten Categories of Books,' *Library Quarterly*, vol. 38, no. 2, July 1968, pp. 261–9. McElroy uses NORC data that were the basis for Ennis's quantitative analysis in the latter sections of his book.

69 Yankelovich, Skelly & White, *op. cit.*, p. 26.

70 For an excellent introduction to the varieties of reader response theory, see J. Tompkins (ed.), *Reader-Response Criticism: From Formalism to Post-Structuralism*, Baltimore, Johns Hopkins University Press, 1980. Also see S. Suleiman and I. Crosman (eds.), *The Reader in the Text: Essays on Audience and Interpretation*, Princeton, Princeton University Press, 1980.

71 N. N. Holland, *The Dynamics of Literary Response*, New York,

Oxford University Press, 1968, p. 310.

72 Though I do not agree entirely with Bleich and Holland, their work shows the value of studying readers. All too often the boldest literary theorists remain bound by the conventions of their profession and deal only with texts, despite intense theoretical interest in arguments that would seem to compel extratextual study of real readers reading.

73 N. N. Holland, *Five Readers Reading*, New Haven and London, Yale University Press, 1975. Chapters 4, 6, and 7 are especially pertinent.

74 D. Bleich, *Readings and Feelings: An Introduction to Subjective Criticism*, Urbana, Ill., National Council of Teachers of English, 1975. See especially pp. 49–63.

75 N. N. Holland, *Five Readers Reading*, p. 219.

76 N. N. Holland, *Dynamics of Literary Response*, p. 93.

77 S. Fish, *Is There a Text in this Class?*, Cambridge, Mass., Harvard University Press, 1980.

78 At the beginning of this period, the *New York Times Book Review* tabulated a weekly bestseller list broken down by major American cities.

79 Thanks to Janice Radway and Peter Rabinowitz for contributing so generously of their time and ideas to help clarify this discussion.

80 E. G. Schachtel, *Metamorphosis: On the Development of Affect, Perception, Attention, and Memory*, New York, Basic Books, 1959, p. 291. Also see A. B. Lord, *The Singer of Tales*, Cambridge, Mass., Harvard University Press, 1960, and B. Knox's review of Moses Finlay's *The World of Odysseus* (1978: reissue), *New York Review of Books*, June 29, 1978, p. 41.

81 See J. Radway, *op. cit.*, for a brilliant discussion of critical responses to romances and their theoretical and empirical shortcomings.

82 Schachtel's essay also claims that what people remember from stories is connected to whatever set of personal relevances they bring to the reading and to the later act of remembering. During the course of this study, I informally questioned people to determine what they had retained from the novels, and a striking example of selective subcultural memory that appears to bear out Schachtel's claim is that a group of young professional women who had read *Marjorie Morningstar* as teenagers all remembered the heroine as someone who showed that a girl could have a career, and forgot that she was heavily punished for moral laxness, abandoned her career, and settled into a traditional marriage. This points to what mass communications researchers as well as reader response theorists and semioticians are increasingly discovering: that communications from the media do not simply *affect* a passive individual but rather are part of an interactional process between what is communicated, an active individual who 'uses' what is communicated in many ways, and the social context in which individuals form their attitudes and opinions. The problems

involved in understanding what 'effects' these bestsellers may have on their audience is, thus, extremely complex. The focus of this study on bestsellers as a social phenomenon, one aspect of a communicative process, acknowledges these problems but does not solve them.

3 Bestselling novels 1945–1955: from entreprerneurial adventure to corporate-suburban compromise

1 S. Shellabarger, *Captain from Castile*, Boston, Little, Brown, 1945, p. 503.

2 T. Costain, *The Moneyman*, Garden City, N.Y., Doubleday, 1947, p. 104.

3 *Ibid.*, p. 19–20.

4 *Ibid.*, p. 433.

5 E. Ferber, *Giant*, Garden City, N.Y., Doubleday, 1952, pp. 415–47.

6 T. Costain, *The Black Rose*, Garden City, N.Y., Doubleday, Doran, 1945, p. 222.

7 L. C. Douglas, *The Big Fisherman*, Boston, Houghton Mifflin, 1948, p. 101.

8 *Ibid.*, p. 144.

9 H. M. Robinson, *The Cardinal*, New York, Simon & Schuster, 1950, p. 188.

10 *Ibid.*, p. 156.

11 *Ibid.*, pp. 311–12.

12 Costain, *The Moneyman*, p. 19.

13 R. Janney, *The Miracle of the Bells*, New York, Prentice-Hall, 1946, p. 35.

14 Often they are 'natural', as in the old phrase the king's 'natural' son – for were they not bastards, there would be no reason for them to have to embark on schemes of self-improvement; their place in life would be preestablished.

15 M. Thompson, *Not as a Stranger*, New York, Charles Scribner's Sons, 1954, p. 65.

16 *Ibid.*, p. 128.

17 Robinson, *op. cit.*, pp. 572–9.

18 K. Winsor, *Star Money*. New York, Appleton-Century-Crofts, 1950, p. 122.

19 Janney, *op. cit.*, p. 28.

20 F. P. Keyes, *Joy Street*, New York, Julian Messner, 1950, p. 51.

21 J. O'Hara, *Ten North Frederick*, New York, Random House, 1955, p. 132.

22 W. Brinkley, *Don't Go Near the Water*, New York, Random House, 1956, pp. 205–6.

23 Ferber, *op. cit.*, p. 159.

24 A. L. Langley, *A Lion in the Streets*, New York, Whittlesey House, McGraw-Hill, 1945, p. 469.

25 S. Wilson, *The Man in the Gray Flannel Suit*, New York, Simon & Schuster, 1955, p. 182.

26 *Ibid.*, p. 5.

27 *Ibid.*, p. 6.

28 *Ibid.*, p. 143.

29 *Ibid.*, p. 26.

30 *Ibid.*, p. 106.

31 *Ibid.*, p. 192.

32 *Ibid.*, p. 277.

33 *Ibid.*, p. 278.

34 H. Wouk, *Marjorie Morningstar*, Garden City, N.Y., Doubleday, 1955, p. 10.

4 Bestselling novels 1956–1968: the varieties of self-fulfillment – the goal achieved

1 A. R. St. Johns, *Tell No Man*, Garden City, N.Y., Doubleday, 1966, p. 193.

2 M. E. Chase, *The Lovely Ambition*, New York, W. W. Norton, 1960, p. 287.

3 J. Weidman, *The Enemy Camp*, New York, Random House, 1958, p. 5.

4 *Ibid.*, p. 261.

5 *Ibid.*, p. 561.

6 J. Steinbeck, *The Winter of Our Discontent*, New York, Viking Press, 1961, p. 108.

7 *Ibid.*, p. 92.

8 *Ibid.*, p. 154.

9 *Ibid.*, p. 104.

10 *Ibid.*, p. 200. It is unclear whether Ethan's participation in the business world can be as limited as he hopes it will be.

11 *Ibid.*, p. 186.

12 H. Robbins, *The Carpetbaggers*, New York, Trident Press, 1961, p. 36.

13 R. Ruark, *Poor No More*, New York, Henry Holt, 1959, p.158.

14 M. West, *The Tower of Babel*, New York, William Morrow, 1968, p. 141.

15 M. McCarthy, *The Group*, New York, Harcourt, Brace & World, 1963, pp. 104–5.

16 J. Updike, *Couples*, New York, Alfred A. Knopf, 1968, p. 454.

17 F. Sagan, *A Certain Smile*, New York, Dutton, 1956, pp. 11–12.

18 West, *op. cit.*, p. 233.

19 Updike, *op. cit.*, p. 458.

20 E. Kazan, *The Arrangement*, New York, Stein & Day, 1967, p. 78.

21 *Ibid.*, p. 150.

22 *Ibid.*, p. 341.

23 *Ibid.*, p. 444.

24 A. M. Lindbergh, *Dearly Beloved*, Nw York, Harcourt, Brace & World, 1962,. p. 160.

25 Chase, *op. cit.*, p. 14.

26 M. West, *The Shoes of the Fisherman*, New York, William Morrow, 1963, p. 29.

27 *Ibid.*, p. 52.

28 J. D. Salinger, *Raise High the Roof Beam, Carpenters and Seymour – An Introduction*, Boston and Toronto, Little, Brown, 1959, pp. 186–7.

29 S. Bellow, *Herzog*, New York, Penguin Books, 1964, p. 307.

30 *Ibid.*, p. 340.

5 Bestselling novels 1969–1975: the failure of success

1 J. Heller, *Something Happened*, New York, Alfred A. Knopf, 1974, p. 16.

2 *Ibid.*, pp. 39–40.

3 *Ibid.*, p. 47.

4 *Ibid.*, pp. 46–7.

5 *Ibid.*, p. 136.

6 Curiously, as work becomes abstracted to the point where there is no sense of making a product, symbolic abstractions in these novels become real and concrete. Heller's hero really smothers his son. Portnoy's Jewish mother really makes him eat at knife point.

7 *Ibid.*, pp. 18–19.

8 *Ibid..*, p. 71.

9 *Ibid.*, p. 206.

10 *Ibid.*, p. 510.

11 A. Hailey, *Wheels*, Garden City, N.Y., Doubleday, 1971, pp. 373–4.

12 I. Shaw, *Evening in Byzantium*, New York, Delacorte Press, 1973, pp. 1–2.

13 J. Updike, *Rabbit Redux*, New York, Alfred A. Knopf, 1971, pp. 29–30.

14 Shaw, op. cit., p. 3.

15 Even their sense of age is different. Rabbit is middle-aged when Craig would still be considered in his youth.

16 Shaw, *op. cit.*, p.367.

17 Updike, *op. cit.*, p. 406.

18 Br'er Rabbit, and the Bushmen's mythical hero are the only other rabbits I know who have achieved widespread popularity. Both belong to relatively oppressed groups who have elevated virtues of cunning and concealment.

19 *New York Times Book Review*, June 30, 1974.

20 R. Bach, *Jonathan Livingston Seagull*, New York, Macmillan, 1970, p. 63.

21 *Ibid.*, pp. 14–15.

22 *Ibid.*, p. 60.

23 *Ibid.*, pp. 53–4.

24 H. Robbins, *The Pirate*, New York, Simon & Schuster, 1974, p. 29.

25 I. Wallace, *The Fan Club*, New York, Simon & Schuster, 1974, p. 155.

26 *Ibid.*, p. 56.

27 J. Dickey, *Deliverance*, Boston, Houghton Mifflin, 1970, pp. 275–6.

28 T. Caldwell, *Great Lion of God*, Garden City, N.Y. Doubleday, 1970, pp. xi–xii.

29 Some, of course, hardly seem to have changed. For example, Wouk's *Winds of War* (1971) and Taylor Caldwell's *Captains and the Kings* (1972) resemble earlier books by these authors, and show few marks of the times. But they are the exception.

30 J. Fowles, *The French Lieutenant's Woman*, Boston, Little, Brown, 1969, pp. 11–12.

6 The social critics

1 T. B. Bottomore, *Critics of Society*, New York, Pantheon Books, 1968, pp. 61, 125.

2 D. Riesman, with N. Glazer and R. Denny, *The Lonely Crowd*, abridged edition, New Haven and London, Yale University Press, 1961 (later reprinted with a 1969 preface added), pp. 3–36, 109–60. W. H. Whyte, Jr., *The Organization Man*, New York, Simon & Schuster, 1956, pp. 3–137, 205–40. C. W. Mills, *White Collar*, London, Oxford, and New York, Oxford University Press, paperback edition, 1956, pp. 63–212.

3 Whyte, *op. cit.*, pp. 4, 63–78, 129–37. All these social critics, themselves men, described the problems of the new social order for men, or assumed that 'men' stand for all humanity. Because their accounts used the generic masculine, I have followed their construction in my explication of their writings.

4 *Ibid.*, p. 397.

5 Mills, *op. cit.*, p. 14.

6 *Ibid.*, p. ix.

7 Riesman, *op. cit.*, pp. 47–55, 60–5, 96–104.

8 Whyte, *op. cit.*, pp. 205–40.

9 Riesman, *op. cit.*, pp. 261–75, 286–303.

10 Mills, *op. cit.*, pp. 87-91.

11 Riesman, *op. cit.*, p. 81.

12 Whyte, *op. cit.*, pp. 196–201.

13 Riesman, *op. cit.*, p. 45.

14 *Ibid.*, pp. 115–39.

15 Mills, *op. cit.*, p. xvii.

16 Whyte, *op. cit.*, p. 397.

17 Riesman, *op. cit.*, p. 18.
18 *Ibid.*, pp. 122, 113, 127.
19 *Ibid.*, p. 113.
20 Mills, *op. cit.*, p. 95.
21 *Ibid.*, p. 95.
22 *Ibid.*, p. 99.
23 Riesman, *op. cit.*, p. 248.
24 *Ibid.*, p. 257.
25 Mills, *op. cit.*, p. 237.
26 C. W. Mills, *The Power Elite*, New York, Oxford University Press, 1956, pp. 304–5. Mills, *White Collar*, p. 237.
27 Whyte, *op. cit.*, p. 288. Mills, *The Power Elite*, p. 309.
28 Mills, *White Collar*, p. 252.
29 *Ibid.*, p. 238.
30 Mills, *The Power Elite*, pp. 314, 320–3. Mills was responsible for the insight that those sociologists who saw the city as a tangle of pathology and social problems came from predominantly rural or small-town backgrounds; therefore, that people's conception of the city has a social basis. (See his essay 'The Professional Ideology of Social Pathologists,' in I. L. Horowitz, *Power, Politics and People: The Collected Essays of C. Wright Mills*, London, Oxford, New York, Oxford University Press, 1963, pp. 525-53.) Yet in his discussion of the city, Mills himself draws on the most pessimistic views of Simmel and the Chicago School. One can only speculate whether it was intellectual despair, or a sense of weariness at his own transplantation from Texas to the inhospitable halls of Columbia, that gave him such a dark perspective on the Metropolis.
31 Riesman, *op. cit.*, pp. 96–104, 107, 108, 157.
32 *Ibid.*, pp. 48–50, 74–6.
33 *Ibid.*, p. 84.
34 Whyte, *op. cit.*, p. 330.
35 *Ibid.*, pp. 301, 313, 314.
36 *Ibid.*, pp. 302, 350–65.
37 Riesman, *op. cit.*, p. 74.
38 Whyte, *op. cit.*, pp. 352–4, 365.
39 Riesman, *op. cit.*, p. 72.
40 Whyte, *op. cit.*, pp. 4, 7, 20–59, 399, 400.
41 Riesman, *op. cit.*, pp. 3–36. The term 'social character' provoked much controversy at the time. I prefer to construe it, as he did, rather loosely – as a device enabling Riesman to link some aspects of personality to social patterns of authority, socialization, and economic organization. In a sense, he too is describing external cultural influences *on* the individual, in spite of the psychological cast of his discussion.
42 Riesman, *op. cit.*, pp.19–25, 137–9, 261–85.
43 Mills, *White Collar*, pp. xiv, xix.
44 *Ibid.*, pp. 263–5.
45 *Ibid.*, p. 283.

46 D. Bell, *The Cultural Contradictions of Capitalism*, New York, Basic Books, 1976, p. 10. R. Sennett, *The Fall of Public Man: On the Social Psychology of Capitalism*, New York, Vintage Books, 1978, pp. 3–4. C. Lasch, *The Culture of Narcissism: American Life in an Age of Diminishing Expectations*, New York, W. W. Norton, 1978.

47 Bell, *op. cit.*, pp. 71–2.

48 Both Riesman and Lasch *assume* that a decline of parental authority has taken place. Social history of the nineteenth and twentieth centuries makes it clear that this is an extraordinarily complex issue that merits much more examination. See, for example, Carl Degler's work on women and the nineteenth-century family.

49 Lasch, *op. cit.*, pp. 31–51, 154–86, 228–32.

50 Sennett, *op. cit.*, pp. 64–106, 125–94, 259–340.

51 Lasch, *op. cit.*, pp. 187–206, 219, 221.

52 Bell, *op. cit.*, p. 28.

53 *Ibid.*, pp. 21, 28–53.

54 *Ibid.*, pp. 19–20, 53, 157–8.

55 *Ibid.*, pp. 130, 61–84, 90, 120–45.

56 *Ibid.*, p. 154.

57 *Ibid.*, p. 155.

58 *Ibid.*, pp. 166–71.

59 It is curious how little they refer to the earlier attempts, except as artifacts of their time. Lasch, in fact, says: 'The critics of the forties and fifties mistook this [bland] surface for the deeper reality' (Lasch, *op. cit.*, p. 64). Sennett, a student of Riesman's applauds him for the creation of 'a social-psychological language for this general and manifold problem' of the relationship between public and private, self and society; comments on the way Riesman has been misread (this is disputable, for many social theorists have found more pessimism in Riesman's characterization of other-direction than Sennett or Riesman himself contend he intended); and then says that *The Fall of Public Man* in a sense turns around the argument of *The Lonely Crowd*. Sennett, in fact, feels that we are moving 'from something like [Riesman's] society of other direction to a society of inner direction' (Sennett, *op. cit.*, pp. 5, 30).

60 Bell, *op. cit.*, pp. 75, 69.

61 Lasch, *op. cit.*, p. xvi.

62 Sennett, *op. cit.*, pp. 6–7, 10–12, 333–6.

63 Lasch, *op. cit.*, p. 12.

64 Riesman, *op. cit.*, p. 250.

65 R. Sennett, *Authority*, New York, Alfred A. Knopf, 1980, pp. 84–120; direct quote on p. 118.

66 Lasch, *op. cit.*, pp. 154–86, 222–4.

67 Sennett, *The Fall of Public Man*, pp. 18–19. This claim tends to gloss over the desperation of eighteenth-century European slum-dwellers, criminals, and violent mobs – all indications that public life and its laws did not seem in harmonious balance to large numbers of people at the time.

68 Bell, *op. cit.*, pp. 155–71. Note especially his discussion of *Faust*, pp. 158–61.

69 *Ibid.*, pp. 89, 87.

70 Sennett, *The Fall of Public Man*. pp. 64–72, 170–4, 175–81, 214–18, for instance.

71 Sennett, *Authority*, p. 3.

72 Sennett, *The Fall of Public Man*, see pp. 28–44 for an extended discussion of method.

73 Lasch, *op. cit.*, pp. 31–51, 125–86.

74 *Ibid.*, p. 234.

75 Mills, *The Power Elite*, see especially pp. 343–61.

76 Bell, *op. cit.*, p. 70.

77 Sennett, *The Fall of Public Man*, pp. 327–33. Whyte, *op. cit.*, pp. 141–67.

78 Lasch, *op. cit.*, pp. xv, 235.

79 *Ibid.*, p. 68. The idea of proletarianization lurks behind some of these formulations. Marx felt that as capitalism developed, the 'middle-classes' would gradually be eroded, and the majority would be forced to join the ranks of the proletarians. Certain twentieth-century developments (economic concentration, the increased specialization or 'rationalization' of the labor process) support Marx's contentions, while others (the rise in standard of living, the proliferation of professionals and service workers) do not seem to. Nonetheless, attempts to understand modern stratification often draw on all or part of this idea, and my sense is that Lasch's emphasis on dependency and his sense of crisis show him at work in a similar universe of metaphor.

80 Sennett, *The Fall of Public Man*, pp. 11, 177–83.

81 Whyte, *op. cit.*, pp. 131–2, 243–62.

82 Mills, *White Collar*, pp. 282–6, 259–65.

83 Riesman, *op. cit.*, pp. 104–7, 149–56; direct quote on p. 141.

84 Lasch, *op. cit.*, pp. 97–8, 171–3, 16–25, 62.

85 Bell, *op. cit.*, for example, pp. 99–128, 136–43.

86 Sennett, *The Fall of Public Man*; see, for example, pp. 47–122.

87 Lasch, *op. cit.*, p. 21. Sennett, *The Fall of Public Man*, pp. 283–7. Riesman, op. cit., p. 76.

88 See T. L. Haskell, *The Emergence of Professional Social Science*, Urbana, Chicago, London, University of Illinois Press, 1977. Also M. S. Larson, *The Rise of Professionalism*, Berkeley and Los Angeles, University of California Press, 1977. For a discussion of the meaning of the word 'society,' and its evolution during the nineteenth century, see Raymond Williams, *Keywords*, New York, Oxford University Press, 1976, pp. 243–7.

89 See his article on 'The Sociological Reality of America,' in *On The Making of Americans*, ed. Herbert J. Gans, Nathan Glazer, Joseph R. Gusfield, Christopher Jencks, University of Pennsylvania Press, Camden, N.J., 1979, pp. 41–62.

90 For a short but lucid presentation of this historiographical

problem, see E. H. Carr's *What Is History*, New York, Vintage Books, 1961.

Bibliography

The dates in brackets following titles in the text indicate the year in which a book first appeared in the bestseller list. These may differ from the publication dates given below.

Adams, R., *Watership Down*, New York, Macmillan, 1974.

Ashe, P., *Naked Came the Stranger*, New York, L. Stuart, 1969.

Bach, R., *Jonathan Livingston Seagull*, New York, Macmillan, 1970.

Bell, D., *The Cultural Contradictions of Capitalism*, New York, Basic Books, 1976.

Bellow, S., *Herzog*, New York, Penguin Books, 1964.

Bellow, S., *Humboldt's Gift*, New York, Viking Press, 1975.

Berelson, B., with the assistance of L. Asheim, *The Library's Public: A Report of the Public Library Inquiry*, New York, Columbia University Press, 1949.

Blatty, W. P., *The Exorcist*, New York, Harper & Row, 1971.

Bleich, D., *Readings and Feelings: An Introduction to Subjective Criticism*, Urbana, Ill., National Council of Teachers of English, 1975.

Boston Women's Health Collective, *Our Bodies Ourselves*, New York, Simon & Schuster, 1973.

Bottomore, T. B., *Critics of Society*, New York, Pantheon Books, 1968.

Bowker Annual of Library and Book Trade Information, New York, R. R. Bowker, 1960–76.

Breslin, J., *The Gang That Couldn't Shoot Straight*, New York, Viking Press, 1969.

Brinkley, W., *Don't Go Near the Water*, New York, Random House, 1956.

Bristow, G., *Calico Palace*, New York, Thomas Y. Crowell, 1970.

Burdick, E., and Wheeler, H., *Fail-Safe*, New York, McGraw-Hill, 1962.

Caldwell, T., *The Listener*, Garden City, N.Y., Doubleday, 1960.

Caldwell, T., *Great Lion of God*, Garden City, N.Y., Doubleday, 1970.
Caldwell, T., *Captains and the Kings*, Garden City, N.Y., Doubleday, 1972.
Carr, E.H., *What Is History?*, New York, Vintage Books, 1961.
Chaney, D., *Fictions and Ceremonies*, New York, St. Martin's Press, 1979.
Chase, M. E., *The Lovely Ambition*, New York, W. W. Norton, 1960.
Cheney, O. H., *Economic Survey of the Book Industry 1930–1931*, New York, National Association of Book Publishers, 1931.
Clavell, J., *Tai-Pan*, New York, Atheneum, 1966.
Clavell, J., *Shogun*, New York, Atheneum, 1975.
Compaine, B. M., *Who Owns the Media: Concentration of Ownership in the Mass Communications Industry*, White Plains, N.Y., Knowledge Industry Publications, 1979.
Contemporary Authors: A Bio-Bibliographical Guide to Current Authors and Their Work, First Revision, vols. 1–108, and New Revision Series, vols. 1–9, Detroit, Mich., Gale Research Company, published between 1962 and 1983.
Contemporary Literary Criticism, vols. 1–25, Detroit, Mich., Gale Research Company, published between 1973 and 1983.
Coser, L., Kadushin, C., and Powell, W., *Books: The Culture and Commerce of Publishing*, New York, Basic Books, 1982.
Costain, T., *The Black Rose*, Garden City, N.Y., Doubleday, Doran, 1945.
Costain, T., *The Moneyman*, Garden City, N.Y., Doubleday, 1947.
Costain, T., *The Silver Chalice*, Garden City, N.Y., Doubleday, 1952.
Costain, T., *Below the Salt*, Garden City, N.Y., Doubleday, 1957.
Craven, M., *I Heard the Owl Call My Name*, Garden City, N.Y., Doubleday, 1973.
Crichton, R., *The Secret of Santa Vittoria*, New York, Simon & Schuster, 1966.
Davenport, M., *The Constant Image*, New York, Charles Scribner's Sons, 1960.
Delderfield, R. F., *God Is an Englishman*, New York, Simon & Schuster, 1970.
Dennis, P., *Auntie Mame*, New York, Vanguard Press, 1955.
Dickey, J., *Deliverance*, Boston, Houghton Mifflin, 1970.
Doctorow, E. L., *Ragtime*, New York, Random House, 1974.
Douglas, L. C., *The Robe*, Boston, Houghton Mifflin, 1942.
Douglas, L. C., *The Big Fisherman*, Boston, Houghton Mifflin, 1948.
du Maurier, D., *Mary Anne*, Garden City, N.Y., Doubleday, 1954.
du Maurier, D., *The House on the Strand*, Garden City, N.Y., Doubleday, 1969.
Eco, U., *The Role of the Reader*, Bloomington, Ind., Indiana University Press, 1979.
Eden, D., *The Vines of Yarrabee*, New York, Coward-McCann, 1969.
Ennis, P. H., *Adult Book Reading in the United States: A Preliminary Report*, National Opinion Research Center Report No. 105, Chicago,

National Opinion Research Center, 1965.

Ennis, P. H., 'Who Reads?', in R. W. Conant and K. Molz, *The Metropolitan Library*, Cambridge, Mass., and London, MIT Press, 1972.

Erdman, P., *The Billion Dollar Sure Thing*, New York, Charles Scribner's Sons, 1973.

Escarpit, R., *The Book Revolution: Books and the World Today*, London, Toronto, Wellington, Sydney, and UNESCO, Paris, George Harrap, 1966.

Ferber, E., *Giant*, Garden City, N.Y., Doubleday, 1952.

Ferber, E., *Ice Palace*, Garden City, N.Y., Doubleday, 1958.

Fish, S., *Is There a Text in This Class?*, Cambridge, Mass., Harvard University Press, 1980.

Forsyth, F., *The Day of the Jackal*, New York, Viking Press, 1971.

Forsyth, F., *The Dogs of War*, New York, Bantam Books, 1974.

Fowles, J., *The French Lieutenant's Woman*, Boston, Little, Brown, 1969.

Franklin, B., *Poor Richard's Almanack*, Mount Vernon, N.Y., Peter Pauper Press, 1936.

Gans, H. J., Glazer, N., Gusfield, J. R., Jencks, C. (eds.), *On the Making of Americans*, Philadelphia, Pa., University of Pennsylvania Press, 1979.

Godden, R., *The Battle of Villa Fiorita*, New York, Viking Press, 1963.

Graham, G., *Earth and High Heaven*, Philadelphia, J. B. Lippincott, 1944.

Greene, G., *The Honorary Consul*, New York, Simon & Schuster, 1973.

Hackett, A. P., *Seventy Years of Best Sellers: 1895–1965*, New York, R. R. Bowker, 1967.

Hailey, A., *Hotel*, Garden City, N.Y., Doubleday, 1965.

Hailey, A., *Wheels*, Garden City, N.Y., Doubleday, 1971.

Hailey, A., *The Moneychangers*, Garden City, N.Y., Doubleday, 1975.

Harbage, A. B., *Shakespeare's Audience*, New York, Columbia University Press, 1941.

Harbage, A. B., *A Kind of Power: The Shakespeare–Dickens Analogy*, Philadelphia, American Philosophical Society, 1975.

Hart, J. D., *The Popular Book*, New York, Oxford University Press, 1950.

Haskell, T. L., *The Emergence of Professional Social Science*, Urbana, Chicago, and London, University of Illinois Press, 1977.

Heller, J., *Catch-22*, New York, Simon & Schuster, 1961.

Heller, J., *Something Happened*, New York, Alfred A. Knopf, 1974.

Higgins, J., *The Eagle Has Landed*, New York, Holt, Rinehart & Winston, 1975.

Hobson, L., *Gentlemen's Agreement*, New York, Simon & Schuster, 1947.

Holland, N. N., *The Dynamics of Literary Response*, New York, Oxford University Press, 1968.

Holland, N. N., *Five Readers Reading*, New Haven and London, Yale

University Press, 1975.

Holmes, M., *Two from Galilee*, New York, Bantam Books, 1972.

Horowitz, I. L., *Power, Politics and People: The Collected Essays of C. Wright Mills*, London, Oxford, and New York, Oxford University Press, 1963.

Janey, R., *The Miracle of the Bells*, New York, Prentice-Hall, 1946.

Jenkins, D., *Semi-Tough*, New York, Atheneum, 1972.

Kantor, M., *Andersonville*, Cleveland and New York, World Publishing Co., 1955.

Kaufman, B., *Up the Down Staircase*, Englewood Cliffs, N.J., Prentice-Hall, 1964.

Kazan, E., *The Arrangement*, New York, Stein & Day, 1967.

Keyes, F. P., *The River Road*, New York, Julian Messner, 1945.

Keyes, F. P., *Joy Street*, New York, Julian Messner, 1950.

Keyes, F. P., *Blue Camellia*, New York, Julian Messner, 1957.

Knox, B., review of Moses Finlay's *The World of Odysseus* (1978: reissue) in *New York Times Review of Books*, June 29, 1978.

Kunitz, S. J. (ed.), *Twentieth Century Authors, First Supplement*, New York, H. W. Wilson, 1955.

Kunitz, S. J., and Haycroft, H. (eds.), *Twentieth Century Authors: A Biographical Dictionary of Modern Literature*, New York, H. W. Wilson, 1942.

Langley, A. L., *A Lion Is in the Streets*, New York, Whittlesey House, McGraw-Hill, 1945.

Larson, M. S., *The Rise of Professionalism*, Berkeley and Los Angeles, University of California Press, 1977.

Lasch, C., *The Culture of Narcissism: American Life in an Age of Diminishing Expectations*, New York, W. W. Norton, 1978.

Lawrence, D. H., *Lady Chatterley's Lover*, New York, Grove Press, 1957. (Third manuscript version, first published by Giuseppe Orioli, Florence, 1928.)

le Carré, J., *The Spy Who Came In from the Cold*, New York, Coward-McCann, 1963.

Lederer, W. J., and Burdick, E., *The Ugly American*, New York, W. W. Norton, 1958.

Levin, I., *Rosemary's Baby*, New York, Dell, 1967.

Lindbergh, A. M., *Dearly Beloved*, New York, Harcourt, Brace & World, 1962.

Literary Market Place: The Directory of American Book Publishing, New York and London, R. R. Bowker, 1982.

Lord, A. B., *The Singer of Tales*, Cambridge, Mass., Harvard University Press, 1960.

Lowenthal, L., *Literature and the Image of Man: Sociological Studies of the European Drama and Novel, 1600–1900*, Boston, Beacon Press, 1957.

Lowenthal, L., *Literature, Popular Culture, and Society*, Palo Alto, Cal., Pacific Books, 1961.

Ludlum, R., *The Matlock Paper*, New York, Dial Press, 1973.

McCarthy, M., *The Group*, New York, Harcourt, Brace & World, 1963.

McElroy, E. W., 'Subject Variety in Adult Reading: I. Factors Related to Variety in Reading', *Library Quarterly*, vol. 38, no. 2, April 1968, pp. 164–6.

McElroy, E. W., 'Subject Variety in Adult Reading: II. Characteristics of Readers of Ten Categories of Books', *Library Quarterly*, vol. 38, no. 2, July 1968, pp. 261–9.

MacInnes, H., *Message from Malaga*, New York, Harcourt Brace Jovanovich, 1971.

Madison, C. A., *Book Publishing in America*, New York, McGraw-Hill, 1966.

Madison, C. A., *Irving to Irving: Author Publisher Relations 1800–1974*, New York and London, R. R. Bowker, 1974.

Mainiero, L. (ed.), *American Women Writers: A Critical Reference Guide from Colonial Times to the Present*, vols. 1–4, New York, Frederick Unger, 1979–82.

Marshall, C., *Christy*, New York, McGraw-Hill, 1967.

Mathews, V. H., 'Adult Reading Studies: Their Implications for Private, Professional and Public Policy', *Library Trends*, vol. 22, no. 2, October 1973, pp. 149–76.

Metalious, G., *Peyton Place*, New York, Messner, 1956.

Michener, J., *Hawaii*, New York, Random House, 1959.

Michener, J., *The Source*, New York, Random House, 1965.

Michener, J., *The Drifters*, New York, Random House, 1971.

Michener, J., *Centennial*, New York, Random House, 1974.

Miller, W., *The Book Industry: A Report of the Public Library Inquiry*, New York, Columbia University Press, 1949.

Mills, C. W., *White Collar*, London, Oxford, and New York, Oxford University Press, paperback edition, 1956.

Mills, C. W., *The Power Elite*, New York, Oxford University Press, 1956.

Mott, F. L., *Golden Multitudes: The Story of Best Sellers in the United States*, New York, R. R. Bowker, 1947.

New York Times Book Review.

Nykouck, B. (ed.), *Authors in the News*, vols. 1–2, Detroit, Mich., Gale Research Co., 1976.

O'Hara, J., *Ten North Frederick*, New York, Random House, 1955.

O'Hara, J., *Elizabeth Appleton*, New York, Random House, 1963.

Potok, C., *The Chosen*, New York, Simon & Schuster, 1967.

Potok, C., *My Name Is Asher Lev*, New York, Alfred A. Knopf, 1972.

Puzo, M., *The Godfather*, New York, Putnam, 1969.

Rabinowitz, P. J., 'Assertion and Assumption: Fictional Patterns and the External World', *PMLA: Publications of the Modern Language Association of America*, vol. 96, no. 3, May 1981, pp. 408–19.

Radway, J., *Reading the Romance*, Chapel Hill, University of North Carolina Press, 1984.

Rand, A., *Atlas Shrugged*, New York, Random House, 1957.

Rechy, J., *City of Night*, New York, Grove Press, 1963.

Riesman, D., with N. Glazer and R. Denny, *The Lonely Crowd*, abridged edition, New Haven and London, Yale University Press, 1961 (later reprinted with a 1969 preface added).

Robbins, H., *The Carpetbaggers*, New York, Trident Press 1961.

Robbins, H., *The Adventurers*, New York, Trident Press, 1966.

Robbins, H., *The Inheritors*, New York, Trident Press, 1969.

Robbins, H., *The Pirate*, New York, Simon & Schuster, 1974.

Robinson, H. M., *The Cardinal*, New York, Simon & Schuster, 1950.

Rossner, J., *Looking for Mr. Goodbar*, New York, Simon & Schuster, 1975.

Ruark, R., *Poor No More*, New York, Henry Holt, 1959.

Sagan, Françoise, *A Certain Smile*, New York, Dutton, 1956.

St. Johns, A. R., *Tell No Man*, Garden City, N.Y., Doubleday, 1966.

Salinger, J. D., *Catcher in the Rye*, Boston, Little, Brown, 1951.

Salinger, J. D., *Raise High the Roof Beam, Carpenters and Seymour – An Introduction*, Boston and Toronto, Little, Brown, 1959.

Schachtel, E. G., *Metamorphosis: On the Development of Affect, Perception, Attention, and Memory*, New York, Basic Books, 1959.

Segal, E., *Love Story*, New York, Harper & Row, 1970.

Sennett, R., *The Fall of Public Man: On the Social Psychology of Capitalism*, New York, Vintage Books, 1978.

Sennett, R., *Authority*, New York, Alfred A. Knopf, 1980.

Shaw, I., *Evening in Byzantium*, New York, Delacorte Press, 1973.

Shellabarger, S., *Captain from Castile*, Boston, Little, Brown, 1945.

Shellabarger, S., *Prince of Foxes*, Boston, Little, Brown, 1947.

Shellabarger, S., *Lord Vanity*, Boston, Little, Brown, 1953.

Shute, N., *On the Beach*, New York, William Morrow, 1957.

Steinbeck, J., *The Winter of Our Discontent*, New York, Viking Press, 1961.

Steinberg, C. S. (ed.), *Mass Media and Communication*, New York, Hastings House, 1966.

Stewart, M., *The Crystal Cave*, Greenwich, Conn., Fawcett Publications, 1970.

Stewart, M., *The Hollow Hills*, New York, William Morrow, 1973.

Stone, I., *Immortal Wife*, Garden City, N.Y., Doubleday, 1944.

Stone, I., *The Agony and the Ecstasy*, Garden City, N.Y., Doubleday, 1961.

Strang, R., *Exploration in Reading Patterns*, Chicago, Ill., University of Chicago Press, 1942.

Styron, W., *The Confessions of Nat Turner*, New York, Random House, 1967.

Suleiman, S., and Crosman, I. (eds.), *The Reader in the Text: Essays on Audience and Interpretation*, Princeton, N.J., Princeton University Press, 1968.

Susann, J., *Valley of the Dolls*, New York, Bantam Books, 1966.

Susann, J., *The Love Machine*, New York, Simon & Schuster, 1969.

Susann, J., *Once Is Not Enough*, New York, Morrow, 1973.

Sutton, H., *The Exhibitionist*, New York, Crown, 1967.

Tebbel, J., *A History of Book Publishing in the United States*, vols. 1–4,

New York, R. R. Bowker, published between 1972 and 1981.

Thompson, M., *Not as a Stranger*, New York, Charles Scribner's Sons, 1954.

Tompkins, J. (ed.), *Reader-Response Criticism: From Formalism to Post Structuralism*, Baltimore, Md., Johns Hopkins University Press, 1980.

Updike, J., *Couples*, New York, Alfred A. Knopf, 1968.

Updike, J., *Rabbit Redux*, New York, Alfred A. Knopf, 1971.

Uris, L., *Exodus*, Garden City, N.Y., Doubleday, 1958. Bantam edition also consulted.

Uris, L., *Topaz*, New York, McGraw-Hill, 1967.

Vidal, G., *Myra Breckenridge*, Boston, Little, Brown, 1968.

Vidal, G., *Burr*, New York, Random House, 1973.

Wakeman, J. (ed.), *World Authors 1950–1970*, New York, H. W. Wilson, 1975.

Wallace, I., *The Chapman Report*, New York, Simon & Schuster, 1960.

Wallace, I., *The Fan Club*, New York, Simon & Schuster, 1974.

Waltari, M. T., *The Egyptian*, trans. Naomi Walford, New York, G. P. Putnam's Sons, 1949.

Wambaugh, J., *The Choirboys*, New York, Delacort Press, 1975.

Ward, M. J., *The Snake Pit*, New York, Random House, 1946.

Weidman, J., *The Enemy Camp*, New York, Random House, 1958.

West, M. L., *The Shoes of the Fisherman*, New York, William Morrow, 1963.

West, M. L., *The Ambassador*, New York, William Morrow, 1965.

West, M. L., *The Tower of Babel*, New York, William Morrow, 1968.

Whiteside, T., *The Blockbuster Complex: Conglomerates, Show Business, and Book Publishing*, Middletown, Conn., Wesleyan University Press, 1981.

Whyte, W. H., Jr., *The Organization Man*, New York, Simon & Schuster, 1956.

Wilder, T., *The Eighth Day*, New York, Harper & Row, 1967.

Williams, R., *Culture and Society: 1780–1950*, London, Chatto & Windus, 1959.

Williams, R., *The Country and the City*, New York, Oxford University Press, 1973.

Williams, R., *Keywords*, New York, Oxford University Press, 1976.

Wilson, S., *The Man in the Gray Flannel Suit*, New York, Simon & Schuster, 1955.

Winsor, K., *Forever Amber*, New York, Macmillan, 1945.

Winsor, K., *Star Money*, New York, Appleton-Century-Crofts, 1950.

Wouk, H., *The Caine Mutiny*, Garden City, N.Y., Doubleday, 1951.

Wouk, H., *Marjorie Morningstar*, Garden City, N.Y., Doubleday, 1955.

Wouk, H., *Youngblood Hawke*, Garden City, N.Y., Doubleday, 1962.

Wouk, H., *The Winds of War*, Boston, Little, Brown, 1971.

Yankelovich, Skelly & White, Inc., *Consumer Research Study on Reading and Book Purchasing*, BISG Report No. 6, Book Industry Study Group, October, 1978.

Yerby, F., *The Foxes of Harrow*, New York, Dial, 1946.

Index

206; expansion of, 155; new, 152, 164; standards of widely achieved, 157; study bounded by, 201
Miller, William, 28, 29
Mills, C. Wright, 9, 10, 64, 150, 151, 152-8, 159-60, 164-5, 206, 221
minority groups, 2
The Miracle of the Bells, 69, 72, 76; *see also* Janney, Russell
mobility, social, *see* social mobility
modernist literature, 44, 54, 57-8, 135, 184, 204; and culture, 170, 180
'modes of experience', 177, 197
The Moneychangers, 127, 134; *see also* Hailey, Arthur
The Moneyman, 23, 66, 73; *see also* Costain, Thomas
Monsarrat, Nicholas, 104
moonshot, 130
Moore, Robin, 104
moral relativism, *see* relativism
motivation, 72-3, 119, 125, 146, 151, 160, 200; overview of portrayal in bestsellers, 193
movie industry, 24-5, 28, 33, 43
movies, 34, 43, 182, 200-1
music, 200-1
My Name is Asher Lev, 120-1; *see also* Potok, Chaim
Myra Breckenridge, 108-9; *see also* Vidal, Gore
mysticism, 115, 136, 142, 146

NORC, 49
Naked Came the Stranger, 37, 139-40; *see also* Ashe, Penelope
narcissism, culture of, 11, 12, 168-9, 172, 174-5, 178-9, 181, 184-5, 199; exemplars of, 181
narrative focus, 4, 7; success as, 93
narrative strategies, 12
narrative structure, 8, 200
New Deal, 2
newspapers, 43, 48, 53
nostalgia, 18, 72-3, 129, 141, 145-7, 164, 168, 199; industrial, 129
Not as a Stranger, 65, 73; *see also* Thompson, Morton
novels, 3-5; development tied to middle class, 36; as fictional representations of relationships, 4; popular, 5-7; possessing imaginative truth, 9; in relation to

the social world, 16, 104-5; as symbolic creations, 46; *see also* bestsellers, literature

objectification, 109, 118-19
O'Hara, John, 79, 126
On the Beach, 103; *see also* Shute, Nevil
Once Is Not Enough, 132, 137; *see also* Susann, Jacqueline
The Organization Man, 82, 151-2; *see also* Whyte, William H., Jr.
organizational melodramas, 13, 102, 143
organization men, 12, 180
organizations, *see* bureaucracy
Ortega y Gasset, 158
other-direction, 155, 158, 163, 173, 183, 222; *see also* inner-direction, Riesman, David

paperbacks, *see* mass market paperbacks
Peace Corps, 105
peer group, 157, 159, 161-3
personality, 12, 166-8, 172; market, 153; molded by media, 160; structure of destroyed; *see also* character, culture of narcissism, other-direction
Peyton Place, 110; *see also* Metalious, Grace
The Pirate, 137-8; *see also* Robbins, Harold
Poor No More, 99, 100; *see also* Ruark, R.
Poor Richard's Almanack, 1
popular novels: as stereotypic, 6; *see also* bestsellers
population growth post World War II, 27
Postal Service reform, 27
Potok, Chaim, 102, 120-1
power, 151, 165; studies of, 206
The Power Elite, 159; *see also* Mills, C. Wright
Prince of Foxes, 68, 71; *see also* Shellabarger, Samuel
private life, 11, 83, 106-7, 114, 146, 168, 179, 196; becomes more important, 117; degraded, 169; invaded by peer group, 162; restructuring of, 199; *see also* public life